# The Darkness That Divides Us

RENATE DORRESTEIN

# The Darkness That Divides Us

Translated from the Dutch
by Hester Velmans

**WORLD EDITIONS**
New York, London, Amsterdam

Published in the USA in 2019 by World Editions LLC, New York
Published in the UK in 2015 by World Editions Ltd., London

World Editions
New York/London/Amsterdam

Copyright © Renate Dorrestein, 2003
English translation copyright © Hester Velmans, 2015
Cover image © Hellen van Meene
Author's portrait © Frank Ruiter

Printed by Sheridan, Chelsea, MI, USA

Library of Congress Cataloging in Publication Data is available

ISBN 978-1-64286-014-6

First published as *Het duister dat ons scheidt* in the Netherlands in 2003
by Uitgeverij Contact, Amsterdam

Twitter: @WorldEdBooks
Facebook: WorldEditionsInternationalPublishing
www.worldeditions.org

Per Luigi Brioschi,
con affetto

and to Kika

# Contents

PART ONE

# Six

# A is for Abacus

We must at some point have made up our minds never to exchange another word with her, because, as if by pre-arrangement, there was always a deathly silence the moment she came into view. We'd clamp our lips shut and look the other way when we saw her coming into the schoolyard or when we passed her in the street, playing hopscotch or marbles all by herself.

When had it started? It must have been the year we learned to read, in Miss Joyce's class. So long ago, anyway, that it was as if a ring, faint but unmistakable, had gradually been drawn round her, marking the spot where she was standing, walking, or sitting: a sign that she had been singled out as a target. As the scapegoat.

Our silence did not mean we didn't have anything to say to her. We wanted there to be no mistake about that, and that's why we often lay in wait for her after school. Four of us, or six, or, if there was nothing else going on, a bunch more.

We'd hide in the shrubbery on the old village green, behind the hornbeam hedge whose leaves in spring were the colour of chocolate. In front of the hedge stood a bench overgrown with brambles. In the old days, when the green was still being maintained, it was a popular spot for courting couples. Now it was mostly deserted. But it wasn't considered particularly unsafe, since it was overlooked by all the houses surrounding the green; anybody could see what was happening out there, unless everybody happened to be looking the other way at the exact same time.

Elbowing one another in the ribs, we hid behind the hedge. The moist earth was crawling with spiders that tried to scramble away on buckling legs when you held a match to them. They made a popping sound as they burned; the shrivelled little ball gave off a measly puff of smoke.

As soon as we saw her coming, we put away our matches and ducked. We were packed so close together that we were just one big huddle of quivering muscle and flaring nostrils.

On the other side of the hedge we heard her pace slacken. Her footsteps slowed until she came to a sudden halt. She was weighing her chances, probably: her after-school tutoring session had run a little longer than usual, dinner smells were already wafting out of the open windows, the street was empty; all the kids had been called inside. Maybe today was her lucky day. She started fidgeting, her fingers plucking at a hem, as if trying to find something to hold on to. Her clothes were always a muddy colour. It was only to be expected of those Luducos, our mothers said, shaking their heads. Men didn't know how to do the laundry, nor did they have a clue about dressing a little girl properly. 'The poor child,' they said.

We stared at each other, our cheeks bulging with excitement. Nobody wanted to go first, or worse, last. That thought spurred us to leap out, all together at the same time, to block her way. Arms crossed, legs planted wide, chins raised. A human barricade.

Her mouth and eyes rounded into perfect Os, her face grew so pale that the freckles looked like ants crawling across her nose, and her carroty plaits, which she had grown long again just to annoy us, sprang loose from the shock.

There was a total silence all around. No sound of telephones ringing in any of the houses. No pan clanging on any cooker. No baby even dared to start crying. No housewife was chatting with a neighbour over the hedge. Even the brambles stopped growing as we thrust the scrap of paper with our latest ultimatum at her, at eye level so that she could read it. She had trouble working out what it said. But we had plenty of time. We gazed at her, relaxed, as drops of sweat welled on her upper lip. When she was finally done deciphering our message word for word, we stuffed the piece of paper down her throat to make sure it wouldn't be used against us. Obediently she chewed and swallowed it. She kept her eyes down, but we were only too aware how blue they were, as blue and brazen as ever, despite her cowering demeanour. The picture of innocence, she was. Oh, she was good. We gave her a shove, sending her stumbling across the deserted square with our promise churning in her gut: 'We gonna get you, scumbag.'

The moment she disappeared from view we were overcome with the urge to shake ourselves like dazed, wet dogs. Suddenly we felt a pressing need for noise. We started making a racket, yelling whatever came into our heads, to convince ourselves we had every right to put her on notice that for the rest of her days her life was going to be a living hell. Tomorrow we would make her pay. Or, better yet, a few days from now. Just as she began to think she was safe again, we'd give it to her good, we would. This year was our last chance: soon we'd be turning twelve, and at the end of the summer vacation we were all going to different schools. At home they had already started gazing at us sentimentally, reminiscing about our happy childhood, which, they said, was very nearly over.

All of us—most of us, anyway—were born here, in the sole modern housing estate of a sleepy little town that would have fallen off the map long ago if a stretch of no-man's-land squeezed between canal and motorway hadn't appealed to a bunch of builders as a prime piece of property.

Our fathers smugly declared they had been the very first residents to move here. Pioneers of sorts, they were. In those days there wasn't another housing estate anywhere else in the whole entire country, I kid you not! The national TV news had come to film the prime minister inaugurating the first house—at least that's what our mothers told us, their eyes still glowing with pride. They'd lost no time spiffing up the place, planting bamboo and embellishing their yards with droll garden ornaments. Then they were off to the salon to have their hair highlighted.

Your dad did have to earn good money if you wanted your own little plot of split-level property here, but in relative terms the prices were a joke. For a similar chunk of dough in Amsterdam, you'd be in a third-floor walk-up with no view. And here you had all that fresh air into the bargain.

That first summer on the housing estate, our parents barbecued up a storm. The whole neighbourhood joined in; after all, pioneers have an obligation to eat well, they have to set an example! Our mums made potato salad by the bathtub, our dads tied on aprons and sharpened their carving knives. In winter everyone pitched in to erect a colossal Christmas tree in the new shopping-mall square,

where the wind howled so fiercely that they'd needed gal-
lons of mulled wine not to get blown off their feet. And by
the time summer came round again, we were born, one
after another, in dribs and drabs, but pretty close in age all
the same, as if the bank had threatened to foreclose on the
mortgage unless a baby was produced by a certain date.

Back in those days we had no idea how that worked, babies getting born. We had no concept of all that's involved,
or of the possible consequences. We simply appeared out
of nowhere, from one moment to the next, to our parents'
immense joy. They leaned over our cribs, they cradled us
in their arms—carefully, because we were such precious
little darlings—and showed us that we really had the best
of both worlds: bathrooms with all mod cons and hygienic
stainless-steel kitchens, but also the countryside outside
our back doors, brimming with cow parsley in bloom and
mud that would ooze into our wellies when we were a little
older, squishy and delicious.

We sucked air into our lungs and screeched with delight.
We hollered so loudly that we could hear one another right
through the walls right and left of us and across the street.
This, too, was part of the deal: little friends our own age,
thrown in for free. What fun it would be to grow up
together—first steps, first words, first tooth, first bloody
lip. And we'd ride our tricycles together! Where else could
you ride a tricycle as safely as down our lane?

We had it made. We were in clover. As if the whole world
knew exactly what we deserved.

The heart of the original village consisted of four narrow
streets around a central square. It was there that our mummies headed every day to do their shopping.

Shaking their highlighted curls, they parked our push-
chairs inside the musty-smelling greengrocer's; the man's

fingers were so swollen with arthritis that he had trouble wrapping the crisp fresh lettuce in newspaper, and if you didn't have the exact change on you, you had to slip behind the counter and help yourself from the till. No place else in the world had such tasty vegetables, our mothers assured him, I really mean it, Mr De Vries. They squatted down in their tight jeans and handed us carrots to suck on. Then they dawdled for a while longer, hoping for a chat; it wasn't as if they had that many people to talk to, but Mr De Vries just went on silently weighing the split peas, and, suddenly embarrassed, they fled from the gloomy shop, needing to put distance between themselves and old age and aching bones and hard work—out, out!

Once safely outside, they collected themselves. They bent down and with flushed cheeks made shushing noises into our perambulators. You could tell how glad they were that we, even more than they, were helplessly dependent on things beyond our control. After all, *they* didn't need anyone to wipe their little bums. They stuffed the lettuce firmly into the pushchair's shopping net, and once again we felt ourselves going bumpity-bump over the cobblestones. Overhead we could see blue skies with the odd cloud here and there that looked like an elephant, or a chicken. Then we'd pop our thumbs into our mouths, because nobody was asking our opinion anyway.

The butcher's. Meat slaughtered on the premises.

The baker's. A country brown loaf.

When our mums were done with their shopping, they'd gather on the village green across from the former rectory. We lay dozing on plaid blankets, snuggled against their hips. Their tanned, pale, or freckled faces glistened in the sun; they dabbed their necks, their voices brayed. Even in our semi-comatose state it made us uneasy, we got itchy, we began to whinge for no reason, just to get their attention. Their panic was understandable. To be twenty years old, far from the big city, banished to a brand-new housing estate in some itty-bitty backwater no one's ever heard of, left to cope all by yourself in this suburban Wild West while your husband was stuck somewhere out there in a traffic jam—but then they would shake themselves, grabbing their painted toenails or the ends of their bleached hair and then tugging as hard as they could, and they were off again, shrieking with hysterical laughter. There was always something to gossip about. There was always some scandal you could freely dish the dirt on, even in the presence of infants. And there were always good snacks, too, to be shared around.

The summer we first opened our astonished eyes, the treat was often strawberries: it was a great year for them, they were as big as duck eggs, the whole world reeked of their sweet, cloying aroma. With their tapered fingernails our mothers pinched the stems from the berries, they bit them in half and gently prodded the pieces into our drooling mouths. The juice ran down our chins, staining our baby knits.

'Watch out for wasps,' Lucy's mother cautioned.

In the sea of maternal bodies she was the only one you could have picked out blindfolded. That was because she smelled of patchouli, whereas our mothers all smelled of Yves Saint Laurent's Paris. Because *our* mummies had our daddies, they had real husbands who could afford to buy them perfume recommended in *Avenue* magazine, and a closet full of sexy summer frocks besides.

Lucy's mum, in her slinky, home-made, invariably black dresses, with her sleek black hair, was the exception in more ways than one, because she was the only one who lived in the old village. Oh, not very long, she replied when asked how long she'd been there, and laughed. Even though our mums couldn't find out as much about her as they'd like, they were fond of her. She was the merriest of them all and could always be counted on to come up with a solution to any problem. She could tell your fortune with the help of a deck of Tarot cards. There was no point looking back, she would say, you should always look ahead at what was next. 'Look, this is the Three of Cups. The card of friendship,' she told our uprooted mothers. 'That's the most important card in the deck.'

In unison we burped and in unison we produced stinky nappies. We slept, we had the colic, we learned you were supposed to chortle if someone cooed 'ta-ta' at you, we stuffed things into our mouths, we grew. We grew like cabbages. At first we reconnoitred the world on our hands and knees, but soon we started walking and pulling breakables off tabletops. We explored electric outlets and discovered the stairs. We said 'Mama' for the first time and were practically hugged to death. Every new milestone was recorded for posterity by video cameras. As far as we knew, the world revolved around us, and every so often we got to blow out another candle on our birthday cake.

Our daddy gave us a brightly coloured abacus, so that one day we'd be able to do sums, to calculate the costs and the benefits, credit and debit and all the rest, or, alternatively, a doll with eyes that shut and real hair, to prepare us for a role no less important. With his heavy daddy-hand he ruffled our hair. He squeezed us close. He rolled around the bathroom floor with us. His face was set in a har-dee-har expression. He sprayed us with the garden hose. On Saturday afternoons we washed the car together, each armed with our own scrub-brush, for the rims. On Sundays we dug in the garden. We planted bulbs and raked leaves. 'Is this paradise, or what?' Daddy asked. But then he'd gaze over our head at the spindly elms poking up in the flat polder landscape, and let out a deep sigh.

At night, when they thought we were asleep, our mummy would snap at our daddy, 'But *who* insisted on moving here in the first place?'

'Oh, not you, I suppose!'

'And now you're home late for dinner every night.'

'What did you expect? Did you think my office would open a branch out here in the boondocks?'

'You're away all day long, while I'm trapped here, cooped up with the kids!'

Through the walls we heard how mad our mummies were. They wanted a chance to show who they were—to the universe, to our fathers, perhaps even to us. They were special, goddamnit; they had talent and potential, far greater than your average Jane! After one of these outbursts you could bet your boots that the next morning we'd find them buttering our bread with a resentful glint in their eyes; it was we, after all, who were tying them down hand and foot. It was because *we* had to grow up in a place where the air was pure and the cow parsley grew that *they* were now stuck out here. We were their cross to bear—day in, day out.

We kept quiet as little mice, watching them muttering under their breath. When you realized that you were somebody's cross to bear, it became hard to get the dry bread down, and your heart started pounding like mad. It seemed that your birth had set off an unanticipated chain reaction. Mummy had become invisible because of you! She was sacrificing herself for you! She had a whole laundry list of motherly grievances! Even hours later your hand wouldn't stop shaking enough for your crayon to stay inside the lines.

When the day had had such an inauspicious start, we'd

often spend the afternoon in the old rectory on the village green where Lucy lived with her mother and the Luducos.

It was a rambling, rather draughty house, with an old-fashioned doorbell pull, a panelled staircase and creaky wooden floors. Lucy's mother, who didn't believe in looking back at the past, had her studio on the second floor. Piles of books and papers lay scattered all over the floor. There were jam jars with dried paints on the windowsills, and the walls were papered with charcoal sketches for her picture books. *Clara 13* was her most famous book, about a cow with a permanent streak of bad luck. All of us had a copy of it at home.

In the darkest corner of the room was a table topped with a green felt cloth. That was the Tarot table. Here your fortune was either made or lost. Here the Five of Wands made you war with yourself, the Wheel of Fortune turned everything topsy-turvy, and the Knight of Cups was known to turn up to save the day. Really, there was nothing supernatural about it, said Lucy's mother, but hey, wait, look, here's the Two of Pentacles, that amazing card that augurs a big change, plus the High Priest, the most protective card of all.

Eagerly our mummies saw their fortunes spelled out for them in the cards. They leaned over the fascinating pictures that told the story of their lives in cartoon-strip form. Meanwhile we stood there gaping at Lucy's mum. She had a dimple in one cheek. Her eyes were cornflower blue. The buttons on her blouse were always half-undone, and when she crossed her legs, you could see a tanned limb through the long slit in her black skirt. Gazing at her, you'd feel so happy and dreamy inside that you couldn't believe she could seriously be somebody's mother. 'Lucy is upstairs, kids,' she'd say, glancing up from her cards. 'Run along up and go play.'

We didn't have to be told twice. We clambered up the staircase whose every tread let out a soft groan.

Since no one can make a living from picture books alone, Lucy's mum had a couple of lodgers living on the third floor. The Luducos, as we called them, were two slow, amiable men of indeterminate age who were constantly on the phone. You hardly noticed their presence, except for their shoes lined up in the corridor. The ones belonging to Ludo were all black leather brogues; the ones belonging to Duco were sneakers in various stages of disintegration. We pinched our noses shut when we passed by.

Lucy's domain was all the way upstairs in the attic.

Her room had a swing hanging from the rafters. There was always a bunch of freshly picked pansies sitting in the dormer window. The floor was strewn with rugs and cushions. Lucy didn't have a Minnie Mouse nightlight like ours, but an artistically swagged string of Christmas-tree lights nailed to the wall above the bed. On the wall opposite, her mother had painted a rainbow, with blue ocean waves underneath, and a ship filled with giraffes, zebras, and lions sticking out their perky heads.

We usually found Lucy sitting cross-legged on the floor when we came in, engrossed in some solitary activity that would immediately strike us as the only possible game anyone would want to play today; indeed, the game without which there wouldn't even be a today. Eagerly we plopped down beside her and spat into our hands.

Under her Indian-cotton dresses Lucy's knees were always a patchwork of scrapes and bruises; she had grubby toes sticking out of plastic sandals and the mud of half a riverbank under her fingernails. She was the exact same age as us, but she'd already experienced so much more. She had discovered a rusty treasure chest filled with gold ducats in the ruins of some old castle; she had battled sabre-toothed tigers; she had sailed a pirate ship, wearing a wooden leg and with a green parrot on her shoulder. She'd spilled hundreds of glasses of orange squash, too, without any dire fallout. Just watch us try *that* at home. At our house, spills always left tell-tale stains on the table-cloth.

We asked our fathers more than once for some clarification on those squash stains. Daddies always seemed to know everything. But even they had no good explanation. Besides, they would always get this funny look on their faces whenever we started on about the way things were done in the rectory, or explained that if something got spilled over there, Lucy's mother just laughed it off. Then our dads would cough and leave the table to walk the dog—our dog King, Whisky, or Blondie.

Lucy told us our dads sometimes lingered on the green for hours, gazing up at the rectory's lighted windows. They'd grab their groins and scratch down there for a while. And then they'd head home again. Back to their own wonderful, modern houses. Saved from the nuisances of living in a white elephant: crumbling concrete, dry rot, and sagging beams. You had to be completely nuts to want to live in a place like that in this day and age, our fathers thought—it's cuckoo.

Lucy saw it all. Nothing escaped her, for she had not only a dormer window but also an eagle eye. She reported her findings to us in the rectory's spacious, overgrown garden every afternoon. Seated on the rim of the sandbox the Luducos had built for her, we listened to her deductions. But when a grown-up came within earshot she'd go all dimple-cheeked, squinting up at them adorably.

'Are you kids having fun?'

'Yeah, we are,' we'd babble, impatient.

'What game are you playing?'

'Eskimos,' said Lucy.

Oh, those kids! The things they say—just this afternoon, for instance! So cute, the stuff they come out with!

And so we were able to exchange, unhindered, a wealth of information while losing our first baby teeth and learning to button our coats and telling our grannies what was going to happen when we turned four. 'When I'm four I'm gonna go to school,' we lisped earnestly. Thinking happily: And then I won't fit in my old bed anymore. Oh boy, when you turned four! The morning of your birthday you'd wake up to find your legs sticking out a mile beyond the bars of your cot. Everyone knew that was what happened.

The nursery school was a few kilometres from where we lived. We walked the whole way there and back every day, stoic as seal hunters, and there we learned to snip, paste, and weave placemats. We also went on a school trip to Utrecht Cathedral. At the sight of the gigantic church organ, Lucy asked, thrilled, 'Is that the Statue of Liberty?'

On the way back we belted out a Russian sea shanty.

*We* didn't need any Tarot cards to see into the future, not even the Three of Cups. It was written in stone: our friendship would last forever.

# B is for Beetle

The summer we turned six—one after another, in dribs and drabs, but pretty close to one another all the same—it wouldn't stop raining. It rained so hard that our toes went mouldy inside our wellies and our fingertips were permanently wrinkly. It rained morning, noon, and night; it rained for every birthday party, right to the bitter end when our parents came to pick us up. Umbrellas on your birthday were a bad omen; everyone knew that. It meant something was hanging over your head, something bad was just waiting to happen.

Only in the night-time did it ever stay dry for a few hours, as if the elements were taking stealthy advantage of the darkness to gather fresh energy. But even then we didn't get a break, because our sleep was still disturbed by the noise of water gurgling down the drainpipes. We dreamed that out in the meadow, where we went to play, the ditch overflowed its banks and swelled into a seething river. The water cascaded over the speed bumps and gushed down our streets. It sloshed against the front doors, it rose and kept rising. When we peered out our bedroom window, we saw bulging fish eyes staring blankly back at us. Alarmed, we dragged a chair over to the window so we could look out. In the moonlit waves we saw ruined lampshades bobbing by; pots that had once held lush houseplants; tablecloths whose colours, cross-stitched by our grannies, had begun to run; welcome mats; old newspapers; and the cushions of the living-room suite our daddies had worked so hard to pay for. Way out in the distance we even caught a glimpse of a cooker adrift, its pots and pans still rattling on top, and, not far behind, an entire family packed like sardines inside a giant enamel colander, paddling away like crazy. Not long now and we'd all be goners.

Upon waking up in the morning it was reassuring, to put it mildly, not to see fish scales plastered to the walls. We were so relieved that at breakfast we went a little wild. One fine day our mothers just lost it. Stop it! I can't take it anymore! For Christ's sake, go play outside, let off some of that steam! Their voices were at such a high pitch that we knew it meant trouble. Nervously we grabbed our macs from the peg, pulled on our boots, and got the hell out of there.

Your mother had to have the house to herself for a few hours every so often or she would go completely round the bend. Her own mother had felt the same, as had her mother before her; it couldn't be helped, mothers as far back as the Stone Age all suffered from the same syndrome.

Heads tucked inside our mac hoods, we ran to our meadow to inspect the water level in our ditch. We hadn't been there in all the weeks it had rained, and were surprised to find a crane and several backhoes parked there. When the summer was over they were going to start building a viaduct there. It had been in the newspaper; our parents had read it aloud to us, including all the pros and cons. So they were still intending to build that bridge? So you mean people thought that by the end of the summer, the world would still exist?

We were just debating amongst ourselves what we should do when Lucy came splashing along. Lifting her knees up high, she stomped down hard in puddle after puddle; at every splash her plaits would whip round her face and she'd shriek with delight. 'Don't you think we should build an ark?' she called to us from a distance.

All the ominous thoughts were at once forgotten. We ran to Mr De Vries's store for some vegetable crates. Then we raided our fathers' tool chests for nails, nuts, bolts, saws, hammers, and pliers.

We worked in shifts, from early morning to late at night. Some of us sawed and hammered. The others had already started digging earthworms out of the mud, catching beetles, pill- and ladybugs, and trapping slugs so big and fat that they almost didn't fit in the jam jars our mothers were kind enough to provide. You had to punch a hole in the lid to give them air; if they couldn't breathe, they'd die. The toads, the slippery yellow-bellied salamanders, the tadpoles, and the sticklebacks were kept in buckets, with some duckweed. After the deluge, every crawling or swimming creature was assured of a safe future, if we had anything to do with it.

And on an afternoon when the clouds hung so low you could practically reach up and touch them without even standing on tiptoe, we started with equal verve on every flying creature there was.

Some way off, next to one of the idle backhoes, we spied the new kid watching us again. We'd noticed him lurking about for the past several days. He was all skin and bones, and his heavy blond hair made his head look at least three times too big for the rest of him. 'Here comes Water-on-the-brain!' we hissed, as soon as we caught sight of him. When he was around we found ourselves talking in louder voices and laughing more than normal. Noisily we bragged about our ark and our animals. We gave each other encouraging slaps on the back while out of the corner of our eyes keeping careful tabs on the new boy hanging out by himself, aimlessly kicking at clumps of grass.

But catching a bird by the tail with some stranger watching your every move was harder than you'd think. We finally plunked ourselves down at the water's edge, panting heavily, for a powwow. Somebody suggested scattering breadcrumbs on the ground and then pouncing with salt and a net. Lucy said we could probably rustle up a net big enough in the rectory's basement. We immediately took her at her word. In that basement anything we ever needed always seemed to be there for the taking, usually in plain view, as if helpful hands had put it out for us.

Waiting for Lucy to return, we were just lighting a bulrush cigar when Water-on-the-brain approached us. He gazed at us with his hands in his pockets. 'So, how's it going?' he asked politely.

We glanced at our jars and buckets. We already had quite a trove.

'How're you gonna catch the pelicans? Or the zebras?'

We were rather taken aback for a moment.

'I can help, if you want.'

To save face, we howled with scornful laughter. Oh, sure! Really? Maybe he knew how to catch a duck-billed platypus! And we didn't have any dinosaurs yet; we'd welcome any suggestions. Yeah, right! We started shouting out the names of animals. We yelled elephant, we yelled lion, we yelled crocodile, we yelled and yelled, all excited at first, but then less so, as it dawned on us that now our ark would have to be at least ten times bigger and, come to think of it, we'd probably need cages, too, if we didn't want to end up being mauled or devoured.

We were still yelling when Lucy returned, dragging a huge fisherman's net behind her. She began spreading it out in the mud without deigning to look at the new boy. It was only when she was done wiping her hands on her jeans that she turned to him and asked, 'And who are *you?*' She was a head taller than him.

'Thomas Iedema,' he answered promptly. 'I moved in last Monday, on Shepherd's Close.' He gestured at the cluster of houses in the distance. The rain had plastered his hair to his oversized skull.

We didn't know whether to feel envy or mistrust. We had spent our wholes lives in one place. Here was a boy who had actually lived somewhere else, which meant he must have seen quite a bit of the world. But hadn't we been told that moving house was for Gypsies? It only led to trouble, and broken crockery.

'My father's got a job here, with the Parks Department,' he went on. 'We used to have a shop, but it closed. So ...'

Impatiently, Lucy asked, 'So what do you want from us, exactly?'

Thomas Iedema shrugged. 'I know about all the animals. My father has this book, it's so cool! It starts with the amoebas. First you have to work through all the invertebrates and arthropods; you're halfway through the book before you get to the mice and such. So if you want, I could ...'

'We could use some of those ducks over there.' She pointed at the ditch.

'Those are moorhens, actually.'

'So? We don't have any of them yet, either.'

Strange, really, that after so many years, this single moment should remain etched so deeply in our minds. It's been a long time since we were mud-spattered kids. The kind of thing we think about nowadays is whether or not to move in together, or whether or not to buy an affordable second-hand SmartCar. But if, on some rare occasion, late at night in bed, we allow ourselves to think about the events we set in motion, wincing with shame, we'll have a glimpse of this one scene, when it all started: that innocent challenge down by the water.

'Or don't you dare?' Lucy taunted. She was moving her hips as if about to start dancing. Her eyes shone.

'He doesn't dare!' we all shouted in chorus.

'Scaredy-cat,' said Lucy. 'It's really shallow.'

Quick as flash Thomas unbuckled his belt, whipped off his trousers and, without a moment's hesitation, slid down the bank into the ditch. Arms flailing, he waded through the murky water. The two moorhens immediately rose out of the water and whirred into the stand of rushes growing on the opposite bank.

We whooped and yelled.

Startled, Thomas lost his balance. He went under. He came up again, his hair matted with duckweed, water pouring out of his nose and ears. He was coughing and spluttering like crazy.

'Hey, stupid!' we jeered. 'You should be on the other side. That's where they've gone!'

Because he was so short, the water came up to his waist. The pelting rain was leaving bubbles as big as tennis balls on the surface. The moorhens quacked in the rushes. Then, suddenly, Thomas let out a yell and plunged head first in the water, throwing up fountains of spray. For a split second his striped shirt ballooned around his neck, then it, too, went under. We saw one foot kick in the air, then the other, and then they too were gone.

We waited.

After a little while we cupped our hands to our mouths. We shouted, 'Hey!'

The water swirled and bubbled.

'Hey, show-off!'

The moorhens re-emerged from the rushes. They paddled into view, their coal-black heads cocked as if to show they felt quite safe again, now that their hunter lay drowned at the bottom of the ditch. If his body was ever recovered, we'd be in big trouble! We just stood there, petrified.

'Out of my way!' screamed Lucy, running up with the bird-catching net in her arms.

Relieved, we stepped aside for her, then closed ranks again. We each picked up a corner of the net, regrouping this way and that since we couldn't immediately agree on the best way to proceed—dredging, dragging, each had his or her own quite valid opinion about what to do, and clung to it stubbornly.

'One two three … *now!*' cried Lucy, jumping into the water with a huge splash. She landed safely, no more than knee-deep in the ditch, and without hesitating bent down and plunged her whole head underwater to reconnoitre, her little bum sticking up in the air.

At her *Now!* some of us had already started casting out the net, but others hesitated, so that the net wafted down in slow motion, entangling Lucy as she tried to stand up again. We were in such a tizzy that, without thinking, we began pulling it in. The net went taut, it cut into our hands, and Lucy went down. The water closed over her head.

We let go of the net. We were in a complete panic. We wanted to go home, we wanted to be in the kitchen watching Mummy shell peas with her steady hands. But we couldn't move. We tried to think of water lilies and other nice things, and then about how great it was that we were going to learn to read, after the summer vacation! Once you knew how to read, our parents had told us, you could have all these vicarious experiences without having to live them yourself. Reading books let you have life doled out to you like homeopathic drops: diluted to the hundredth degree. Which was definitely a better option, sometimes.

Suddenly, with a great roar, Thomas shot up out of the water. Coughing his guts out, he flung something black up on the embankment. He panted, 'A rat, quick, get a bucket on top of it!'

Just a few feet away from him, struggling furiously with the net, Lucy, too, was on her feet. Flailing wildly with her arms, her legs planted wide in the water, she finally managed to disentangle herself. Indignantly, she cried, 'Wasn't it a *moorhen* you were supposed to catch?'

The next day they each had a ring on their finger drawn in magic marker. If you dared so much as *think* 'Thomas Water-on-the-brain,' you'd get a vicious kick in the shins from Lucy. His name was now Thomas the Rat. He came up to her chin, and the work on the ark was abandoned.

Toward the end of that drenched summer, a few weeks later, we all received an invitation to the engagement party. At home there was some uncomfortable laughter when our folks tore open the envelope and read the card to us. You could tell Lucy had told her mum exactly what to write.

'Should we give them a salt-and-pepper set?' our own mums sniggered to our dads. 'Or maybe a toaster?' To us they said, waving their hands, 'Oh, run off and play, for goodness' sake,' which made us prick up our ears, because we wanted to report back to Lucy later what they'd said. But Lucy was much too preoccupied with Thomas to listen to our stories.

Enviously, we wondered what those two could be up to. At Lucy's house just about everything was permitted, as long as her mum wasn't disturbed while at work in her studio. She didn't pay any attention to the kids that came over. She didn't expect you to sit and have something to drink with her in the kitchen first, either; you could just go ahead and do whatever, she didn't care. Lucy's announcement of their engagement was probably the first time her mum had even noticed Thomas.

Maybe the two of them were busy building a cabin in the rectory hallway; maybe they were even finding out where babies came from! The latter was a mystery that had become of increasing interest to us of late, especially since we never seemed able to get a satisfactory answer at home. You came out of your mother's tummy, yeah, obviously, there were pictures to prove it, a whole album full. But the way you got *into* that tummy in the first place—that was such an unbelievably gross story that you knew right off they must be pulling your leg, no matter how serious their expression. We were sure it involved a completely different scenario, something to do with gravity, or something. Didn't our fathers always tell us everything had a scientific explanation?

Without Lucy to play with, the days were long and tedious. Every time we started some game with high hopes, it always ended up getting horribly bogged down, now that Lucy wasn't around to fine-tune the rules if necessary. Afternoons that should have been perfect for a game of Ali-Baba-and-the-Forty-Thieves ended in chaos and angry tears. All our treasure hunts, races, and dress-up sessions went sour. And every time we snuck over to Thomas's house on Shepherd's Close to try kidnapping him, we got there too late. He'd already gone off to play somewhere, said his mother.

She was a short, squat woman, with beady round eyes that looked as if she was about to apologize for something, and she always had a rag in her hand to polish our fingerprints off the door jamb. According to our mothers, who were past masters at sniffing out information on newcomers in record time, she was dirt-phobic. She never set foot outside, they said, except to shake out her dust mop.

Why on earth someone with that kind of problem would marry a groundsman, who tramped home every day with mud on his shoes, was the sort of thing they loved to speculate about. 'Maybe he's really good at it,' they whispered, covering their mouths. At what, Mummy? What's he so good at? Oh, child, that's none of your business.

Sometimes we'd catch sight of the man who was really good at none of our business, maintaining the grounds of the housing estate, or on the village green. He wore a broad-brimmed yellow sou'wester on account of the rain, that hid his face completely. There was something about him that made you think of a buffalo, the way he charged at the wild roses and barberry bushes. The kids living on Pitchfork Hill had seen him with their own two eyes (cross their hearts and hope to die) pulling out great handfuls of stinging nettles without gloves on or anything! We were terribly impressed. We decided that if we upset Thomas even in the slightest, the nettle-man would break every bone in our body, and suck out the marrow, too.

The engagement party was set for Sunday afternoon. It was supposed to be an English tea party. We weren't exactly looking forward to that part, because tea always gave us such a woolly tongue. But at four o'clock our mothers firmly parted our hair with a wet comb or else tamed it with a couple of festive barrettes, they gave us the thoughtfully selected presents to carry, and told us to have a good time 'and mind your manners and don't forget to say thank you at the end.'

At the rectory, the door was opened by the Luducos,

dressed in black tails and bowties. Their sparse hair was slicked back with gel, which made their kindly faces look even more clueless than usual. 'May we take your coats, sir, madam?' they asked us.

We stared at them open-mouthed.

'Today we are the butlers,' Duco whispered. He was still wearing his stinky sneakers; that's how we could tell it was him.

In the hall Lucy and Thomas were busy tickling each other to death, so we stepped into the living room. Our spirits immediately rose. Such a spread of pies, cakes of all kinds and all sizes, and white-bread finger sandwiches cut into triangles! We were allowed to help ourselves to as much as we liked, said Lucy's mum, and if anyone didn't like tea, there was orange squash, too. She was padding around on bare feet and had a bright-red scarf knotted around her head, which made her look even less like somebody's mother than usual. You couldn't imagine *her* ever sacrificing herself for Lucy, or becoming invisible or anything.

The news about the orange squash came as a huge relief. We completely forgot to shake hands. We fell upon the food, ravenous.

As we were stuffing our faces, Lucy and Thomas entered the room, their hair all messed up. 'I had him begging for mercy,' laughed Lucy. Lovingly, she started pummelling his big round head.

'But *you* peed in your pants!'

'Not true!'

'Do try to leave your fiancé in one piece, darling!' said her mother. 'And now, let's raise our glasses to you two, shall we? Does everyone have tea or squash? What about our butlers?'

'We're having iced tea,' said Duco, with a grin. He raised his glass.

'Cheers!' Ludo, too, waved his glass. When he looked at Lucy, all these little laugh-lines appeared around his eyes. He nodded almost imperceptibly, as if to say, 'Ah, that Lucy!' At home our daddies sometimes acted that way, too, if they were feeling particularly proud of you. It gave you the delicious feeling that you were capable of just about anything; fathers could do that just by gazing at you a certain way. That Ludo sure would make a great father one day. He sometimes gazed at Lucy's mother with that same kind of look in his eyes—you know, the way mothers love to be looked at. Is that a new dress you're wearing, darling? Have you done something with your hair? That colour looks *great* on you. No doubt about it: Ludo would definitely make the grade. Only he'd better get a move on with it. He was no spring chicken.

'Right, my little turtledoves,' said Lucy's mother cheerfully. 'Here's to the two of you!'

We all cheered *Hurray!* at the top of our lungs.

Next came the opening of the presents. It was so embarrassing—our mothers had bought them things like a Barbie's wedding gown, or toys for playing father-and-mother. There was also quite an assortment of Tupperware. Weird. We didn't get it.

'Oh you lucky things,' said Lucy's mother. 'I'll have to borrow those from you sometime. So tell us, Thomas, do you feel settled in yet? Do you like it out here?'

'I didn't, at first,' said Thomas. 'But now I do.'

'You can tell your mum and dad that I'll come over to meet them very soon. Oh blimey, I should have invited them, shouldn't I!'

'You can invite them to the wedding,' said Duco.

Ludo asked, 'And do your parents like living here too?'

'Yeah, they do. Our house in Opzand wasn't like here. Everything's so new and clean here.'

'Opzand?' Lucy's mother suddenly looked as if she'd sat down on a thumbtack.

'Really? We used to live there too!' said Ludo enthusiastically. 'In one of those old cottages down by the dike. We used to say it was ...' He looked at Lucy's mother for help, but she didn't seem to notice. She downed her glass in two, three big gulps. She'd gone all white.

'Idyllic,' said Duco, 'that was the word, Ludo. But I don't remember any family by the name of The Rat.'

'Silly,' said Lucy fondly, 'that's not his *real* name.'

'But isn't that what it said on the invitation?'

'My last name's Iedema,' said Thomas.

'Iedema!' cried Ludo. 'You mean the florist?'

Duco snickered. 'Well, well! What did your parents think of Lucy's card?'

'I didn't let them see it,' said Thomas. 'No need for them to know I'm with *her*.' He rolled his head in a gesture that took in the whole messy room, including the spider webs in the corners of the ceiling.

'I don't believe it,' said Ludo. 'Lucy has snagged herself an Iedema!'

'I still remember it like yesterday, the time your father ...' Duco started to laugh, his eyes crinkling with mirth.

Lucy's mother stood up so abruptly that her chair nearly toppled backward. 'I am really disappointed in you, Thomas.' Her voice came out sounding throttled. 'I don't like sneaky children who do things behind their parents' backs!'

There was a baffled silence.

'But Mum,' said Lucy. 'It's only because his mum gets so worried about him getting dirty. She was already in such a state the time he came home dripping wet ...'

'Dirty? Who's dirty? Are *you*? Well, well, isn't *that* a nice thing for a boyfriend to say!'

'What's got into you?' asked Ludo, astonished.

'I won't have that little sneak in my house. I won't have Lucy going around with the likes of him. If I'd known, I'd have ...'

'Hey, wait a minute, wait a minute,' said Duco. 'We were having a party.'

'Anyway, we're already engaged, so there!' cried Lucy. 'Too late!' She pulled a rude yah-boo face at her mum.

We were so agitated we couldn't help going into hysterical laughter. The Luducos started laughing too; *they* didn't have to set a good example, or raise anybody. The more everyone laughed, the more it felt as if Lucy's mum must have been kidding.

We spent the rest of the afternoon playing up in the attic. We must have spent an hour playing the Monkey Game, and then The Duchess's Visit. We played as if our lives depended on it. That was always the best solution, we'd found, if you didn't understand what was bugging the grown-ups.

# C is for Crisis

It was only a matter of days now before we'd finally, finally, be learning to read and write. This milestone involved stiff, brand-new clothes, and also pencil cases, gleaming rulers, and big boxes of markers, pens, and coloured pencils. We sharpened our pencils to razor-sharp points. Lucy was the only one who wasn't getting a new set; there were always plenty of pencils lying around her house—enough, anyway, to highlight important words in red or blue till kingdom come. They were big, fat, round sticks, those— the real thing, they were; our own thin, hexagonal pencils looked kind of mingy in comparison, even if they were now honed like daggers. And *that* was what really counted, we assured one another, for you never knew when you might need a weapon to defend yourself. Take Lucy's mum, for instance.

She hadn't set foot outside the house since the engagement party. That was because, Lucy reported, the Ten of Swords had suddenly turned up on the Tarot table—the dude with all the swords stuck through his gut, the card of catastrophe and ruin. Which was why her mother had wisely decided to stay indoors. Better safe than sorry; no need to throw yourself deliberately in danger's path! Danger could be lurking anywhere, really—behind Mr De Vries's counter, on any of the four streets of the village, or even out here on the green, right at her own front door.

We spread the word, increasingly concerned. Thomas was especially worried. According to him, the circumstances called for drastic precautions. But there was no need for him to go around acting as if putting the rectory on heightened alert had been his idea; we had all arrived at the same conclusion. Not long now, and we'd be at school all day; we could hardly be expected to keep an eye on things from there. When and if the danger foretold in the cards finally did show up, Lucy's mother would have to face it on her own. What we had to do now was help her arm herself to the teeth. She'd be so grateful that she'd gather us up in a great big bear hug. Her shirt partly unbuttoned, the red scarf wound around her head like a brilliant flame. We would clamp our legs around her hips and get all woozy from the patchouli smell.

The trees in the rectory's front garden were already turning colour. We were pelted with shiny chestnuts as we darted up the gravel path. Scattering in alarm, we ducked, prowling like tigers, keeping in touch by walkie-talkie. We looked left, right, and left again, because that's what our mums had drilled into our heads, and, doubled over, sprinted to the front door—those heavy, banged-up, scratched double doors.

It was Duco who opened the door.

He wasn't shaved.

He looked surprised.

So did we. Our fathers had been at the office for hours; they were probably sitting in an important meeting, or dictating a memo to give someone a good dressing-down. It worried us that Duco wasn't at work; fathers were supposed to be in the office, but on the other hand, the Luducos weren't fathers, they didn't do real work, just something to do with stocks and shares or something. Once we had that straight, we felt right as rain again.

'Have you come to play with Lucy?' Duco asked in an unusually dull voice, as if he couldn't take it any more.

For appearance's sake, we nodded.

It wasn't until we were inside that we could tell how right the Tarot cards had been. There was an uneasy atmosphere in the house that smacked of whining and moping, quarrels, sulks, and negotiations. In the corridor the pictures hung all askew, as if when nobody was looking they'd been trying to shake their way out of their frames, in case they had to beat a hasty retreat. Instead of the usual enticing aroma of the Luducos' breakfast, the only smell coming from the kitchen was the sorry stench of cold ashes. Alarmed, we thundered up the staircase with the creaky treads.

Lucy and her mother were sitting in the first-floor studio among a jumble of papers, paint jars, and Tarot cards. The curtains were drawn and there were barely any lights on, which made the room seem murkier than usual. Even the cool drawing of *Clara 13* over the mantelpiece looked as if someone had smudged mud all over it.

Lucy, seated on a stool at the drawing table, was just cajoling, 'But *Mum*, why don't you just stop reading the cards?'

'As if that makes any difference,' said her mother. 'Don't be silly.' With an irritated sigh she rolled her eyes up at the ceiling festooned with plaster grapes and curlicues.

Our ceiling at home had designer fixtures, lighting fixtures that cost—well, our fathers said, don't even ask, you don't want to know. In our homes everything was different. And suddenly, out of the blue, we felt as if we had landed in a strange country with all sorts of edicts we didn't know, where ornate plaster and darkness were the rule, not polished steel or halogen. Panicked, we all started talking at once.

Lucy's mother stared at us, baffled. 'What *are* you talking about?' she asked. 'What about them, my pencils? *Why* do I have to sharpen my pencils?'

We were so excited, we were ready to burst. There was danger lurking right outside those drawn draperies! Skulking always, maddeningly, just out sight, which only made it even more chilling! But wait a minute, wait, slow down: what good was a pencil, actually, in the face of real danger? What *had* we allowed ourselves to be talked into? Only your little sister would fall for something *this* lame. 'It was Thomas's idea!' we yelled, stammering with shame.

Lucy's mother whipped around to look at Thomas. 'Okay. I don't get it,' she said crossly. 'What *is* this famous idea of yours exactly, *what* is this racket about?'

Thomas clasped his arms behind his back and puffed out his chest. Eagerly, he began: 'Well, say you run into the enemy.'

'*What* enemy?' She stared at him as if he were one of the arthropods in his father's book, one of the creatures that came way before the mice. 'I thought you were talking about my pencils.'

'I was,' said Thomas, his big head wobbling from side to side. ''Cause, let's say you don't want the enemy to see you. Well, then all you do is, you poke him in the eye with your pencil. Then he's blind as a bat, see? And then you make a run for it.'

It was brilliantly put. We had to hand it to him. We all looked at Lucy's mum expectantly.

She seemed to be thinking it over, doodling on a piece of paper with a piece of charcoal. The marks on the paper kept getting darker and uglier.

Lucy stood up. 'Well, we'll just go up to the attic, then,' she said uncertainly.

The charcoal snapped in two. 'No you won't,' said her mother. 'I have been giving you the benefit of the doubt, Thomas, but now it seems that you're not only a little sneak, you've got a screw loose as well. You do come up with some sick ideas, don't you, Thomas. Don't you understand how dangerous that is? Why, it was just recently all over the newspapers, somebody was *murdered* that way! With a ballpoint pen in the eye!'

She was steaming mad now; we could practically see puffs of black smoke coming out of her ears. 'I said to Duco just the other day, how can that happen? How is it possible—that an ordinary, everyday object like a ballpoint pen could actually kill someone?' She looked back at Lucy. 'Okay, that's enough. I won't have you hanging around with that little creep anymore, Lucy. Do you hear me?'

'But Mum!' Lucy started protesting.

We tried to look deeply preoccupied with pious, virtuous thoughts. *Just remember*, they used to tell us at home, *life doesn't come with a user's manual.* You could never tell what tomorrow would bring, but if things were going your way, you might as well make the most of it.

But nothing stands in the way of true love. That very afternoon we saw the two of them going off together, hand in hand. With her long, skinny legs and her shoulders indignantly hunched, Lucy looked just like a strutting heron. To keep up with her, Thomas had to take two extra skips for every one of her strides.

They made straight for Shepherd's Close. There they installed themselves in the garden shed out back, where Thomas's father stored his dirty work clothes. A sneak peek through the little window showed that they were sitting comfortably on a couple of overturned buckets and, with great gusto, were engaged in dismantling a potato crate with a pair of hedge shears.

At last the day dawned when our mothers were to take us to the big school. Since it was our first day, our teacher, whose name was Miss Joyce, allowed our mums to accompany us into the classroom, a room with tall windows that let the autumn sunlight in. It felt very solemn in there, like in church. Maybe that was why our mothers' faces were graver than usual. As we hunted for a place to sit, they kept hooking their hair back behind their ears and licking their lips. The desktops were scored with angry, indecipherable marks left by children long ago.

Thomas was the only one of us escorted to school by his father. He was so very clean that he gleamed from head to foot, as if his mother had scrubbed him with disinfectant so he wouldn't bring home any germs. His father's head was bare, he wasn't wearing his sou'wester, which made him look a lot less intimidating; he looked like someone you'd known all your life, like the Luducos. He stood in front of the classroom with his hands in his pockets, chatting with Miss Joyce in a loud, self-confident voice. He didn't seem to mind that everyone could hear what he was saying. 'Sadly, mine's like a leaky sieve, you know, though one does learn to live with it,' he said. 'But I'm chuffed Thomas doesn't seem to take after me in that department.'

We craned our necks to see that leaky thing of his. The thought that he might be wearing a nappy under his overalls made us collapse all over each other in hysterics.

'Behave yourselves!' our mothers hissed. But we paid no attention, because in here Miss Joyce was the boss, and she was talking to Thomas's father matter-of-factly, as if that leaky thing of his weren't in the least bit funny. If she was that open-minded, she probably wouldn't even bat an eye-lid if you asked her where babies came from. We were suddenly seized with a great fever for learning.

'Perhaps you could give us a tour of the parks and gardens someday,' said Miss Joyce. 'We'd all enjoy that, wouldn't we, boys and girls?'

'Yeah!' we cried. 'Great!' We drummed on the desks with our fists.

'Okay, and now it's time to say goodbye,' she went on cheerfully, 'because I believe we're all here.'

That was when Lucy barged into the classroom. Her hair wasn't plaited. She wasn't carrying a backpack, either, or a yoghurt snack. She slid into the desk next to Thomas.

Our mothers were perturbed. They murmured, 'Lucy, did you come all by yourself? Is something wrong? Your mummy isn't ill, is she? We haven't seen her for ages! Is there anything we can do for her? Come on, tell us!'

They were so insistent that it made us proud. We generally thought of mothers merely as people who ignored you when you said something sensible, but it seemed there *was* more to them, then, after all. Only, what were they thinking they could do for someone who was going to have to take on the Ten of Swords?

'Ladies! You too, sir,' Miss Joyce admonished them. 'Out, please.' She consulted the list that lay on her desk. 'Was I supposed to have a Lucy? Was I?' she muttered to herself.

The leaky father was last in the line of parents filing out. He gave Thomas a quick thumbs up. Then he, too, left the room.

Miss Joyce picked up a piece of chalk and listed our names on the blackboard.

If you recognized your name, you were entitled to come to the blackboard and draw a little star next to it with a piece of coloured chalk.

'Thomas!' He was the first to call out his own name. He jumped up clumsily. The chalk on the blackboard made a screeching, bird-like sound, which made us think of the egrets and sandpipers in our meadow. Thinking about all the stuff we already knew or had figured out for ourselves made us feel a lot better. We were going to be detectives when we grew up, or beauticians, and you didn't need to know how to read or write to be those. We crossed our arms and leaned back.

'So your father was right about you,' said Miss Joyce with a smile. 'It's a good thing too, Thomas.' Then she looked around the classroom, as if to say, 'Who's next?'

Barbara and Tamara guessed wrong, and so did Floris and Joris. Safranja, however, scored, and Sam with the shaved-chicken neck nailed his, too. Vanessa, at the blackboard, glanced triumphantly over her shoulder to see which of us dummies hadn't been up yet, and then drew a silly little heart next to her name. Some people really had everything going for them. Because Vanessa also had a cat that had cancer of the ear. The vet had lopped off its ears two weeks ago and cauterized the stumps. So now the cat had a new lease on life, and Vanessa was the only kid in the whole wide world to have a cat that looked like a hamster.

'Come on, children,' said Miss Joyce, 'who's next?' She tapped the floor with the tip of her shoe to encourage us. Across these floorboards, she told us, hundreds of children before us had taken their first steps in becoming readers; this floor had been here long before the polders were pumped dry, back in the time when most everything out yonder still lay beneath the endless sea; that's how old our school was, as old as the hills—you could tell from the way its name was spelled: School of Ye Bible.

The Bible, we knew it well. It was God's word. God said, 'Let there be light,' and then all the stars in the sky had lit up, twinkling as bright as can be.

'What about me?' Lucy suddenly cried. 'Where am I?'

Thomas started reading off the rest of the list.

'No, don't help her,' said Miss Joyce. 'It doesn't really matter if you know how to read or write your own name yet. It's just to give me some idea.'

'Lucy isn't even up there,' said Thomas.

Lucy squealed, 'You see!'

'Oh, child,' said Miss Joyce. 'Of course you are.' And she pointed.

Thomas's lips moved. 'That says *Lucky*.' After a moment he added thoughtfully, 'There's no one here called Lucky.'

'Aha,' said Miss Joyce. Her face lit up, just like one of God's stars up in the sky. Beaming, she went on and on about why the 'why' sometimes sounds like 'ee' and about how the 'see' in the ceiling looks like half a circle, or you'd have 'keel' and her own name would be 'Joyk.' It really made no sense at all. Letters, she said, could be tricky; they had a will of their own—one time they might sound like this and next thing they'd sound like that. But we could count ourselves *lucky* we weren't in China: we had only twenty-six of them—letters, that is—and you hardly ever needed the *q* or the *x*; you could live to a ripe old age and never need to use *x* or *q*. 'There's nothing to it, really there isn't,' she promised, smiling at us somewhat damply.

It was true. One moment we were still ignorant know-nothings fidgeting in our hard seats, longing for some distraction, and the next we were reading about See and Spot, Spot and Dot, Spot and Dick. How did we do it? Had Miss Joyce unlocked a little shutter in our minds to release some fairy dust that magically gave us the power to decipher the letters, letters that, when strung together, formed whole words, even? Has she used some secret formula that made us—we, who never missed a trick—forget everything else around us? We no longer saw the worn floorboards or the faded walls of our classroom; we no longer even noticed the dead-carrion smell in the corridor.

'*Mmmmmmoon*,' went Miss Joyce at the blackboard, on which she'd drawn a gaily smiling moon.

'*Mmmmmmoon*,' we all hummed after her, intrigued.

'And what if I took away the *mmmmmm* and put in an *essss* instead?' Her arm, in the sleeveless checked blouse, came up. She erased the M. But we'd never forget it, never, that M. Coming from the mouth of Miss Joyce, that *M* just made you want to do your very best.

'*Sssoon!*' she said. 'See?'

'*Sssoon!*' we agreed, in chorus.

We were her very first class because she'd only just finished her studies. That was why we had to be her little helpers, she said. Because everything was new to her. The chalk, the notebooks, the bell. And when she said that, she laughed, exposing her teeth—she was a bit buck-toothed, though, to her credit, she didn't seem to mind. She went and sat down at her desk at the front of the classroom and looked at us hopefully. 'Open your books,' she said.

The Safe Way to Read was the method we followed.

The *Safe Way Reader* started you off on the word *I*. What a concept, using *I* as the foundation for learning to read, said Miss Joyce, all excited—wasn't it a neat idea? And that little word *I* would lead you to all the other words! As soon as you could read *I* you had practically all the words in the whole entire world at your fingertips!

The Safe Way sometimes liked to have a little fun, too. For example, you'd get a picture of children armed with fishing rods pulling white bits of paper out of a pond. The balloons filled with letters coming out of the kids' mouths showed which words were supposed to go on which scrap of paper. *I fish hat. I fish rat. I fish sock. I fish fish.*

I fish fish—that was a good one! Even the little boy in the picture thought it was funny. He had a mop of thick blond hair, just like Thomas's. The girl fishing next to him was the spitting image of Lucy, with plaits and freckles. She wore a bright yellow jacket trimmed in purple, just the sort of thing the real Lucy always wore. The other children didn't look like anyone we knew.

Miss Joyce had noticed the resemblance too. 'What did Thomas fish?' she asked.

'Fish!' we yelled at the top of our lungs.

'And what did Lucy fish?'

'Sock!' we howled in chorus.

Clearly, immediately upon hearing of Thomas's and Lucy's engagement, the Queen had ordered all the old primers shredded and new ones printed with the right illustrations.

Every afternoon the lights in the classroom came on a little earlier, and when we walked home from school the leaves crunched beneath our feet. Long-forgotten scarves, mittens, and hats were dug out of hall closets. The bakery smelled of cinnamon and allspice, and Mr De Vries sold pumpkins and gourds, which our mothers displayed in the window in nice antique baskets. At night the temperature sometimes dipped below zero, and then the next morning the roofs were sprinkled with sugary frost, like gingerbread houses. On other mornings the fog was so thick on the way to school that if we hadn't been holding on to the tips of one another's woolly mufflers we'd have got lost in the fog. You had every reason to hold on tight, because if you were unlucky enough to disappear into the fog, you'd melt and dissolve right down to your last toenail, until a puddle was all that was left of you; everyone knew that. Every remaining drop of you would quickly have to be collected in a brass bucket and saved until an old crone who knew what to do about it came along, or else you were a goner, forget about it.

Every day, as we walked past the rectory, we saw that Lucy's mother's bedroom curtains were still drawn. She was in bed, said Lucy, because she had the flu. On the one hand that was good news, because that meant she wasn't in any imminent danger. But the flu was such a commonplace thing that we really couldn't get too worked up about it.

What made this flu unusual, however, was that it just went on and on. Weeks went by—in our reader we were already at 'Dan in his Hut'—and still her fever hadn't gone down. Our mothers would have been happy to go see how the patient was doing, but as long as there was still the possibility of contagion, Lucy's mother didn't want any visitors. Happily, talking on the phone was permitted, so our mothers were still able to find out what the cards had in store for them. Whispering, the receiver pressed to their ears, they protested—what about the well-disposed Page of Wands, or the generous King of Pentacles? But once they'd hung up, they would sit back, disappointed, and sigh that still, it was different, wasn't it, to see the cards with your own two eyes, and besides, in some respects it was easy for Lucy's mother to say, being a single woman with no husband and all.

Then, crushed yet still hopeful, they'd look up their horoscope, and as they leafed through their magazines we saw no end of words flip by which we hadn't yet learned in our *Safe Way Reader*. It was hard sometimes not to lose heart. But Miss Joyce assured us on a daily basis that we were making great strides. Such a great job we were doing on 'Dan in his Hut'! She was awfully proud of us.

'Dan is at the gate.'

'Dan picks up sticks.'

'Dan carries sticks to the hut.'

'Excellent,' said Miss Joyce. 'Okay, Lucy, your turn.'

Lucy followed the words with her finger. The tip of her tongue protruded from her mouth. '*To. The. Nut*,' she grunted.

'The *Hu-Hut!*' we cried, irritated. We were dying to find out how the story ended, and if there were any Red Indians in it. That Dan was such a slowcoach anyway; with Lucy and her bungling we'd never get there.

'*Hut?*' she repeated, perplexed.

Whereas we could see the words jumping off the page like brightly coloured marbles, each with its own meaning, Lucy had made no progress at all since the very first day of school; she could only tell what a word meant if there was a picture to go with it. She simply didn't get it. Even though Thomas spent every afternoon after school practising with her, she *still* couldn't even tell the difference between *moon* and *soon*!

It made Miss Joyce sad sometimes. As she handed back our first report cards, she glumly remarked when she got to Lucy's desk, 'You really should try a little harder, honey. Or else your folks will think it's my fault.'

'Oh they won't, miss, don't worry,' said Lucy. She opened her report card and peered intently at the writing, frowning.

The sight of it made us throw up our hands in despair. What good was Lucy to us if she couldn't tell the difference between *rock* and *dock*? If she was the dumbest of us all, who in future would come up with our projects, who was there for us to look up to and obey? If this went on, we didn't stand a chance of discovering a chest of gold ducats in the ruins of an old castle; we probably wouldn't even get in a decent round of Donkey Derby, ever again! It was enough to make you want to vomit. Maybe we ought to give her a good shaking, to get her brain up to speed. Hey, Lucy! We gonna *get* you, if you don't watch out! If only she weren't as strong as six gorillas. If only that dork Thomas would try harder in the daily tutoring sessions. Which gave us an idea, suddenly. What if Lucy's mother found out that the two of them spent every afternoon together? She'd have a fit, she would. 'Oh, you want to go play outside, do you? *I* know what you're really up to ...!'

*Oh, you do, do you?* Our own mothers were nuts about that expression. *Oh, you do, do you?* was usually followed, at the very least, with a smack upside the head, and a hissed, '*That'll* teach you!'

Teaching, the Safe Way: that was what it all boiled down to.

As soon as school was out we gathered in the bicycle shed, armed with pen and paper. We couldn't agree on the exact spelling of 'shed,' but we decided it should be clear enough to anyone reading the letter. Whoever read it would recognize at once that it came from some anonymous good Samaritan who only had everyone's best interests at heart, even if it led to the shit hitting the fan.

Entering the front yard of the rectory, we snuck up to the front door as quietly as we could. We pushed the letter through the letter box. Just to make sure, we took turns peeking through the flap to see if it had landed squarely on the mat, in full view.

We ran all the way home, elated. There would be bangers, mash and kale for dinner tonight—it was that kind of weather—and maybe our dads would give us a few euros as a reward for the excellent report card Miss Joyce had sent home with us today.

The next day was Saturday, so we had the day off. There was a stiff breeze; it was just the day for playing *Titanic*. We were standing around on the village green, in the process of casting the different roles, when Lucy came storming out of the rectory, her plaits blowing straight up in the wind. Cupping her hands to her mouth like a megaphone, she bellowed, 'Crisis! Crisis!'

We immediately stopped what we were doing.

She flopped down on the bench over by the thorn bushes. 'I'm *cooked*.'

'You don't say,' we said evenly, poking each other meaningfully in the ribs.

She raised her hands. Her mum! Her mum was having *such* a hissy fit! Miss Joyce must have phoned her yesterday afternoon to prepare her for that shitty report card, because she'd been in a terrible state when Lucy got home. She'd been apoplectic, practically purple in the face. No one had felt like cooking; there'd been nothing for dinner.

It wasn't until late at night that Lucy screwed up the courage to show her the report card. When she read it, her mother suddenly went icy calm. Or rather, it seemed to energize her. 'I'll tell you one thing, Lucy,' she said, in the tone of someone who has just had an idea that's been a long time brewing, 'I'm not going to sit back with my arms crossed and watch your future be jeopardized at that backward village school. You belong in a better school, in the city. Right away! We can't afford to waste any more time, with you not learning a damn thing. I'm going to look into it at once.'

Lucy jumped down off the bench and started kicking the bushes right and left. 'She says we're going to move!'

We stared at her, nonplussed. 'But she's got the flu,' we objected, 'and there's the Ten of Swords, too. Don't tell us she ...'

'That only proves how serious she is,' cried Lucy hoarsely. 'But I'm not leaving, you hear? I'm going to stay here, watch me. I'll just go into hiding. I'll run away and go hide over at Thomas's.'

We hastened to offer her our own basements, and then our attics, where it would be nice and snug for her because of the boiler being up there. We said we would sneak upstairs three times a day with a plate of sandwiches and a tangerine for her. We made it sound as comfy as we could, guiltily aware of the fact that Thomas's house would be the first place they'd go look for her, thanks to our brilliant anonymous letter. Except that it was possible her mother might not have read it yet, with all this other stuff going on.

'Lucy!' Ludo called, standing on the rectory's gravel path. 'Come inside, I've made you a sandwich!' With his hair blown back and his shirt collar flapping in the breeze, he cast a worried look up at the old chestnut trees in the front yard, which were creaking in the wind.

Lucy said in a low voice, 'I'm running away tonight. When my mother thinks I'm asleep.' Then she turned and ran inside.

# D is for Death

The wind picked up even more toward evening. In the gardens the bamboo swished back and forth. Rain exploded against the windows like water bombs. 'It's *nasty* out there,' said our mothers, closing the drapes and lighting candles. They padded around in stocking feet, neatly folding the scattered newspapers, plumping the sofa cushions, and rearranging the chrysanthemums in the vase on the table, to show the elements they weren't scared.

This had a contagious effect on our fathers. They got up to inspect the window sashes and door hinges. They opened the fuse box and peered inside a while. Then, rubbing their hands, they poured themselves a well-deserved beer and a glass of sherry for Mum. 'Come on, love, come and sit down here.' They were always at their best as a couple in what they considered an emergency.

They were so clueless that it took your breath away. They hadn't the faintest idea of the real dangers lurking everywhere, all the time. They were like Adam and Eve in the Garden of Eden, ignorant of evil. But we had long ago decided there was no point disabusing them of their illusions. It would be as mean as picking up a defenceless kitten by the scruff of the neck and dangling it out the attic window. If we shared with our parents what we knew about life and the universe and all that, they wouldn't know what hit them.

It was endearing, but annoying too, at times.

We sat down next to them on the couch. We sipped our hot chocolate. We agreed that the new Honda in the shiny brochure was really something. We talked about the sales coming up. We whined a bit when it was time for bed. But our thoughts were with Lucy the whole time.

Once under the covers, we anxiously listened to the howling wind. It was a wind that never died down, an angry, stubborn wind. We pictured the wind tugging at Lucy's hair as she clambered out of her attic window. Arms akimbo, she balanced in the gutter, her plaits whipping around her face like snakes, her clothes flapping in the gale.

We jumped out of bed, grabbed the first stuffed animal we could reach from the sill, and dove under the blankets again. Suddenly, the thought of Mum and Dad sitting downstairs, chatting about trivialities without the foggiest notion of what was happening, gave us a safe feeling, as if there really was nothing to worry about. But their innocence wouldn't stop Lucy from sliding down the gutter spout. It wouldn't prevent the wet ivy from slapping her in the face, making her lose her grip on the slippery downpipe and land on the ground with a crash.

'Ouch,' she squealed, scrambling to her feet in the rectory garden. Her face drawn in pain and apprehension, she shook her wrists a few times and then bent down to feel her knee.

Just then a thin wedge of light flashed across the lawn; someone pulling back the living-room curtains a crack. Lucy promptly pressed her back up against the wall. Was it her mother looking out the window, squinting into the darkness? Or was it one of the Luducos, wondering what had fallen off the roof? It could have been anything. A dead limb ripped off a tree by the wind. The lid of a dustbin careening through the yard. An exhausted crow tumbling out of the bruised sky. Going out to inspect the damage really wasn't a very appealing prospect in this filthy weather. The curtain was drawn shut again.

Just to make sure, Lucy waited a while longer. Over the howling of the wind she could now hear the voices in the living room, that's how loud and angry they were. She listened, aghast. There was a huge fight going on in there, an argument that matched the storm in its ferocity and made the walls quake. The whole house shook like a nuclear-power plant about to blow. Why were her mother and the Luducos screaming at each other, when normally they were the most conciliatory people in the entire world? It sounded as if things were being said that were better left unsaid, sour recriminations that had been pent up for so long that they'd begun to ferment and were now being spewed out in one big belch. The harsh words just kept coming; Lucy couldn't make head or tail of what they were saying, it was all just a great barrage of fury. Maybe she should go back inside and tell a funny joke or something. But just as she was considering that option, she heard, clear as a bell, her own name yelled out accusingly. Startled, she clapped her hands over her ears. Whatever it was that was being fought about so bitterly, it had something to do with her.

On tiptoe so as not to make the gravel crunch, she turned and ran into the street. Behind her the rectory grew smaller and smaller. She raced as fast as her legs would carry her, putting as much distance as possible between her and her mother poring over the Tarot cards to determine the most auspicious time for their move to the big city, and the Luducos yammering and wringing their pale hands because they were losing their lodgings.

We tossed and turned in our beds as Lucy bolted from the old village, leaving behind the patchouli scent, the string of Christmas lights over her bed, the juice you could spill without anyone raising an eyebrow, the tea you didn't have to drink, the picture of *Clara* 13 in the room where stories came to life. On her way to the house you weren't allowed to enter until you'd wiped your feet a good sixty times. To the linoleum that had been scrubbed to within an inch of its life. To the chlorine bleach that fizzed angrily at you.

Had the same thought suddenly occurred to Lucy, too? Her pounding feet started sounding like a tune that's lost its rhythm; or, you might even say, like a song sung backward. Her steps faltered and slowed. But the wind grabbed her by the scruff of the neck, pushed and prodded her in the back, and drove her on as if she were a dry autumn leaf. She started thrashing her arms and her legs. She tried to dig her heels into the pavement. But the wind roared, *On, on you go! You are mine now, because just a minute ago you were using me as your cover, and now you'll have to pay!*

We hugged our plush giraffes and bunnies to our chests. We were in such a state that we wished we could stick our thumbs in our mouths, but you weren't supposed to; if your teeth grew in crooked, you'd never make it very far. Our mothers never tired of reminding us of that, tapping a fingernail against their own pearly whites. They were always fretting about our future.

And who, meanwhile, was supposed to worry about the present?

We, of course. Really, it was all up to us. But our eyelids were growing so very heavy. We knew we had an obligation to stay awake with Lucy in her hour of need, but the urge to fall asleep kept growing stronger, just like the wind. We, too, put up a mighty struggle, and we, too, lost the fight.

But ours was not a peaceful sleep. Hovering somewhere between sleep and wakefulness, our minds dreamed up the weirdest scenarios. Lucy ringing the doorbell at Shepherd's Close, as if it were the most natural thing in the word.

She lucked out; it wasn't that walking dust mop that opened the door, it was Thomas's father. He was just as relaxed, just as self-assured, as in the classroom the first day, talking to Miss Joyce. Come on in, kid. A glass of milk? And a biscuit? Oh, don't worry about the crumbs. What did you say? You're coming to live with us? But of course, you're very welcome. The first thing I thought that day you arrived late for school was, That girl could have been my own daughter.

We sat up in bed, blinking. That Lucy, she always did manage to land in clover. Things had a habit of going her way. She was indomitable.

She sat down in the living room, making herself at home on the sofa covered in a starched, clean linen sheet.

'Do you want to listen to some music, Lucy?' asked the stinging-nettle man, stretching his back, hands laced behind his neck.

'Sure,' said Lucy. She felt like the queen of the castle.

'What would you like to hear?'

At home they never asked her what she wanted to hear. At home she had to put up with the Rolling Stones or Satie, or whatever else the adults were in the mood for. From now on *she* would be in charge of the mood. The music she now chose would be hers and hers alone, charged with the significance of this moment: Thomas's father saying she could stay with them, forever.

We must have nodded off again for a bit.

Now she was sitting on his lap, wide-eyed; it wasn't only the music she liked that interested him, he also wanted to know her favourite colour, what she liked to eat, and which fairy tale she liked best. Everything she said fascinated him.

'Red,' she said, 'or, no, orange.' She hadn't ever really given it much thought, but she was definitely the kind of girl who would go for orange—a hectic, dangerous colour.

Where would she like to go, if she had the choice? To the island of Robinson Crusoe and his man Friday, of course.

Her favourite animal was the moose.

Her favourite thing to wear was her Winnie the Pooh sweater.

Sport: soccer.

Season: spring, the first time you're allowed outside without a coat.

Ice cream: pistachio.

She gave the answers thoughtfully. She was like a page in a colouring book being filled in bit by bit. It became more and more obvious what she was: she wasn't the dumbest kid in the class who was going to be sent to another school in disgrace; no, on the contrary, she was someone with exceptional taste and ideas. Not that at home they hadn't been interested—quite the opposite. But her mother always assumed she knew what Lucy had to say before the words even passed her lips. Even before she opened her mouth, her mother had already jumped to some conclusion. You never got to understand yourself that way.

He laughed when she told him. His arms, hugging her chest, had big muscles from pushing the mower. He smelled of woodbine, earthy and wild.

What she would do with a million guilders.

What she'd never have the guts to do.

What she was best at.

What kind of things she collected.

What she'd most like to know.

Breathlessly, we sat up in our beds again. Here's your chance, Lucy! Here, finally, is the answer, offered to you on a silver platter.

She didn't have to think it over, not even for half a second. 'Where babies come from,' she said, nestling even more snugly in his lap.

Outside, the wind howled as if it had had a door slammed shut on its fingers. Inside, our parents blew out the candles, they carried their glasses to the kitchen, they turned off the lights, they brushed their teeth, and went to bed.

When we woke up that Sunday morning, we knew we must have dreamed the whole thing, because when we passed the rectory, we could see Lucy sitting in her dormer window, hugging her knees, her back pressed against the window frame. We yelled up at her, but she didn't react. She knew, of course, that we couldn't wait to make her pay for being such a braggart. Oh, going to run away, was she? 'Sissy!' we yelled. 'Scaredy-cat!'

The rest of the rectory's windows were still curtained, which somehow made the house look as if it harboured a secret that didn't tolerate daylight. The yard was littered with dead tree limbs. It was as if the storm had raged more fiercely here than anywhere else, with special evil intent. Spooky!

We raced off to our field, or at least what was left of it, now that the work had started on building the viaduct. It had long been stripped of all grass. Gone, too, were the stones under which we used to find the yellow-bellied salamanders. The ditch where Thomas had caught his rat had been drained dry. There was just grimy yellow sand everywhere. So this was what our dads called progress.

Glumly, we trudged across our former kingdom. And then we saw him. He was lying at the foot of the viaduct's first, only half-completed, pier—on his side, as if asleep, his head buried in his arms.

Oddly enough, we all had the exact same thought: that it must be one of the Luducos, gone out last night for a stroll, forgetting his keys. Ah, well, he'd have thought considerately, I won't get anyone out of bed, I'll just catch some winks out here. The man was of the same height as Lucy's lodgers, with the same thinning hair.

It wasn't until we got closer that we realized who it really was, and what was wrong with him. We jumped back in horror. From a safe distance we peered to see if there was any blood, but we couldn't spot any. Even so, it was fairly obvious that Thomas's father was as dead as a doornail.

# E is for Evil

The next Monday morning we started on a new chapter in
our reader, all about a mouse called Koos, but we couldn't
concentrate. We kept having to peek at Thomas's empty
desk. Halfway through the lesson, Miss Joyce sighed that
there was no point pretending it was a day like any other.
We'd better take out our crayons and make a lovely picture
for Thomas to show him how bad we felt for him.

With a loud clatter, we got out our crayons. But then the
classroom went very quiet. The idea that granddads died
and then never took you fishing again was hard enough to
fathom, but … your dad? Dads weren't supposed to die,
were they?

With clammy hands we drew a sou'wester lying abandoned on the ground in a stand of tall stinging nettles.
Down in a corner we drew Thomas with tears rolling down
his fat cheeks, with his mom next to him. Out of respect
we went back and erased her broom.

After a little while, Vanessa asked in a small voice, 'Did
he have cancer, Miss?'

Our teacher sat down, facing us on the bench where
Thomas and Lucy normally sat fondly bashing each other's

brains out. 'I really don't know,' she said.

Lucy wasn't at school that day, either. That was as it should be, naturally, if your fiancé's father had died. You were supposed to stay home and weep, with a black veil over your face. The tears you shed beneath that black veil turned into crystals, which you were supposed to store under your bed in a special little box, so you could take them out every so often and, smiling wistfully, watch them sparkle in the light.

Miss Joyce sighed again. She said, 'I'm afraid I know just as little about it as you. But I don't think he was ill. If he had been, he wouldn't have been able to hold down such a demanding physical job, landscaping in all kinds of weather, rain or shine.' She pulled the sleeves of her cardigan down over her hands. 'Luckily, it hardly ever happens, but it *is* possible, my pets, for someone's heart just to stop, or for something to suddenly go wrong in the brain.'

We, too, pulled down our sleeves. We swayed just as sadly from side to side as our teacher. It did help a little. Then we just sat for a while, saying nothing.

She said, 'If he'd been found earlier, who knows, he might still be … It was unfortunate that it happened during the storm, when no one else would venture outside.'

It was another reason Lucy had to be shedding bitter tears right now. If only she had run away from home as she'd said she would! Because in that case she'd have crossed the field on her way to Shepherd's Close. She'd have bumped into Thomas's father, out for a stroll or smoking a fag he wasn't allowed to light up at home. She would have seen him suddenly clutching his chest, and she'd have called for an ambulance. She'd probably even have been allowed to ride along in the ambulance, with the sirens going and all.

'Where is he now?'

'In the ground, isn't he?'

'No, silly, he's in heaven!'

Miss Joyce said, 'His body is being examined by a special kind of doctor to find out why he died. It's the law.'

We perked up. Right at this very moment, he was being sliced into little pieces and examined under a microscope. Then, as soon as those doctors found out what had malfunctioned, they'd fix it. Then they'd stuff everything back inside and sew him up again neatly. And then they'd give him a huge electric shock, and then he'd open his eyes and get up from the operating table.

'And after that,' said Miss Joyce sadly, 'they'll take him home in a coffin, and then anyone who wants to can go there to say goodbye.'

At lunchtime, nearly all of our mothers showed up in the schoolyard. As soon as they saw Miss Joyce, they thronged around her, arms waving in the air. As if it wasn't horrible enough, they cried, they'd just heard a piece of even more appalling news, first from Mr De Vries, who had a son who was a policeman, and then again at the baker's, whose middle daughter was married to Mr De Vries's son.

They had immediately decided that the children could no longer be allowed to walk to school and back by themselves. They had already worked out a carpool. They made our teacher swear she'd watch us like a hawk at recess, and be extra careful herself, for that matter. 'Because he didn't die from natural causes,' they whispered behind their hands. 'It was foul play!' They couldn't bring themselves to say any more; the very thought of it made them gag. With grim faces they grabbed us, lifted us onto the back of their bikes, and raced home. We didn't know what had hit us.

Wherever you looked, you saw mothers with their kids on the backs of their bikes, or mothers dragging their progeny along on the pavement. On every street corner people stood in little huddles, whispering. The streets were buzzing with the shocking word that nobody had ever expected to use with regard to an acquaintance or a neighbour, even if he was only a superficial acquaintance or a relatively new neighbour: *murder.* Murder on home turf! Murder in the pioneer housing estate the prime minister had inaugurated in person, before the cameras of *The Evening News*, brandishing a great big symbolic key made of gold-painted plywood! He had spoken of a new way of life. A new, safer era for our country.

The newspaper cuttings were still pinned to our kitchen cabinets. If we climbed on a stool we could touch them; by now they were as dry and wrinkly as an oak leaf pressed between the pages of a book and then forgotten. The cuttings drew a lovely picture of the picturesque new housing enclave, a place that avoided the urban blight of slums, poverty and decay. Here there were no homeless people, no crazies with matted beards (whether borderline or completely insane) sleeping in your doorway because the shelters had run out of room, no junkies or dealers on every bridge, underage prostitutes with laddered black stockings, pickpockets, preachers of the apocalypse, alcoholics, bicycle thieves, foreigners with hungry eyes, foreigners with vacant eyes, foreigners out to steal your car radio, foreigners out to rape your daughter, pimps walking around with a menacing swagger, or apartment dwellers who are so upset at the infernal racket their neighbours make that they resort to smearing the communal stairs with green soap.

Here everything would be different, the newspapers promised. No dark, dangerous alleys in *our* neighbourhood. No riff-raff in *our* streets. No risk of the menace that elsewhere could ambush you in your own home. And now?

Now that promise of a safe life was smashed to smithereens. But where could our shocked mothers turn to recoup their loss? If only reality came with an on-and-off switch, like the TV, which they always hastily turned off when something unpleasant came on, like the recent news report about those kids who had been lured into the woods by some man.

Instead of making us lunch, our mothers gathered in one another's living rooms with unkempt hair that would soon reek of smoke and cigarettes. They talked in low voices. Out in the corridor, we pressed our ears to the wall.

What, they asked one another, could possibly have led to this criminal act? If only they had the facts, a motive, the reason. Because what if there was a dangerous lunatic at large, ready to claim another innocent victim tomorrow? What should they do? And, by the way, shouldn't one of them go over to Thomas's mother, to see how she was holding up? They sighed deeply. They crushed out their cigarettes. They huddled a little closer together. Then, finally, they got down to the nitty-gritty. 'A *pencil*,' they said. 'Who would ever think of that?'

Mr De Vries's son and his colleagues didn't need an autopsy of Thomas's father's heart, or of his blood vessels, or his lungs. His stomach didn't have to be pumped to check for anything more unusual than the leeks, meatballs, and vanilla pudding he'd had for dinner that fateful night. They'd immediately known what the pathologist and his helpers had to examine, because there was just one very visible injury. All they'd needed was a pair of tweezers.

They couldn't help whistling through their teeth when the pathologist pulled the pencil out of the deceased's left eye. It had been driven into the eye with such force that the point had broken off against the inside of his skull. It was a fat, round, red colouring pencil.

He must have died instantaneously.

When at five o'clock that evening the details of the murder were published in the newspaper, our mothers could no longer keep it from us.

After tea we managed to give them the slip and snuck out of the house. We met up on the green. Hiding behind the beech hedge, we kept the rectory under surveillance. We waited patiently, confident that the police would come to the same conclusion as us. After all, there weren't too many people who used that kind of pencil; it was only too obvious the murder weapon had come from this house. The killer must have stolen it from the studio. Or maybe he'd pinched it from Lucy's backpack.

There were two of them, and they arrived in an ordinary, unmarked car. Their faces were ordinary too, and their windbreakers were so ho-hum that it almost made you fall asleep. It was all very different from what we'd seen on TV.

They were inside for an hour, at least.

We could feel our hair growing, that was how little else was happening. We hadn't expected them to take this long over the identification of stolen goods. Though they had to be careful not to erase any fingerprints, of course.

Suddenly the rectory's front door opened. Flanked by the two detectives, Lucy's mother came out. She walked resolutely down the path, carrying an overnight bag, the kind mothers always took with them when they had to go to hospital to have another baby. One of the detectives held the car door open for her. Just as resolutely, she climbed into the back seat. We couldn't see the expression on her face because her long, straight hair hung down like a curtain. It was as if she just had to go somewhere, and was thinking, How lucky that these nice gentlemen can give me a lift!

We all rose to our feet to gaze after the car. When it disappeared round the corner, we looked back at the house.

The rectory seemed to tower even higher than usual over the surrounding houses. We flung our heads back, but we didn't see Lucy in the attic window gazing after her mother as she was driven away. We tiptoed up to the blue stoop and pressed our ears against the door. Inside we heard creaking sounds, the house sighing and quietly groaning, as usual. We rang the doorbell.

It took a while before we heard footsteps in the hall. Either Ludo or Duco pulled open the door with some effort, as if it had suddenly grown considerably heavier. We hardly recognized him. His eyes were bloodshot, his cheeks were sunken, his hairline seemed to have receded at least another four inches, while what was left of his hair was sticking straight out on either side of his head. He tried to say something, but his mouth was too trembly to get any words out.

Unceremoniously, we shoved him out of our way and thronged inside. 'Lucy!' we cried into the dark, cavernous hallway.

Ahead of us, at the end of the corridor, a faint shimmer of light spilled from the semi-closed kitchen door onto the tiled floor. Stumbling towards it, we flung the door all the way open.

Lucy was sitting at the kitchen table with her head buried in her arms. Her back was arched like an angry cat's. Her bony vertebrae poked through her sweater. Her legs were clasped around the rungs of her chair as if she were afraid she'd float up to the ceiling otherwise. Ludo—we could tell from the shoes it was he—sat next to her, rubbing her back.

The kitchen smelled of ginger biscuits and chamomile tea. As usual, there were piles of dirty dishes on the granite counter. The hum of the water heater was a hum as familiar as our own heartbeat. The last of the stickers we had stuck on the fogged-up window a while ago were peeling off. For a while there, they had been giving out stickers with every purchase: petrol or chips or detergent. We'd been over the moon about it at first, collecting them greedily and swapping them in elaborate transactions—blood was spilled over those stickers!—but in the end we got fed up with them, we wound up just sticking them anywhere, indiscriminately, on any convenient surface, there were just too many of them, it was *raining* stickers, and still our mothers insisted on bringing them home with a tireless zeal that embarrassed us no end, they kept buying more stuff just so they could saddle us with even *more* of those wretched stickers; all in all, it had been a complete farce.

In the doorway, Duco said, 'I couldn't stop them.'

Ludo looked up as if he'd only just realized we were in the kitchen. Then he shook Lucy's shoulder gently. 'Honey,' he said, 'your friends are here.'

But she didn't raise her head from the tabletop, which was a mess of white rings made by juice glasses.

Ludo said, 'It *is* sweet of you to have come over right away.'

We glowed with pride. The Three of Cups, the card of friendship: that was the most important card of all.

Duco walked over to the cooker. He started turning on the burners, one after another.

Ludo went on rubbing Lucy's back. He didn't explain what else you were supposed to do in this situation, besides coming over right away.

Duco told us, 'We're about to eat.' All four burners were now blazing away. The gas hissed. But we didn't see any pan of potatoes, nor even the faintest sign of dinner preparations.

Yet, for some reason, we had suddenly lost the nerve to ask why Lucy's mother had gone with the police, or where. Too embarrassed to open our mouths, we scuffed our feet on the floor. Our eyes darted here, there, and everywhere, trying to find inspiration for something to say. But all we saw were the Luducos' crumpled faces and Lucy's winter-white neck, and it was hard to say which of those was the most pathetic.

'Oh honey,' Ludo muttered. 'Oh my little girl.'

Shuddering, Lucy hunched her shoulders a little higher.

Duco stared at the blue gas flames.

Our parents were waiting for us at home; surely Lucy would understand that. In countless houses mothers were beginning to fume, glancing at the clock. They were starting to hurl complaints about like tossed frisbees: Jesus Christ, I'm not running a hotel here! Then, beginning to get worried—there was a murderer on the loose, after all—they grabbed coats, scarves, hats, gloves, and flashlights. They ran into the street. They called out our names. They bumped into each other in the dark, and cried out in alarm, 'Yours too?' Suddenly weak at the knees, they propped one another up, fear clutching at their hearts. *Anything*, they'd do anything for us: wash our dirty socks and knickers, clean up our messes, donate their last kidney to us—'That's what a mother is for, darling.' They'd do *anything* to have us back. But something as simple as walking over to the rectory to rescue us from that awkward scene in the kitchen? The thought never even entered their heads.

Frightened, we grabbed one another by the hand. All we could hope for now was that Lucy's mother would shortly hitch a ride home. As soon as she walked in, everything would go back to normal again. But as Duco went on staring at the flames as if paralyzed, and Lucy began to sob under her breath, it finally hit home: we had probably seen the last of her, for the time being.

The authorities promptly started showing up. Lady social workers in grubby sweaters with their hair in a bun marched in and out of the rectory. They took notes and wrote reports. They had to grudgingly concede in the end that it would be best for Lucy to stay where she was. Especially in light of the fact that the Luducos had immediately stepped up to the plate and offered to look after her. A mother accused of murder—it was such a dreadfully traumatic thing for a six-year-old to have to go through that further changes in her living conditions could prove dire, if not fatal. Peace and quiet, and an orderly routine in a familiar environment: that was the ticket. At least for the duration of the preliminary investigation, which could drag on for months.

They signed their report with a flourish, and left.

We read, *The dog has a bone*. We read, *What do I hear?* We read and we read, as if the only way we could keep the world turning was by deciphering new words and learning their meanings. Miss Joyce slowly paced back and forth among our desks. Every time she walked by Lucy, she'd tug her plaits straight or fold her collar down neatly. At recess she sometimes gave her a banana.

Lucy wouldn't speak. She chewed on her fingernails. All her drawings had prison bars.

Thomas had returned to school with a note from his mum. The teacher had read it, nodding sadly, and then assigned him a new seat at the back of the classroom. There he now sat every day all by himself, being what he forever would be: a fatherless boy. You could hear it in his voice when it was his turn, when he droned in his rapid but vapid monotone, 'See, the fox is in the box. The fox sees the dog. The dog runs up the tree. The tree is in the wood.' You could tell how much he missed his father, especially when he read the words 'tree' and 'wood,' and he was starting to scare us—his sadness scared us, his anger and his despair. During break he went off by himself in the playground, kicking at pebbles the way he had once kicked at clumps of grass in our field. Lucy, slumped against a wall, watched him, her eyes burning in her pale face like two pieces of glowing coal. He ignored her. He looked right through her. As far as he was concerned, she didn't exist.

The rest of us, who used to know everything there was to know about Lucy, now knew next to nothing. Day in, day out, we'd hang around, trying to wangle some information out of her. More than once we spotted the detectives' car parked out in front of the rectory. What were they doing there?

She wouldn't answer us. She bowed her head and kept her mouth shut.

We tried to imagine her mother in a smoky interrogation room, a blinding spotlight trained on her face. The thought gave us hope. The interrogators were bound to fall head over heels in love with her, that was a given. She'd end up winding them around her little finger. She would simply roll them up and tuck them in her pocket. Before we knew it, she'd be home again. And then Lucy and Thomas would sit together again in the front row in Miss Joyce's classroom, as usual. Lucy would be talking a mile a minute again, glaring at anyone who so much as thought of mocking her fiancé. It would probably annoy the hell out of us; still, anything was better than this quiet, dazed Lucy with the bowed head. This was a turn of affairs we'd certainly never asked for. None of us was any the better off for it.

Our parents bought Christmas trees in the town square. They treated us to doughnuts in a pedestrian mall that was so draughty that the powdered sugar flew everywhere. Then we went window-shopping; Mum grabbed Dad's sleeve firmly when the jeweller's window display came into sight.

For weeks, festive lights twinkled indoors and out, angelic music played, bells went ding-a-ling, the world smelled of pine needles, mulled wine, and toasted almonds.

On New Year's Eve we had our first glass of champagne. Our fathers got to their feet to toast the new year, one that would hopefully prove safer for everyone, with more police patrolling the streets. 'We're lucky; *we* still have each other,' said our mothers. 'Let's always remember that, and be thankful for it, too.' Then we had to pretend we had the hiccups, if we wanted to avoid a round of hugs and kisses.

Next came a cold spell, with deep snowdrifts. We were pulled to school on our sleds. We got ice skates, because when you were six it was high time you learned to skate. You'd thank your parents someday. You could hear the water slapping softly against the ice from below. It was scored with grooves that tripped you up. It was just a question of gritting your teeth and trying to keep going.

Sometimes we'd spot the Luducos pulling a listless Lucy across the ice. Methodically, assiduously, the Luducos would swing their legs, left, right, left, as they dragged her along. At the far end of the pond they made a pirouette, then they skated back smartly, with Lucy in the middle. Over the open ice they went, left, right, left, the Luducos in hats that probably dated from the First World War, and our Lucy with a scarf tied across her mouth. A scarf that said: I will not talk.

What *was* she keeping from us?

Sometimes Thomas's mother would come to the pond,

too, to watch from the sidelines. After all, bacteria are killed by the cold. But she never spoke to anyone, and in the end, people gave up trying to get her involved in the fun on the ice.

There was no one to pull Thomas across the dark expanse, nobody to teach him how to dig the toe of your skate into the ice to come to a screeching halt. Half the time he'd just stand and watch next to his mother on the frozen grass, with such a look of yearning in his eyes that the rest of us were inclined to press our foreheads into our own dads' stomachs. But Dad shook us off; he was busy trying to impress the new lady next door, who had no idea how he smelled when he got up out of bed in the morning. He was talking in this cool, amused way. Out of the corner of his mouth came a message meant only for us, a message we had to lip-read so he wouldn't have to say it out loud: *Scram. Go on, scram, get lost!*

And when the ice melted and everything turned green again, the criminal investigation was finally completed and the trial could begin.

Soon enough, the newspapers talked of nothing else.

# F is for the Facts

Indignant about the verdict—surely a terrible miscarriage of justice—our mothers immediately started circulating petitions. If it had been *their* daughter, they said, they would have done the exact same thing as Lucy's mother. Now that the motive for the murder was known, they had only one thing to say, and that was that they, too, would have stabbed the living daylights out of Thomas's father with whatever object happened to come to hand.

Our fathers scratched themselves somewhat uneasily behind the ears. They'd never realized they were married to women who approved of murder and homicide under certain conditions. In a reasonable voice they tried to object, saying the law *did* exist for a reason. The woman could have filed a complaint against Thomas's father—that's the way these things were handled in a law-abiding society. If not, democracy would soon become a free-for-all. Civilized society would go to hell in a handbasket. Taking the law into your own hands was contrary to the principles of international human rights. Every person had the right to a fair trial; the legal recourses were perfectly adequate.

Our mothers placed their hands on their hips. Oh yeah?

Oh yeah? And what if it had been our own Vanessa, our Safranja, or our Sara? What if it had been *our* little girl? Poor Lucy, only six years old and already damaged goods! Jesus Christ, surely no punishment was harsh enough for that kind of atrocity! And besides, why should the taxpayer be saddled with the cost of feeding and housing a pervert like that? To have him enjoy a nice long holiday in some cushy cell?

But now *she* was sitting in that cell, our fathers demurred.

Our mothers stamped their feet. Precisely, it was a gross injustice and it had to be put right! Why was Lucy's mother languishing in Bijlmer Jail? Because some man hadn't been able to keep his hands and the rest where they belonged for a change, that's why! You couldn't turn on the television or open the newspaper without having your nose rubbed in it over and over again! Always the same story! And this one was a father himself, as well! Oh, sorry, we mean *had been!* Their eyes flashing with fury, they slammed the door behind them and took their petitions to the mall to make the most of the Saturday crowds.

When they hadn't come home by six o'clock, Daddy made us crackers with cream cheese. All well and good, he said, but there was no need to take it so personally.

Too late: our mothers had discovered sisterhood.

They no longer had the time to come and sit on our beds when we'd had a bad dream. They were no longer available for sore throats or scraped knees. Their meetings went on until late in the night. They pored over the newspaper articles and editorials, comparing and contrasting them until they had reconstructed the statement Lucy's mother had presumably made in court, from beginning to end. Where the accounts conflicted, our mothers simply split the difference. When a question came up that even the prosecutor hadn't been able to resolve, they hit upon the answer. That was because they were able to fill in every hole in the story straight from the gut; they didn't need anyone telling *them* what it meant to be a mother.

Their conclusion was that it had been an emotional chain reaction. There had been no premeditation on Lucy's mother's part; she'd had no plan, she hadn't known what she was going to do. There had been no time. She hadn't even put on a coat. She had simply dashed out of the house, driven by her maternal instinct.

They couldn't check with her if they'd hit the nail on the head, naturally. But according to the explanation they'd cobbled together, and which they managed to turn into a convincing story through sheer force of imagination, it must have happened as follows: their friend had been about to turn in when she'd heard a strange noise outside. It sounded like the moaning of a dog that had been hit by a car. Startled, she'd gone to check it out. She didn't see anything unusual out on the road. But as she strode back up the garden path, she heard it again. She debated whether she should wake the Luducos. And then she spotted Lucy.

Her little girl, whom she'd thought tucked safely into bed, was lying rolled up in a little heap under a privet bush. She was clawing at the earth as if trying to dig a hole she could sink into and disappear. She was whimpering pitifully.

Horrified, she had carried the traumatized child inside. There, not knowing what else to do, she had run a hot bath. But Lucy had refused to take her clothes off. She'd stood in the middle of the bathroom, teeth chattering, stiff as a board, hugging herself. And then the whole story had come pouring out.

Lucy's mother knew she had to stay calm. That only a calm and composed reaction from her could make the world bearable again for Lucy. So she had gently lowered her into the bath, sponged her back, and quietly sung to her. And after that, she had put her to bed with a sleeping pill. The child had almost immediately nodded off from sheer exhaustion.

Pulling the attic door shut behind her, she was still intending to wake up the Luducos; it was her turn to weep and groan and get it out of her system. But the next thing she knew, not really realizing what she was doing, she was already out of the house, spurred on by some primitive urge further inflamed by bitter self-reproach. Could she have failed more drastically as a parent? Her little girl had run away from home! She had to put things right, fix it, undo the damage.

Assaulted by someone the kid had run to for shelter! A great wrong had been done to Lucy, an injustice of the worst kind. She had a red haze swimming before her eyes. She thrust her hands into the pockets of her cardigan, but found nothing there except a couple of pencils and crayons.

She had already left the centre of the old village behind, she felt sand crunching underfoot, she was running up to the new housing estate, stumbling and cursing. The wind blew paper and other debris into her face, she had to halt for a second to wipe the tears from her eyes, and then she spotted him, in the orange glow of the construction floodlights. He was standing in the lee of one of the piers of the new overpass, smoking a cigarette.

She thought, coolly, Sure, out for a breath of fresh air to get rid of the smell of sex! Slowly she walked up to him. She raised her arm. And just as she was about to tap him on the shoulder, he turned round.

He didn't even have a chance to register surprise or alarm. The moment his eyes met hers, he was done for. His were the eyes that had lusted after her child.

Afterward she went home, drained. She decided she would cook up a special breakfast in the morning. Pancakes for Lucy and scrambled eggs for the Luducos, who had no inkling, sleeping the sleep of the innocent, as always, their shoes lined up neatly in the corridor like good boys and girls.

Our mothers felt as if they had been there themselves. They seethed with indignation and solidarity, and at home the sisterhood was now a presence at every meal, like an uninvited guest who doesn't have the decency to keep quiet. There was a fair bit of fist-banging and dish-rattling. Grim slogans like *Dictatorship of the prick* were bandied about, and when it was time for the washing-up, we'd hear protest songs coming from the kitchen along the lines of *Bollocks to balls!*

It was all making us more and more anxious. If we understood correctly what was meant by 'emotional chain reaction,' then it looked as though soon there would be nothing for us to eat but cream-cheese crackers. We'd have to stuff our own clothes into the washing machine and work out which knobs you had to push. We'd come home from school every day with a latchkey on a string around our necks, back to a house with not a single pumpkin in the window. There'd be nobody to clap her hands in admiration of our drawings, or to praise us for how fast we could read an entire page from top to bottom!

Our mums had completely flipped out on behalf of a mother who—admit it—had never really understood how a mother was supposed to behave. We remembered the way she would coolly stay at her drawing table even when we were in the process of reducing the place to rubble. Her bare feet. The tea that was never offered. The dirty dishes in the sink. The dust along the mouldings. The skirt with the slit up the side. The purple lipstick. The long, sweet-smelling hippie hair.

'And don't forget those Luco boys of hers,' said our fathers, cross-eyed with spite. 'Lodgers, my foot! And with a child in the house, too.'

'Please! Where did you get *that* idea? It just goes to show you've got a one-track mind!' our mothers bitched back, in their it's-always-the-same-story-with-you-isn't-it voice.

'Simple. I know human nature. You sit there yakking your heads off, but what do you *really* know about her? Did you ever ask her what happened to Lucy's father? Well? Isn't it possible she helped that one into his grave as well?'

Oh, everyone's life will have a few loose ends, our mummies remarked, this time a bit less stridently, because they had to rid themselves of the pesky thought that it was true that Lucy's mother had never been very forthcoming about her past.

Our mothers couldn't get to sleep at night. They paced up and down in their dressing gowns, then sat down at the kitchen table with pen and paper. They made notes and lists of priorities. They drew little arrows up, down, and sideways. They tried to plot a course for themselves through the minefields of the patriarchy. Sure, the scales had fallen from their eyes. But that didn't mean that a whole new world order had suddenly emerged, or that they were ready to change course. They had only their sisterhood to cling to. And even that wasn't without its problems, because when all was said and done, sisterhood was supposed to include *all* women—including the filthy pervert's wife. Who—to look at it another way—was herself a victim, surely. In a different sense, perhaps, but none the less tragic for that.

They remembered how in the winter she had come to

watch the ice-skating. Had her awkward silence really been a scream for help?

To everyone's astonishment, Thomas's mother showed up right on time to the coffee to which, for appearance's sake, 'the whole neighbourhood' had been invited. Her neck was covered in red blotches, she was lugging a large handbag and wearing rubber gloves that everyone politely pretended not to notice. After all, her germ phobia had now acquired a new, symbolic significance.

Love, our mothers thought glumly, was a funny business, wasn't it? They stirred their coffees while working up the nerve to say something.

She, too, was visibly struggling in that unfamiliar living room. She seemed on the verge of tears, like a little kid who realizes too late that she's come out without boots or mittens when the weather turns nasty.

Our mothers' hearts went out to her. Timidly, they asked her if she was doing all right now.

'It's a nightmare,' she burst out. 'A complete nightmare. For Thomas it's even worse, of course. To lose your father that way—so suddenly, too! They used to sit together, you know, every night, with their noses buried in their nature books, and then, all of a sudden ... You have to know that my husband was seriously dyslexic, couldn't do much more than look at the pictures, so he was especially proud of our Thomas being such a good reader, he told me once, he said ...' Tears were streaming down her cheeks. 'He said, "Thomas is a new and improved version of me."'

Our mothers put their cups down. They noticed their hands were shaking.

'Such a wonderful father, he was! Nothing was too much for him. On the first day of school, he took Thomas to school just so he could see what kind of clothes the other kids around here wore. So that Thomas wouldn't stick out like a sore thumb. I get out of the house so rarely, I really can't take care of that sort of thing.' She wagged her yellow gloves helplessly. 'What's to become of him now? I told him he can have goldfish. But a boy needs his father. How are we going to manage when he gets older? Or do you think I should have promised to get him a dog, for him to wrestle and play with?'

For a moment she seemed just as taken aback by her own loquaciousness as our mothers were. But now that the silence was broken, there was no stopping her. 'He's so ashamed. He's afraid people will believe the stuff in the newspapers about his father. Surely the poor kid doesn't deserve that? That, on top of everything else? He keeps asking me if we can't move, if we can't go somewhere where nobody knows us. And I keep telling him, "If we left now, it would only make people think that what they said about Daddy in the papers is true." All those lurid, sensational articles.' Leaning down, she pulled a stack of newspaper cuttings from her handbag.

Outside, we hopped up and down, trying to see inside. We recognized who was in there. We ducked down again when Thomas's mum began reading out loud. She read in the same rushed, vapid monotone as Thomas. Finally it was quiet; she'd finished reading the whole lot. We hoisted ourselves up again to peek under the venetian blind.

Our mothers sat there as if this was the first time they'd heard those newspaper stories. With downcast eyes they were pushing back their cuticles, or just staring at their knees.

Thomas's mother stowed the cuttings back inside her handbag and said, 'The fact that it now seems that her whole story was based on lies and fabrications—that's easy to miss, isn't it? Thank God the court didn't fall for it, but in the meantime her version was reported in all the rags, all of it. It's what's "in" these days, it's what they like to write about, that kind of story. You know, sexually abused children and all that. Of course she was clever enough to jump on that bandwagon. But my poor little boy at home, he reads everything! Tommy, I keep telling him over and over, the things it says there, nothing as nasty as that ever happened, I swear, Tommy. Tomster, my husband used to call him, "Hey, Tomster, how's it going?" But if I say Tomster now, he gets cross with me, so I just say Tommy-dear, just listen, listen to Mummy now: they *never* found anything on that little girl, any DNA evidence … How am I supposed to explain those things to him, I so did want to spare my child all that filth, six is much too young, he still believes in the stork and everything …'

'Oh, but so do ours,' said our mothers gratefully. 'At their age—they're still little kids!'

The second round of coffee was poured.

'They didn't find any DNA evidence,' she repeated emphatically. 'And the little girl's testimony wasn't very convincing, either. She was just making it up as she went along. Her story was just full of holes. Thank God they called me as a witness as well. I know my husband, don't I? I *knew* him, I mean. Of course he wasn't always the most faithful of husbands, but there it is, women found him attractive, he couldn't help it.'

Our mothers remembered they used to speculate he must be good in bed, and they blushed.

'He often gave me cause for jealousy; but then I, in turn, didn't always do right by him, either. Ours wasn't a perfect marriage, but he did love me, he always came back to me in the end. If he'd had these kinds of … cravings, I'd have known about it. He always told me everything. So I also knew right away when he started having an affair with *her*.'

Our mothers looked at each other, nonplussed.

'Didn't you know? That bitch, that murderess, used to live near us, in our former village. May God forgive me for telling the judge about it, but I felt I was obliged to. She'd been hell-bent on stealing my husband. When she found out she couldn't have him, she came and yelled obscenities through the mail slot, and more than once, too. It was a relief when she moved away, let me tell you. If only we'd known where she'd gone, because if we had, we would never have moved here, and Thomas would still to this day have a father.' When she'd finished, she stood up, brushed off her skirt, and said goodbye, shaking everyone's hand with her squeaky canary-yellow glove.

We ducked just in the nick of time before she stepped outside.

On the other side of the window it was quiet for quite a while, even after she'd long disappeared from sight. Our mothers just sat there, crestfallen. They'd been ready to put everything on the line for the cause of justice; they had even put their domestic harmony at risk. Had they bet on the wrong horse?

Miserably, they remembered what our fathers had said. You thought you knew someone, but deep down, what did you really know about her? All those happy hours in the rectory, all those intimate tête-à-têtes, when they had poured out their heart and soul to her. Hadn't it been a true friendship, then? Had she been fooling them for all these years? They started giggling nervously. What did they care, really, what may or may not have happened long ago? Even if it were true that Lucy's mother had once been dumped by a man, which they didn't think very likely— not on this planet, anyway—wouldn't she have taken her revenge right then and there? Why wait and do it years later, when by pure coincidence the guy who rejected her—yeah, the hell he had!—crossed paths with her again? No, they couldn't see any logical connection between what happened back then and what had happened now, nothing to set off this sort of chain reaction.

Our mothers could appreciate that Thomas's mother would leave no stone unturned to clear her husband's name, if only for the sake of that poor boy of hers. For that reason alone, her words carried pitifully little weight. Yes, that was right, wasn't it? Didn't the facts speak for themselves, after all? Little Lucy had confirmed the facts under oath. Okay, so maybe the child's testimony hadn't been completely consistent, but what did you expect? Because how would someone her age find the right words? As a mother, you could only fervently hope that your child would *not* be able to come up with the right words for this sort of outrage!

Just look at that poor little girl, so pale and withdrawn these days; if that didn't prove it for once and for all! It just broke your heart, it did, to see her trudging through the village clutching Ludo's or Duco's hand. A recent article in *Parents Today* had stated that abused children are often haunted by the notion they are responsible for what was done to them. Just think how guilty a little tyke would feel if her mother wound up in the slammer on account of what had happened! Especially a little girl with an imagination as lively as Lucy's. A fertile mind, while extolled by educators everywhere, could also be a terrible cross to bear.

'We'd better keep an eye on her, it may all prove too much for her,' our mothers urged one another, because here at least was something practical, something to sink their teeth into. The more steeply Lucy went into decline, the more reason they had to believe in her mother's innocence—to believe in their friend, who would not be going barefoot in the grass for the time being, who was looking at twelve years behind bars. How was it possible, for God's sake, for a complete innocent like her, with no prior convictions, to get sentenced to twelve years?

They had no idea, none of them.

But the longer they stewed over it, the more the question dug in its heels and then threw itself back in their faces. How, indeed? Chagrined, they recapitulated what they knew. Lucy's testimony, the lynchpin around which it all revolved, turned out on closer inspection to indeed be a little shaky, a bit muddled. It hadn't struck them that way before, but that may have been because all their attention was focused on their friend's predicament. They would have to reconsider everything.

Outside, we children had run out of patience. We began banging on the window and pulling funny faces.

Sighing, they said, 'Ah, there they are, our little brats.' They forced their lips into a smile and waved at us to come inside.

We climbed into their laps, we tugged at their hair, we squished their cheeks between our hands and squealed that it made them look like guinea pigs.

'*Must* you always demand so much attention?' they complained. 'You're little terrors, the lot of you!' And as soon as the words were out of their mouths, everything suddenly fell into place, and they could see the entire drama, clear as glass.

The mother, always at her drawing table, wholly absorbed in her work.

The child, frequently left to her own devices for long stretches of time.

The mother who just *had* to finish that picture.

The child who consequently was free to watch TV programmes the other children weren't allowed to see—like the news, showing one sleazy sex scandal after another.

The mother, feverish with inspiration, working on behind her closed door.

The child with the lively imagination, bored to death downstairs, pining for attention.

The thought of it sent our mothers into a complete tailspin; they stared at one another in consternation. They had always considered Lucy such an unusual child, even when she was very young, so strong-willed you couldn't distract her like other babies, and those eyes of hers, always brimming with schemes and wild stories.

And as a mother, you always believed your child without question; that was something they knew from experience.

# G is for Garlic

Miss Joyce decided we ought to have something to take our minds off it. We needed a distraction. There was more to life than that one tragic incident. There still were other things in the world. Happy things. Things you could accomplish together, putting your shoulders to the wheel as a team. A joint project: that was the ticket. A project that, with the end of the school year coming up, would win us accolades to boot. A project so contagious and fun that it would make everyone for miles around smile again.

We heard her proposal with interest. It sounded as if it might just blow our parents away. And so we gave the Big Letter Show a big thumbs up.

For months we worked on the show in the greatest secrecy. In Arts and Crafts, we constructed huge letters of papier-mâché, which we painted all the colours of the rainbow. Music was devoted to the songs we'd be singing; in Gym, we practised the dances. It was devilishly hard. First we'd take on the animal kingdom: DOG, CAT, BUG, FISH, and GOAT. Then, the foods we eat: PLUM, FLOUR, CAKE, HAM, and MILK. You had to dance your guts out, then step forward on cue and display your letter up high in the air, so that—*shebang!*—you were all lined up just right so that the audience could suddenly read your word. In the next bit, representing the human body with NECK, CHIN, NOSE, and ARM, the *E*, the *N* and the *C* had a hell of a time constantly changing places. In between, the *Q* had a solo, as did the *X*, while in the background the rest of us raised our hands with puzzled expressions on our faces. The finale had us spelling out BRAVO, with Miss Joyce as the exclamation point at the end, and tons of streamers and confetti.

We were *so* ready for prime time.

Our only problem was Lucy.

We really thought the least she could do was give some sign that she was happy that she didn't have to move away. After all, she had what she wanted: she was still home, as ever, in our village. And we were the best company anyone could wish for. You could have loads of fun with us, you could build arks, we weren't sissies, we had a trapeze act and *Simon Says* and we were as dependable as the Bank of the Netherlands: you could hang us upside down from the monkey bars and we *still* wouldn't ever snitch on you. So there was no reason she couldn't confide in us and tell us what exactly had happened that night. Our mothers, too, kept saying the same thing: only Lucy *really* knew what happened; she alone knew the score. 'Why don't you ask her?' they said. 'Just ask her, why don't you.'

It really galled us, the way she insisted on playing deaf and dumb. It made no difference whether we brought up the subject in a roundabout way or got straight to the point. But that wasn't the way it was supposed to be among friends, was it? Among friends, you weren't supposed to keep secrets to yourself; on the contrary, you were supposed to share them. Because we knew, having learned about the bread and fishes in Miss Joyce's Religious

Instruction, that the more you shared, the more there was to go around. If Lucy shared her secret with us, it would only get even *more* secret, it would end up being the biggest, awesomest secret in the whole wide world. On the street, people would step back in awe when they saw us pass by, wearing grave expressions: 'There go the children who know the secret!'

Spitefully, we watched her stuttering and stumbling through another reading lesson. Without Thomas to help her, the alphabet appeared to be a completely impossible hurdle for her. Through clenched lips she swore the letters turned their backs on her. But when we peeked over her shoulder, we realized that our mothers were right: that girl had a much more active imagination than was good for her. 'Miss!' we cried out anxiously. 'She's going to ruin our show!'

'Lucy has special trouble reading. She can't help it. She's receiving remedial help, and she really is trying her best,' said Miss Joyce, but she looked as if she only half-believed it herself. The truth was that she preferred success, and we couldn't really blame her, either.

The night of the performance on the last day of school, our parents were just as excited as we were. Nearly all the dads came home from work earlier than usual. Nearly all the mums put on a brand new T-shirt and lip gloss. Then we all walked to school hand in hand.

We were, our fathers said contentedly as we walked along, the very model of a perfect family again.

Our mothers cracked a sour smile. It wasn't that the ball and chain had proved to be a more irresistible force than the sisterhood. It was more a question of perception, the stark realization that certain responsibilities rested on a mother's shoulders alone: if you didn't stay right on top of your children when they were young, there was a risk they'd grow up twisted, mentally and morally. Instinctively, they tightened their grip on our hands. And a message promptly snaked its way from our fingers, up their arms, to that special brain cell that's primed to receive and decode maternal signals: 'Yes, you'll always come first, that's just how it is. I'll always have to sacrifice my own needs for yours.'

When we reached the schoolyard we saw Thomas arriving with his mother. They went inside with their heads down, as if they were ashamed they were no longer a complete nuclear family. We squeezed our daddies' hands as firmly as we could, but Daddy's hand didn't have the same kind of message-receiver as Mum's.

And now Lucy, too, came walking up, between the Luducos. Lucy's plaits were tied with two enormous bows of sheer organza. Ludo, rubbing his hands, was saying to nobody in particular, 'It's going to be fantastic, you'll see.'

Duco said, 'Because we've made some great preparations!' He pinched Lucy's cheek.

'Duke,' she muttered, 'you shouldn't always give everything away, man.'

'Oh, well,' said Duco, 'but surely your friends can see for themselves what I mean?' He winked meaningfully at her oversized bows, which were hard to miss.

Just then, Miss Joyce announced from the doorway that the cast had to come inside *im-me-diately*.

Show time!

In the locker room behind the gym, we pulled on our navy gym shorts, lovingly washed and pressed for the occasion. We couldn't contain ourselves, jumping on top of each other with excitement, just like last week, when we'd hidden Lucy's underpants behind a radiator when she was in the shower. What a laugh! She'd had to go around with a naked bum the rest of the day. We'd lain in wait for her during break, and every time we caught her we'd pulled up her skirt. We had even managed to send her flying one time, and forced her legs open as she lay there on her back. She'd tried to cover it with her hands, but she was no match for all of us. It was there for everyone to look right into. Everyone pointed. *That* ought to jog her memory, we jeered. When she persisted in keeping her mouth shut, Vanessa had come running up with the broom from the janitor's cupboard. 'A good thrashing is what she needs.' Vanessa was, of all of Lucy's best friends, her *best* best friend, so we did what she said.

After a while, Thomas, who'd been watching with his hands in his pockets, had turned and walked away. And a little while later, Mr Klop, the Year 2 teacher, came and pulled us off her. He snarled at Lucy that she should come to school properly dressed. 'Just because your mother isn't around to look after you—that's no excuse. You're old and wise enough to know girls don't walk round with a naked fanny. Or else you're just asking for it.'

'I'll be watching you, my darlings,' Miss Joyce said encouragingly, standing in the wings of the stage that had been built in the gym especially for our performance. 'Remember, whatever happens, just keep dancing. If you keep going, nobody will notice if there's a slip-up.' It was her first production ever, but she was as professional as anything.

Now came the piano's first rousing measures. We grabbed our letters; we were raring to go. 'One, two, three,' Miss Joyce counted, 'and a-one, and a-two, *now!*'

We burst onto the stage for the wild opening, wriggling and tumbling about the platform like vermicelli. We were the primordial stew, so to speak: we represented the Chaos that existed before the Word. But then the music gradually slowed down. The melody grew sweeter and sweeter, and just as sweetly did we deposit our letters on the ground, then proceeded to teeter on our tippy-toes, stretching our arms up in the air, reaching for knowledge, and sang how much we wanted to Learn to Read.

'*Aaah*,' went the audience. Cameras clicked. Video cameras whirred.

'Letters!' Miss Joyce hissed from the wings.

Quickly we picked up our letters again and hugged them to our chests, as if holding a precious gift. We put on the most learned expression we could come up with. Voilà: we had discovered the Word.

The applause hadn't yet died down when the animal kingdom's merry polka started up. Our feet pattered across the floor, we bounded left, right, and all over the place, and then, at the exact right moment, the *D*, the *O*, and the *G* surged forward as the rest of us fell back. DOG! Well done; and now, quick, quick, time for GOAT. The *O* had it easy, it could stay in place. The *G* did a quick sideways shuffle, the *A* wobbled a bit, but then found her footing again, and *T* was also on the ball. Class act! Solid as a house!

But BUG bollixed it up big time. The *B* and the *U* were already in their positions downstage, swinging their hips. '*From dawn till dusk, I bite, I bite, I bite,*' they belted out at the top of their lungs, while the rest of us started kicking like mad at *G*'s lanky legs to get Lucy moving in the right direction. The Luducos would have done better helping her practise her moves rather than tying those lame bug-bows in her hair.

There was a smattering of laughter from the audience.

'Just get on the end, Lucy,' Miss Joyce called softly.

The piano started again on the lead-in to *I bite, I bite, I bite.* We marched in place with forced smiles plastered on our faces.

Our fathers and mothers began whispering. They craned their necks to glare sternly at the Luducos seated at the back of the hall. Hey, you two! Do something, can't you? Come on, help her out! The silly girl's hogging the lime-light! Good grief, are you blind or something?

The Luducos' faces were as pale as two eggs. They stared back, bewildered.

Our mothers heaved hopeless sighs and ostentatiously turned back to the stage. Our fathers followed suit, only to find themselves staring at the back of Thomas's mother's head; she was ensconced in the first row in a high-necked grey blouse. What a shame, our dads couldn't help think-ing, to have this chunky old bag, this drab mouse, as a trade-in for that sexy, mysterious hellcat. They felt as if they were the ones who'd received a twelve-year sentence— twelve long years without a glimpse of Lucy's mother.

'On the end, Lucy!' Miss Joyce prompted a little louder, a little less patient this time.

Now G finally found her spot on the other side of the U, and the three bugs sang hopefully, *'Don't swat, don't swat, don't swat me please!'* Lucy was waving her letter over her head like a flaming torch. She seemed pretty pleased with herself; the problem was that she was holding the U upside down. We were really going to have to watch her. For cripes' sake, this wasn't a game of Pirates or Cowboys-and-Indians. The object right now was to wow the grown-ups who doled out our pocket money!

Next there was a rumba dance that could go seriously wrong if you got out of rhythm. This interlude was neces-sary to give the kids backstage who didn't have a letter role in the next part ('Foods') a chance to change into some-thing edible. We had a dancing head of lettuce, an apple, a parsnip; we looked like the veggie display in front of Mr De Vries's shop. Lucy was a head of garlic in beige crêpe paper, her face hidden by the tops of the cloves tied round her torso. It was all in the details, said Miss Joyce, it was all in the details.

As soon as the vegetables came dancing on, Garlic started showing off. She was as limber as anything. She could snake her arms around, splay her legs, and at the same time arch her back until the back of her head touched the ground. As long as she didn't have to use her brain, she was in her element. Standing at the edge of the stage, she kept kicking her legs higher and higher, as if she wanted to prove something.

'Well now!' buzzed our parents, impressed. 'Look at that one! Is that your Safranja? No, it certainly isn't our Sara, she's the leek.'

Quickly we intoned the Song of the Plum, a four-part round that thundered back and forth across the stage. The dancing vegetable stall parted obediently into two wavy lines to make way for the four letters. Only that confounded Garlic ignored the rehearsed choreography. She stayed front and centre, whirling her arms about like a waterwheel. We sang louder, working up to the climax. There was nothing for it, it was time for PLUM to move downstage—we were almost at the end of the song. The P, L, U, and M were already thrusting their shoulders forward. They were ready to barge right over that Garlic if necessary. Our singing grew louder; we sang our little hearts out, all agog to see how this would end.

'All vegetables stand aside!' cried Miss Joyce in a warning tone.

PLUM shifted into high gear, high-stepping up to the footlights.

In the midst of doing a pirouette, Garlic glanced over her shoulder. Then took a flying leap into the wings.

Afterward, our parents said they assumed it was all part

of the show. Someone whooped, guffawing, 'Plum jam!' as the whole PLUM team tripped and fell, tumbling off the edge of the stage.

There was a moment's silence. But then the piano started up again, a boisterous improvisation to distract the audience.

'Dance!' hissed Miss Joyce. 'Smile!'

We had given her our word; she didn't have to worry, we'd make sure she had every reason to be proud of herself and of us. But when Garlic came skipping back on and started doing some kind of Cossack dance, it was the last straw. We swarmed across the stage and tackled her.

Our parents, still as clueless as ever, thinking they were watching a re-enactment of some forgotten historic vegetable battle, started clapping. Or maybe they were applauding the PLUM crew, who were scrambling to their feet, crestfallen and dazed. Maybe they were laughing so hard at all the dented papier-mâché that they didn't even notice Miss Joyce storming onto the stage and pulling us off Lucy, taking the opportunity to give each one of us a good shaking. 'Just keep going!' she hissed. 'MILK, at your posts!'

Half in tears, our voices quavering, we started the next song, but soon our feet found the rhythm again and then we were dancing once more, automatically, in a whirl of panting letters and smashed foodstuffs. The M was broken, but he was able to camouflage it pretty well. Garlic was in the worst condition. Only the top of her costume was still intact, the rest was in tatters.

'Just try and make the best of it,' Miss Joyce cried. 'Improvise if you have to. Don't give up!'

We slogged our way through MILK as best we could, bruises and all. Next, we started on CAKE, our eyes scouring the audience for our parents, who must have caught on by now, surely, that it was all getting to be a bit much for us, that we wanted to go home and cuddle on someone's lap? But when, boogieing and warbling, we finally managed to locate Mum and Dad, we saw that they weren't looking at us at all. The entire audience was staring, mesmerized, at Garlic.

Wiggling her hips, she was doing a suggestive bump-and-grind to the music. Improvise, the teacher had shouted, and that Garlic didn't need to be told twice. With all the showmanship of a seasoned burlesque dancer, she smoothed out the tattered crêpe paper remnants of her costume one by one, as if they were veils, twirled them briefly around the tip of her finger, and then tossed them carelessly over her shoulder.

'Is that your Vanessa?' our parents called out to each other, bug-eyed with admiration.

As we were still trying to extol the delights of CAKE, a Garlic-stripper was stealing our show! At home you got in trouble for throwing a sock on the floor, but our parents were charmed by this striptease; they thought it was hilarious. They were just about climbing on their chairs. In a minute they'd get out their cigarette lighters, like at the end of a rock concert.

Our voices faltered. Our song died away. The only sound left was the piano and the rustling of crêpe paper.

With a slow, seductive shake, stomach thrust forward, Garlic flung her penultimate veil over her shoulder. Parading from left to right, arms spread wide, she took in the applause. Then she raised her hands and yanked down the ruff of cloves that had concealed her face, and shook out her plaits. Her eyes shone: wasn't that great?

The hall suddenly went so quiet that you could hear the piano pedal squeak, but the music had stopped.

Everyone in the audience was thinking the same thing; the thought floated above our mums' and dads' heads like the cartoon-bubbles in our first primer, the ones that contained sentences like '*I fish fish*' that made us laugh so hard we'd practically fall off our chairs.

With a smothered gasp, Thomas's mother heaved herself from her chair. She made a movement as if attempting to lean forward and backward at the same time, and then, in awesome slow motion, she collapsed in the aisle.

'Mummy!' yelled Thomas. He jumped headlong off the stage in his cucumber costume and raced over to her. 'Mum! Are you hurt? Mum! Say something!'

There were calls for water, for a doctor.

Several of the mothers rushed forward. 'Move over, big boy, give her some air.' They pushed Thomas aside; they hunkered down and swiftly began unbuttoning the grey blouse. More and more people swarmed around her in the aisle. We too slipped down off the stage and threaded our way between the adults' legs. We saw Thomas's mother's big white breasts spilling out of her bra. Someone was slapping her on the cheeks. If she opened her eyes, she'd have a heart attack, for sure: all those panting mouths spewing bacteria right in her face, all those unwashed hands pawing at her, and, lastly, the most unpardonable thing of all: all those eyes ogling her exposed body, which for years had slept trustingly, submissively, in her late husband's arms.

All the grown-ups were so busy robbing her of her last shred of dignity that only we children saw the Luducos finally bestir themselves. Barrelling up to the front, they reached up, their white wrists sticking out of their sleeves, grabbed Lucy, who was still planted in the middle of the platform as if she had no idea she was the one responsible for all the commotion, and pulled her down off the stage.

# H is for Hell

All summer long, postcards kept arriving for us with 'xoxo from Lucy' written on the back in Ludo's or Duco's handwriting. They'd left on holiday right after the performance, and seemed to be planning to take the longest trip of the century.

It was with mixed feelings that we traced their peregrinations, from destination to destination, on the inflatable globe Dad had given us. Sometimes a duplicate postcard, showing the same sun-drenched village or castle, made us think they must be on their way back. But soon there'd be another postcard waiting on the doormat, indicating they had changed course, as if at the last moment they had recoiled at the thought of going home. Maybe they'd already been on the bus or train home a number of times, only to do an about-turn when they caught sight of the thunderclouds hanging over the village. There was bright sunshine everywhere else, but in our village the skies were heavy with the dark misgivings our mothers were now airing on a daily basis. Since her Garlic turn, Lucy was suspected of all kinds of things not meant for our ears.

Vanessa, who wanted Thomas to be her boyfriend, told

him that what it came down to was that Lucy was an even worse liar than we'd ever suspected, and a far bigger drama queen as well. For his birthday in August, she sawed a plywood heart for him that was as thick as a double cheeseburger. Her mother let her paint her fingernails for the party, and curled her hair.

The birthday party was a rather paltry affair. Thomas's mother poured glasses of watery lemonade for us in the garden, and we each got a wafer-thin slice of cake. The dress she had on was so spotlessly white that we kept our hands folded behind our backs as a precautionary measure. The dress was because she had accepted Jesus as her Saviour. She said it was the only way she could deal with what life had thrown at her.

Before we were allowed to take our glasses from the scrubbed wooden picnic table, we had to join together to say grace. 'Amen,' said Thomas listlessly. He was sitting in the unmown grass next to a neglected boxwood shrub. The sunlight fell mercilessly on his home-cut hair and the clothes bought for him by his dad, which he was already growing out of.

'Amen,' we echoed half-heartedly.

Then his mother gave him his present.

He turned it over and over in his hands. You could tell he hadn't been expecting anything, that he had already resigned himself to suddenly being poor; he was a born philosopher, or so our mothers were fond of telling us. At home, even a hint of a whine in your voice would set them off: Oh, certainly, sir, madam, your highness, but what do you suppose *Thomas* is eating right now? Do you have any idea, your majesty, how much pocket money other children—let's not name names, okay?—can expect to receive? Oh, do excuse me, your lordship, but there exist children in this world who don't WANT IT RIGHT NOW, you know, who don't NEED IT RIGHT NOW, who don't keep whining for stuff NOW, NOW, NOW! Who may never again ...

Thomas picked at the tape on his package with his fingernails. The wrapping paper was used; it was all crushed and creased. Slowly, he unwrapped it. The book that emerged wasn't new, either. The corners curled up. It was an encyclopaedia of the animal kingdom, as thick as your fist.

'I wrote something in it for you,' said his mother, sounding even more apologetic than usual. She was nervously twisting the dish towel she'd been using to polish our glasses into a big knot.

He opened the book. He read out loud, '"Daddy's book, for Thomas's seventh birthday, from Mum".' He looked at her incredulously. 'It's mine now?'

'Yes, from now on it's yours.'

'Jiminy Cricket,' he said fervently. He jumped up from the grass and hugged her.

'Are you happy with it?' she asked, relieved.

He nodded. Big fat tears were rolling down his cheeks. He just stood there in the middle of the garden, bawling! His arms hung at his sides like two stiff boards, his hands were balled up into fists, and his toes dug into the grass.

'Here,' said Vanessa, hastily offering him her present. She was blushing with anticipation. 'Here you are, Thomas. For you ...'

He slapped her hand away.

'Oh, my poor darling,' said his mother. She stooped to pick up the present. She didn't know what else to do.

Thomas cringed; he seemed to be shrivelling up into a little ball. Soon he'd be just a hollow space, a hole brimming with missing and yearning.

His mother, bending down, took his chin in her hand. 'Daddy still sees you, you know,' she said softly. 'I'm sure he's thinking right now, I'm so proud of my big seven-year-old son. And every time you open your book to look at the pictures, he'll be right there with you, and ...'

'Not true!' screamed Thomas. 'He's dead and getting eaten by worms!' He picked up the book, opened it, and hurriedly started leafing through it. 'It says so in here, see for yourself, Mum!'

She raised her hands defensively. 'That's ... but it's just his *body*!' She spat out the word as if it were a broken tooth. She looked at us for support. We quickly occupied ourselves counting the wasps that were sluggishly buzzing around the empty lemonade glasses.

'The invertebrates,' Thomas was muttering feverishly to himself. 'Here.' He held up the book.

The photo had been taken in extreme close-up. You could see every ridge, the glinting slime, the semi-transparent gelatinousness. But the worst thing was the greedy, yawning mouth. It wasn't hard to imagine a grown man disappearing down that hole. One gulp and down he goes. The monster would hiccup with a lazy belch, and then, thanks to the spasms of peristalsis, work its prey deeper and deeper down into its gut before finally, after it was finished digesting, contentedly pooping it out.

'I don't see it that way,' said Thomas's mother. She was trying to sound calm.

'But that's the way it *is*!'

Suddenly we realized what he meant, and our hearts started racing. Vanessa, too, got it; she began picking furiously at her polished grown-up nails.

For Lucy was the only one who knew what it was like to disappear down the gullet of one of those ravenous monsters. She must have told us a hundred times, soberly and in great detail, about the time she'd been swallowed by a boa constrictor, one morning last year in the rectory garden. It was only thanks to her Swiss Army knife that she was still alive today. The memory brought a lump to our throats. Because who else could tell you a story as riveting as that? Okay, maybe Lucy had a hard time spelling BUG; but you had to hand it to her, she did string words together better than anyone else when it came to conjuring up fantastic adventures, each more convincingly real than the next. Just as real and convincing, in fact, as the dragons that were invisible to the grown-ups, but that hid behind the bathroom door at night, swishing their tails and puffing wisps of smoke from their nostrils, lying in wait with the patience of ages.

What did it matter, really, that she'd ruined our show? We suddenly missed her so keenly that it made the hair on our necks stand up. Lucy! Come back, Lucy! We can't wait to hear about your adventures! Were there any bears?

Thomas shut the book. He noisily snorted a bubble of snot back up. He snapped at his mother, pityingly, 'You don't get it, stupid.'

With her eyes lowered, she tugged on the ends of the dish towel. 'You're only saying that because you miss your dad. That's why you're behaving like this.'

Without another word he turned and trudged into the house, dragging his shadow along after him. You could tell from the way his shoulders jerked that he was crying again.

We watched the scene in alarm. It seemed that missing someone turned you into an awful crybaby. Luckily *we'd* never let it get to that stage.

After the summer hols, we got Mr Klop as our Year 2 teacher. Mr Klop stank of onions and called us 'hot-shots' when he was in a good mood. He had a new baby at home and was often up all night, so he wasn't in a good mood very often. He believed in self-motivation and he didn't like whiners and moaners. If you did something that didn't sit well with him, he sometimes pulled your hair really hard.

What wouldn't we have given to have Miss Joyce back, who had turned us into such softies! The first few days we took our complaints to her during lunchtime, but she had a new class of kids who adored her now; she had no great use for us anymore. It was shocking to see how swiftly she'd shifted her love for us, her little lambs, over to a bunch of complete strangers. We'd been sure that what we had with her was forever. But blink once, twice, and—poof!—gone was the history you'd had together, as if it never happened.

Lucy's homecoming, too, had been a disappointment. After her round-the-world trip, we had expected to have the old Lucy back again, the Lucy of the boa constrictor—fearless, cunning Lucy, not this pale, skittish creature. We longed for the days when she would punch you in the mouth if you so much as looked at her the wrong way, but we just never managed to get a rise out of her.

'Your mother's a murderer!' we yelled encouragingly. 'You're nothing but a butcher's brat!' Or we'd shout, 'Slut! Slut! Dirty slut!' We once even tossed her up and down in the air behind the bike shed for such a long time that our arms felt as if they were coming out of their sockets. It was killing us, it really was. What were we supposed to do with this exasperating zombie who reminded us so much of the Lucy we'd lost, so that we were turning into weak pussies, filled with desperate longing? She *owed* it to us to become her old self again, and if she wouldn't do so voluntarily, then we'd just have to make her.

But not for nothing were we constantly lectured at home that sticks and stones will break your bones but words will never hurt you; no matter how we scolded and yelled, it had not the slightest effect on Lucy. Naturally, getting her arse kicked a little couldn't be expected to faze someone like her very much. She probably hadn't even noticed. We'd have to find another way.

You had to hand it to Mr Klop: he was a terrific storyteller. The moment he rose from his chair to perch on one buttock on the corner of his desk, stroking his nose pensively, we all sat up. He told us about men who came here many years ago, the Batavians, travelling down the river in a hollowed-out tree trunk. They wore bear skins, they gambled and guzzled beer as if there was no tomorrow, and they had founded our country. That last bit interested us less. The fact that our country existed was obvious; after all, we lived here, didn't we?

'Oooh, sir,' we wheedled. 'Tell us another one.'

He paced up and down between the rows of desks, in his element. The pitter-patter of the rain against the windowpanes made the classroom feel cosy. We tucked our feet up under us. Ever since we had found the pen Mr Klop had lost days ago—the green one with the silver top—inside Lucy's school desk, we couldn't do a thing wrong in his eyes.

'Okay, then. Let's talk about Boniface, then,' he said. 'He was murdered in the town of Dokkum.'

We wobbled in our chairs with excitement. 'How did he get killed, sir?'

'With a sword?'

'With an axe! Wasn't it, sir?'

He stopped pacing. 'Retards! Knuckleheads! You should be asking WHY he was murdered! The how doesn't matter. Why! That's all that matters. You should fall under the spell of the eternal WHY. That's the root of all knowledge, you fatheads. That way you'll also learn that for every action, there's a reaction, because everything is cause and effect. Nothing ever happens for no reason. Get it?'

'Yes, sir!' we yelled at the top of our lungs.

'Any questions? No? Then I'll pick a volunteer. You, over there. Lucy!'

She sat up with a start. She was still a little pale from the action at break time, out in the rain. Today we had outdone ourselves; it wouldn't surprise us if her spleen were permanently shot. She said haltingly, 'But—what if those … Vavay-bians had just paddled in the opposite direction?'

Mr Klop raised his hands to heaven. 'We were already at Boniface. But okay then, back to the Batavians. Well, they just travelled with the current.'

'Why?'

In a few short, vehement strides he was at her side, standing by her desk in the very last row, next to the crafts cupboard, and yanked at one of her dripping plaits. 'Because water flows *downstream*, you ninny! Because every river flows into the sea. That's why they wound up here. Christ Almighty, if we'd had to rely on bright lights like you back then, our country wouldn't now exist.'

'She said Vavay-bians instead of Batavians,' giggled Vanessa.

This was our cue. We all started laughing. We made wild *Va-va-voom* noises and began wiggling our hips.

The teacher stuck his neck forward and snapped at Lucy, 'As usual, miss, you are not very helpful in keeping peace and order in the classroom.'

'But you said it yourself. Vavaybians. Vavaybians in a hollow tree trunk!'

'Oh, did I really? I think it is high time, miss, that you learned to pay a little more attention to the truth. Maybe you should go and think about *that* for a while out in the corridor. Out!'

'But I didn't *do* anything!'

'No, always the picture of innocence, aren't you; it's the story of your life! Go on, out! You can count how many boots there are in the corridor. There are plenty of them out there.'

Conscientiously, we bent over our notebooks as she shuffled reluctantly out of the classroom to miss yet another lesson, her umpteenth. We hoped the teacher, who was being driven up the wall by her ever-growing stupidity, would go up to the blackboard and show us one more time how to write 'Batavians.'

Our mothers were fit to be tied about the boots. 'All twenty-eight pairs!' they kept saying to one another. 'And not just a little water, no, filled up to the brim! The little hoodlum!' Bristling with indignation, they gave the Luducos the low-down when they bumped into them in the village, describing Lucy's revenge down to the last detail.

'Ah well, kids will be kids,' Ludo began in a conciliatory tone, putting down his bag of carrots on the pavement, as if he needed to have his hands free to defend himself.

But Duco, wearing an uncharacteristically grim expression, went on the counter-attack. 'Speaking of kids, how come we never see yours in the rectory anymore? They always used to come and play after school.'

For a second, our mothers didn't know what to say. Safranja's mum finally said, 'But doesn't Lucy get tutored after school? Surely you don't expect the others to wait around for her to finish!'

'Perhaps not, but what about on the weekends?' Duco insisted.

Nobody said anything.

'Surely not ...' he went on, now stuttering with embarrassment, 'not because Lucy is being blamed for her mother's ...'

The turn the conversation was taking didn't sit well with our mothers. They really had no desire to be reminded of the existence of a friend on whom they had so abruptly turned their backs, without even thinking of sending her a postcard from time to time, to ease the loneliness of her incarceration—but what else *could* they have done, all things considered? Their voices went shrill. It was obvious, they said, that the gentlemen knew very little about how to raise a child. To tell the truth, they'd been rather surprised when, upon Lucy's mother's conviction, the Luducos were appointed as the girl's legal guardians. As professional parents, they thought that perhaps the social services ought to be told of the way Lucy had been behaving of late. For her own good. Someone had to keep an eye on that one, or she'd end up becoming a problem. A child who was capable of such extreme mischief ...

'*Extreme?*' said Duco. 'Oh, come on! She sprinkled a little water in a few boots!'

Ludo nodded. He was baffled as well; a little water in a few boots, that's what he, too, thought they had said.

Extreme, the mothers repeated angrily, yes indeed, extreme! Because any child who was that naughty had to know perfectly well that she was stepping over the line. That was pathological behaviour; it meant she was deliberately asking to be punished, and when a child asks to be punished, it stands to reason she must have a guilty conscience; it was as obvious as the nose on your face.

They crowded accusingly around the Luducos on the pavement, those two prats who never noticed anything, who went round with blinders on, who didn't even know that Lucy had patiently stood at the little water fountain in the school hallway filling one boot after another; those dopes who on that fateful night hadn't realized, either, that the girl's mother had run out of the house in a murderous rage; those two milksops who should have stopped her, who could have done something so that our community wouldn't have been tarnished by its association with an unspeakable atrocity, with goings-on just too vile for words. Thanks to these two losers, a father was lying six feet under, a mother was in the clink, and all the children were robbed of their innocence. Good eggs like them were always the worst. They made the most awful mess of things; it just went to show you.

It wasn't as if our mothers didn't know all about it; didn't they have one of those couch potatoes at home themselves, one of those wimps who, given half a chance, would look the other way and try to wriggle out of his responsibilities, one of those men who couldn't be goaded into action even if the world were going up in flames before his very eyes? Their own mothers had been saddled with husbands like that as well, and before that, *their* mothers, and so on and so on. Dreadful, but what could you do?

They were *that* close to kicking the Luducos' shopping basket into the gutter. How they'd love to pry a paving stone from the pavement and hurl it at their heads! They could see themselves inciting a public lynching, right here, across from the bakery, and the fury they were feeling made them convinced that they had every reason to do so.

Ludo, trying to appease them, said, 'We'll have a word about it with Lucy.'

Duco picked up the shopping basket.

The two men took off in such a hurry that you could see their knees knocking together.

That evening, our mothers boasted that they had only to snap their fingers for Lucy to be removed from the Luducos' care.

'And then what?' asked our fathers, puzzled. 'What good would *that* do?'

That was *so* typical of men, our mothers declared. They were incensed. They sent us out of the room and gave Daddy a good telling-off.

As for us, the prank with the boots had filled us with renewed hope. Because hadn't that act of defiance made Lucy's irrepressible Lucy-ness emerge from hiding? The audacity of it—it was her way of finally getting her own back, and just in time, too, because patience wasn't exactly our strong suit. If she'd gone on any longer without giving us some sign that we were justified in believing her old self still existed, then we'd probably have written her off as a lost cause and left her alone.

Now, however, we could count on a happier outcome. The trick was not to allow her to backslide. Enthused, we considered our options. Our brains were bubbling over with one scheme after another. We went round with a red *S* pinned to our chests and a cape flowing from our shoulders. And that was even before we were fully aware of our powers. A stunt like the pail bristling with earthworms, for instance, hadn't even occurred to us yet. But somehow we already knew we'd be endlessly inspired; after all, Lucy had always brought out the best in us.

Mr Klop didn't teach Religion; theology wasn't his thing. He told us he was a Darwinist—the survival of the fittest was his creed. Kids who whined and moaned the moment they got a little splinter in their finger would never get very far, in an evolutionary sense. Such sissies were, in the greater scheme of things, strictly superfluous, and therefore consumed more than their fair share of precious oxygen, which, considering there was a hole in the ozone layer, was a big problem. The fact that the rainforest and the polar cap were going to pot was entirely their fault.

And so, every Tuesday morning at eleven—the period

reserved for Religious Instruction—he would decamp with a good book on genetics under his arm.

Thomas's mother could probably use the money she earned teaching us Religion; what's more, thanks to having Jesus as her Saviour, she seemed to have conquered her fear of dirt. But she wasn't particularly good at teaching. Last year, in Miss Joyce's class, it had been pure bliss to listen to the stories about Moses in the rushes, and Egypt's seven or ten plagues. It had been a refreshing respite, a welcome break from swotting. But with Mrs Iedema, all we ever heard about was just that one boring bloke who always did exactly what his father wanted him to do. It wasn't exactly riveting.

We sat through the entire weekly Jesus-hour longing for Mr Klop's spit-bubble fuming, but out of respect we remained quietly at our desks, singing psalms. Even the raising of Lazarus was kind of boring, at least the way Mrs Iedema told it. As for the prostitutes, who intrigued us quite a bit, according to Mrs Iedema all they ever did was wash people's feet.

It was often all about humility and mercy. Mercy was a big theme. He who could not forgive his enemies would never enter the Kingdom of Heaven, said Mrs Iedema, staring right at Lucy. Her entire face started quivering. Mercy was hard work, you could tell.

Lucy quickly looked the other way. Religious Instruction always had her acting like a complete basket case. Whenever the subject of eternal damnation and hellfire came up—the only times our teacher really livened up—Lucy would stick her fingers in her ears. To tell the truth, we thought it was pretty creepy ourselves. To burn was bad enough. But *forever*? Even a single hour felt so eternal that it left us limp and exhausted. We were ever so thankful when Mr Klop finally flung open the door and announced, rubbing his hands together, 'Noon! Right, kids, we have fifteen minutes left to accomplish something useful.'

Happily rattling off the five-times table once again, we told ourselves that we really had no reason to be scared of hell. Hell, after all, was meant for the wicked, the corrupt, and the Pharisees. We, on the contrary, weren't *really* doing anything wrong when the teacher's back was turned to write something on the blackboard, were we? Or out in the schoolyard, when the shouts of scores of kids drowned out all other noise? Still, scattering afterwards, sweaty and out of breath, we sometimes did get that funny feeling—you know, the feeling you get after you've blown up a frog by poking a straw up its bum; suddenly we didn't feel so terrific.

As a matter of fact, we were beginning to hope that Lucy would finally throw in the towel. But what were the chances of that? Just look at the way she insisted on going to the loo during break every morning, although she knew perfectly well what was in store for her there. Or the way she'd drink her carton of milk every day, even though we'd put soap in it over a hundred times. Or like that time with the matches. Or all the other times. Even if we had made her write out *I'm sorry I'm wasting your oxygen* on a million cigarette papers, she'd simply have done it. She walked into every ambush, every trap, with eyes wide open; she seemed to be courting danger on purpose instead of trying to escape it. What was she playing at? There really was no need to rub our noses in it day after day; we were perfectly aware of how gutsy she was.

It got harder and harder to think of something that would top the last torment. On days when, for some unknown reason, the sad smell of snuffed candles hung in the air, we'd anxiously ask ourselves if we were actually still the ones calling the shots. Had the roles been quietly reversed? Was *she* the one making *us* jump through the hoops now?

You couldn't always be sure who or what started it, even if Mr Klop maintained that things never just happened for no reason.

Obstinately, she just kept coming to school every day. It got more and more upsetting. If only she'd tell on us! Just once! Watching her staggering unsteadily back to the classroom after gym, we prayed she'd complain about us to our teacher. We kept having to push the envelope further, hoping it would force her to release us at last.

Only, who would ever listen to her? Which of the adults would ever believe her? 'You have to take anything that Lucy says with a grain of salt,' was the general consensus these days.

# I is for Isolation

One mild morning in May, we found Mr Klop waiting for us in the doorway to the classroom with such a black look on his face that his eyes looked like purple jelly beans. A fat vein stood out on his forehead, and he was working his jaws as if he was getting ready for the sermon of a lifetime. Words were to our teacher what cudgels had been to the Batavians.

Our fingers nearly failed us as we nervously unbuttoned our jackets and hung them up. Loops broke off, buttons clattered to the floor. Cowed, we shuffled inside and tried to find our seats in as orderly a manner as possible.

Mr Klop shut the door. He marched to the front of the classroom and gazed at us, legs spread wide, rocking his torso slightly from side to side. Accusingly, he stared at the desk where Lucy was supposed to be sitting. We glanced over our shoulders. The spot next to the craft-supplies cupboard was empty.

You could have heard a pin drop.

After a while, he said, 'There's someone on his way here to see you.' That was all. Then he went and sat down.

We didn't dare move a muscle.

Mr Klop started cracking his fingers one by one, an ominous frown on his face. Suddenly he leaned forward. 'If anyone in this class has done anything to cause me shame'—he said it very quietly and very slowly—'there will be hell to pay. I repeat: hell-to-pay. Is that clear, you little snakes, you viper's nest?' He cupped his hand behind his ear.

'Yes, sir,' we breathed.

Behind him, on the blackboard, the nine-times table was waiting for us. If he'd been in a good mood, he'd have announced, 'Nine—a tricky bastard, that one. But are we maths wizards, or aren't we? Come on, let's show that wanker a thing or two, shall we?' Hopefully, we kept our eyes fixed on the numbers, waiting for some sign of a thaw.

The minutes ticked by, on and on. Our clothes started giving off steam. Outside the fogged-up windows, people were strolling up and down the street, on their way to whatever, carefree as only adults could be. For them there was never a cloud on the horizon.

Suddenly, Vanessa burst into tears. 'We were only trying to help her, sir,' she snivelled.

Mr Klop said nothing. He glared round.

'And she was asking for it, too,' Sara added.

'It's true!' squeaked Safranja.

'What, exactly,' he asked icily, 'was she asking for, then?'

Just then, Duco entered the classroom on squeaky sneakers, clutching a plastic carrier bag. His forehead was slick with sweat. His expression was a bit less good-natured than usual, which made him suddenly look like a different man from the one who used to pick us up when he found us crying halfway up the rectory stairs because they were too steep, and then, with a hand on our bums, helped push us up.

'Good morning,' said the teacher. He stood up. He seemed

to be debating whether to shake Duco's hand. Then, with a flourish, he offered him his own chair.

Duco shook his head. 'Good morning, children,' he said. His voice quavered a bit.

'Let's get right down to business, shall we?' asked the teacher. 'Niceties are wasted on this lot. And they've been in the hot seat since nine o'clock, so they should be good and ready by now. Blow your nose, Vanessa. It's too damn late to start crying now.'

'Was it you?' asked Duco, startled, staring at Vanessa. 'Lucy didn't want to name names, she didn't want to tell on anyone.'

'Did you punks hear that?' The teacher aimed a vicious, random kick at one of the front-row desks. 'What have you done to deserve *that*, you sneaky bastards?'

Duco stared at him in dismay, hugging his bag to his chest. He hadn't been exposed to Mr Klop's methods on a daily basis, as we were. He was clearly flustered.

'And those two over there,' the teacher pointed, 'were in on it, too.'

Sara and Safranja cowered.

'I don't get it,' said Duco softly. 'You used to be crazy about her.' His eyes roved around the classroom. 'You *all* were, as a matter of fact.' Suddenly, his eye fell on Thomas. 'Did *you* put the other children up to this?' He walked up to Thomas, his hand stretched out in front as if trying to befriend a dangerous dog.

We noticed that the hem of his raincoat was coming out.

Thomas had turned white as a sheet. He wasn't one of the ringleaders, actually. He usually wasn't even one of the spectators. We often beat him up because he made *us* do all the dirty work, the crybaby.

'There's no point turning your mates against Lucy. Can't you see that?' said Duco.

'You're not going to get your father back that way,' Mr Klop clarified.

Thomas promptly pushed his fists into his eyes. We all knew what he was thinking, because we liked to refresh his memory often enough: if Thomas had never planted the idea of the pencil in Lucy's mother's head, his father would still be alive today. If the grown-ups only knew! If you even so much as hinted at bringing it up, he'd tear a page out of his father's big animal book for you to make you shut up.

Maybe it was time to up the ante on the bribe he had to pay. He had already given us nearly all the invertebrates; soon we'd get to the mice, and then you were almost through the entire animal kingdom.

Duco turned to Mr Klop with an anguished expression. 'Ludo and I thought it was on account of the extra help Lucy is getting after school that the children never come over to play anymore. That's what Lucy told us, too. But we shouldn't have bought her story, should we? Because it's clear there's something else going on.'

'Tutoring does take up quite a bit of time, naturally.' Our teacher pursed his lips. 'And it can, indeed, cause a child to become somewhat isolated. Which does sometimes lead to disruptive behaviour.' He looked as if he finally understood why he so often had the urge to grab Lucy by the plaits and yank her to her feet. The realization seemed to come as a relief. 'They start demanding attention in a negative manner, and one thing leads to another. They are children, after all—it isn't anything rational.' He glared at us spitefully.

He didn't realize that we saw right through him. Grown-ups never did. Sure, they had the power to scare the living daylights out of you, to send you to bed without any supper, or to slap you with detention; but they had no idea we could tell, from the faintest inflection in their voice, if they were being sincere or not. After all, from the time we were in the cradle, we'd had to listen to their lies and fabrications, their evasions and excuses, their attempts at self-justification, their getting away with all sorts of stuff and showing themselves in the best possible light.

Duco put down his carrier bag on Mr Klop's desk. He wiped his sweaty forehead with his sleeve. 'Children,' he said, and it was painful to hear how sincere he was in what he was about to say, 'the reason I'm here is that Ludo and I feel this just can't go on.' He opened the bag, looking close to tears. Then he pulled out Lucy's two plaits, with the coloured elastic bands still in place. They looked very scrawny in his big grown-up's hands.

We gasped.

'Her lovely hair,' he said in a smothered voice.

Vanessa started crying again.

Trying to control his voice, our teacher said, 'Come up here, the three of you.'

The girls slunk up to the front, cowering.

'Explain yourselves, please,' said the teacher, roughly lining them up in front of the blackboard.

Vanessa stammered that yesterday, after school, the three of them had just had been shooting the breeze with Lucy—girls' stuff, you know—after she got out, having finally finished *The Safe Way: Book II*.

We were so on edge we nearly burst out laughing. Yeah, we could just see Lucy talking about girly things! She knew more about the tusks of a mammoth than about patent-leather Mary Janes.

Exactly, said Sara. That was *exactly* what they'd talked about! They'd been explaining to her that she looked a like a dork, the way she was dressed. She looked silly. Didn't she?

Safranja nodded vehemently.

And then they had given her some friendly advice, and suggested that she do something about those plaits, for a start, because her hair was just hopeless. They'd offered to cut them off for her right then and there.

'But she's *always* had plaits,' said Duco. 'Always.'

'They aren't *in* anymore,' whispered Vanessa. 'They made her look like a nerd.'

Duco bit his lip. He looked from the guilty threesome to the rest of the girls in the class, as if trying to commit every hairdo to memory. Then he said, humbly, 'Of course Ludo and I don't know much about what's in and what's out. And it isn't easy for a girl, having to grow up without a mother.'

We couldn't help thinking of Bijlmer Jail. We used to drive past it on our way to Amsterdam to visit our grandmas; we would see the prison's tall white towers with our own two eyes. So that's where Lucy's mum was now, behind one of those window slits. Did she remember us, playing in the sandbox in her garden, or scarfing down pancakes with syrup in her kitchen? Was she counting on one of us to bake her a cake with a file hidden inside? Or had she forgotten us, the way you forget the words to a song you once learned long ago?

'So, what are you going to do to make it up to her?' asked Mr Klop. 'Have you given it any thought?'

The girls were silent, heads drooping.

'Well, I'll leave that part up to you,' said Duco. He started putting the plaits back in the bag. Maybe he was going to preserve them in a box when he got home, nestled in soft tissue paper. Then he could take them out with his clumsy, pudgy fingers from time to time, and ask himself guiltily why he hadn't kept up with what was in and what was out.

Mr Klop walked him to the door. He said, 'I hope you

understand that I have no way of controlling what they get up to after school.'

'Of course I do,' said Duco. And he meant it.

The mothers of Sara, Vanessa, and Safranja went to the rectory with an offering of buttery shortbread. They spent the evening in the Luducos' parlour, strewn with a year's worth of old newspapers. In bright, energetic voices, they deplored what had happened, their eyes darting from the dusty windows to the open can of tomato soup that, for some reason, had been left on the mantelpiece. They took turns excusing themselves in order to inspect the state of the lavatory. There was no soap by the sink. In the hall they ran their fingertips along the wall tiles.

When Lucy came in to announce she was going to bed, they pulled her onto their laps without so much as a by-your-leave. 'To be honest,' they said, as they discreetly sniffed at her pyjamas and took mental note of her dirty feet, 'it looks much better on you, that cropped little head. You *do* like it, don't you? Well, then!' They smiled, saying one really shouldn't make a mountain out of a molehill. 'And you *will* remember, from now on, won't you, love, that all you have to do is say no when something's about to happen that you don't like? A big girl like you? Come, Lucy, surely you can do that! And by the same token, we *have* always found it a little hard to believe, that last year you were, *you* know … Anyway, we'll let bygones be bygones, and so now tell us, how are you doing now with the reading?'

They were too quick for the Luducos, who had to pour the coffee, ask if anyone wanted milk or sugar, and offer the shortbread. They were always just a fraction late in trying to intervene, those two big lugs, huffing and puffing from the effort of being such good hosts.

'I've read *Clara 13* four times already,' Lucy answered, curtly, with triumph in her voice.

'Five times, if you count the time you read it to us aloud,' said Ludo.

'But isn't that book mostly pictures? She really ought to be starting on *Jip and Janneke* by now,' Vanessa's mother said, concerned.

But Lucy had no intention of slogging her way through the morass of difficult words just to read boring stories about ordinary children with ordinary parents. She hadn't the slightest inclination to get banished to the tidy ecosystem of a normal family life, which all mothers seemed to want for their offspring, with nothing more dramatic in it than a runaway dog. She said, 'At least *Clara 13* is real.'

'Of course it isn't real, child. Your mother made the whole thing up.'

There was a painful silence.

'Lucy meant,' Ludo rushed to her rescue, 'that Clara keeps having all this bad luck, and there's nothing that can be done about it. Which is just the way it sometimes happens in real life.'

'But it's a *cow*!' said Sara's mother, as if she'd never heard of such a thing.

'We happen to be extremely fond of cows, here,' said Duco.

The mothers made a mental note of this cryptic assertion, to add to their dossier.

'And then, at the end, when she learns how to fly ...' Lucy spread her arms wide, her face suddenly beaming. Her armpit was visible through a rip in her pyjama top. '*That's* real,' she repeated. Then she sat back, and yawned.

'Does she always go to bed this late?' Safranja's mother asked Duco.

'Well, actually, you're the ones keeping her up. She was

on her way to bed half an hour ago ...'

'All right, do your best tomorrow, Lucy, won't you, now?' the mothers called in chorus.

She gave the Luducos an ardent kiss, raising the mothers' antennae again. Two middle-aged men living with a little girl who pranced about in her tattered pyjamas virtually half-naked! Whatever next! After all, during the Big Letter Show, they'd all been able to see for themselves how very precocious Lucy was.

Then they said yes, please, to a glass of white wine.

'If it hadn't been for *Clara 13*,' said Ludo, doing his best to salvage *something*, 'she'd probably never have persevered so bravely with her reading. She sleeps with that book under her pillow. Sometimes, we say to each other, it's as if her mother *knew* Lucy would need that book someday. As if she had read it in the cards.'

It must be the wine, the mothers thought dizzily. Really, as a rule they practically never thought back to those mornings in the dusky room on the first floor anymore, where they'd had their lives spread out before them in pictures and symbols. But that was then, when their hearts would start to beat a little faster when The Magician turned up ('Take charge of your own destiny!') or the volatile Wheel of Fortune ('Soon you will see a big change'). And this was now. And now they knew what could come of it if you took these things too seriously. It could lead to your daughter getting her hair shorn off at school.

Why the social workers had only once come to check up on the Luducos—on a Friday afternoon, when the sky was streaked with wispy clouds that made you think of playing with matches—became a source of endless speculation. It was hard to imagine those two putting on a particularly clever or convincing show. There must have been something else, something our mothers couldn't quite put their finger on. Christ, what right did the poor bastards have to be Lucy's guardians? The mothers would have given anything for a peek at the social workers' report. They would just have to accept the fact that they weren't about to see the last of Lucy, that thorn in their sides. Just the thought of her made their cheeks flush an angry crimson. Getting such nice little girls as Vanessa, Sara, and Safranja in trouble—how *could* she!

The mothers kept insisting the three friends had acted with the best of intentions. After all, aren't girls always messing with one another's hair? The Luducos should never have made it into such a big deal. And it was just too silly for words that Mr Klop, normally far from a pushover, had allowed himself to be strung along. God Almighty, shouldn't girls of Lucy's ilk expect to get their hair shorn off sooner or later, anyway? Given that history tends to repeat itself?

We listened to them glumly. We had expected quite a different outcome. We'd thought everything would be out in the open, once and for all, now that Lucy was walking around with a disfigurement for everyone to see. But even now, it seemed, she'd kept her mouth shut about the other stuff—hadn't spilled the beans, not even to the Luducos. Maybe she was ashamed of being tormented on a daily basis for the entire school year. Or maybe she was simply determined never to tell on anyone she'd been on a school trip with to Utrecht Cathedral or the Liberty Monument, or sung sea shanties with for as long as she could remember. In the Mafia, people had a similar set of principles.

Thinking about it at night in bed, the hopelessness of the situation made us feel sick. We pulled the pillow over our heads, waiting for sleep to release us into oblivion.

If you weren't asleep by the time the clock struck twelve,

said Mr Klop, you'd turn into a werewolf. You'd burst out of your pyjamas, and with drooling fangs and a hairy hide you'd go on a rampage; you couldn't stop yourself. You might even wind up dragging your own baby sis from her crib and tearing her to pieces: the urge was simply stronger than you.

We jumped out of bed to turn the key in the lock, just in case, and shut the window tight. Before drawing the curtains again, we stared out at the street with its tidy front yards and shiny parked cars. Everything looked so peaceful, so normal and ordinary, that we just couldn't understand how we could possibly belong here, since we could already hear our pyjama seams popping and feel the pitch-black bristles growing out of our chest. Maybe we'd been switched at birth! Perhaps our *real* self was somewhere else entirely, biting its nails in despair, wondering if we'd ever find it again.

Vanessa, indignant, said that it was all Mrs Iedema's fault. Didn't she teach us that we had to show forgiveness? Well, what could be more forgiving than helping your own boyfriend's ex make herself look a little more presentable? 'If even *that*'s not the right thing to do, then I don't know what is,' she said.

She was right. You had to forgive, and keep forgiving.

And then it was almost inevitable. We didn't need the clock to strike twelve; just the sight of that pale, freckled nose and close-cropped head was enough to set us off. It was stronger than we were.

In Mr Klop's class it could be touch-and-go sometimes, because he was now grimly watching our every move. But he couldn't keep an eye on us forever. Just a few more weeks, and then we'd no longer have to worry about those suspicious eagle eyes of his. Then the days would just keep on coming, one after another, as usual. Days so hot that the cobblestones smelled of gunpowder; wet days, grey days, blah days, days as cold as a razor blade; gazillions of days without hope or anything to get excited about. Lucy and us, we still had years and years to go.

PART II

# Twelve

# J is for Jail

At regular intervals I would receive a fat envelope of draw-ings in the mail from my mother. After carefully smooth-ing out the creases, I tacked them up on the walls of my room with the drawing pins Duco bought specially for that purpose. It was a single row at first, but soon turned into two rows, and then three. In the end her drawings stretched from the skirting board all the way up to the ceiling. I had to climb on a chair to look at the top ones, and for the lowest ones, I had to lie flat on the floor on my stomach.

I got to know exactly the way everything looked: her cell, the bed, the metal desk, the chair, the wardrobe that listed sideways a bit, the toilet, and the door with the peephole and the sliding hatch. The fenced-in prison yard where she jogged in circles, the bare recreation room where she watched the telly in the evening, and the prison canteen where she could buy teabags or chocolate. She made a whole comic strip out of it, with lots of detail, and it was often quite funny, as if to say, 'It's not *that* bad in here.'

There were also portraits of the prison guards, and of the hairdresser who cut her hair four times a year—a West

Indian lady as broad as a manatee, with gold teeth and jungle-print leggings. My mother always pasted a lock of her own hair right under the portrait of the hairdresser. Sniffing it greedily, all I could detect was a whiff of dust and grease, which I took to be the smell of the workshop.

The workshop where my mother whiled away her days put the finishing coat on advertising signs and chair frames that were manufactured off-site. The workshop was filled with big machinery. It was a fun place to work—this I inferred from the radio that was prominently featured in all her workshop drawings. It had big, fat, musical notes coming out of it, punctuated by exclamation marks.

Some drawings also had writing on them. 'Hardening of the powder coating takes place at elevated temperatures (160-200 degrees centigrade). The powder coating is recyclable, which makes it a better choice than lacquer.' I had trouble deciphering the long, unfamiliar words. I didn't understand what she meant by them. Was it a secret code or something? Or maybe it was some sort of *Clara* 13 for adults. It had been so long since my mother had seen me that she probably thought I was all grown up by now.

To do the spraying, she wore a safety helmet that made her look like an astronaut or a deep-sea diver. ('We are able to achieve optimal spray quality [norm SIS 05.59.00] Sa 21/2 and Sa 3.') She also had on gigantic gloves reaching halfway up her arms. ('Dipping the product in acid after the alkaline bath improves the rinsing property, and thus the adhesion.')

Sometimes a foreman's report slipped in among the drawings. Over the years, my mother was taught Sawing and Filing. She learned to Drill and Punch. She learned to Weld and Solder. She was taught Metal Bending (Wire as well as Pipe). All these skills she depicted in loving detail for me in her drawings, signed with a smiley face. It never said 'Love from Mum.'

Sometimes I'd lie in bed examining those smiley faces for a good half hour with my magnifying glass. If the grinning mouth in the latest missive was off by even a fraction of an inch, I'd have the darnedest time getting to sleep. I'd keep tossing and turning, with only the muffled sounds of Ludo and Duco moving about somewhere downstairs to lull me: their heavy step, their deep male voices. They were often up until all hours of the night with their charts and spreadsheets. They calculated consolidation points and emerging trends. With the help of benchmarks and bottom lines, they noted every movement of every stock and commodity they invested in. It calmed me to think of their figures and their percentage points. It occurred to me that the numbers, at least, could only be explained one way: they were either up, or they were down. It gave you something firm to hold on to.

My communications with my mother weren't in the form of letters either. In reply to her drawings, I sent her bright collages pieced together from pictures I cut out of newspapers and magazines. A field of happy sunflowers framed by a border of sturdy Black & Decker tools from a DIY brochure. A cowboy on horseback, swinging a lasso at Snoopy, innocently dozing on top of his doghouse. Sometimes I'd cut out balloon captions from comic strips—'Hi beautiful!' or 'Come on, Jethro, hurry! Aunt Sidonia's asking what's keeping you!'—which I'd paste onto a blank sheet of paper with my glue stick. I also managed to work in a lot of jeeps and elephants, to show my mother that she needn't worry about me: I was perfectly fine. When they broke my arm at school, even before the cast was dry I'd sent off a collage of at least twenty sprawled and wrecked bikes, because I'd managed to convince the Luducos that was the way it had happened, and they took turns visiting my mother every month, mournfully and faithfully, like a couple of beaten dogs.

She never wrote, 'Would you like to visit me sometime?' The only kind of thing she ever wrote, scribbled across a cheerful drawing, was, 'A product can be significantly improved by such treatments as galvanizing, electroplating, and epoxying.'

We were in complete agreement, she and I. We didn't need to see each other face to face to know what was best for us. The story that lay pressed between the covers of our mutual silence had best remain what it was: a closed book.

# K is for Klutz

I often had the feeling we were living our lives with bated breath. All three of us had come to fear the sudden, the unexpected. In order not to be caught off-guard, Ludo, Duco, and I organized our time into set patterns. We didn't want any surprises. Every day had its own rhythm, its own rituals and significance. Very early on Saturday morning, when there was hardly anybody in the village yet, we did the entire week's shopping. On Sunday afternoons we played Monopoly for hours on end with the radio playing in the background, over a bottle of wine for the Luducos and a Coke for me. We sat and we watched the news on the telly every evening, each privately wondering at the fact that the world situation had stayed pretty much the same, as if what had happened to us hadn't tipped the scale in the slightest. Every report card was an occasion for a box of chocolate-covered marshmallows, no matter what it said. Every successful stock-market transaction called for a round of cream cakes. The little red tub in the scullery was reserved for bicycle-tyre repairs, the blue one from under the sink for soaking splinters that had become infected. Easter egg hunts at our house were so easy you could find the eggs with your eyes closed, and Duco got me a set of yellow ribbons for my plaits, which had soon grown back again.

It was a slow, languid kind of life, lived in a hazy state of suspension, but it made me feel secure. The moment I arrived home, to be greeted by Ludo and Duco, the Monopoly hotels, and my own little felted-wool egg-cosy, I was safe. We never talked about that night. Still, I could tell they couldn't help thinking of it sometimes: they'd suddenly go all awkward and shy, and not let me out of their sight, and spoil me rotten. Of course I didn't really deserve to be coddled like that, but it was nice. I couldn't help thinking that if someone went to such lengths for you, he must really care for you.

This predictable rhythm, and all our sleepy routines, came to a crashing halt shortly before my twelfth birthday. I had always assumed that twelve years really meant twelve years, and that was that. But that turned out not to be the case. It seemed that you only had to serve a portion of your time, and that you could cut your sentence down even further with good behaviour.

'But that's a fortnight from now!' Duco exclaimed, when Ludo returned from the monthly prison visit with the stunning news. Duco was sitting on the couch doing a crossword puzzle. His pen stayed poised in the air.

Ludo hadn't even taken off his coat. He stood in the doorway, breathing heavily. 'I decided to take a taxi home,' he said. 'I just didn't have the patience for the bus today.' He said it as if it were the most normal thing in the world—this, from someone who never threw away the package unless he'd checked to see if there were any coupons to clip inside.

Duco put down his pen. He fumbled for his handkerchief in his trouser pocket, nodding at me. 'Well, Lucy, it looks as if we'll soon be a foursome again, what do you think of that? Crikey!'

Oddly enough, all I could think of just then was the half-finished collage lying in my room upstairs, on which I'd pasted a large cruise ship from a travel brochure. I wouldn't have to finish it now. My boat would sail forever across an empty sheet of paper, on its way to nowhere.

The next morning, Ludo and Duco were suddenly galvanized into action. They whirled around in a frenzy, lugging rubbish bags filled with old newspapers, tablecloths with cigarette burns, and a lot of other indescribable junk. Then, over my protests, they dismantled the kitchen's empty-tin pyramid. Over time it had turned into quite a sport, that daily challenge of adding another tin to it without upsetting the increasingly precarious structure. After dinner we'd often sit for hours adding and subtracting, Ludo peering over his spectacles—'No, try propping it up first under there, on the right; careful, Lucy!' The empty kitchen corner was a sorry sight, and that night I dreamed that they dumped me into a rubbish bag too, and put me out with the trash.

When the whole house was tidy, they took out a couple of fossilized shammies and gave windows that hadn't seen a sponge in six years a thorough cleaning, inside and out. For the first time in ages, the light poured in untrammelled, and we could see how dirty and neglected everything was. We had been too preoccupied with our own problems to bother with the dusting and household chores, which would have interfered with our everyday reality. For the Luducos, missing my mother had been a constant duty, which had given them a hollowed-out and harrowed look. They'd never had much flesh on their bones, but now it just made your eyes ache when you saw them appear at breakfast in the morning in their underwear. Duco would give Ludo a listless little nudge: 'We do have to try to eat, old boy. Here, have some muesli, you love it.'

As for me, working down my bowl of yoghurt, I was usually too distracted thinking about what might happen at school that day to worry if our household was running smoothly.

But now we rolled up our sleeves. We were a great team; we'd always known we were. Working side by side, we cleaned the crusty cooker, we scrubbed layers of gritty grease off the bathtub, we mopped the tiles in the hall until their original colour was revealed, we stripped the sour-smelling sheets off the beds, we scoured the refrigerator's mouldy recesses. And all the time we were working our fingers to the bone, my heart was hammering like crazy. I didn't know if I was happy or terrified.

Once the house was sparkling clean, we took the bus into town. Ludo and Duco bought themselves a whole stack of shirts in crackling Cellophane and, in their excitement, enough socks to last them into the next ice age. Next they wanted to kit me out from top to toe, too. I had to turn them down since I really wasn't entitled to anything nice, though I couldn't tell them that, naturally. They were disappointed they couldn't buy me anything. 'You do need new underwear, and that's that,' said Duco firmly.

Underwear I could handle, that shouldn't be a problem.

In the girls' department, they weren't in the least bit embarrassed about sorting through the racks of underwear. They blithely stuck their hands inside the knickers, pulling at the fabric to test the stretch, bending their bald heads together. 'Black is the most practical,' said Ludo, who always did the laundry.

At the till, I reached up and gave them each a peck on the cheek—just like that, I didn't know why myself.

'You *are* getting to be a big girl, Lucy,' said Duco. 'It won't be long before you're towering over us.' He held my jacket hood as we walked outside.

And, strolling down the busy high street to the bus stop, I realized I didn't want my mother to come home at all.

The next day we found her waiting for us by the prison gate. In a shapeless beige raincoat, an overnight bag waiting next to her on the pavement.

It was a beautiful spring morning. Behind her, the tall white prison façade gleamed in the sun. I decided it didn't look that bad, for a slammer. In there, my mother had learned to Mill and Drill. In there, she'd slept two thousand nights in the bed beside the listing wardrobe, behind a locked door, with a guard on the other side of the peephole. It was in there that she'd done all the hundreds of drawings that wallpapered my room, except for the one in which she stood bonking her head against the wall for twenty comic-strip frames. On the reverse side she'd drawn a polar bear pacing up and down, swinging its head from left to right. The pictures had dotted lines around them, with a little pair of scissors drawn in: you were supposed to cut them out, then collate and staple them together at one end. If you flipped through the resulting little book with your thumb, it was just like watching a cartoon.

She used to make the same kind of booklets for me when I was little. I had kept one in which I was jumping rope, complete with Pippi Longstocking plaits bouncing up and down.

But I wasn't really in the mood for a cartoon of a head-banging woman and a pacing polar bear—really I wasn't. I'd lost that one as soon as I could.

The towering buildings were whipping up a stiff wind, blowing my mother's hair into her face so that she didn't see the taxi. I had a moment to watch her unobserved. Her lank, dark hair was quite a bit shorter than before, but I already knew that from the drawings. What she had failed to draw were the grey streaks running through it. Or how pudgy she'd grown, in spite of the jogging. She didn't have a waist, and the flesh in her face was no longer stretched tight over her bones; it looked kind of bloated, as if she was puffing out her cheeks. There was a pouch under her chin. Her complexion, which had been rosy, was now sallow. There wasn't a trace left of the girlishness that had once set her apart from the other mothers.

Just as I had finished absorbing her new appearance, she tossed her head back to sweep the hair out of her eyes. Two birds soaring through the cloudless spring sky caught her eye. Reading her lips, I could tell she was saying 'Oh!' in delighted surprise. Then she glanced our way just as the taxi drew up.

Ludo pushed me out of the cab ahead of him. I felt his excited breath on my neck. I had to fight the impulse to clutch the sides of the door and dig in my heels.

Behind me, Duco said, 'I wish we'd brought flowers.'

I got out, feeling a little dizzy. She'd be expecting a kiss from me. It was the least anyone could expect.

She stood frozen in the same pose, facing me. She was standing less than two feet from me. Her face was riddled with fine lines, like an old painting. She didn't move, but looked me over, up and down, quick as a panther. 'Lucy,' she said, after a moment. Nothing more.

Ludo gave me an encouraging prod in the back. But twelve horses couldn't have made me move. I dug my nails into my palms. 'Hi Mum,' I said. I tried to find the right tone, but had no idea what that was supposed to sound like.

She blinked. Then she bent down to pick up her bag.

'Give me that case,' said Duco.

My mother smiled uncertainly. She put her bag down again. And then she spread her arms, drawing all three of us into a rough bear hug.

Thanks to all the Metal Bending, she'd developed muscles of steel.

In the spanking-clean house she kept exclaiming about the most ordinary things. She couldn't stop nattering about everything she saw, and her new, hoarse voice sounded as if, for years, she'd been doing a lot more shouting than talking. What an unheard-of bliss, to be allowed simply to move from room to room in our house! As well as the fact that none of those rooms stank of other people's bad breath, or body odour, or farts. Not to mention not having to listen to all the tedious, senseless squabbles. Or that it was neither so horribly cold that the urine inside her kidneys froze, nor so terribly hot that it made her head throb. That she could sit all morning by the open terrace doors if she chose, gazing out at the garden all fresh with dew. That she could turn off the radio whenever she felt like it. That she could take a shower in private. That there wasn't a constant din of metal clanking on metal. That we had coffee that tasted like coffee, soft toilet paper, and a telephone that she could use any time she wanted. Just being able to rise or go to bed when it suited her, she said, was heaven.

I couldn't look at her when she said that sort of thing, I just couldn't. The very thought that she had lied, had lied through her teeth in every one of her drawings, was too much. But at the same time I was ashamed of the thought. Because the things she had done, the things she'd been capable of—it was so awe-inspiring that it I couldn't even get my head around it. When I tried to picture what it had been like, my brain felt as if it would explode. How, after all that, was she still able to laugh? How on earth did she stand it, being locked up behind bars for six long years? I had to admire her strength, but for some reason, her presence was nearly unbearable. I kept worrying that I'd run in the other direction when I saw her, or do something else that would hurt her or disappoint her horribly. I just hoped she wouldn't notice I was doing everything in my power not to have to be alone with her.

Ludo and Duco made it easy for me the first days of her homecoming. They never even spent a minute at their desks in their own rooms. Eagerly, they brewed pots of tea, opened bottles of wine, buttered pieces of toast, and tirelessly massaged my mother's neck. They didn't seem to even notice how everything about her had grown coarse and frumpy, and I was jealous, not just of them, but of her, too—of all their unshakable, unconditional love, solid as a rock. I watched them enviously, half hoping for some hesitant gesture, some halting phrase that would reveal that at least *one* of them wasn't totally okay with the new reality, either. But I hoped in vain.

It felt strange, to say the least, to be a foursome again. Every time I set the table I'd forget to put out a plate for her. She saw me return to the cupboard to rectify my mistake because, pretending to leaf through a magazine, she peeked at me over the top, the way people do who find themselves sitting in the same waiting room. In the morning I'd brush my teeth in my attic, spitting into a plastic cup so that I wouldn't have to run into her in the bathroom, wearing her old white bathrobe, the robe that had hung on the back of the door all this time, patiently waiting for her return. Picturing myself as that robe, and then picturing my mother sticking her arms up my sleeves and wrapping my soft ribbed cotton folds around her naked body, I stiffened with repugnance. When I met her on the stairs, I'd hastily step aside with a forced smile on my face.

But in the evening, after a long day at school, I was often too spent to keep my guard up. So, by the end of the first week, she was able to seize her chance, waylaying me in the hall. She stopped right in front of me. She stared at me with her clear blue eyes. I had forgotten about their brilliant colour; I'd also forgotten the dimple in her cheek. Sometimes I just didn't know *what* I remembered. She asked me, very quietly, as if trying to pry a secret out of me, 'So tell me, how are things with *you*, Lucy?'

I blushed beet-red right down to my toes at this sudden interest of hers. 'Just great.'

There was a pause; then she said awkwardly, 'Well, that's good.'

From the kitchen, Duco called us to dinner.

Her hand, which had been reaching out to find mine, faltered. 'Don't worry, we'll get used to each other again,' she said in a different, cooler voice. 'It's just a matter of time. Don't you think?'

'Sure,' I said politely. There really was no point in contradicting people. It only made them turn on you.

Duco again yelled that the pancakes were ready. He always spread them with lashings of jam, icing sugar, and a dab of butter. When everything in your life went wrong, all you had to do was think about Duco's pancakes and you were happy as a lark again. But of course I'd have to tell him I didn't care for any. I hoped he wouldn't take it personally, and decide I was getting to be a horrible teenager. He had come into my room the other day to ask why I was being so surly with my mother. Soon he wouldn't love me any more.

In the kitchen, Ludo had put candles on the table. His

short-sighted eyes twinkled. As far as he was concerned, everything was A-okay.

My mother sat down. She picked up the napkin from her plate with her rough factory hands. The tips of her fingers had become flat and stubby. It was hard to imagine that these same fingers, manicured and all, had ever dealt the Tarot's Celtic Cross to help people get a handle on their lives. Those people had trusted her blindly. She had been their crutch and their comfort, once. And in the eyes of the world she was nothing but a common murderer now.

I shuddered so violently that the table shook.

'Cold?' asked Ludo, affectionately running a hand through my hair.

I shook my head.

Duco began serving up the pancakes with an *I did it!* expression on his face. He was our kitchen maestro, but even for him, it was quite a chore to produce a meal that didn't call for a can-opener. Our entire joint repertory consisted of nothing but pasta, salad with olives, string beans, and, of course, pancakes, because they were *de rigueur* whenever it was somebody's birthday. For birthdays our Dukie would cook up a storm. Over the last few years, he'd doled out gazillions of mouth-watering pancakes at the kitchen table. But then he'd amble over to the window and stand there next to Ludo, staring out, while the pancakes grew cold and soggy and the garlands drooped. They hadn't ever grown used to our new situation without Mum.

'Delicious,' said my mother, digging in.

Duco winked at me.

I cut my pancake into little pieces and started pushing them around my plate. I gathered that when they'd visited her, they'd never told her about our neighbours giving us the cold shoulder. I had no idea what else they could have talked about once a month, year in, year out, sitting at opposite ends of a table under a guard's watchful eye, but definitely not that.

'So, is there anything special going on, tomorrow?' she asked.

'What do you mean?' asked Ludo.

'Tomorrow is the Queen's birthday, isn't it? There must be all kinds of festivities.'

'Oh, that,' said Duco uneasily.

My mother drowned her pancake in more syrup. 'Well, I *will* have to set foot outside the front door one of these days, won't I?'

After a brief silence, Ludo said, 'But why so soon?'

'I've been cooped up inside for six years. Actually, I can't wait to see Mr De Vries again.'

'He died. I told you at the time, remember?'

'What I mean, my dear boy, is that I have no intention of keeping myself cooped up in here, as well.'

Ludo and Duco exchanged glances. To judge from their faces, it had suddenly occurred to them that the time of her incarceration may well have been the least complicated period in their lives; at least they'd known exactly where she was, and hadn't had to worry about her getting herself into trouble.

'Queen's Day!' said my mother. 'I've got such great memories of that day from when I was little!'

'I haven't got the right clothes!' I exclaimed in alarm. At school, you were expected to wear patriotic colours on Queen's Day. Mostly orange, for the royal House of Orange. I jumped to my feet.

My mother stretched out a hand toward me. 'I'll find something for you to wear later,' she said. 'Just eat up first, sweetheart, finish what's on your plate.'

I shrank back before she could touch me. 'I'm perfectly capable of taking care of it myself,' I said sullenly. 'Like I always do.'

The schoolyard was a hive of activity: all kinds of amusements had been laid on. Bobbing for apples and Pin the Tail on the Donkey for the little ones, contests and races for the older kids. There was a booth selling flags, hats, and tooters, and a stall offering, for a modest sum, orange squash for us, orange bitters for the parents, and orange cupcakes for all.

I was only there because Mr Turk, the Gym teacher, had told me earlier in the week that I ought to join in more. 'It's no wonder everyone thinks you're antisocial and stuck-up; you're bringing it on yourself, you know.'

Since someone had immediately rammed a hat on my head that flopped down over my eyes but which I was wise enough not to try and take off, I kept bumping into people and getting an earful. But swearwords can't hurt you, as we all well knew.

'Take that silly thing off, girl, and look where you're going!' Mr Klop ranted, grabbing me by the scruff of my neck. 'And, now that I've found you, please note that you're signed up for the three-thirty relay race. According to Mr Turk, you're in serious need of some physical exercise.'

Next to Mr Klop stood Miss Joyce, dressed in red-white-and-blue from head to toe, a walking Dutch flag. Beaming, she said, 'What a super idea, Lucy. Your team will be so pleased to have the benefit of your long legs.'

I stared at her with bitter hatred. At least Mr Klop and most of his successors didn't try to hide the fact they were complete bastards, but that bitch Joyce was a sneak of the worst sort, all fake cheeriness. Even if she found me thrashing about with my head in the toilet, she'd manage to give it a positive spin. 'I already did two hundred and fifty push-ups for Mr Turk yesterday,' I cried.

'It could have been five hundred,' said Miss Joyce philosophically. 'And remember: exercise does wonders for the figure. It may not be of concern to you now, but someday, you'll see, everyone will envy that cute figure of yours.'

Right. *There* was something to look forward to. *That* would make life interesting.

Seething, I made a beeline for the ring-toss and the dart-throw, to work off steam. I scored a solid one hundred per cent on the nose in both, but the mothers giving out the prizes told me crossly that they were only for the little ones, and that a big girl like me ought to be ashamed of herself for wanting to make off with a stuffed animal.

Stupid of me: I hadn't counted on the fact that I'd have to hang around here all day. I hadn't brought anything to eat or drink with me and didn't have any money. It was hot. The huge crêpe-paper bow was already sticking to my neck, and my orange suspenders, which I'd cut down from an old pair of Duco's, were making my shirt cling uncomfortably to my torso. I wanted to sneak inside to slake my thirst at the water fountain in the loo, but every time I ventured up the deserted steps, I'd suddenly find myself with a whole conga line on my heels, raring to have some fun at my expense, so that I'd have to make a hurried retreat.

It wasn't until the end of the morning, when the marching band arrived with great fanfare, that they stopped paying attention to me. I started sifting through the rubbish for something to eat. In one of the dustbins I found a yoghurt drink that had hardly been touched, and lots of half-eaten cupcakes. I didn't even care that Thomas and Vanessa, furtively sharing a fag behind the dustbins, could see me scraping the leftover crumbs from the wrappers. Vanessa shook her head in disgust. This summer, Thomas was going on a trip to Scotland with Vanessa and her mum; she'd been boasting about it for weeks. Okay then, fine, it would give the three of them something to tut-tut about, me rooting about in the rubbish like a pig.

Having eaten my fill, I watched the toddlers run an egg race on their pudgy little legs. Whenever things got so bad I just couldn't take it anymore, the sight of those cute little tykes, blissfully playing their heads off or just scampering about, invariably cheered me up. They were happy nearly all the time, and for no earthly reason. Sometimes you'd see one of them walking along and then suddenly start to skip, just for the love of it. I often pondered whether there was a way to stop them from getting bigger and meaner. The sweets they were amazed to discover tucked into their jacket pockets came from me. I was happy to spend all my pocket money on them, because it was such fun to see their little faces light up. They thought there was a good fairy in our school. It was too bad that I couldn't think of anything more practical, something they could really use.

When I heard the announcement that the relay race was about to start, I made my way over to the double track that Mr Turk had chalked on the playground's paving stones. One runner from each team had to sprint across to the far side, tap a teammate's hand, and run back to thrust the red relay baton into the next runner's hand.

The teacher blew the whistle, and we were off.

Mrs Iedema, who was the referee at my end, raised her flag to show that the first runner was back. I elbowed my way to the front to grab the baton so that I'd be the second runner, but my teammates yanked me back in line by my plaits. Of course—I was going to have to go last, so that if we lost, they could blame it on me. Blankly, I let them shove me all the way back into last position. My orange bow ripped. And just as I was plucking the last pieces of shredded crêpe paper off my neck, I spotted my mother standing just a few yards away.

She stood back from the other parents, who were spurring on the relay racers with loud shouts of encouragement. She was wearing that rubbishy raincoat again, she had on sunglasses, and she was by herself; she must have slipped out of the house while the Luducos were busy at their desks.

How long had she been standing there? Had she seen me foraging in the dustbin? Had she noticed I was never with any of the other kids, and that nobody had talked to me all day except to yell at me? Had she seen me lurch blindly through the crowd with that silly hat crammed over my eyes? Had she seen me getting told to get lost wherever I went? Was she thinking to herself, And here I was imagining Lucy would be able to hold her head above water!

My teammates ran back and forth. There was a lot of yelling and cheering.

'Don't just stand there dozing, you!' cried Mrs Iedema. 'You're up next!' She wasn't looking directly at me; she avoided having to look at me whenever possible.

I pulled myself together and began concentrating as hard as I could. I was going to run like the wind, I would fly faster than a cannonball, I'd win the race and they'd all cheer and yell and slap me on the back. My mother would go home reassured.

Sara came jogging back from the far side, lagging half a lap behind her opponent. 'Run!' I screamed, digging my toes into the starting line, my hand outstretched, ready and set.

'Sara! Sara! Sara!' chanted the onlookers, as if she was in the process of breaking all records.

As she crossed the line, instead of tapping me on the arm she gave me a punch in the stomach. Doubling over, I lunged for the red baton tumbling through the air in agonizing slow motion. I saw it flip over and over, and it wasn't until just before it hit the ground that the similarity suddenly struck me. It looked exactly like a pencil. I recoiled. I felt I was choking.

Then, with a loud crack, it snapped in two under my foot.

The victory cheers of the other team were drowned out by the pandemonium that broke loose on our side. All the usual profanities and even a few brand-new ones were hurled at me. I didn't care. I couldn't touch any red pencils. That was the only thing that mattered. I could sometimes get around some of the other prohibitions, but not this one. Shielding my head with my arms, I tried backing out of the circle. But Mr Turk grabbed me by the collar to give me an unholy shaking. 'Did you *have* to be a spoilsport again?' he cried, his face purple with rage, six weeks' detention written loud and clear on his glowering brow. 'You just couldn't resist, could you!'

'That child is incorrigible,' said one of the parent onlookers loudly. All the fathers and mothers were glaring at me.

Then my mother suddenly stepped forward. Calmly, she pried me from the Gym teacher's clutches, straightened my collar, and said, 'Aren't you overreacting a bit?'

The Gym teacher didn't recognize her at first. No one did, in fact. They stared at her as if she were the Scarlet Pimpernel, or some ancient, mythical agent of revenge.

'I've just come to tell you all,' said my mother, taking off her sunglasses and stuffing them in her coat pocket, 'that I'm out of prison.'

Mr Turk took a step back, bumping into Mrs Iedema, who had turned ashen. There wasn't a peep out of any of the kids. The mothers' knees shook. The fathers' eyes bulged.

I was sure that my mother had no idea how scruffy she must look to these people. I nearly wept with shame, and then, before I knew it, with sudden fierce pride. My mum was thumbing her nose at the lot of them. She knew it didn't matter what people thought of the way you looked on the outside. You might very well be a good fairy on the inside. Gazing round, taking her time, she said, 'And now that I'm back, I'm going to be watching you people to see how my daughter is treated. You'd better count on it.'

Mrs Iedema, lips drawn in a thin line, hissed, 'The nerve. The bloody nerve.' Her hand was pressed to her chest. There were beads of sweat on her forehead. 'How *dare* you show your face here again!'

'I live here,' my mother said dryly. 'And I've served my time.' She looked round again, from one person to the next. At her former friends, and at their husbands, the ones who used to moon about outside the rectory at night, supposedly walking the dog.

Nobody stirred. There they stood, our neighbours and acquaintances, staring foolishly at the tips of their shoes, wearing their orange rosettes in honour of the Queen's birthday, their hats, their red-white-and-blue face paint; such patriots they were.

Finally Miss Joyce piped up, indignant, 'We've gone through a lot of trouble trying to help Lucy with her reading. And we *have* made quite a bit of progress. Haven't we, Lucy?'

'Oh shut it, bitch,' said my mother in her harsh prison voice. 'It's a disgrace, what I've just witnessed here with my own two eyes. Don't think I'm leaving it there. I'm ready to make a huge fuss. You'll be hearing about this.' She put her arm around my shoulders, an arm that felt so heavy it nearly slammed me to the ground.

I was so proud of her that I tingled from head to toe, as if I had an electric current running through me. Nobody could lay a finger on us. Together we could show the lot of them what was what.

Mrs Iedema burst out, 'But that child has only herself to blame. Only herself or her disgraceful mother!'

'Mum! Don't!' said Thomas. He'd rushed to her side and was pulling at her sleeve.

But Mrs Iedema was finally standing face to face with the devil who had destroyed her happiness. In a rage, she continued, 'Don't tell me it's normal for a girl her age to have nothing but sex on the brain! Like mother, like daughter! Or do I need to spell it out?'

My elation immediately went up in smoke. My heart was pounding. I didn't want it to go there.

My mother gave a condescending laugh. 'Bullshit!'

The other mothers gasped. *Bullshit?* For years they had anticipated this moment, and for years they had rather dreaded it. They had made vague resolutions, only to reject them again, flummoxed. If they did ever have to face their friend again, they would handle her return as circumstances dictated at the time; that was the collective verdict. But could *this* creature really be their former friend? This … this fishwife?

'Complete and utter bullshit,' said my mother, 'to detract attention from what's been done to Lucy.' She stared defiantly at the bystanders.

But Mrs Iedema wasn't done with her. 'And what about what's been done to *my* child? Hasn't Thomas lost his father?'

'Mum, please!' said Thomas, his face all white. 'Let's just …'

'The poor lamb!' Vanessa's mother's voice rang loud and clear. 'Always trying to protect his mama.'

'Thomas would still have a father,' cried Mrs Iedema wildly, 'and I'd still have a husband, if you …'

At the top of my lungs, I yelled, 'Anyway, the pencil was Thomas's idea!'

Thomas flinched.

'Lucy!' my mother hissed in dismay.

But it was true! And had Thomas ever come to my defence? If I spilled the beans, it was because he deserved it! He definitely deserved it!

'And what is that supposed to mean?' Mrs Iedema was seething. 'What kind of insinuation is that?'

'Oh come, leave the poor boy alone!' cried Miss Joyce.

The parents craned their necks anxiously. 'What are they talking about?'

'They're trying to pin the blame on Thomas!'

'You're kidding!'

'Not on Thomas, surely?'

The assembled mothers were baffled. But instinct told them something really low and mean was going on here: blaming an innocent child for an adult's crime!

Their disgust couldn't help rubbing off on the fathers, who had been staring at my mother open-mouthed. It had been a close call for them, as well; she could very well have wrecked their families, too. What did the bitch think? Did she think she could still wind them around her little finger? Please! Respect is something that has to be earned.

Instinctively, the parents moved in closer, shoulder to shoulder. Together, they stood for a society that still had room for common decency, virtue, and family values.

My mother grabbed me by the hand. 'I think you misunderstood,' she began. 'What Lucy meant was …'

But even the teachers had had enough by now. Fresh out of prison, then shows up out of the blue, thinking she's entitled to kick up a fuss? Ha! A convicted murderess wants to read *them* the riot act? As if they hadn't always done their duty, in all good conscience! 'You'll be hearing about this,' she'd said. About what, might they ask? And since when did scum like her get to call the shots?

I didn't see who was the first to throw something at us. All I saw was the apple core that hit my mother somewhere at chest height. And after that, we didn't even stand a chance.

# L is for Lewis

The minute we got home, we quickly locked the door behind us. We tossed our stained clothes into the washing machine. We iced our bruises. I was given a soothing compress for my throbbing head, which had a sizable plug of hair ripped out of it. Speechless, the Luducos brewed a pot of chamomile tea.

We'd barely recovered our breath when, that same evening as soon as it grew dark, a brick came flying through one of the windows. Since we didn't know if it was just an afterthought or a prelude to a whole new set of ordeals, we took the precautionary measure of barricading the windows and doors by piling all the furniture up against them. Ludo drew me onto his lap and whispered soothing nonsense in my ear to lull me to sleep. His cheek tickled mine. He smelled of peppermint.

The next morning, since we no longer had a breakfast table or chairs to sit on, we had a picnic on the floor of the gloomy living room. Somehow we all managed to act as if it was the most normal thing in the world. Even Ludo, the most finicky of the four of us, folded his creaky legs beneath him without comment and gamely chewed on a piece of toast.

Because even if it seemed as if our lives had been abruptly turned upside down, or had even suddenly blown up in our faces, the truth was that it had already been this way for us for years. My mother's homecoming only served to shed light on the truth, a truth as indisputable as it was brutal. In some weird way, I felt relief. At least now all the cards were on the table.

We spent the first day in our bunker playing Monopoly by candlelight, one game after another. We bought hotels, railway stations, and water-treatment plants, which gave us the bracing feeling that we were still full participants in the functioning of society. The fact that it was on a regular weekday, not a Sunday, that we were moving our pieces around the Monopoly board made us reckless with excitement.

Duco bought Amsterdam, lock, stock, and barrel. His breathing got heavier and heavier. Afterward, we heated up a frozen pepperoni-and-mushroom pizza in the oven.

During dinner, whenever the adults weren't paying attention, I'd take a quick nip from their wine glasses, to make sure they didn't get too tipsy. They had to keep a clear head, it seemed to me. But after a few gulps, I started wondering what for, in fact. We all had some very rough years behind us. We were entitled to a little relaxation.

We soon got used to the lack of daylight, the way one gets used to anything in the end. After twenty-four hours, we couldn't imagine living any other way. There was even something comforting about it. We slept like logs, anyway, and sometimes we'd even nod off in the middle of a game of cards or a meal.

In the darkened living room, my mother seemed in her element. She sat contentedly with her back against the wall, her legs, which were still lovely, stretched in front of her. The soft light of the candles set out all over the floor erased the lines around her mouth. Even her hoarse voice sounded different in the semi-darkness—sweeter, more seductive. But whenever I felt her gaze on me, I'd get the jitters. She'd better not even think of blaming me for all this. Who, after all, was the one who'd made such a huge fuss in the schoolyard? *She* was the one who started it.

The third night, Duco wondered, 'Shouldn't we be *doing* something?'

'Phone someone, you mean, or what?' said Ludo.

'Boys, boys!' scoffed my mother. She didn't see the need to waste more words on it. Every time she said 'Boys!'—her pet name for the Luducos—in that tone, I couldn't help playing the old game: trying to figure out whose eyebrows I'd inherited, which of them had given me my narrow shoulders, my long legs. Ludo and Duco usually got the exact same number of points, as long as I left out certain things, like Duco's crossword puzzles.

'We'll have to do *some*thing, won't we,' said Duco, but he didn't sound very convinced. 'What do you think, Lucy?'

I didn't know. I just couldn't take reality very seriously at the moment. Only once in a while, when I'd decide to check the kitchen cupboards, the surreal fog in which we found ourselves would briefly lift. We had lots of tins of baked beans, fortunately. Beans were very nutritious. But the loo-paper supply was getting dangerously low.

Exactly one week later, at ten-thirty in the morning, the telephone rang. It sounded like an alarm clock going off. It suddenly reminded us that an outside world did exist. We looked at one another uncertainly. Then Ludo answered it. He was the most conscientious member of our household; he couldn't help himself. His face fell. 'Mr Turk,' he said stiffly.

My mother grabbed him around the waist and pressed her ear next to his.

'Certainly,' said Ludo into the receiver. 'But surely you must understand that, given the circumstances, Lucy will not be able to attend ...'

With a sharp tap on the cradle, my mother disconnected the call.

Duco turned to me, wide-eyed with alarm. 'No need to panic. No need to panic,' he said, squatting down beside me. He'd been terribly shaken when it had finally dawned on him that the Queen's Day incident couldn't have been a unique occurrence. He'd asked me, bewildered, why I hadn't ever told them what went on at school. I hadn't been able to think of a plausible reason. 'Were you ashamed, was that it?' he'd asked, and I'd nodded. I was just relieved that he had no idea of the scope of it, or the details. And he'd never find out, either, because otherwise he'd never, until the end of time, sleep another wink. He'd already been so terribly upset the time I'd come home with my plaits cut off. It had taken quite some ingenuity and quick thinking to keep the two of them in the dark. I had lied and cheated and feigned indignation whenever they'd tried in their own way to find out about what was going on in my life. 'Oh man, stop bugging me, it's none of your business.' It had been the only way to stop them from rushing to my defence. I shuddered to think what would have happened if they had.

Ludo said to my mother, 'What did you do that for? That Turk chap was mentioning compulsory attendance and the law. If Lucy stops going to school, we're in big trouble.'

'Oh, my darling,' she scoffed, 'what else did you expect?' She yanked the phone cord out of the socket in the wall.

'I don't know,' said Ludo. 'Keeping a child home when the law says she should be at school ... and especially in her case ...'

'In her case?' My mother raised her eyebrows. 'What, because I've done time? Well, then let me tell you the first lesson they teach you in the slammer, right off. When everyone's out to get you, and you're up against the lot of them, you can't win. So you'd better prepare yourselves— our former friends will do everything in their power to get rid of us, now that they've all decided that we're scum. They're going to squeeze us out of this community like a pimple.'

There was a silence. Then Ludo said, 'Then we'll get the police involved.'

'Yeah? And then? Do you think they'll post a cop outside to guard our house permanently? And a bodyguard for Lucy, too, when she's at school? Anyway, is that what we want? Do we really want to live that way, under constant surveillance?'

'But we have our rights,' Ludo said wildly. 'For God's sake, surely we haven't ...'

'As if that makes any difference in this situation.' My mother started pacing up and down. 'Mark my words. Our life here is over. We might as well cut our losses and run.'

I couldn't get to sleep that night. I listened to the house creaking. The plaintive squeak of a gutter—was there someone up there, prowling across our roof? Was it the wind howling round the chimney, or was there a posse of vengeful vigilantes on our roof, intent on smoking us out with stink bombs?

I'd never thought about it that way, about them wanting to squeeze us out like a pimple. Yet they so enjoyed teasing and picking on people that they'd probably miss us terribly if we, as my mother had put it, cut our losses and ran. Cripes, how pissed they'd be! Lucy, come back, come back!

I hated the idea. Really I did. It had taken me a great deal of effort to learn to survive, to make myself indifferent and hard. But I'd stayed the course, and I was rather proud of what I had achieved. And just as I was on top of my game, and wasn't bothered by anything anymore—not even being made to swallow a bucketful of earthworms, not even scavenging for food in dustbins—along came my mum to upset the apple cart. And I could so easily have made it into the *Guinness Book of Records*! Had all that grinning and bearing been for nothing, then? Wouldn't anybody ever reluctantly grant, 'One thing you've got to give Lucy, she never surrenders'? Instead of that, I could see them rubbing their hands with glee: 'We sure managed to run *her* out of town, the scared little sissy.'

And to think that my mother, of all people, had helped them get there!

Were they all sleeping peacefully, with a clear conscience? Wasn't there anyone in the entire village tossing and turning with remorse or regret? Didn't they realize what hopeless failures they were at being true Batavians? And what about Mrs Iedema, always harping on forgiveness? Surely there had to be someone out there willing to forgive and forget, so that we could at the very least not have to leave?

In year two, Mr Klop had taught us what a chain reaction was. If you nudged the first domino in a row of dominoes, making it fall over, all the other dominoes would follow suit; there was no stopping it. The same went for wildfires on the prairie: wildfires were just as impossible to stop, they'd spread in all directions until there wasn't a sprig of grass left standing. Or take the way vampires kept creating more vampires by biting people in the neck, who'd then turn round and bite even *more* people in the neck, turning *them* into vampires, and on and on to infinity. The whole world was teeming with such chains of events; the minute they were unleashed, you were powerless to stop them. Once your fellow citizens kicked you out, there was no going back.

The next morning, my mother had dark circles under her eyes, but her voice sounded resolute as she announced over our picnic breakfast that she hadn't come out of jail just to be condemned to house arrest for goodness knows how long, without any kind of trial. Endless deliberation was a luxury she couldn't afford; every day cooped up inside was one too much for her. 'Let's take the bull by the horns and just get out of here. That's what it's going to come down to eventually, in any case. We'll just be doing ourselves a favour by taking off, and the sooner the better.'

Today, Ludo completely agreed with her. All you had to do was look at our furniture barricades to see that she had a point, he said. It didn't really matter in the long run how we got into this mess. What mattered was to get ourselves out unscathed. We had to save what there was to salvage, before things got even worse.

'Worse?' I said.

'That Turk-chap can't wait to send the authorities after us. And what then? Before we know it, they'll have you in some foster home,' said my mother.

'But where are we going, then?' I asked, distraught. Every time she decided to save me, I went from the frying pan into the fire.

'Someplace where we can start over with a clean slate.'

'Abroad,' Duco concluded, rather too promptly. My mother must already have talked it over with them.

'Yes, that's probably the best solution. Just moving on to the next village or the next province certainly won't make things better,' she said. 'The Netherlands is such a small place, sooner or later your past will always catch up with you here.'

The three of them were putting on quite a song and dance for me. But I couldn't really think of a good rebuttal. It was true that wherever we went in The Netherlands, it was likely there'd be someone who remembered that sensational murder case, and that would be the end of being left alone. We'd have to change our names. We'd have to wear sunglasses at all times, and we'd never be able to let down our guard.

'Just think of it as an adventure, love,' Ludo said to me. It was obvious he felt relieved at the prospect of being treated like a normal human being somewhere out there, instead of a piece of shit, simply for being a part of this family. I suddenly got a lump in my throat at the sight of his dear face with those silly spectacles. I forgave him on the spot for having cooked all this up behind my back with *her*. I punched him in the shoulder. 'Okay, Ludikins.'

'Besides, we're all out of jam,' said my mother, scraping the last dregs out of the jar and spreading it on a cracker, 'so we'll just have to spring into action.'

'We're almost out of toilet paper, too,' I said.

'It's always the women who see the practical side,' Duco said to Ludo.

A shadow stole over my mother's face. Then she said, 'We've got to. Right, Lucy?'

I nearly choked on my tea. Since coming home, she hadn't ever alluded to it, not even once. And now she had done it in the Luducos' presence! We were never to mention it again, that was the deal. She'd promised. Otherwise, life would be untenable, for all four of us. We'd just shrivel with horror and dismay. We'd never again be able to get ourselves out of bed in the morning, we'd never again have the strength to open a tin for dinner, and, worst of all, we'd never again be able to look one another in the eye.

I started babbling a mile a minute, to change the subject.

'Can't we go to Florida? They have pelicans and flamingos and crocodiles and ...' Was it crocodiles, or alligators? I could never tell the difference, you'd need a book about the animal kingdom like Thomas's in order to... Appalled, I held my breath.

'We aren't millionaires, lovey. We're only very modest traders.'

'But extremely competent ones, Ludo, let's be fair,' said Duco. 'So you and I can earn a living anywhere, as long as there's a phone.'

'Where would *you* like to live?' my mother asked him.

'Um ... Tuscany, perhaps? Lounging under a cypress tree, doesn't that appeal to you? Olives? Chianti? Museums?'

'Hmm,' she said. 'Very tempting. But which of us speaks Italian?'

'We'll just take a language course. Italy's definitely an option, as far as I'm concerned.' Ludo looked excited.

I gazed at the drawn curtains and at the furniture piled up against the doors and windows. Were they nuts? We weren't just planning a holiday! 'Where would we take that language course? And when?'

'We're just trying to keep it light, Lucy,' said Duco, 'because we'll get terribly depressed otherwise. Come on, now it's Mum's turn.'

My mother rubbed her forehead. 'You know, it doesn't really matter to me where we go. As far as I'm concerned, anywhere as long as we don't have to bump into lots of people all the time. I've had enough of the so-called civilized world. I want peace and quiet, for all of us.'

'Oh, well.' Duco took her hand. He was already picturing the perfect idyll: our little family whole again, in the back of beyond somewhere, so that he'd never have to share her with strangers again.

'Why don't we take a look at the atlas?' Ludo proposed.

The die was cast. As soon as you start finding dog turds and dead rats in your letter box, you stop being too choosy. The chosen location was a Scottish island somewhere way out in the ocean, at the remotest edge of Europe: Lewis. It was just a stab in the dark, but you'd be hard-pressed to get any farther away from the civilized world.

And so we left like thieves in the night, once Ludo and Duco had sold enough shares to pay for the move and the tickets. We took only the bare essentials with us; a second-hand dealer would take care of the rest for us.

A taxi drove us to Schiphol. I gazed back at my old dormer through the cab's rear window for as long as I could, remembering how I'd climbed out on that fateful stormy night and slid down the rain spout, because I hadn't wanted to move away. It felt like a hundred years ago, but it had just been the year we learned to read with Miss Joyce. The year that made it clear I was dumbest one in the class. I hadn't even been smart enough to fudge it; every time I had trouble deciphering some word, I'd mumble, 'You-know,' but the teacher never bought it; she'd drawn up long lists of my you-knows to help her analyse the problem. If you'd asked me, she'd have been better off showing me how to tell the difference between a *d* and a *h*.

If I hadn't objected to our moving away that time, it would all have been different. It was too awful to even think about. And now I had to move anyway.

At the airport, Duco bought me a magazine. Ludo took me over to the perfume counter to help him choose something for my mother. I sniffed all the bottles the salesgirl uncapped for us, but none of them smelled of my old mummy, the one from before that night.

She sat next to me on the plane. She was leaning back on the headrest and her eyes were closed, but in her lap her roughed-up fingers wouldn't keep still. Was she worrying about what she was getting us into now? Or was she sad because we'd been forced to move out of our rectory? The home where she'd painted a mural for me, and hung a string of Christmas lights over my bed? Mum and I had stood there, wobbling side by side on the mattress springs; she only had to move her foot for me to collapse, and if I jumped, crowing with delight, she had the hardest time keeping her balance, as if we were tied to each other by a piece of string. Her cheerful instructions: 'Nurse Lucy, would you be so good as to hand me that hammer? And would you kindly stop jumping up and down? Or I'm afraid our patient will die.' When it was done, we turned off the ceiling light. Then we gazed together at the effect of the Christmas lights casting patterns in the dark. 'Just right,' she'd said. 'Just like Lucy.'

When the flight attendant brought us our breakfast, I shyly asked my mother if she'd like my fruit salad. It looked delicious.

In Edinburgh there was a rental car waiting for us. It was going to be a long trip, because we had to drive all the way north, where we were to take the ferry.

Duco drove. At every turn in the road, he'd tell us how terrifying it was for someone with a mouldy, seldom-used driving license to have to remember to stay on the left.

'You're doing fine,' Ludo would respond every time, and give his shoulder a squeeze. He and I were in the back seat, because we weren't any good at map-reading.

The rolling landscape whizzing by looked gorgeous in the spring sunshine. There were little lambs in the meadows. There were thatched cottages everywhere; they looked so cosy and snug that you just knew the inhabitants were the nicest people. I could see the four of us in one of those little doll's houses, with climbing roses and a rain barrel in front, and pink geraniums spilling from the windowsills.

After driving for several hours, we stopped off in a village that was just one street, so that what you saw was what you got. The adults wanted coffee; I asked for chips, which came wrapped in newspaper instead of in a paper cone. I thought that was pretty cool. I was starting to have a little more faith in this expedition of ours.

Back in the car, I dozed off with my head on Ludo's shoulder. I thought I heard him say, 'Sorry, Lucy, being no good at reading maps is a trait you must have inherited from me,' but then all four of us were wading along the beach. We all had on bright-red swimming trunks and we all had happy faces.

I didn't wake up until we were driving up the rattling ramp of the car ferry that was to take us to our destination. I sat up. I thought of my unfinished collage—the one with the ship that had been doomed never to sail anywhere—and suddenly it occurred to me that it now had a destination after all, which meant everything was going to turn out all right, in some warped, fantastical way.

Stiffly, we got out of the car. We climbed up to the top deck and stood at the railing. The sun had disappeared behind the clouds and there was a stiff wind that tasted of iron and salt. Seagulls screeched. The boat tooted. Everything suddenly started moving. We were off.

'Just look at that,' said my mother. 'Simply extraordinary.'

She was talking about the steep, forbidding rock walls rising up on either side of us. On land there was no sign of human habitation. There were hardly even any trees or bushes. Everything was barren. Everything was hard. Everything was grey—the rocks, the sky, and the water.

And waiting for us somewhere out there was the Isle of Lewis, just as bare and hard and grey.

# M is for Moon

We spent the first night in a hotel in Stornoway, the island's main town. The place stank of overcooked cabbage, even upstairs in the bedrooms. The sheets on my bed were damp. The bedside table held brochures for any tourists crazy enough to come here.

With a sinking heart, I studied the photos of grim piles of mossy stone, crumbling lighthouses, and rock-strewn roads with rain puddles rippling in the wind. The captions were almost impossible to decipher. Tràigh Mhór, Roinn a'Roidh, Abhainn Grimestra, Eilean Chaluim Chille, Teampuill Mholuidh; surely they couldn't be the real names of places or things? How would I ever ask for directions here if I ever got lost?

For hours I stared at the unintelligible words, shivering in my sagging bed. A word that was impossible to read was like an out-of-focus photograph; you know there must be a meaning hidden in there somewhere, but what it is remains exasperatingly hazy. I just didn't get why writing was ever invented, or why smoke signals and the tom-tom had been made obsolete.

On a whim, I started tearing a few pictures out of the

brochures. I didn't have any glue with me, but I managed to make a collage using toothpaste. Or it may have been my tears that made it all stick: a dilapidated lighthouse, with the Clach na Truiseil—some sort of rock, from the looks of it—pasted on it sideways, and the place name Stiomrabhagh, and all the other horrible words, words I'd never be able to read even if I lived to be a hundred.

I slipped the collage under my mother's door. It took such a load off my chest that I fell asleep immediately.

Driving to the estate agent's office the next morning, Mum didn't let on that she must have got up criminally early in order to make a drawing for me by way of reply. It was a beautiful sketch of a lovely bay surrounded by chubby dunes. At the foot of the dunes, at least a thousand little flowers had been coaxed to bloom in coloured pencil. On the beach, pink and blue shells twinkled in the sun. And along the seashore ran a girl, pulling along an orange kite high up in the sky.

I absolutely adored it. So she had never stopped loving me, she still loved me, somehow, in spite of everything! The thought of it suddenly made me feel I was exactly like that figure in the drawing: just an ordinary little girl with plaits.

'Step on it, Duke!' I cried, elated.

At the estate agent's, we were given a key and directions. The agent advised us to stock up on supplies in town. The house had a freezer, he told us.

In the supermarket, I pranced past the frozen peas; I nearly did a somersault in front of the fish fingers. I balanced two frozen Black Forest cakes on my head. At the till, I leaped on top of Ludo, shrieking with laughter. 'You're the *man!*' I yelled.

'Silly billy.' He pulled me back on my feet, laughing.

'Lucy,' asked my mother, 'would you like some of those chocolates, or some toffees?'

But I was already being wheeled out of the shop by Duco in the loaded cart, the two of us belting out the national anthem in as fast a tempo as humanly possible.

When we were done with our shopping, the back seat was packed to the ceiling with frozen chickens and other foodstuffs. Ludo and I barely had room to squeeze in.

As we rode along, Duco pointed at a sign by the side of the road. 'Anyone who knows how to pronounce that deserves the Nobel prize.'

'That's Gaelic,' said my mother. 'Only one local in a hundred can still speak it today.'

'In that case, we won't have to bother with it. We'll just talk to the other ninety-nine.' Duco grinned at me in the rear-view mirror.

So they must have discussed it, last night in bed. They'd talked about me, how best to set my mind at ease about all those funny names. My toes curled up inside my rubber boots from sheer pleasure; it felt great, to be the one everyone else was concerned about.


Our new house didn't have a thatched roof, and there weren't any geraniums in the windows. It had once been white, but you couldn't tell unless you used your fingernails to scratch at the walls, which were just as sooty inside as out. Instead of one of those cheerful rain barrels, the garden had a mountain of peat in it, reaching up to the roof. The house was built at the edge of a vast, grey peat bog, criss-crossed with muddy drainage ditches. From the minuscule windows you had a distant view of low-lying hills beneath the leaden sky, monotonous and sombre.

We weren't city folks—we were used to quite a bit—but this really was living with nature. The wind blasted right through the walls, stealthily driving the drizzling rain through the chinks and cracks. There was moss growing in the sagging gutters. It smelled just as swampy inside as out.

The adults announced, poker-faced, that they simply loved it. They could see an austere, rough, and hard-working existence for themselves here; the simple pleasures of a roaring peat fire and home-baked bread. 'The peat colonies!' said my mother. 'It couldn't *be* more appropriate!'

'Hey, get real, will you?' I said in alarm. 'There's no way we're actually going to *live* here, is there? You can't be serious!' I pointed at the rickety wooden table and the patches of damp on the walls of the hole that was evidently the kitchen, since it had a colossal cooker rusting in one corner.

'I don't see why not,' said Ludo.

'It's just perfect,' my mother declared. 'And when summer is over, you can ride the bus to school in Stornoway. In the meantime, we'll have plenty of time to help you brush up on your English.'

'She already knows quite a bit of English,' said Duco. 'From watching telly. Right, Lucy?'

'But it's a complete pigsty in here!' I yelled in despair. How could they not notice the dilapidated windows bulging and rattling in the draught, or that the skirting boards were as riddled with holes as Swiss cheese? 'Everything is old and grubby and worn! I bet there isn't even a ...'

With her new muscles of steel, my mother grabbed my arm. 'That's enough, princess. I refuse to hear any more whining. Where I've just come from was a *lot* less comfortable than this. Don't you ever forget that!'

Her reproach left me gasping for air. She might as well have said it out loud—'It's all your fault, Lucy.'

'Come, love,' said Duco, to change the subject. 'Let's go

return the car to Stornoway, just you and me.' Now it was he who was holding me by the arm. Next thing I knew, we were sitting in the car, peering through the steamed-up windshield.

Duco drove slowly, even though keeping to the left could hardly be a problem for him out here, since the road was so narrow. It meant he was working on giving me a sermon.

'You probably think I'm a bad sport,' I said sullenly, to help him get on with it.

He gave my knee a squeeze. 'I just think it's too bad you can't be happy about your mother being home with us again. That's what's bothering you, isn't it, and not the move? Ludo and I thought you'd be jumping for joy.'

I started biting my nails.

'Cat got your tongue?'

'Look out, sheep!' I yelled.

It was a sad, muddy sheep. It was planted in the middle of the road, its wool dripping wet, bleating.

Duco honked the horn.

The sheep turned its lean snout to glance over its shoulder. *So?* it was thinking, bored, *what's new?*

Duco honked again.

The sheep wagged its backside, which was clotted with crusty dreadlocks. Then it fired a volley of droppings at the car before galloping off, its hind legs flailing in all directions, onto the deserted moor.

'See that?' I said triumphantly. 'We haven't even been here an hour and we're already getting shat on.'

'That's no big deal, it won't put me off. Not after all the poopy nappies of yours I had to change.' He looked at me askance. 'You have no idea, do you, how often I had to save you from your own excrement.'

Adults, when they reminisced, always turned the dumbest things into some kind of heroic feat. They were apparently under the misapprehension that you had never heard them sigh, or sometimes even swear, when you'd made a big load in your nappy. They just assumed babies were blind and deaf, so that later they could fool you about everything that happened when you were little. 'It was Ludo who used to change my nappies,' I said coolly.

'How would *you* know!'

I kept my mouth shut. But I remembered everything. I certainly remembered the way my mother was always coming over to lean over my crib, her mouth drawn in a thin, worried line, presumably trying to figure out if I looked like Ludo or Duco. I remembered word for word what she would tell me when we were alone, with urgent, halting breath, because she just *had* to get it off her chest, because her heart would never have healed otherwise. How could I ever forget that?

Duco rammed the car back into first gear. 'It feels like only yesterday. And now you're almost twelve.'

'May I turn on the radio?'

'Twelve is a tricky age. Already so tall, and yet still so very young.'

'Come off it, Duke.'

'It's true, isn't it? Twelve is the age at which a girl really needs her mother. You'll be getting your period soon.' He said it in the most unembarrassed way, as if he were still sponging and powdering my private parts on a daily basis. 'And when that happens you're better off with your mother about, I assure you. Take it from me.'

Some houses came into view, each just as dilapidated as ours. Nearly every front garden was littered with old washing machines, expired tractors, rusty cement mixers, leaky boats, and broken fishing traps. You also saw the occasional scrawny chicken high-stepping among crumbling walls with tufts of dirty wool stuck to them.

'Is this the downtown?' I asked sarcastically. 'Is there a coffee shop here, where I can go smoke weed, later on?'

He finally lost his temper. 'Don't be such a pain in the arse!' he growled. Then he pressed the pedal to the floor.

I immediately shut up. It wasn't easy to rile the Luducos, but when it did happen, the consequences could be pretty dire. Once they got good and mad, there was no going back. They so rarely asserted themselves that they didn't know their own fury, let alone have the ability to keep it in check. So I kept my lips clamped shut and stared out the window at the electricity poles sticking up higgledy-piggledy among the houses. Their wires dangled down in untidy loops. The power would probably go out here at the drop of a hat, and the stuff in the freezer would be in constant danger of defrosting.

That night, as I lay under the rafters of our new roof, a drab little moon shone into my room that made me think of The Moon of the Tarot, the card of secrets and betrayal. Fog drifted in from the sea in dense, menacing tatters.

# N is for Neighbour

There was just one good thing about the new situation: since the school year was not yet over, I had most of the day all to myself. I couldn't bear the thought of having to deal with other children right now. They'd have my guts for garters as soon as they got the chance. When I saw them coming across the moor after school got out—there were surprisingly and alarmingly many of them—I'd hide in the house, in the sad realization that I didn't have any skill set to be proud of anymore, not a single thing I was good at that would win me respect. It had been so long since I'd hung out with other kids that I no longer knew how you went about doing it.

Since there wasn't much else to do, I spent most of the time on one of the many little beaches, strewn with calcified seashells half-buried in the gritty sand. When it rained, I sought shelter under the big rocks, huddled in my rain gear. It rained most of the time. Although it was already well into spring, my fingers were permanently stiff from the cold and my nose ran incessantly. I tried lighting fires, but there was hardly any wood to burn, and the little there was, was soaking wet. I'd occasionally come across a dead seagull.

When the weather wasn't too beastly, I often walked all the way to a place called Callanish, on a road rutted with deep brown puddles. The only person I ever encountered was the postman, who also delivered milk in his red car. On a low hill in Callanish there stood a formation of stones that looked like the menhirs that *Asterix*'s Obelix always seemed to be lugging about in the cartoon, except that these were twelve times the size. There were dozens of them, and they'd been honed by the salty west wind into all kinds of weird twisted shapes. There was one with a fissure so deep that you could stick your whole arm into it, up to your elbow. Standing on tiptoe, I always hoped there would be a letter for me inside. You never knew—someone, somewhere, might be thinking of you.

Silhouetted against the pewter-grey sky, the prehistoric stones looked just like giants. It gave me a safe, comforting feeling to sit at their feet. If worst came to worst, all I'd have to do was whistle through my fingers, and then, with a loud creaking and groaning of their stone limbs, they would come to life. They'd lift me up on their shoulders as if it were nothing, and with thundering steps they'd carry me off, bounding along the shoreline fragmented into an infinite number of islands, where the bullies and harassers could never follow.

My mother and the Luducos thought the reason I kept myself aloof from the other kids was that my English wasn't yet good enough, and they'd waylay me at every opportunity with long lists of vocabulary, which they made me repeat after them. But they themselves weren't that keen on contact with the outside world, either. They wanted to start off slowly, so that they would gradually ease into the community, they said. Like some seedling pushing its shoots up from the earth so stealthily that no one notices, until suddenly a substantial plant has taken root to which everyone has unconsciously already grown accustomed, so that nobody will ask any questions. So it came as quite a shock when, after ten days or so, this fellow came knocking on our door.

He wore a shabby oilskin and a cap with a visor. He told us he lived down the road, in one of the cottages with the unpronounceable names, and after that revelation, he pointed at the horizon. 'Aye, so we're next-door neighbours,' he specified in a sing-song accent. He had come, just in case and in the spirit o' friendship, to show us exactly where his property began and ours ended, so that when we went to cut the peat we wouldn't accidentally encroach on his land.

'How very kind,' said my mother from the doorway. 'But we have a supply of peat that should last us years.'

Our neighbour took a few steps back to cast an appraising eye over the mountain of peat next to our house. 'It mebbe last ye till the end o' May, but only if the weather remains as mild as it is the noo. Personally I wouldna count on it.'

'But once the peat is gone, we'll just switch to some other kind of fuel,' said my mother. 'I don't think we'll ...'

'What is it ye'll be burnin', then?' asked the neighbour in surprise.

It suddenly dawned on my mother that, in a place where peat was free for the taking, there probably was no earthly reason for any other kind of fuel to be sold. After a short pause, she said, 'Please, come inside for a moment. I'll put the kettle on.'

I helped her set the mugs on the table, and the cake plates. I even smoothed down the plastic tablecloth. We had to make a good impression. We should try not to louse it up from the get-go.

'This is Iain,' my mother said to Ludo and Duco when

they came into the kitchen, both red-eared from being on the phone. 'He's going to teach us how to cut peat.'

We didn't have far to walk; the peat backed right up to our fence. It looked like a piece of cake, the way Iain produced a whole set of uniform bricks of turf with just a couple of slashes and tugs. But as soon as you tried hacking at the stuff yourself, it proved to be a heavy and difficult job. The bog was less spongy than it looked; it was riddled with tough roots of heather and petrified plant remains. My mother was the only one of us whose arms didn't give out in the first five minutes.

The Luducos and I were glad when it started to rain. We suggested we all go back inside.

'Wait, let me show you the dryin' first,' said Iain in his sing-song accent. 'Because that's quite a skill, it is, to get the hang o'.'

'Wouldn't it be better to do that when it's not raining?' asked Duco.

'Och, you might wait till kingdom come! And besides, it's the wind as does the drying, so a wee bit o' rain won't make a difference.' Iain pulled the blocks of peat from the trenches with his bare hands and nimbly stacked them into rows, like roof shingles. 'And then you've got to drain 'em, that's the trick, see, by digging a channel. Else it will all rot right under yer nose. Look, like this.' The blade flashed. The rain lashed at us in stinging squalls.

My mother began stacking a row of peat bricks. 'This isn't easy,' she panted.

'But once it's stacked right, you can leave it be for several months,' said Iain. 'So there's the advantage, see.'

'And then what?' asked Ludo, staring at the pink palms of his hands.

'Then you have to turn them, of course.'

My mother tried hacking out a channel. 'Is this deep enough, do you think?'

'It's a fine start.' He grinned. The rainwater streamed down both sides of his cap.

She went on cutting. 'So tell me, how much peat will we need, altogether?'

He narrowed his eyes and stared at our house. 'You're sitting right in the wind up there, so there must be a strong draught up yer lum. At least twice the volume of the house, I reckon.'

'But nobody else around here has that much peat,' said Duco in surprise.

'Oh, but they will, come September.' His rs were soft as butter. 'We are burning the last of it now.'

My mother wiped a muddy hand across her forehead. 'In that case we'd better take this on as our new hobby, boys.'

'But first, a nice cup of hot tea,' said Ludo.

'You go on ahead, I'll come inside in a minute.' My mother planted the blade in the ground with a twisting motion, then straightened to toss a clump of mud over her shoulder.

'No, not like that, or you'll do yourself an injury,' said Iain.

I'd really had it. The wind was whipping the rain in my face in gust after gust. Nowhere else in the world did you get as drenched as you did here. I ran after Ludo and Duco, who were hurrying inside with their heads tucked in.

At the gate, I looked back. Iain had his hands clasped around my mother's on the hatchet. They were standing hip to hip in the pouring rain. Then he began slashing the blade into the soaking-wet fen with easy, rhythmic movements: in, out, deeper and deeper, faster and faster, in, out.

My mother laughed, breathless.

Iain was holding her from behind, pressing her back to his stomach. Stepping backward, together they hacked their way into the moor. Faster and faster, deeper and deeper, they hacked themselves clear, clear of the Lud-ucos, and clear of me.

Afterward, Iain came inside for a cup of tea. He didn't seem to notice how shabby our kitchen was. He hung his drip-ping oilskin over the back of a chair as if he were at home, rolled up his sleeves, and planted his elbows on the table. His hairy arms bulged with massive muscles. The same hairy arms in which my mother had just disported her-self.

Ludo brandished the teapot. His glasses dangled from a string around his neck. 'Anyone for another piece of cake?'

Iain wouldna say no. Chewing, he went on and on about the upcoming peat harvest. The entire family, including the bairns, would head for the peat hag. It was hard work, but a good time was always had by all.

'Did you hear that, Lucy? That will be a good opportunity for you to make friends.' My mother's cheeks were still red.

Iain glanced at me. It was obvious he didn't think anyone would want to be friends with me. They'd all laugh at me. I'd never be able to compete with them in the peat-cutting department. I'd already lost before we had even started. I hung my head.

'What's the matter?' asked Duco. He looked at me closely. 'Don't you want to?'

I shrugged my shoulders.

'Do you take the whole family with you too?' my mother asked Iain.

'Na, we've just had a wee bairn, so the wife wilna' be join-ing us this year. It does make a difference, though, one less pair o' hands.'

'Well, I'll be glad to give a hand,' she said. 'I think I've already got the hang of it.'

'Oh, but I can think of another solution,' said Duco. 'Couldn't Lucy babysit? It would give your wife a chance to get out and about a bit. Lucy is great with little kids, aren't you, Lucy?'

He was such an incorrigible chump, I *knew* he had no idea he had just killed two birds with one stone.

Their house was built very close to one of the smaller beaches. A great mound of peat leaned precariously against it. In the yard, planters made of stacked tyres held scrawny plants blown sideways in the wind.

Rowan had dull, lanky red hair and gnarled hands. From her skeletal frame dangled two surprisingly large breasts, flopping around untethered inside her blouse. Her face made me think of a sunken pudding. Was this Iain's wife? It was altogether unlikely that she could be the mother of such a pretty little girl as Iola, who, from the moment I set eyes on her, seemed perfect to me, from her round little head right down to her adorable shrimpy toes.

As Rowan pulled on two cardigans on top of each other in the dark, messy kitchen, she started giving me instructions, of which I understood hardly one word. She mumbled even worse than Iain. She pointed at a plastic nappy bucket in the corner, stinking up the place. Whenever her sentence ended on an up note, I'd quickly nod yes. By the time she was stamping her feet into her boots, my head was spinning. She leaned over the crib one last time. Her flat face lit up. She cupped the little baby cheeks in her hands. 'Goodbye my flooer, bye my wee doll, bye my bonnie bairn. Will ye be a good lass for Lucy, who's come to look after ye? In't that nice of Lucy? Ye'll have a nice time, won't you, the two a'ye.'

Then she turned to me again and told me at least three last, totally incomprehensible things, with an encouraging, and at the same time worried, look.

'Okay,' I said. 'No problem.'

As soon as she shut the door behind her, I lifted Iola out of the crib and sat with her on my lap on one of the straight-backed wooden chairs. It was chilly in the kitchen, but for the first time in ages I felt myself getting all warm inside. I couldn't get enough of the baby's shiny little ears, her cute little nose, her miniature fingernails. Everything about her was still perfect. She'd never yet hurt a soul. And nobody had ever harmed a hair on her head. It was unbearable to think what could happen to her someday. If she'd been mine, I'd never have been able to sleep another wink. I couldn't imagine how any mother ever did.

I dangled the toffee I'd brought for her in front of her little face, holding it by the rustling paper twist, and started telling her about the stones of Callanish, which were actually mighty giants, though you might not think it. Appearances can be deceiving. She'd better remember that. You couldn't tell by looking at me at first, but deep down, I was basically a good and brave person, even if I did have something on my conscience that was so unspeakable that just the thought of it immediately set off a whole set of new penalties and prohibitions.

She looked at me expectantly.

Was it that non-judgmental gaze that made it so tempting to spill your guts to a baby? Newborns had such a mild and wise look about them, as if they were the ones that already had a whole lifetime behind them. Nothing surprised or disgusted them, and they could forgive every human sin. Strange to think, really, that everyone started off being so smart, only to end up so terribly stupid; the other thing that was strange—scary, even—was that you were apparently doomed to forget everything you had ever known, seen, or heard as a baby. Maybe I, too, would wake up some day no longer able to remember what was whispered in my ear as I lay in my crib. Once that happened, how would I ever be able to make sense of my life?

I looked down on Iola's round little head. She didn't look much like Iain, but even less like Rowan. Genes were funny things, after all, as my mother liked to remind us—they could deceive you; for example, they might skip a few generations and endow a child with features belonging to ancestors so distant and forgotten that the result was quite unrecognizable.

The baby glanced at me sleepily, gave a deep sigh, and then, with a grunt of pleasure, squirted out a big load in her nappy.

It was a disgusting feeling. I quickly lifted her from my lap and deposited her on the table. I looked round the chaotic kitchen. Nowhere did I spy any clean nappies. Was that what Rowan had meant when she'd pointed at the bucket in the corner? That she was out of nappies?

I picked up the bucket and tipped it into the sink. The water was brown and scummy, and gave off a strong stench of ammonia. Soap—you'd expect to find some soap in a kitchen, wouldn't you, or was soap as hard to come by as sunlight in these parts?

On the table, Iola began to wail. Desperate for a clean nappy, she flailed her little arms so wildly about that the back of her head bonked on the table. 'Shush now, sweet pea,' I said over my shoulder. 'Be a good girl, then I'll give you your toffee.'

The only thing I found in the cupboard under the sink was dishwashing liquid. I squirted this liberally on the nappies and then stirred with a wooden spoon that I found lying on the counter. In this howling wind they'd dry in less than an hour. 'At our house, Ludo always does the laundry,' I told Iola. 'The first time he did it here, the wind blew everything off the line. They're still finding our socks all the way over in Harris. It never occurred to him to use clothes pegs. He's such an absent-minded professor, you know.'

Iola went on wailing.

I opened her safety pin, lifted her by her two little feet and swept the nappy out from under her. I'd mop the floor later. Now I lifted her off the table by her little arms, depositing her in the sink. I held her little bottom under the tap. The cold water made her gasp. Then she started screeching again. Using the corner of a tea cloth that was about to disintegrate with age, I wiped her little bum clean. Then I wrapped her in the blanket from her crib. I put my mac back on.

It was hard getting the door open while carrying both Iola and the bucket, but I couldn't leave her in the house by herself, could I? I was here to look after her.

Outside the wind, thundering in from the bleak grey sea, just about bowled us over. I leaned into it, my head tucked low. You did have the odd day when there was no wind, but then there was usually a heavy fog instead, that turned the sun into a wan, watery moon. I didn't know which was worse.

I wrestled my way to the stockpile of peat. With great care, I managed to clear a safe little nest for Iola between the peat blocks. After snuggling her in there, I gave her three big kisses on her adorable upturned nose. Then I carried the nappies over to the washing line.

All in all, it was turning out to be a pretty good day. It gave me a great sense of satisfaction to see my nappies, all clean again, flapping in the wind. And I still had hours ahead of me to play with Iola, and to tell her about the time I'd caught a fairy in a glass jar, and kept it alive with dewdrops and sugar sprinkles.

I squatted by the peat pile to pick up the baby again. My heart started pounding. Wasn't this where I'd cleared a space for her between the blocks? No, I'd left her somewhere up a little higher. Or no, wait, lower down, of course. But was this where it was? I took a few steps back. Anxiously I scanned the identical bricks, the endlessly zigzagging stack. It was a landscape without any recognizable landmarks. Iola was an energetic little thing, but much too young to crawl away on her own. She had to be in the same place I'd left her.

'Iola?' I said softly.

The wind howled across the peat pile. It tore a brick from the top of the pile and sent it tumbling, taking several others with it in its fall.

I opened my eyes wide. This couldn't be happening. It just couldn't. 'Iola!' I cried. I began pawing at the bricks in a total panic. I tried to move aside the outermost blocks without causing an avalanche, but they were so dry and flaky that they promptly crumbled in my hands. The wind blew the dust into my eyes and my mouth. Coughing and choking, I scrabbled at the pile. The mountain was dauntingly long and wide. I had to go at it systematically. I had to keep my cool. I *had* to. And I would. If only I'd. If I'd just.

Tears were rolling down my cheeks. The baby had trusted me. She had believed in me. She'd thought, As long as I'm with Lucy, nothing bad can ever happen to me, because Lucy is so big and strong.

I made agonizingly slow progress, inch by inch, foot by foot. Every second of cautious poking felt like an hour, an hour in which Iola was long past the stage of no return. I was going to find her suffocated, crushed to death. 'Give her *back* to me!' I sobbed at the unresponsive peat.

Sand and fragments of heather-root crunched between my teeth. The wind pounded its fists upon my back. Behind me the sea droned on monotonously. Yet it also felt as if everything had stopped moving or making even the faintest sound. As if the whole world were holding its breath.

I had to go for help.

They'd kick me to death.

Rowan would murder me.

And then, out of the corner of my eye, I caught a flash of pink. Her blanket. I whipped my head around. Over there! All the way at the end. Where I'd left her on purpose, because it was the most sheltered spot.

Stumbling, slipping and tripping over fallen bricks, I raced over to her.

She was lying in the exact same spot where I'd left her. With fizzy lips she lay there, gazing at the flapping nappies. You could see them reflected in her huge, clear eyes.

I picked her up and hugged her close, panting with relief.

I was shaking so violently that I could barely keep a grip on her.

I plunked her down in the nappy bucket, blanket and all, and flopped down in the dust beside it, gripping the handle as if my life depended on it. I couldn't stop shuddering. I would *kill* anyone who ever tried to harm Iola. I'd wipe them off the face of the earth. I'd defend her to the death, even if that meant going to jail. And suddenly I understood, in every fibre of my body, why six years ago my mother had been so convinced that the barristers and the judge would believe her story. Because if they were threatening to go after your child, you didn't care what happened to yourself anymore; there was nothing you wouldn't do. It was more than a mitigating circumstance—it was a law of nature. She'd barely had to think it over; she'd been certain it would work. She'd hastily instructed me how I should answer all their questions. There had been very little time and we'd both been very upset, but she had managed to ram the whole pack of lies firmly into my head. I could still repeat them, word for word.

Next to me, Iola squealed, and instinctively I turned to look at her. She looked back at me, grinning from ear to ear, utterly content in her bucket.

# O is for Outside

The next day, like every other Sunday, a dead calm settled over Lewis. The entire population was off to church, in black coats and with devoutly bent heads. The peat bogs were deserted again. Scattered across the moor, like will-o'-the-wisps fluttering in the wind, were the plastic bags the peat-cutting families had brought their lunches in the day before. One would occasionally get caught on a bush, but never for very long; the wind always managed to tear it away.

I sat hugging my legs in the kitchen window, watching the grossly uneven tug-of-war.

Ludo and Duco were sitting by the Aga, engrossed in their books since breakfast. They had blisters as big as pigeon eggs on the palms of their hands, and they ached in places where, they said, they'd never known they even *had* muscles.

The peat sputtered and hissed pleasantly in the Aga. And, if you concentrated, you could see a dusty beam of light making its way in—not actual sunshine, of course, but definitely quite a bit more light than usual, as if someone up in heaven had kindly left a shutter open a crack.

Yesterday, Rowan had been delighted that I'd done the washing for her, and that I'd even mopped the kitchen floor. But she'd been even more delighted to see Iola chewing on one of my plaits as if it was a salami. She could see for herself I was a first-rate babysitter. She'd ask me to come back again soon, she'd said. I'd been so elated that I'd run all the way home.

I heaved my legs off the window ledge and, with my toes, poked Duco's stockinged feet, which were roasting by the cooker's open hatch. 'Hey, Duke, old man. Anything fun on the agenda for today?'

'I'm reading, pussycat.'

I gave a kick in the other direction. 'Ludikins?' I whined hopefully.

'Lucy.' He grabbed me by the ankle. With his other hand, he turned the page. 'Will you make us a cup of coffee?'

I put the kettle on. I ground the coffee beans. I poured milk into the little pan. By then I'd had it with being the perfect daughter. 'The weather's super-duper nice, anyway.'

Ludo put his book away. He took his glasses off. He rubbed the bridge of his nose. 'Such enthusiasm, all of a sudden!'

'I think it's pretty cool here.' I poured the water on the coffee.

He gave me a probing look. Then he said with a smile, 'I'm so glad.' He picked up his glasses and his book again.

'What are you reading anyway, egghead?'

'A book, Lucy, I'm just reading a book.'

First I poured the whipped milk and then the coffee, because if you did it the other way round, according to those two, it didn't taste nearly as good. Just as I was handing them their coffees, my mother entered the kitchen with a basket of peat. Briskly she began feeding the cooker with more peat. 'Hey, lazybones,' she said over her shoulder.

'This would be a perfect day for starting that vegetable garden of ours.'

'But it is the Lord's Day,' said Duco. 'If you so much as stick a spade in the ground today, you'll get lynched.'

'You mean you don't feel like it,' said my mother, rather sharply.

'Duco is right,' said Ludo. 'Surely you don't want to ...'

'The two of you are always pooped before you've even begun.' She tossed the basket into a corner. 'It's impossible to get you to do *fuck all*. All you ever want to do is sit around on your arses all day.'

I still wasn't used to her using words like that. I quickly climbed back onto the window ledge.

Outside, the wind was still winning, the plastic bags still losing. A lonely sheep plodded past the stacks of peat.

I could hear my mother pouring herself a cup of coffee the wrong way—first the coffee and then the milk—and pull out a chair at the table. Her movements sounded brusque. 'Well, in that case I suppose I'll just sit around on my arse for a while, too.'

The mood in the kitchen had suddenly turned tense. I was terrified a fight was about to break out. If only the Luducos would say something to make everything go back to normal! But they were silent. Maybe their own fathers had always remained tight-lipped the same way, and that was because *their* fathers before them had done the same. It was something you never stopped to think about, really, but it turned out that everything was a consequence of something else. It suddenly made me feel terribly depressed, to think that the whole of existence was really just one big chain reaction. It wouldn't surprise me if, in the future, I found myself doing stuff exactly the way my mother always did it. And what if I had children myself someday, what if they in turn had children, as well?

'Goodness, Lucy,' said my mother. 'What are *you* brooding about? You look as if you've just seen the Loch Ness monster.' Her voice had lost its belligerent tone.

I looked up. Out of the corner of my eye I saw that the Luducos, unruffled, had gone back to reading. Maybe I had just imagined it. 'Nothing,' I said curtly.

She stared at me across the kitchen table, with those eyes that had this hungry look in them these days.

'What are you looking at?'

'Your hair. Shouldn't we try some different styles, more appropriate for secondary school?'

I wanted to say, Mind your own business and worry about you own hair, but of course I couldn't.

'Why don't you start taking out your plaits? I'll go fetch a hairbrush.'

Reluctantly, I stood up and started pulling the elastics off my plaits, thinking, I bet that without them Iola won't recognize me anymore.

Coming up behind me, my mother said, 'Here, come and stand in the light.'

Without turning round, I took a few steps back. 'Like this?' I asked sullenly.

'Yes, Lucy.' Then she began brushing my hair.

I held myself stock-still.

Her brushstrokes were calm and regular, but also so firm that my skull immediately began to sting. She still had the knack. A hundred brushstrokes before bed every night made your hair shiny, healthy, and strong. What great hair you have—such abundance.

Mum and I, in the rectory's cavernous bathroom, wrapped in white terry towels, with dripping-wet hair, standing side by side in front of the mirror with determined looks on our faces, each holding a glass with a beaten egg. Ready, set, go! Shrieking with laughter. Rub it in quick, massage it in well. We're a *sight*, oh stop it, what if the boys saw us looking like this! But the boys didn't have to know our little secrets. Just us girls. What *wouldn't* you do to make sure they loved you? And then finish it off with a vinegar rinse. Don't forget, okay?

My hair crackled and squeaked from the roots to the ends so that I couldn't even hear the Aga's hiss anymore.

My mother grabbed my shoulders. 'Turn around.'

Feeling self-conscious, I kept my eyes on the floor. She was standing so close to me that her chest nearly touched mine. I felt her lifting up the hair on either side of my face. She smiled. 'I know, that's what I'll do.' To my relief she let go, but only to pick up some hairpins lying on the table. Then she began to pin up my hair, quickly and firmly. Moments later, she was cupping my chin in her callused hand and turning my face to the side. I felt her eyes sizing me up. Probably a welcome change from Soldering and Epoxying, anyway, I thought, clenching every muscle in my body.

'My lovely Lucy,' she said softly.

Duco, by the cooker, whistled through his teeth.

Ludo said, 'The boys had better stay home.'

My mother made a few more adjustments. 'It looks really darling like that. Go take a look at yourself in the mirror.'

The way they were all beaming at me was embarrassing. I ran into the icy bathroom. I saw at once that she was right. My hair looked really good like that. I looked like a girl in a magazine. So that's the way my mother wanted me to look; this was the Lucy she wanted. The elated grin vanished. The last time anyone had messed with my hair, I had fallen for it too. I'd believed Vanessa and her friends; I had really thought—what an imbecile!—that everyone would start being normal to me again once I changed the way I looked. In a frenzy, I began pulling out the hairpins. The hair fluffed down along my cheeks, shiny from the brushing. I braided it into two plaits again, as tightly and stiffly as I could. Iola liked it that way.

'Oh,' said Ludo, when I came back into the kitchen.

My mother said nothing.

I burst out, indignant, 'Yeah, really! There's no way I can go around looking like *that*!'

'It looked good on you, though,' said Duco.

'What do *you* know about it, anyway? You of all people! Look around—nobody wears their hair up out here. What did you think—in this shitty wind? Do you really think you can walk around in a fancy hairdo in a *gale*? Dream on!'

'Cool it, Lucy,' he warned.

'You want me looking like an idiot, don't you! So that people will wonder, Is she a little cuckoo, or something? Because who wears their hair that way, in this weather? The hairpins will blow away the moment you step out!'

'Nobody wants you to go around looking like an idiot,' said my mother. 'Why would we?'

'That's right,' said Ludo, 'why would we?'

'Couldn't you stick up for me just *once* for a change?' I was fighting back tears. The traitor!

'But you do have a point, about the wind,' said my mother.

'You said it!' I cried, all discombobulated. 'See? She said it, too! And when *she*'s the one saying it, you believe her, don't you!'

'What, exactly, are we talking about now?' Duco asked in a put-upon tone.

'That you always believe *her*!' The words exploded from my mouth like bullets, but they flew right over the Luducos' heads. They did hit my mother, however. 'Okay, enough of this nonsense,' she snapped. 'We're going to have lunch now. Why don't you set the table.'

'But surely nobody's denying that it can be extremely windy here,' said Ludo, apparently trying to pick up the thread again. 'It's what the Hebrides are known for. Everyone knows ...'

'Oh, stop it,' said my mother.

She had brought me here on purpose, to this windy island, where it was always just as stormy as it had been that terrible night. So that I'd be constantly reminded of that other stormy night. And also of the fact that we two were forever sworn to silence. Not only did I have the power to crush her with a single word; she could also destroy me the exact same way.

Over the next several days I was kept on my toes by a host of self-imposed penances that made life pretty difficult. I had to jump through all kinds of hoops in order to comply with them without attracting too much attention.

I cleared off and just wandered around the island without any particular goal or plan in mind. At Callanish, little blue flowers that looked too delicate to survive came poking out of the ground, as the death-defying broom put forth its first plucky blossoms. I discovered several new rock-strewn bays, but everywhere it seemed to be the same story: the sea battering the beach with the same dumb, stubborn force; the same scrawny birds running along the shoreline on their tall, spindly legs, furiously pecking at the sand; and the same danger of getting trapped in the mudflats' quicksand. I almost lost a boot in it, once.

One morning I spied Rowan and Iola in front of their cottage. Rowan was balancing the baby on the gate. I waved, but neither of them saw me. I stood there watching them until they went back inside, back to the cold cooker and the stinky bucket in the corner. Knowing how they lived in there made me feel a part of their lives, as if we had known one another intimately for the longest time.

And every day when I got home, just before the school let out, I'd find my mother in what she now called 'the vegetable garden' but which was still just a boggy piece of ground. She dug and turned the soil as if she never got tired. She was going to plant the radishes over here, and over there, the potatoes. And then she'd wipe her hands on her blue jeans, pick up her hatchet, and spend a couple of hours cutting peat. When I saw her striding across the moor, it struck me that, with all the fresh air and exercise, she was rapidly getting back to her former shape, although with a difference—not quite as slender, not as soft. She looked a bit like a tree buffeted by the wind, sturdy and unbending.

From my window lookout I kept a close watch on the comings and goings of the peat-cutting families, who got started every day around four o'clock, when their work was done. Rowan was never with them. I was dying to tell her that I'd gladly babysit for Iola any afternoon, but was terrified that doing so would immediately create an Iola-taboo, once the other penances noticed that that one would hurt me the most.

I had tea with Lude and Duke, who'd come downstairs for a brief break, oblivious. I seemed to be the only one who noticed that my mother and Iain were deep in conversation by one of the drainage ditches they had excavated together. Iain had his hands raised to the sky and my mother was shaking her head.

'Don't you think it's time Mum started drawing again?' I asked, slicing the fruitcake. 'It isn't fair, you men having to earn all the money.'

Duco said she had a lot of catching up to do.

Ludo pulled me toward him by my plait and started tickling me in the ribs.

But I wouldn't play along.

A few days later—it had been raining buckets all day long, but now a pale sun had broken through—I found her waiting for me at the gate with a big orange kite. The exact same kind as the one in the drawing she'd made for me in Stornoway, I noticed immediately.

'Look, Lucy!' she whooped, barring my way. 'It's suddenly occurred to me that the wind is good for something after all.'

First the business with my hair, and now this; surely she wasn't trying to make up for all the lost years? But Mrs Iedema used to tell us that every new day gave us a fresh chance to be a good person, so I let her thrust the spindle into my hand.

'Isn't it great?' My mother smiled at me.

When I still refused to answer, she walked onto the moor with long strides, dragging the kite along by its bridle.

Caught off guard, I remained by the gate as the string started whirring, unspooling rapidly in my hand. She had used a rolling pin from the kitchen as a winder, the kind of thing only she would think of. Suddenly the string was taut. 'Ho, stop!' I called; I couldn't help it.

The string between us was stretched so tight that I felt it humming. Every movement my mother made was transmitted along the string to me, as through an umbilical cord. Then she let go of the kite.

It shot up into the cloud-streaked sky like a comet, with such a strong tug that the rolling pin was nearly yanked out of my hands. I clutched the handles tightly and tried to let out some line. The kite was already up as high as it would go, right over my head; if I didn't watch out, it would flip over. Its pull was as strong as a team of oxen. I was standing on tiptoe; my arms were just about getting pulled out of their sockets.

'Can you hold on?' Stumbling over the rutted ground,

my mother came racing back to where I stood. She slung an arm round my waist just as I felt myself being lifted off the ground, and lunged for the spindle with the other hand. 'No, don't!' I screamed. The kite promptly began to flounder. It's sometimes possible to reel in the slack as it plunges, but not with someone pulling at you. I began hauling in the limp line as if my life depended on it; hand over hand, I towed it in. 'Start winding!' I yelled, my eyes fixed on the line flopping back and forth in a big loop. When I was little, we'd sometimes send a message on a piece of paper up into the sky along with the kite. One time I wished for reindeer mittens, and the next night, when I went to bed, I found a pair on my pillow. They must have blown in through the open window, Mummy said.

As I clawed the string in, hand over hand, she rewound it swiftly onto the spool. Slowly but surely the string stretched tight again. I snatched the spool out of her hand and started running in order to make the kite catch the wind again. Okay, let it out slowly now. The kite began climbing obediently. It rose, nice and diagonal, and without any abrupt jerks. It ended up so perfectly steady, high up in the sky, that it seemed to be pinned to that cloud up there with a pushpin.

My mother came and stood next to me.

I could hardly speak, bursting with pride. 'You gave it too much line, at first,' I managed. 'They zoom like rockets when you do that.'

'Oh, was that what went wrong? Strange though, you wouldn't think a person could forget how to fly a kite, would you? Oh well, well done.'

Together we gazed up at the sky.

'Do you like it?'

I nodded.

After a while, she asked, 'Are you starting to feel at home here?'

'Yeah, it's okay.'

'And have you met any nice kids yet?'

I launched into an enthusiastic description of Iola. About that darling little skull of hers, not much bigger than an upside-down teacup, and how happy she'd been, sitting in the bucket. Once she got me started, I could hardly stop.

She coughed. 'Okay, but what about kids your own age? Have you met any?'

'Not yet, but I'm in no hurry.'

'Lucy ...' She hesitated. 'Listen, it isn't good for you to be by yourself all the time. We need other people, so that our own thoughts don't start to drive us crazy.' She looked at me out of the corner of her eye.

The kite needed all my attention just then.

'There's no reason on earth why anyone would want to make your life miserable out here. That's another reason we moved, you know. To give you a fresh start.'

I felt her hand on my neck. With her rough fingers she started rubbing the little hollow in my neck, between my two plaits. 'You never confessed to the boys how bad it was for you at school, did you?'

'Oh, it wasn't *that* bad,' I said, agitated. Next thing, she was going to say, 'Is this what I went to prison for? So that you could make an even bigger mess of your life?' I gave the string an unnecessary tug.

'Were you afraid that ... er ... bad things would happen if Ludo and Duco knew how badly you were getting teased?'

I bit my lip. I started hauling in the kite.

'Oh, not yet! Hand it over, if you don't feel like it anymore. Oh, look, up there, a rainbow!'

On Lewis you could see a rainbow at least sixty times a day.

'I think that rainbow ends right at Iola's cottage. Oh, by the way'—her voice changed—'you should never give toffees to a little tot, you know. Rowan was quite upset, Iain told me.'

'But she said I could come back another time!' I cried. I'd thought Rowan hadn't noticed me digging the stringy toffee out of Iola's throat in the nick of time, just before she walked in the door. Maybe she'd been peeking in the window, to make sure I was doing everything exactly to her liking.

'Are you sure you understood what she told you?'

'Yes, Mum, I swear!'

'That, by the way, is another reason you should be making friends with other children, to improve your English. The fastest way to pick up a language is by speaking it. Then you don't run the risk of any misunderstandings.'

I was almost sobbing, 'I swear, it's true, she said I could come back and babysit Iola anytime.'

She pinched my neck. That meant she would help me. She'd go to Rowan and tell her I knew how to get a huge kite to fly even in the worst kind of weather—so, if there was anyone you could trust with a baby, it was me. 'Look,' she said, 'here comes Iain. Let's talk it over with him.' She let go of me. 'Iain!' she called.

And then it dawned on me that I'd been tricked. She had distracted me on purpose, so that I'd forget what time it was. Because it was four o'clock; people were suddenly swarming onto the fen from all directions. They were all gazing up at the kite dancing in the wind, and then they all looked down and straight at me, caught like a fish on the end of my mother's line.

# P is for Penis

They said 'Mrs' to my mother and 'Guv' to the Luducos. They wore stiff brown Harris-tweed coats and caps, made water-repellent with applications of sheep's fat. They had ropy arms, wind-chapped lips, and mosquito-bitten necks. Boldly, they picked up jellyfish from the beach and whacked them in one another's faces for fun. Even the little ones were sure-footed as they climbed across the slippery, seaweed-draped rocks. Their names were Verity, Hamish, Janice, Fergus, Rory, Struan, Fiona, Lachlan, and Gavin. Whenever their parents didn't need their help with the cutting, they'd come by to pick me up. They came to the door and asked in shrill voices if I was home, and if Mrs or one of the Guvs would please ask me to come down.

At first, I'd hoped they were only interested in the kite. But once that novelty had worn off, they still kept coming for me, like a pack of dogs you just can't shake. I didn't know what would happen if I refused to go along. Since I didn't have to go to school, I was already different; to make myself even more different probably wasn't such a great idea. So I'd trail after them on leaden feet.

They had built a driftwood fort on the beach at Uig. The

gaps in the walls were chinked with peat. A rusty sheet of corrugated metal, tied on with fishnet, served as the roof. Inside, it stank of the petrol Gavin kept in there. Gavin was the leader. If anyone ever expressed the slightest doubt about that, Gavin would pick up the dented jerrycan and take a big swig of petrol into his mouth, light a match, and spew out a fountain of flame. That would shut anybody up.

You couldn't stand inside the fort; you had to crawl in on all fours. Once inside, you were packed in so close together that you couldn't help getting into a conspiratorial mood. Here schemes were concocted that boded little good for any animal that dared to crawl onto the island of Lewis. Here a bloody and complicated plot was hatched against Mrs Walker, the headmistress of the primary school. There was a great deal of swaggering and bragging and one-upmanship. There was tons of smoking and drinking and dead-serious strip poker. It was the law according to Gavin.

Gavin was Iain and Rowan's eldest son. He had Rowan's flat face, a lazy left eye, and incredibly long arms. He moved in an odd, jumpy way, like a frisky rabbit. Like the rest of the big boys, he already attended the secondary school in Stornoway, and he put nothing less than the fear of God into me.

I did my best not to draw any attention to myself. If I was ordered to dig a trench or a ditch, I dug a trench or a ditch. If I was sent out to gather cockleshells, I gathered cockle-shells (used for munitions, since the fort was in a constant state of high alert), even if that meant traversing the mud-flats, which were even more treacherous at Uig than elsewhere. I'd plant my feet carefully in the footprints of the troops walking ahead of me. I copied what they did; I kept my mouth zipped and my ears open. I shuddered to think that I might misunderstand what someone had said, and then do something wrong that would turn me into a target. At home, I urgently practised the local dialect. I sent Duco into stitches one night by telling him, 'Dead keen on yer wee dram, are ye no'?' He said I was making great strides.

In contrast to my former classmates, none of the children out here asked me any sniggering questions about the precise nature of the Luducos' relationship with us. In the eyes of Gavin's gang, they were simply the 'lodgers.' All the Lewis islanders rented out rooms whenever they could, thankful for every broom cupboard and every chicken coop they possessed. Practically every house had a crooked B&B sign on a post somewhere amid the rusted scrap metal out front. With any luck, said Verity, who sometimes had sex with Gavin in the fort while the rest of us dug trenches in the rain, you could rent out your own bed to your ma and pa in the summer months, and then they could sublet it to the tourists. The fact that we had two Guvs lodging with us was, in her eyes as well as the others', just proof that my mum was a shrewd one.

It seemed she had thought of everything.

I soon found out that Gavin and his gang were cruel and vicious in an almost detached way, as if they were acting largely out of ingrained habit. Life had to be dealt with aggressively because whoever landed the first punch had the advantage—but other than that, it was nothing personal.

In some weird way, that boosted my confidence. Back in my swashbuckling days, when I used to command pirate ships, I had always tried to impress the same kind of attitude on my crew. Upon boarding an enemy vessel, you were duty-bound to wipe out every Tom, Dick, and Harry, not just the captain, who merely had the misfortune of being the skipper. Then you hoisted the flag with the skull and crossbones, and convened in the captain's cabin to drink to your victory with a hearty glass of rum.

I saw myself standing in the bow again, with the bright-green parrot that I'd rescued from the rainforest perched on my shoulder. Those *rains* had been wrapped so tightly around its legs that I'd had to slash it free with my pocket-knife. That poor bird had been so happy to be rescued that it never left my side. You could do a powerful lot of good in the world, as a pirate.

Remembering my former adventures steadied me. I no longer waited for Gavin's deputies to come and fetch me; I set out for Uig every afternoon of my own accord, and waited among the wind-flattened juniper bushes for the others and whatever was going to happen. If they didn't show up, I wasn't relieved but disappointed.

Our activities depended on the weather. If the rain was about to wash you right off the face of the earth, you just went right out on an expedition, to the lochs and burns where, on Gavin's orders, we emptied the traps in the icy water and nicked the fish before anyone noticed they had any in them. But when the weather was dry, we stayed inside our fort. That way the enemy was never able to predict our movements.

Inside the fort, the gang killed time telling tall tales. About the island of Luchruban, which was inhabited by a race of misshapen dwarves. Or about The Maiden's Stone in Habost, where you had to leave a little milk in a hollow tree for the evil fairies, because if you didn't, they would smite the cattle with the bubonic plague. One unusually muggy afternoon, the topic of the bog-beastie came up. The bog-beastie was a flasher who roamed the machair with a stiffie.

'Ever heard of it?' Verity suddenly asked me in a loud voice. She had a smirk on her face. She started shaking out her flaxen hair. Her Vanessa-hair.

A short, fierce tremor of whispers went around the fort. Then the place went completely quiet. They were all watching me closely.

The sudden attention made the blood congeal in my veins. What did they want from me? Was I supposed to do something, to prove something, to justify my presence in their midst? 'What did you say?' I asked timidly. I only knew the meaning of machair—what they called the wildflower meadow bordering the beach. I didn't know what the other words meant.

'Ye ken what a flasher is, don't you? And a stiffie?' Verity snickered. 'Hey, Gav, why don't you gie her a peek.'

As the others jeered, Gavin opened his fly.

'Oh, that thing!' I said, with as much indifference as I could muster.

Swinging his willy from side to side, Gavin scooted over to me on his knees in his jerky way. '*Oh, that thing!*' he repeated, somewhat miffed. 'Could ye no' find a nicer way to put it?'

'She'll ken fine tae do wi'it,' Lachlan surmised.

My armpits began to prickle with sweat.

'Well?' demanded Gavin, moving his hips back and forth right in my face.

At the tip there was a kind of blind eye, staring at me moistly. There was a thick blue vein running up the side. It gave off a rancid smell. It was even nastier than the way my mother had described it to me. Or maybe I wasn't remembering it right. I'd been just six years old, and in a complete panic, besides.

Smirking, Gavin leered at me. The others waited, their mouths hanging open in suspense.

You were supposed to take hold of it. That was it. That's what my mother had told me.

I didn't dare. I didn't want to, either. Except … if I could put Gavin in a good mood, then maybe he'd put in a good word for me with Rowan. And then she'd let me babysit for Iola again. I stretched out my hand. I closed my fingers around his swollen member.

A hissing sound escaped the onlookers, but nobody said a word.

It was a lump of throbbing muscle. I couldn't bear to look at it. But looking up at Gavin was even more out of the question, because I suddenly realized what was supposed to happen next. For an instant I was filled with such horror that I couldn't move. But that really was what she had told me.

I forced myself to lean forward. The blind eye was now even slimier than before. It had a little thread of drool dangling from it. I bent down and closed my lips around it.

'Jesus,' someone whispered, somewhere in the back of the steamy fort.

I thought I was suffocating, I thought of Iola with the toffee stuck down her throat, and my mouth filled with the salty taste of tears, and then suddenly I tasted something else as well, just as Mum had told me. 'He made you swallow it. That's why they won't be able to find any trace of it.'

I swallowed.

'Ho!' Gavin gasped. His face glistened with sweat and his breath was coming fast. It took him a few moments to bring his glassy eyes into focus again, as if he were slowly waking up from a strange dream.

'Hey, Gav,' Verity began, indignant.

'Hey, Lucy!' Struan and Lachlan cried at the same time. 'Have another go?'

I felt a strand of Gavin's slime drooling out of the corner of my mouth, but I didn't dare wipe it off just yet. My mother had told me that I'd had to do it twice in a row. She had given me very precise instructions on what had happened in between, and I'd even managed to repeat it word for word to the police when they questioned me. But now that it was real, I didn't think I'd be able to stand it if Gavin pulled down my underpants and felt me up with his cold fingers. His fingernails were always black.

In a daze, I recoiled, but collided with a wall of firm bodies. The fear took my breath away. Of course. Of course the same thing was going to happen as that time at school, when they'd all ganged up on me and pulled my legs apart, yelling *slut! slut!* just because I had said exactly what my mother had instructed me to say. I wanted to scream, but no sound came out. Gavin already had a hold of me, I couldn't escape his clutches, he was pulling me close— and began wiping the corner of my mouth with the stiff sleeve of his brown jacket, shaking his head and saying, 'Ye canna go hame to yer Ma looking like that, can ye lassie! Or ye'll be grounded, for sure.'

Then he fished around for his thing, stuffed it back in, and zipped up his trousers. He sprang to his feet, full of fresh energy. Snapping his fingers, he made a commanding gesture. 'Okay, men. Back to the mines.'

The others got out of our way as he pushed me outside ahead of him. His hand on my arm was a sign that I now belonged to him. I was shaking right down to my toes. I felt sick and so sweaty that, once we were out on the beach, I immediately zipped open my jacket for the rain to cool me down. It took me a while to grasp what Gavin was saying to me. He was telling me I was promoted to Extra-Special Commando.

That night, I was abruptly woken by a strange sound, as if someone were shuffling about the house, dragging his feet. I listened with bated breath. Did I hear my name being called, faintly, like a whisper on the wind?

I flung back the blankets, jumped out of bed, and crossed the cold linoleum to the window. The draught made my nightgown flap against my legs. Softly I moved the curtain aside. I didn't see anything at first. It was uncanny how dark the nights were out here, with no street lights, and with that perpetually overcast sky. They were old as the hills, those clouds; they'd been blown here all the way across the Atlantic Ocean, doggedly gathering strength. Not even the fiercest storm could blow them apart.

But then my eyes got used to the darkness. So it wasn't long before I spotted him. He was standing in the vegetable garden, by the fence. At first, I thought it was the bog-beastie that had come staggering up to our house out of the machair. But then I saw he was wearing a sou'wester. He was holding a bunch of stinging nettles.

With my hands over my eyes, I stumbled back to bed in the dark and buried my head under my pillow. He couldn't do a thing to me. He was dead. He honestly couldn't do a thing to me!

The next morning, Duco said my eyes looked funny. He felt my forehead and sent me back to bed with a hot-water bottle.

# Q is for Quantum Mechanics

Two weeks went by before I was allowed outside again. When I ventured out on shaky legs to inspect the state of the world, I found that the peat had all been harvested and the flat land next to our house had turned into a gently undulating landscape—mountains of peat drying in the wind, with patches of dark water glittering in between and clouds of midges hovering above.

The days had imperceptibly grown longer, and the thermometer by the kitchen door was up to a whole sixteen degrees. The balmy weather seemed to have gone to Ludo's and Duco's heads. Mustering all their strength, they'd hammered together a fence next to the house, hoping it would act as a shelter for sunbathing, but they quickly discovered that wherever the wind couldn't reach, hordes of nasty little insects would suddenly come out of nowhere. The midges were so tiny that it was easy to understand why Iain called them 'smidgies.' They'd bite you right through your clothes, and there was no point trying to slap them away—there were billions of them. Fire and smoke, said Iain, were the only things that would keep them off.

You could scarcely turn around these days without finding Iain sociably draped over the vegetable-garden gate, shooting the breeze with my mother. On his advice, she had limited herself to cabbages the first year, instead of attempting to grow the strawberries I'd been begging for. Following his instructions, she had planted Savoy cabbage, because it did well in acidic soil. 'Shouldn't he go home from time to time, to be with Rowan and Iola?' I asked her.

I was sure that Duco's tippling—he was drinking far too much again, as he had when my mother was in jail—must have something to do with Iain; Duco always got plastered when he worried about her. I still vividly remembered our weekly early-morning excursions, huffing and puffing, to the recycling bins in the square with the bag of empties. 'Got to get rid of the evidence, Lucy, before Ludo catches me sinning.' The memory filled me with a profound sense of despair. How come adults kept making the same mistakes over and over again, and how come everyone then seemed to turn a blind eye, except me?

Ludo had rustled up a bicycle, an ancient bone-shaker lacking a baggage carrier, with back-pedal brakes, dating from the year dot. When he noticed how wobbly my knees were, he proposed taking me for a ride. 'I know just the place you want to go,' he said mysteriously.

I hopped on the crossbar in front; I still fit in the space between his arms. Gazing at the familiar hands on the handlebars, I felt I was little again, and quite safe.

We biked up the long road riddled with potholes. There was a smell of honey in the air. Behind my back, Ludo was breathing heavily through his nose. Every time I leaned back a bit, he'd put his arm around me and ask me if I wasn't too tired. I'd shake my head, although to tell the truth, I felt wiped out. But the anticipation of where we were heading kept me upright.

'Look!' I cried out, when we were still quite a way off. 'Look, Ludo, there they are!'

The bend in the road revealed them, just as magnificent and immovable as ever. They had simply stayed the same, while I had changed into someone who had had sex. Sex was a big deal, if you believed Struan's and Lachlan's stories. They'd give anything to get some. So I should consider myself a lucky girl, to have it simply fall into my lap. But for some reason, the fact that it was irreversible really bothered me. I could never change back to the way I was before. I was tied to it now, forever. I was happy to see that the giants didn't turn and run from me in disgust, anyway.

I jumped down off the crossbar. I stumbled, zigzagging, through the tall plumy grasses to greet each one in turn: the hunchbacked giant, the giant with the hooked nose, the giant with the beard. There were forty-seven of them. I trailed my fingers along all the cold ridges and the polished protrusions, along the brightly hued concave arteries of stone and the faintly glittering embedded crystals. 'Hello!' I kept saying softly. 'And hello to *you*, too!'

At the foot of the largest stone, right in the centre, Ludo had sat down to unpack our picnic: home-baked sourdough bread, sheep's cheese, an apple each, a thermos of tea. Not only was my energy starting to come back, but I suddenly felt hungry, too. I sat down on a boulder and greedily tucked into a sandwich.

Behind us, the waves were crashing onto the countless little islands along the shore. In a meadow a little further on, a sheep bleated. And maybe, somewhere just out of sight, an industrious seagull was at this very moment laying an egg containing a little screecher that some day would poop on our heads. But not just yet.

We ate. We took turns blowing on the hot tea Ludikins had poured into the cap of the thermos. The drizzle made his glasses look like frosted glass. He gazed pensively over the rims at the giants. He was the kind of person who always knew exactly when to keep his mouth shut.

When I was little, the question of which one I would eventually marry sometimes kept me up at night: would it be our Lude or our Duke? For Ludo, I pasted blue sticker-dots on a piece of origami paper; on Duco's they were red. The answer would thus ultimately be revealed, or so I hoped, and then I'd go and live in some little village with the winner, in a rectory with creaky stairs and green tiles in the hall.

My mother had seen the origami papers with the dots, and said, 'The love of one good man is a gift from God; and you and I are lucky enough to have two. We have to take good care of them.'

And now I had Gavin. It depressed the hell out of me. Maybe I could teach him to keep his fingernails clean. Only, my mother always said, you should never try to change someone. There was only one person you could change, and that was yourself. And she had proved it too, as I should know. She'd proved it when she'd suddenly been smitten, had suddenly fallen so unexpectedly and un-intentionally, so madly, feverishly, desperately in love, that her entire being had been consumed with desire, longing, and a mad craving, and that the stolen hours they had spent together had been all that she'd lived for. I knew all the details by heart, I'd heard them so often.

At first, of course, she'd been convinced that it was out of the question, if at home you had more than enough love as it was. But that conviction soon faded. When you had it this bad, you deserved more than a few stolen hours. You had the right to a whole lifetime together. And before she knew it, turning that right into reality came to seem just a matter of time, plus a few formalities, such as the severing of existing relationships on either side. The two of them, he and she, were meant for each other, there were no two ways about it. At home, in the little house below the dike, she'd been by turns so withdrawn and so elated that the others were beginning to notice. Time and time again, she'd been on the verge of telling them everything, especially since the outcome seemed preordained. But she kept dithering. Destroying other people's happiness and shattering their trust was a monstrous thing to do. Maybe it was kinder to keep the illusion going a while longer; the grief that would inevitably follow would be long-lasting enough, as it was. And then—it turned out that she was pregnant.

Her lover lit a cigarette when, starry-eyed, she told him. Calmly, he said that he had never meant for their relationship to become serious, and that this might be a good place to put a stop to it. As an expectant mother, he presumed, she wouldn't want to go on sleeping around. She was flabbergasted. Because the child was his, she was certain of it, the alien seed always won out, everyone knew that, something to do with evolution, she was stumbling over her words, she'd look it up for him, the foreign seed was the fittest, for the sake of the survival of the species, the child was his, she was one hundred per cent sure of it. He shrugged his shoulders; it did seem a bit far-fetched to him, considering the overabundance of sex in her life. And with a friendly pat on her arse and thanks for the nice time he'd had, he put on his coat and went back to his wife.

Blankly, she, too, started buttoning her clothes. She must have misheard him. Or *he'd* misunderstood *her.* That was it; she hadn't made it clear enough. He thought she wasn't ready to give up her old life. But she'd rectify that, oh absolutely, right this minute. Before he'd even reached home, the telephone had begun to ring. Before he got to his work at the florist's the next morning, she was waiting by the door. Before the postman came, there was already a pile of envelopes on his doormat. She left no stone unturned. For weeks she stalked his every move. She appeared out of nowhere next to him, in the café, in the supermarket, at every stoplight, and round every street corner. When he stopped venturing outside on foot, she left little notes under the windshield wipers of his delivery truck. When he shut himself up inside his house, she snuck along the path to his front door at night and shouted through the mail slot that they were meant for each other. She pleaded and she begged and she threatened and she wailed and she implored, so single-mindedly and incessantly that one fine evening he dumped a bucket of water on her head from the bedroom window.

Only then did it finally dawn on her that she should set her resolve on a different outcome: forgetting him. But the village was small; there was always the chance of running into him unexpectedly, and then it was possible she'd lose all self-control. She had to leave. And now, suddenly, her pregnancy, which she could no longer hide, and which presented a perfectly good explanation for her peculiar behaviour of late toward the two men she had almost lost, turned out to be a great excuse: it made perfect sense that she would want to move to a bigger house. Emotionally exhausted, she watched her two 'boys' pack up the boxes, each equally proud of the child in her belly, too much in love, too amiable, and too tolerant to wrangle over which of them might be the father, the father of the unborn little girl to whom, over the course of the next long and agonizing months, burning with shame and longing, she would whisper her secret over and over again.

'Penny for your thoughts,' said Ludo suddenly. He was holding out an apple.

I stood up abruptly, brushing the crumbs off my jeans. 'I've just got to check on something.'

The fact that people had secrets was one thing. But to saddle *you* with them, that was criminal. They turned you into their accomplice without even asking. I could lie before I even knew how to talk, and that was the truth. If Ludo and Duco had known about all that, they'd have washed their hands of me ages ago. And yet there was a part of me that had always assumed my mother had simply made up that story, that it was a fairy tale just like all the others she used to tell me, except without the and-they-lived-happily-ever-after ending. It wasn't until I was six that I accidentally discovered that it had really happened. How should I have known? Merely by having her whisper it to me for nine long months, over and over again? But they bombarded you with so much stuff before you were born! Bach cantatas played especially for you; stomach massages; positive, welcoming thoughts; fleeting memories; suppressed fears and crazy dreams—you had to work your tail off to understand any of it, to categorize and sort it all out, and to top it all, you were expected to listen to them jabbering their heads off, too!

When Gavin and I had kids, I would handle it quite differently. I wouldn't burden the poor little tykes with unsolicited information that would only complicate their lives. I wouldn't breathe a word about how their father's lazy eye gave me the creeps, the way it kept turning the wrong way, or how his other eye, the blind one, mesmerized me. Not a word. As far as I was concerned, they were allowed to enter the world with a blank slate. What use were all those confessions? It was much more fun to have a mother who simply made things up. For that, they could count on me. In the morning at breakfast, for example, I'd say, 'The giants were rumbling up a storm last night. I bet there's a letter waiting over there for you today.'

I threw my apple core away. I traipsed through the wet grass to the stone with the crack in it. If that was what you were supposed to do, I'd leave notes for my kids inside that crack someday, but for some reason I was convinced that I'd have the kind of children who were so adored by everyone that they'd need a wheelbarrow to collect all their post.

'Lucy!' cried Ludo. 'It's really coming down now! Come on, let's go home!'

Glancing over my shoulder, I saw that he had started packing up. He stowed away the thermos in the knapsack, with what was left of his apple on top. Our Lude still didn't seem to get it, that in the Hebrides you could litter to your heart's content; nobody gave a damn.

'Hey, Lude!' I yelled. 'Ludikins! Relax!'

'Are you coming?'

Hastily, I stuck my arm into the mossy crack. Fumbling about in there, I felt something rustle between my fingers. My heart just about skipped a beat. I pulled out a postcard.

It was a postcard showing the giants of Callanish. They looked exactly the way they looked in real life; every one was there, even the biggest one, with its dramatic face. On the back of the card it said in large print, 'For Lucy, who's finally feeling better, thank goodness.'

Someone had thought of me and sent me this card! I immediately felt twice my size. I thought to myself, somewhat surprised: I exist. It was an incredible feeling, but the weirdest thing was that I'd never felt it before. I had never stopped to think that I was someone—me. Crikey, what a responsibility!

Ludo, grinning, was waiting for me by his bike.

'Look!' I said excitedly, handing him the card.

Just then, we heard the put-put of a motor, and we both looked back.

A moped came tearing down the road, driven by Gavin.

I couldn't help stepping back.

He stopped. 'Hiya, sir,' he said to Ludo.

'Hello, Gavin,' said Ludo.

'Hiya, Lucy.' He said it nonchalantly, but his face suddenly went all red. 'Feeling better?' He was doing his best to talk proper English.

I nodded.

He fidgeted a bit with his headlight. His nails were not only black as soot, they were also all raggedy.

'Did you just get out of school?' Ludo asked amicably.

'Yeah. Man, we had a shite test on quantum mechanics. I didnae hae a bleedin' clue.' He wiped his greasy hand on his thigh. He shot me a shy glance. 'Hop on, if you like. I've got errands to do, for me ma.'

'Another time, perhaps,' said Ludo. 'Lucy is only just back on her feet, and it's started to rain pretty hard now.'

Gavin glanced up at the slate-grey sky as if he'd never seen it before. 'It's no' a real storm.' He screwed up his face with the effort of articulating every word correctly.

Then all three of us were silent for a while.

'Aye, but wet it is, fer sure,' Gavin finally qualified further. He looked to Ludo for support, who was standing there with his rucksack like some overgrown boy scout.

'And that being the case, we really must get going,' said Ludo, briskly getting on his bike.

Suddenly I really felt like getting on the back of Gavin's moped; I had no idea why. Or maybe it was because now that I knew I existed, a moped suited me better than an old bicycle with back-pedal brakes.

'Come on, love,' said Ludo. He pulled me up on the crossbar in front of him.

'Hey, Gav!' I cried.

He looked me in the eye for the first time.

'Gav, will you pick me up tomorrow on your way to the fort?'

His cheeks turned crimson again.

'Will you?' I insisted. Simply and merely by existing, I could make the leader of Lewis's Special Commandos blush. It was weird, but it also felt great.

'Fine,' he said. He revved the motor.

'See you, then, Gavin,' said Ludo.

'Yeah, bye,' said Gavin, and he took off, navigating skilfully between the ruts and potholes in the road.

Ludo pushed off too. Slowly, we got up to speed. We had the wind against us. In two minutes he was out of breath. The drizzle had turned into buckets. 'Can't you go any faster?' I asked.

'I'm doing my best.' His breathing was laboured. 'Hey, Lucy. What sort of thing do you kids get up to, in that fort?'

'Oh, you know.'

'You know what?'

'We drink and we smoke and we play strip poker.' The truth, after all, was often the last thing people would believe; I should know.

'Oh, so I don't have to worry?'

'No, don't worry.'

'Oh, good. I was afraid that you might be sitting around solving quantum mechanics at Gavin's behest, or having other serious discussions.'

'Gavin looks like a rabbit.' It gave me a nice feeling to say his name out loud; it felt like a little electric shock.

Ludo laughed. He took his hand off the handlebar and rested it on my dripping head. 'Ah, Lucy,' he said. 'Still such a funny little thing, aren't you, when you come right down to it.'

That evening, I made my famous soup.

My famous soup was prepared with the help of a can opener.

'This is, and always will remain, the best soup,' said Duco, smacking his lips. 'Come on, admit it, you could never turn out such scurvy-looking meatballs if you tried making it yourself.'

'But you *did* prepare a home-cooked meal or two in the six years I was away, didn't you?' asked my mother. 'I hope so.'

The Luducos and I tried to look as non-committal as possible. My mother didn't need to know everything. Lude, Duke, and I, we had things that belonged to just the three of us. Like the song we sang while raking leaves; or the best way to pull off a plaster; or the fact that you were supposed to pour the milk in first, before the coffee. It was too bad, really, that my mother wasn't part of it.

I got in an even better mood when, later that evening as I went up to bed, I found the giants' postcard in my back pocket. I had to smooth it out; it had become a bit creased. It really was a fantastic card. I wondered how Gavin could have known about my wish to find mail in Callanish. Maybe he'd once seen me standing next to the stone with the crack in it, and had jumped to the right conclusion. I read the text once more. And then—'*Idiot!*' I berated myself, crushed; of course Gavin didn't know a word of Dutch.

I felt myself deflating, like a punctured tyre. So it had just been faithful old Lude. But I was sure I'd never told him about my secret postbox. Had I spilled the beans, then, in a delirious fever? I couldn't afford to have that happen. When I'd had those terrible nightmares six years ago and would wake up in the middle of the night screaming, Ludo and Duco had taken turns sleeping in my room with the dormer window for a while. I'd been terrified every time I opened my eyes that I might have shot my mouth off. 'He isn't just some character in a fairy tale that some mothers tell to their babies! He's *real!*' Or that I might have moaned, 'Alien seed!'—that disgusting expression that made me shudder even to think of it. In the end, I'd scarcely dared fall asleep. It was pretty rough, for someone who was only six. Kids who were only six years old weren't supposed to have a care in the world.

I still believed that.

# R is for Royalty

The next afternoon, I heard the fitful sputtering and bang-ing of Gavin's motor from miles away. I watched him through the kitchen window as he approached. He stopped just outside the garden gate. He had a grey scarf knotted over his nose and mouth, which made him look like a bank robber. His red ears stuck out on either side of his cap.

I grabbed my jacket off the coat rack and ran outside. The moor glittered in the hesitant sunlight. Right above my head, a lark was chirping its optimistic song.

Gavin pulled the scarf down and remarked, by way of greeting, 'Y'allright?' He started waving his arms as if try-ing to clear the air to make room for even more words, but then stopped abruptly. His bashfulness made his wander-ing eye wander even more than usual.

To break the ice, I asked politely, 'So, how's the quantum mechanics?'

'Whit? D'ye ken Planck's Constant, and such?'

I tried to make myself look as clever as possible. Planck's Constant, I repeated to myself, thrilled. It sounded like some kind of game. The hunt for Planck's Constant. Maybe we could give that a go, instead of going back to the fort, which I had to admit I was rather dreading.

He revved the engine. 'Are ye coming, then?'

With a sinking heart, I climbed on. It was a short ride.

The others were kicking a jellyfish that had washed up on the beach. The little ones were splashing along the water-line and trying to crush as many shells as they could with their wellies. Ian Dury blared from the radio: *'Hit me with your rhythm stick.'* Verity was rather conspicuously French-kissing Struan on top of a cockle-crusted rock. You could see the drool running down Struan's chin.

I had expected Gavin to start barking orders right away, everyone back to the galleys, but he just said mildly, 'It's much too nice out to work today.'

'In that case, let us enjoy the sun,' I said. I sounded like someone's great-great-grandmother, and to make up for it, I quickly pulled a face and crawled inside the fort.

There was nobody else in there.

'All right, then,' said Gavin, behind me.

I turned to face him, on all fours. I could see the crusty corners of his chapped mouth. 'Or shouldn't we first ...' I blurted.

'Whatever you like. Mebbe this time you first want to ...' He wiped his sweaty upper lip with his hand.

'No, I ...'

''Cause you deserve it.' He suddenly looked determined. 'Where do you want to lie down, over there, or over here?'

My mother hadn't said anything about lying down. I'd never be able to reach it that way, and maybe I'd be doing it all wrong.

'Let me think,' I said, panicking. But I couldn't think of anything except to sit down next to him, my legs stretched out stiffly in front of me.

We sat there for a while, staring ahead.

In the end, Gavin said grimly, 'Well, let's get on wi'it, eh?'

He turned to me and stuck his hand between my legs.

I nearly let out a scream.

Kneading my crotch with one hand, he pushed me down flat on my back with the other. Then he stuck his tongue in my mouth.

I shut my eyes. I kept thinking with all my might: I exist.

Gavin was slobbering at me like a Great Dane as he edged his way on top of me. His spit tasted very different from mine. Our noses kept colliding. I was terrified I'd bite him by accident. My jaw was starting to wobble from the effort of staying open. My neck was going stiff.

'Ah, lassie,' he muttered, 'ah, my bonnie wee lassie.' He fumbled with my trousers, he unbuttoned the top button, his fingers were on my bare belly, he pulled the zipper down, his hand slipped inside my knickers, and in a helpless reflex I heaved him off me by flipping myself over on top of him, but then I felt the bump of his thing against my stomach and in alarm started repeating to myself, Planck's Constant, Planck's Constant, while he huffed in my ear, 'Hey, wait, you're smashing me wrist!'

'Yeah, so get your hand outta there!' I squealed, overwrought.

'You could have telt me, ye ken, if ye wanted to be on top. Bleedin' hell, you're an animal, so ye are.' He said it with awe.

I wanted to roll off him, but he was holding me by the hips and started jiggling me back and forth across his groin with a blissful expression on his face. 'Will you let me come inside, Lucy, just for a sec?'

My anxiety was making me even crabbier. 'Now what do you want!'

'What do you think? I know ye've done it before!'

My heart sank, because I couldn't help thinking, Only with a broom. It shocked me, being forced to think that sort of thing about myself. I didn't want to be someone who'd had that sort of experience, ever. I said, 'Oh, go ahead.'

He was quiet a moment. 'Are you sure?'

I nodded.

He started pulling my trousers down, and my knickers. It wasn't easy, because I was lying on top of him, stiff with fear. His palms were wet. 'Will ye no' take off your shoes?' he asked.

I kicked my shoes off energetically. It was a relief to be able to do something.

'And now like this, no, like that, wi' your knees.'

I pulled up my knees one by one so that he could pull down my trouser legs. We were a good team. Except that it felt pretty strange to be lying there with a bare bum, on top of someone who was still fully dressed and even had a scarf around his neck and a cap on his head, in a foul-smelling fort on some beach on a windy island called Lewis.

Gavin asked, 'Uh, so, what ye say we do next?'

'You know.'

'Okay.' Under my stomach, his fingers fumbled for his own zipper. After squirming a bit, he said, 'Hey, Lucy?'

I closed my eyes; I thought it was more romantic that way.

'Gie us a hand, eh ... uh ... I'm no' sure ... see, I ...'

'What?' I pushed myself up on my arms to look at him. 'Don't you know what to do?'

His face had gone beet-red. 'Didna think ye'd get mad.'

'You're sixteen, nearly!'

He looked sheepish. 'But the lassies from here canna go as far as you. My dad says you Dutchies'—he toiled to get the words out one by one—'that you're very, uh, permiscuous.'

Another fucking word that didn't show up on any of the fucking lists I was supposed to cram into my head every night. Why didn't they ever teach me stuff I needed to know? 'Say again?' I asked, irritated.

'Permiscuous,' Gavin repeated.

'Oh, that.' My arms were so tired that I let myself fall back on top of him, defeated. His hands promptly landed on my buttocks. I panicked again. 'Wait a minute, wait.'

'What now, lassie?'

'Right, wait a minute, I mean, tell me, is that permiscuous-thing the reason your dad is always going after my mum?'

'My dad?' He sounded shocked.

'Yeah, your dad!'

Under my belly, Planck's Constant promptly shrank. Furious, Gavin wriggled his way out from under me. He sat up. 'Hae you seen them together, then? What were they doing?'

'He comes round almost every day,' I babbled. 'I've been telling my mother it's got to stop, but she says she can't help it. He's got it bad, that's for sure. Can't *you* make it stop?'

'Christ,' he groaned, from the bottom of his heart. 'What an eejit. And am I supposed to tie the bugger to a chair, to make him stay home?'

'Well, you know, maybe you could ...' I thought it over. I saw Rowan's flat face before me. 'Does your mum have a birthday coming up or anything, so that you could get her a sexy nightie or something? So that she could tart herself up a little ...'

He stared at me with bulging eyes. 'Go on! They're *married*, for Chrissakes!'

'They may be now. But next thing you know, he'll leave her. Dude, you have no idea, people who are in love—! One day, *poof!* he'll be gone. You've got to keep an eye on him.

You can't let him go out alone anymore.' I started pulling on my jeans again.

He didn't even notice. 'It's me ma oughta be keeping an eye on him, not me!'

'Fine, but she can't, if she can't go out,' I said. That wasn't what I'd been driving at, honest—the thing just fell into my lap. 'So what can we do about that? Hey, why don't we offer to look after your little sister? That way your ma will be free to do what she needs to do.'

I was so wild with joy that I nearly made the mistake of telling my mother I was going to babysit Iola after all.

She was pulling weeds when I got home. She didn't notice me, and for some reason I hung back, watching her from a distance, keeping one foot in front of the other in order to create the impression I was just walking up, in case she suddenly looked up.

She was tranquilly hoeing between the rows of Savoy cabbages, grown from the seedlings Iain had given her. From time to time, she bent down to pull a weed from the soil by hand. She radiated the calm, the dedication, of someone performing a task that gives her immense pleasure. Carefully she picked up a stone that had landed among Iain's cabbages and tossed it into the wheelbarrow. Again she stooped, picked something up, inspected it carefully. Was it a ladybug? If it had seven spots on its wings, she could make a wish.

But what did she have left to wish for? By the looks of it, she was perfectly happy.

One of my feet began tingling unpleasantly because of the way I was standing, as twisted as the Egyptians in Mr Klop's history books. Here I stood, for no reason other than seeing her happy as a pig in clover. What *right* did she have? How did *she* deserve to be at peace with the world and with herself? Why were the nightmares for me and not for her?

She looked up. Catching sight of me, just for an instant she seemed to have to make herself overcome some reluctance. She didn't like being spied on. Yet she managed a smile. 'Hey there. Did you have a nice afternoon?'

I knew she wouldn't hesitate to rat me out to that Iain of hers if I told her about Iola. Who'd pass it on to Rowan—as soon as he could spare a moment for Rowan, of course. My mother was going to have to stop throwing a spanner in the works all the time. My life was my own now, and mine alone. 'It was okay.'

'That doesn't sound very enthusiastic. Tell me?'

'There's nothing to tell.'

'There's always something to tell.' She was leaning on her hoe, but her calmness was now a pose—some agitation had made its way into her gaze; with me around, she no longer felt completely at ease. Something dark and unspeakable hung in the air between us, separating us from each other like a wall.

'Well?'

I shrugged. My leg was asleep and I couldn't get it to move.

In a shrill voice, she suddenly demanded, 'How much longer are you going to keep up this sulky behaviour of yours?'

'I'm not doing anything.'

'Of course not, never, but meanwhile ... You're really starting to get on my nerves, do you know that? Bloody hell, I feel as if I'm living with a walking time bomb. I never know what to expect, with you. How do you think that makes me feel?'

What did she mean? Did she mean she was afraid I'd spill the beans? Was that it? Didn't my own mother trust me?

The thought was so alarming that I found myself fighting back tears. How *could* she think such a thing? How could she, after everything I'd done to keep her secret safe? It had been for her sake that, on that terrible night, I'd ... no, I refused to think about it, I refused. There was no point looking back, she had taught me that herself! And yet that was precisely what I'd done that night, I had looked back, and there he'd been, sprawled on the ground, it was real, it was really real, just as real and just as true as the fact that my life had been one big fat lie from the word go.

'Lucy!' Duco suddenly called from the doorway.

I blinked.

'Am I ever glad you're finally home! I was about to ring the coastguard.' His scruffy face was turning red with relief—our Lucy, home safe.

'Don't be silly,' my mother snapped at him. 'She's quite capable of looking after herself. And now get lost, because your pride and joy and I were just having a little tête-à-tête.'

A look of uncertainty crossed his face. 'Is something wrong, then?'

My mother stuck the hoe into the ground. 'I can't say I'm ecstatic about the way she's behaving. I suppose it was too much trouble for you, to look after her upbringing while I was in prison?'

The Duke looked as if he was starting to count to ten. He was staring fixedly at the hunchbacked hills lying huffily in the distance.

'You've spoiled her to death, both of you. It was easier that way, I suppose? Just keep pretending everything's hunky-dory, nothing but sweetness and light! And who wouldn't, in your place? Ever since ...'

'Stop!' I screamed.

She turned back to me. 'Let me tell you something, miss

Princess-and-the-pea: I'm back now, and I'm not putting up with your moods any longer.'

Before I turned three, Duco had taught me how to make a phone call, because I was so eager to copy what Ludo and he did. He'd snapped a picture of me once with the receiver in my hand and a pencil stuck behind my ear. He still carried that photo in his wallet.

I ran inside past my mother, straight into his arms.

The first time Gavin showed up on the beach with Iola tucked under his jacket, his troops were gobsmacked. They started jeering, 'Hey, who's the nanny now, Gav?'

Unperturbed, he undid a couple of buttons to pull Iola out. She had on a pale-yellow romper suit. 'Look, ugly-face,' he said to her tenderly, 'there's yer underlings. Say hello.' Waving her little arms from side to side, he glared around the circle.

'Hi Iola!' I cried.

'That one there's no underling, that's Extra-Special Commando Lucy.'

I felt myself blush with pleasure. I existed. And not only that, I was someone to be reckoned with.

'Yeah, Blowjob Specialist!' Verity was laughing so hard she almost fell over.

Gavin ignored her, nestling Iola in the crook of his arm. With his free hand, he groped in his back pocket and, as if drawing a gun, pulled out a bottle. Deftly, he stuck the nipple into the greedy little mouth. 'This bairn'll drink anyone under the table. I'm just sayin', we're not gonna gae soft, just because she's underage.'

'Well, as a matter of fact, we're expecting an attack any moment,' Struan began.

'Now that the head o' state is here'—Gavin scooted Iola a little higher up on his arm—'we have immunity.'

'Shit,' said Verity. 'So we laid all those mines for nothing!'

'Private Verity is assigned to nappy duty. Any other volunteers?'

'Me, me!' cried Fiona, age five. She was jumping up and down in her wellies on a dead seagull.

'We need you for more difficult work,' said Gavin kindly.

'Right, gae real,' yelped Verity, with her hands on her hips. 'Yer aff yer heid if you think I'm going to wipe the wean's bahooky for you …'

'D'ye ken the word "insubordination"?' Gavin asked her coolly. 'D'ye ken the words "court martial"? D'ye ken the words "firing squad"?'

To my surprise, I suddenly realized that I understood everything he said. It was as if a little key had been turned inside my head; I wasn't hearing gibberish anymore. It was all as clear as anything. What had I been so worried about? I'd never have to grope for words again, now that I could read them effortlessly off Gavin's lips. It had to be a sign of true love.

'I already had to change three bairns today, at home!' Verity's voice rose with indignation.

I elbowed her in the ribs. 'I'll do it for you, if you like.'

'Tss!' she went huffily. 'Show-off.' But I could see the relief in her face.


After an explosive but quickly settled debate, the fort was turned into a palace for Her Majesty Iola the First. It acquired a little front stoop, from which she could view the parade on festival days. The oil barrel we used to sit on when playing cards was put to new use as the cradle-of-state. We laid a path of seashells from the palace entrance down to the royal fountain, which was powered by a bicycle pump. To her great delight, little Fiona was named First Royal Water-Pumper. Using pallets that we dragged all the way back from the dump at Brenish, we built a royal coach. It wasn't easy, yoking all the bucking and kicking little kids together, but once they were harnessed, it was more than worthwhile. Verity ran alongside them with a whip.

In honour of Iola's coronation, we organized tournaments every free moment we had. We screamed ourselves hoarse during the jousting and the sword fights. Lachlan was phenomenal with a lance. I was given the honour of handing out the prizes, since Gavin had decided I was the Queen Mum. Every morning when the others were off at school, I cut and pasted laurel wreaths for the victors. I took my role so seriously that, once or twice, I addressed Ludo and Duco condescendingly as 'my good people.'

The prospect of the approaching summer vacation made everything even more divine. When summer came, Iola would stretch out her little arms to me every day inside her palace. I'd give her a bottle and then burp her on my shoulder. I'd pull her little romper off expertly each time she pooped in her nappy. On the beach I'd dig a hole fit for a princess, for her to disappear into right up to her neck. I'd take her for a ride in the surf on the oil barrel. And all on account of getting myself designated as the Commander-in-Chief's girlfriend. They all said it: 'Lucy is Gav's lassie.' Gavin would grin from ear to ear when he heard them say it. 'She's a bonnie wifey,' he told Stru and Lach.

But he never tried getting inside my knickers again, not since I'd once let it slip that, when the summer was over, I'd be starting secondary school. 'Lucy, Lucy,' he'd said, appalled, 'when you're twelve years old yer not supposed to have sex the way you've been having, kiddo. Trust me, it's just no' right, it's agin the law. We'll knock some proper manners into ye yet.'

Kissing and petting were acceptable when you were twelve, so that was what we spent our time practising now.

That was something you should become good at, anyway, he believed, and it didn't do nobody any harm. After we were done, we'd share his bacon sandwich.

At first I'd sometimes bring my own sandwich from home, because I was sure our larder was better stocked than Rowan's, but he wouldn't hear of it. He wasn't the kind of man who'd allow himself to be kept by a woman—certainly not by a woman who was only twelve years old. It was lucky, he said, I didna look my age. 'Because you're so tall and know so much about Planck and such, you *seem* much older.' His troops presumably laboured under the same delusion, and he saw no reason to set them straight.

I felt happy and special. Nobody could try anything with me, not with Gavin around. I decided not to tell him I had been engaged once before. In all honesty, even I preferred to think about that whole episode as little as possible.

# S is for Summer

At the start of the summer vacation, all the B&B signs were repaired and hanging straight again. Everyone was getting ready to milk the tourists arriving daily by ferry at Stornoway and swarming over the island's high roads and low roads.

Verity's parents sawed out a window in the side of the old caravan in their yard and hauled it over to Callanish to sell hot soup, tea, and scones. Stru's dad got his kilt out of mothballs, greased up his bagpipes, and made a killing playing *Auld Lang Syne* on the side of the road. Iain had managed to get his hands on a batch of the famous Harris teddy bears, which had fallen off the back of a lorry. My mother had made a sign for him. Swinging in the wind, creaking loudly, it promised that the bear of your dreams was to be had for a song in Rowan's kitchen.

On the beach at Uig, too, business was booming; we sold rough chunks of gneiss that might or might not have a fossil hidden inside, and pale-blue scallop shells. The First Royal Water-Pumper collected the pound coins with such a hungry look on her face that most holidaymakers didn't have the heart to ask for their change. The more primitive and pathetic we looked, the healthier the cash flow, said Gavin, so it was a piece of luck that Fiona had just lost all her front teeth.

The funniest moments came when I'd overhear someone speaking Dutch. The Dutch tourists hadn't the foggiest, of course, that anyone understood their loud comments. Middle-aged ladies dressed in sensible brogues, in particular, couldn't get over seeing us on the beach with an infant in a bucket.

I went home every night with a bundle of cash in my pocket. But the best thing of all was that there were no longer any penances hanging over my head. It was quite simply the best summer in the entire history of the world: everyone was happy, the mothers kept putting an extra slice of bacon in their children's sandwiches, and on Sundays, the entire island had new black coats to wear to church.

The only one not rubbing her hands with glee was my mother. Having all those nosy parkers around made her nervous, she said. She started reading the cards again for the first time in years. And every time she did, the Two of Pentacles would turn up—the card of restlessness and change, the card of travellers and wanderers.

'Why don't we just pack our bags?' she asked.

It made me think of the lengthy trip the Luducos and I had taken six years earlier: of all the lemonade we drank in all the outdoor cafés, of the strange, colourful bills I was given to buy souvenirs—a seahorse-key chain, a doll in national costume. They had really done their best to distract me. That was the reason for our trip, they told me: to give ourselves and other people the chance to forget what had happened. It was best to forget. The one thing we weren't allowed to forget was that I had lots of friends, and so they insisted on sending postcards to the kids in my class, signed with my name. They let me pick them out, one cheery postcard after the next.

Back then, there was nothing I'd have liked better than to stay away for good. But now I was someone who received postcards, and I had Gavin, and my responsibilities as First Lady and Queen Mum. So I told Duco there was no way I was going, even if my mother were to get her way.

'She won't,' he said, uncharacteristically grim. 'We have no intention of uprooting ourselves every time her majesty's nose gets out of joint.'

He and I were sitting behind the new windbreak. We were gazing out over the moor, which was looking drab and brown in the light of the setting sun, slapping, for form's sake, at the midges swarming round us. Duco had a bottle of whisky next to his chair. The smell of frying meat wafted out through the open kitchen door. My mother and Ludo were preparing dinner.

Ludo's voice suddenly came loud and shrill over the simmering cooking sounds: 'Really, can't you talk about anything else?'

'Ludo's had it with her too,' Duco remarked. He poured himself another one. 'Let him deal with it.'

He didn't seem to remember that, in our family, it wasn't considered right to eavesdrop on other people's conversations. If you happened to overhear something not meant for your ears, you either had to say 'Ahem!' loudly enough to make your presence known, or else you had to get out of there in a hurry. Otherwise you'd live to regret it. Because, count on it, my mother used to say, you're likely to hear something you'll wish you never knew.

Right now, in the kitchen, she was saying something unintelligible. She probably had her head in the fridge.

'That may be what *you* want, but that doesn't mean it's automatically happening.' Ludo's voice came through loud and clear.

'Well said,' muttered Duke.

'And especially not now,' said Ludo, 'now that Lucy is finally beginning to find her niche.'

'Lucy?' my mother replied. Even the way she was laughing back there was impossible to miss: her gruff, rough jailhouse bark. The sound came whizzing around the edge of the kitchen door and walloped me on the head. 'Weeds always grow back, remember. That should be obvious by now, shouldn't it? Or were you expecting me to sacrifice myself for her *again*?'

My ears were burning.

Next to me, Duco emptied his glass. 'Let's go for a little walk,' he suggested quickly.

We got to our feet and wandered off.

Duco held my hand firmly in his as we walked across the moor. We were both a little short of breath. Our hands stuck together with sweat. After a little while, he said, 'She's upset because of all the day trippers. She's worried about being recognized by Dutch tourists, which could set off a whole new round of gossip about us here.'

'Can't she just can lay low for a while?'

'We keep telling her that. In a month, the place will be deserted again. She can just stay indoors until then; that would be the best solution.' In the old days, his voice would have told me that this was the answer to his dreams— Mum having to stay indoors, where she'd be constantly in his sight. Now he just sounded annoyed.

But I didn't want Ludo and Duco to start hating her, either. Then it would all have been for nothing. I had to try to get her to be a bit nicer to them.

He gave my fingers a squeeze. 'And you have to be on your guard as well, not to bump into any Dutch people. Maybe we'll have to keep you indoors for the time being too.'

I stood still. 'But didn't you just ...'

'Well, your mother thinks differently.'

My life had never been this good, and now here she was, about to ruin it again for me. I yanked my hand free.

'We may just have underestimated it a bit,' he said. 'It seems that escaping the past isn't as easy as we first thought.'

As we were doing the washing-up that evening, I told my mother I wanted to cut off my plaits. She nodded thoughtfully, rinsing a pan. After a moment's silence, she asked, 'And wouldn't you like a little colour in your hair, as well, just for a change?' Then I knew she had seen right through me, and the way she could read my mind sent cold shivers up my spine.

She dried her hands. 'Sit down, let's just fix it right now.'

I sat down at the kitchen table, where a pile of clean dishes was waiting to be put away in the dresser. The rest of the dinnerware was still soaking in the sink. But to my mother, this had priority.

'It's high time we did something about your hair, I've already told you that.' She draped her tea towel over my shoulders and took a pair of scissors out of the drawer.

I sat there as if turned to stone. That other time, I could have sworn it just made her feel good to touch me and fuss with my hair, the way she used to, before, but now she was giving herself away; it was this she'd been working up to, she was as cunning as a fox.

'Would you like to save them?'

I shook my head. I already had one pair of lopped-off plaits, from the first time they'd been cut off. How many memento boxes of cut-off hair did anyone need to carry around with her all her life?

She must have been paying attention in jail when the

West Indian hairdresser cut her hair; she was swift and deft. One lock of hair after another floated down past my burning cheeks on the way to the floor. The only thing I heard was the snip-snip of the scissors. Soon, all my hair was scattered all around me on the kitchen floor—there was no going back.

'Do you want it chin-length, like a pageboy?'

'Just chop it all off.'

My mother didn't respond. She went on snipping, calmly and carefully. Now and then, she'd step back to weigh the effect. She frowned and she concentrated. It made me very uneasy, to see her taking such care with it.

'Your hair looks cute no matter what you do to it,' she said. 'There, done. Look at me?'

Reluctantly, I opened my eyes. I'd expected her to look at me triumphantly, with spite, but her face had quite a different expression; I couldn't immediately put my finger on it. Quickly, I turned round to get out the dustpan and brush. As I swept up my hair from the floor, I felt her eyes on me still. It made my arms heavy and slow.

I carried the dustpan outside to the dustbin by the peat pile. It suddenly felt as if there was much more open air out here, now that I'd lost my plaits. It made me feel exposed, insecure. Coiled in the green dustpan, the hair looked as if it had never had anything to do with me. As if it had never patiently grown from my very own skull, as if I'd never washed it twice a week and then rinsed it with vinegar. I dumped it in the dustbin. I wouldn't need my mother to brush my hair ever again, anyway. And it was then that it finally dawned on me what her look, just now, had meant: it had been a look of regret, sadness, and pity.

Gavin thought my new hairdo was pure dead brilliant. He said I looked at least fifteen. Sitting on the steps of the royal palace at Uig, he kept running his big hands through the short tufts on top of my head to make them stand straight up. According to him, I'd easily get into the disco in Stornoway, looking like this. The fact that I was now somebody who was being asked to go out on a date filled me with a profound sense of awe. At home, we didn't believe in God, but now I had the distinct sense that he definitely did exist. Maybe I could ask him to do something about Iain and my mother. Maybe you didn't always have to do everything yourself.

Gavin danced Iola on my knee. He promised to bring back some purple-sequinned disco socks for her, size zero. Iola crowed. She had finished her bottle and was a bundle of energy. She was so busy cooing that she didn't even miss my plaits. 'And then we'll paint her nails with glitter polish!' I yelled. I was suddenly so very happy—I never knew you could be that happy. The reason people had dirt under their fingernails here was only because of all the peat blown in the wind. You couldn't help it, it was on account of the soil and climate; even if you were a royal family, you couldn't escape it, even if all you did all day long was to lag about on the royal throne.

Gavin gave Iola a big smacker on the top of her head and ruffled my hair again before applying himself to the preparations for the naval parade. Gazing after him, I melted; I was melting because I was lucky enough to have the love of a good man so early in life. I felt as warm as a slice of bread in a toaster, and Iola, sitting on my lap, probably felt the same way. 'Look,' I said to her, 'boats.'

Under Gavin's direction, everything that could float, or might possibly float, was being dragged across the sand— heaps of mouldy logs, but also some washtubs borrowed from home, and little Fiona arrived rolling an empty beer keg nearly as big as she was. The wind lashing her cheeks had turned them purple. There was snot dangling from her nose. But when she saw me sitting up here, a big smile stretched across her face from east to west. 'Lucy!' she yelled. She came running up to me. 'I like your hair!'

'You do?'

She nearly snapped her neck nodding yes. She felt her own hair, which was tied in two pigtails on either side of her head. She looked exactly like Pippi Longstocking, or just like me at her age. 'I want to look the same,' she said firmly. Pulling a big pocketknife from her pocket, she handed it to me without further ado.

Out on the beach, Verity was watching, glaring at me in her usual spiteful way.

'You'd better talk it over first with your ma,' I said. 'And, besides, it's better to use scissors.'

'There's a wee scissors in my knife,' said Fiona. She showed me, bursting with pride.

I laughed. 'They're only big enough to cut your nails.'

'Hey, super-cool knife, Fi,' said Verity, who'd suddenly materialized at our side, snatching it out of her hands.

'Gie us it!' Fiona yelped. She kicked Verity in the shins.

'What's a wee bairn like you doing with a thing like this? Ye'll cut yeself, if ye dinnae watch oot.'

Some people always had to go and spoil things for other people. That was life—you had to accept it—but if they started picking on little kids, they were messing with me. 'I used to have a knife like that, too, when I was little,' I snarled. 'The exact same kind, when I was her age.'

'Oh yeah?' asked Verity, hands on hips. 'So tell me, what d'ye use it for, then?'

Breathlessly I started telling them about how I'd used my knife, once, to slash my way out of a boa constrictor that had swallowed me on the garden path.

'Stupid! I'm not talking about made-up stuff, I mean for

*real.*' She took a step closer and started prodding my shoulder with one finger, as if touching me disgusted her. With her other hand she waved the knife in my face. 'Let me tell you something, right? You dinna amount to a fuck. No' a fuck. You may impress wee shites such as Fi here, but other than them, you're fooling nae wan.'

'Oh yeah? Oh yeah?'

'Gav is just kiddin' on, take my word for it. He'd never fall for a little shite like you, with your pathetic stories for wee bairn. Swallowed by a boa constrictir, eh? Gi' us a break! D'ye still believe in Santa Claus, then?' She glared at me through narrowed eyelids. 'What a bletherskite you are. What a babby! What have ye ever done besides sheet in yer nappy?'

'Gavin's taking me to the disco, I'll have you know.'

Her face fell. She turned around. She cupped her hands to her mouth. 'Gav!' she yelled across the beach. 'Gav, a' you a child molester, or is Lucy a liar?'

The others all promptly dropped their floats and tubs. Smelling a fight, they came in closer.

'Verity's a big fat liar!' Fiona bawled. 'Lucy got swallowed by a snake! She did!'

I hugged Iola tight. She was my shield. As long as I was the Queen Mum, nothing bad could happen to me.

'Go on, then, tell us some more of yer heroic exploits!' Verity stuck her chin out. Her Vanessa-blond hair bounced up and down. 'Did ya fight tigers, and sail pirate ships, an' that?'

Gavin came running up, mowing everyone out of his way with his long arms. 'D'ye fancy ending up in the brig?' he barked at her. 'I kin take care of it, no problem.'

'Oops, there's our bairn-diddler. But ho, our Gav cain't get it up for a real *wo*man. Totally nada. So ye've got to make do with wee uns, innt'at right?'

Gavin, furious, snapped his fingers. But his men didn't react. They were doubled over, in stitches. 'Is't true, Gav?'

I had to shut the viper up before she totally undermined his authority; you didn't have to tell *me* what a chain re-action was. 'Hey, shut your big trap, you!' I began ranting at her.

'And what if I doon't?'

'Then you'll have to answer to me!'

'Oooh, oh deary me, I hope I survive! What were you doing the day Bambi's ma was shot?'

'Hey Verity, you got yourself a price on your head!' Lach-lan slapped his thighs, his fish-eyes popping out of his head with mirth. He was leering from her to me and back again. That was the moment Iola on my lap chose to kick her little feet, hiccup once or twice, and then throw up her entire bottle. Her Babygro was drenched in sour milk. 'Gavin!' I cried. 'Burp-rag, quick!'

'Oh, he's quite the father, our Gav,' Verity declared. 'That's what you get when you only hang out wi' weans.'

'Shut your mouth, bitch,' I said. 'Or I'll nail it shut.' I made to stand up.

'Help! Gavin's wee bairn's after me! And she's capable of anything!'

And then I said it. I said she had better remember that I once killed a man, and that I hadn't even needed a knife, just a red pencil.

'Oh, wow, that's really something,' said Verity. 'Had ye lost yer blue pencil, then?'

Iola gagged again. Then she started crying pitifully.

'She has to go home,' said Gavin brusquely. 'She in't feel-ing well.' He wouldn't look at me as he snatched the baby out of my arms.

'It's true, I swear,' I told him, on the verge of tears.

'I'm off.' He hitched Iola onto his hip.

'Don't forget your *other* Smurf,' yelled Verity, pushing me toward him.

He jabbed me back with his elbow. He hurried away from me with Iola in his arms.

'Gav!' I cried.

He pretended not to hear. He sprinted across the beach to his moped. The wind was whipping the sand into mini-twisters.

In the distance, along the shore, a group of tourists in brightly coloured macs was coming toward us. They were walking along as if they didn't have a care in the world, as if *they* had never wanted to dig a hole in the ground and make themselves disappear. They were just ambling along as if they hadn't a clue what it was to realize you were responsible for someone else's downfall.

'Gav,' I repeated once more, dazed.

'Hey, Lucy?' Struan asked. 'Tell us about the pencil, how'd ye do it?'

The others promptly descended on me like a flock of vultures.

'Was there loadsa blood?'

'What did you kill the bloke for, anyway?'

'Had he nicked sommit of yourn?'

'What did he want with you?'

I tucked my head low between my shoulders. I tried with all my might to think of safe things.

'And did they arrest you, then?'

'Did they give you a hard time in the interrogation?'

'You must have been in the slammer a long time, right?'

'Did you they gie you anything besides bread an' water to eat, in jail?'

'Bread wi' maggots in it?'

'How many times did you try to escape?'

'Hey, Lucy? Come on! Tell us! How many years did you get?'

They hissed and booed when I jumped to my feet and ran off. I raced along the beach as fast as my legs would carry me. The sand was soft and heavy underfoot. I had to shake them off my tail, I had to … except that I couldn't take the shortcut through the machair right now; but even if there hadn't been that particular taboo, I wouldn't have dared go that way anyway, because that's where the flasher with the stiffie was sure to be waiting for me.

The blood throbbed in my ears. Slogging my way through the sand, I reached the narrowest section of the beach, where three tourists were leaning over a puddle. They were so blond that they had to be Dutch. Dutch burghers who probably remembered every detail of the sensational murder case, the true facts of which had never come to light—annoying, nosy Dutch people. As I passed them, I tucked my head down as far as I could. A lady and a little girl with ash-blond hair, and a slight boy with a huge head, who was jabbing at the puddle with a fishnet on a pole. '… Invertebrates and arthropods,' he was saying in Dutch. 'They come before …'

I nearly tripped over my own two feet. Blindly, I ran on. My thoughts tumbling over one another. Get out of here. Get away!

The curve of the bay was already in sight. If only I were allowed to glance back over my shoulder, to reassure myself I'd been mistaken about that threesome! But I wasn't allowed to do anything except run, run as fast as I could, and there was nowhere for me to go except to get away from then, and away from now.

# PART III

# Eighteen

# T is for Time

On my eighteenth birthday, the Luducos took me out to dinner. We'd all been very much looking forward to the outing; it was quite a big deal for us, because reserving a table in a restaurant was something we didn't do very often. After much discussion, we'd settled on the restaurant in the Angus McCleod Motel in Tarbert. We had heard that the scallops there, plucked from the sea by Angus himself, were bigger and more tender that the plumpest mussel.

You only turn eighteen once, Duco kept saying, and then Ludo just couldn't resist pointing out that the same went for every birthday of your life. Their squabbling was a good diversion; that way, none of us had to be reminded that this would be the last birthday we'd celebrate together, as a threesome, for the foreseeable future.

That night I wore a dress that had been advertised in the mail-order catalogue as 'irresistible'—moonlight-silver, with a killer décolletage—and my first pair of stilettos. I had smeared on enough lipstick to leave prints on at least a dozen glasses, bound to send many a waiter into transports of desire. Lude and Duke each wore one of the many ties I had given them as presents over the years on festive occasions, because it was so hard to know what else to give a man. All three of us looked so fabulous that I couldn't get over it.

We sailed into the restaurant as if it were the most normal thing in the world for us to eat out. I paused for a moment in the doorway, giddy with excitement. In my moonlight dress, I felt daring and sexy. After coffee, I was going to order a brandy in one of those special snifters, and I'd smoke a filter cigarette that I'd languidly crush out after taking three puffs, just to have a waiter rush over and put a clean ashtray in front of me. I'd thank him in that special, bored way that showed you were a woman of the world. He'd never for a moment suspect that my knowledge of that kind of thing came from magazines, and soap operas on the telly.

I let my breath out slowly and looked round.

The walls were weeping a yellowish grease. The five or six little tables were set with grimy paper tablecloths and grubby dishware. A tape recorder cranked out deplorable music. The only other patron was sitting in a dark corner, leaning over his plate with one arm slung around it in a protective manner. From the kitchen came the sound of breaking dishes.

Angus McCleod did not, apparently, read the sort of magazine from which I had gleaned my illusions. After all, fishing was his main livelihood. He had a cutter anchored in Harris harbour, freshly tarred. Perhaps it was because he was already sufficiently exposed to the elements in the daytime that he kept all the windows of his restaurant tightly shut. It was extremely warm and stuffy in there.

Ludo rubbed his hands together. 'Ah, we're about to get ourselves spoiled rotten.' He looked like a little boy who's looking forward to jumping in the pool with a record-setting splash.

With a flourish, Duco pulled out a chair for me. 'Milady,' he said. He was wearing aftershave. His sleeve brushed my bare shoulder as I sat down, and for some reason I suddenly felt right down to my stiletto heels what a lucky girl I was.

A girl in an apron dress shuffled over to us after Angus yelled from afar that there was a table ready to order. She gaped at us in silence for a while. Then she asked, 'Are ye folk from Monte Carlo or sumplace?' She didn't wait for an answer. Picking her ear with the end of her pencil, she announced that there was just a fixed menu: the famous scallops, followed by steak sautéed in butter with roast potatoes, and cheesecake and strawberry ice cream for dessert.

Ludo asked for a bottle of champagne and Duco said that he couldn't possibly think of anything more appropriate. They beamed at each other.

The girl shook her head. 'The only thing I have is what the boss calls baby-champs.'

'Let's do it!' declared Duco.

A little while later, she brought us the Babycham. We raised our glasses. 'Eighteen,' sighed the Luducos, together. 'How time flies!'

It was lucky that, with them, you didn't have to worry about profound reflections or reminiscences. 'Cheers, gentlemen,' I said. I took a sip. And another one. It tasted like apple juice. 'Mmm.' I didn't want to disappoint them.

Duco twirled the glass between his fingers and gazed at the flaccid bubbles. 'An interesting year.'

'When you come back in the summer hols next year,' said Ludo, 'we'll do this again.'

'Next year! What's the point talking about next year, when we're having such a good time right this minute, the three of us?' grumbled Duco, somewhat ruffled.

'Loosen your tie, old boy,' Ludo told him. 'You're sweating.'

'It's suffocating in here,' I said, ever the conciliator. But I, too, was suddenly feeling the heat rush to my face at the thought that I wouldn't be seeing them for an entire year.

When the meal arrived, we planted our elbows on the table, fell on our food like seasoned mariners, and gorged ourselves in silence. Ever since my mother's departure, we had gone back to our old ways with the can opener, so we ate with great relish. The scallops were downright delicious. Every bite we took endowed the greasy restaurant with just a smidgen more glamour. Or maybe it was just us—three bashfully twinkling stars in this shabby firmament.

'Heavenly,' I said with my mouth full during dessert.

'Fresh strawberries would have been even better, of course, wouldn't you agree?' asked Ludo. Duke and he glanced at each other, smirking. You'd think they'd been practising a special snap of the fingers at home that would now bring my favourite berries pelting down from the ceiling. When I was little, they used to have a whole repertory of magic tricks. They could get an egg to disappear in a glass of water. They tied a ring on a ribbon, with a double knot to make it extra secure, then, with a mysterious expression on their faces, they waved a black silk scarf over it three times, and *hey presto*! Right in front of my astonished eyes, the ribbon and the knot were parted. They could make lemonade change colour; their nimble fingers turned twenty cent pieces into euros for my piggy bank; and they always guessed which card I had picked from the pile they asked me to choose from. Nobody else in the world could do what they could do—nobody.

I must have been at least seven when, one afternoon, I discovered a box in Duco's desk drawer. On the cover was a picture of a black top hat with little gold stars dancing round it. My curiosity getting the better of me, I opened the box. Nestled in neat little cardboard compartments, I found an egg and a glass, a ribbon, a ring, a silk scarf, and all the rest, plus a booklet with illustrations that left nothing to the imagination.

With a ringing in my ears, I rammed the cover back on the box. Ludo and Duco weren't real magicians at all! They didn't have supernatural powers, they weren't all-powerful, they couldn't turn water into wine, they weren't above the law—Mr Klop's laws, the laws of cause and effect and of action and reaction, everything one long, irreversible chain reaction. They had gulled me and pulled my leg, they had … But then, another thought flashed through my mind. The magician's art was nothing to sneer at, actually. It was a genuine skill, and it didn't just fall into your lap. You had to practise and practise. If I was having such trouble with those stupid exercises in our *Safe Way Reader*, when reading was such a piece of cake for all the other kids at school, could you blame the Luducos for still being in the process of mastering something as complicated as magic? The three of us just weren't that quick on the uptake, that was all there was to it.

What this was, simply, was their practice box. Every night when I was upstairs asleep, they sat downstairs in the kitchen, testing each other on the vanishing egg or the knotted ribbon. Their goal was to become all-powerful magicians, to bend everything and everyone to their will. Once they'd mastered it, nothing bad could happen to us anymore. We'd be above the law—all laws.

Duco gazed at me across the table, smiling. 'Still, soon you'll be able to have all the strawberries you want.'

'Yes,' I said dreamily. The supermarkets in the Netherlands were chock-full of strawberries. I'd push my shopping cart along miles of alluring edibles instead of having to choose between two flaccid turnips in the cool box at the Timsgarry gas station, or having to make do with yet another distant offspring of Iain's original Savoy cabbage from our garden.

'And that,' said Ludo, 'brings us to your birthday present.'

'Just give it to her now. There's no need to sing happy birthday first.' Duco was beaming as if he were the one about to receive a gift. 'You'll never guess, Lucy, never.'

Lude extracted an envelope from his breast pocket and handed it to me without further ado.

Inside was a photo of row after row of strawberry plants. The plants I had tried for years to grow in the vegetable garden, but which had refused to thrive. Blame it on the lack of sunlight, but they seemed to attract every kind of mould, and had never made it far enough to bear fruit.

'A strawberry field,' Duco announced triumphantly. 'We bought you a strawberry field in the Westlands. On the Internet.'

Ludo took out another envelope. 'It's a parcel of land on an organic farm. Here, this is the deed.' He watched me breathlessly, as if he suddenly wasn't sure if the gift would be well received.

I was speechless.

Duco said, 'It wasn't easy to find, but we thought you'd like a piece of land rather than a greenhouse.'

My very own strawberry field. Only the Luducos— because you only turn eighteen once—could have thought of something like this. Something this absurd. Something this fantastic. Something this impractical. 'How does it work?' I asked, for lack of words that could even come close to expressing how excited I was. 'Am I supposed to ...'

'You don't have to look after it yourself. You can go there

and roll around in the strawberries every day if you like, naturally, but if you choose not to eat them all yourself, the profit from the harvest of this field is yours to keep. We've worked out that you can easily live off your land for several months of the year.'

'Strawberry fields forever,' said Duco. He laughed, pleased with his joke.

In a voice choking with emotion, I said, 'That was good thinking on your part.' Year after year, their gift would reach out to me like a pair of strong, safe arms—as long as there were people who liked to eat strawberries, anyway—and provide me with the safety net of a steady income.

'It will be a hard slog for you once you're studying, sweetheart,' said Ludo. 'Earning your keep on top of it isn't really doable. This is a much better solution.'

'I'm going to go there to have a look at it as soon as I arrive! I'll take the train there first chance I get. And when I get there, I'll give you a ring and I'll tell you how much I ...'

The girl in the apron nudged my arm because she wanted to clear my plate. She had strong body odour. 'Coffee?' she asked offhandedly, addressing nobody in particular.

'Just a minute, miss,' Duco said. Then he turned to me again. His voice softened. 'Yes, yes, you'll give us a ring and then you'll tell us how much you ...?' I could tell from his eyes that, for him, in some sad, tired way, this was the moment of truth. That he wanted to hear it once, just once, which really wasn't too much to ask—just one time in the life of an eighteen-year-old. This was our last chance.

I couldn't. I didn't say it. Even if it was true. Because that it was true was a given. It was as true as Lewis's incessant wind and the waitress's BO; as true as the walrus that had washed ashore recently and distressed everyone with the eerie, human sound of its desperate moaning; as true as the note my mother had left on the mantel—so true that you couldn't avoid it.

But I couldn't say it. It was totally out of the question. Otherwise we'd land in a minefield.

After dinner, we went to Angus's café next door. It turned out to be a dark, serious watering hole with soot-blackened walls. Lining the two longest walls were wooden benches that looked as if they were made of driftwood that had come washing up on some chilly day. The only decoration was a plastic plant on the zinc-topped bar. The attraction in there wasn't the atmosphere, evidently; chatting was something you could do on your own time. Three men in pea coats and caps were seated on one of the benches in deathly silence, systematically drinking themselves into a stupor. Their manner of lifting the glass to the mouth revealed a habit so ingrained, it had to have been inherited; they drank the way their fathers had drunk before them, and before them their fathers' fathers, and their fathers in turn, and so on, until you ended up at Adam, or thereabouts.

Lude and I installed ourselves on the empty bench while Duke went to order for us at the bar. I tried to sit in such a way that my cleavage remained decent. The air, saturated with malt and smoke, made my eyes sting, but that didn't prevent me from noticing I was being ogled from the other side with bleary interest. I started feeling even woozier than before. I thought, I'm probably tipsy.

Duke came back with the drinks. He'd bought three double whiskies. The first sip made me sneeze.

'You've got a long day ahead of you tomorrow,' said Ludo, 'so perhaps we ought to go a bit easy on the ...'

'Tomorrow! There you go again,' said Duco. 'When do we ever go out? We're finally out on the town, and you don't even know how to have fun.'

'I *am* having fun,' said Ludo indignantly.

They could bicker like a couple that's been married a hundred years, but it never amounted to much. I couldn't help laughing.

'Are you laughing at me?' asked Ludo. 'Making fun of me? Today of all days?'

'She turns eighteen only once. Let her laugh as much as she likes, is what I say.' Duke tossed his whisky back and got up to fetch another round.

'Dukie!' I called after him. When he looked round, I twirled my finger in the air. 'Buy the whole place a round on me, won't you?' I was stunned at how suavely I carried that off.

On the opposite side of the bar, the international sign language had been recognized. Under the brim of their caps, three pairs of eyes followed Duco to the bar. He returned with a bottle and some glasses.

'Celebratin'?' asked one of the men eagerly.

'A birthday girl.' Duke poured so generously that the whisky sloshed over the rims. His face was sweaty and his shirt collar was askew. He came and sat next to me and put his arm around my shoulders.

The threesome took their caps off their heads to toast me, exposing their weathered faces, gnarled as tree roots. Their toast was long and flowery, with lots of 'sláintes' and health, wealth, and happiness in it. It even made the plastic ivy gleam a little, and probably sent the pimply-faced kid behind the bar (possibly Angus's son) into a reverie, dreaming of whitewashed walls and a jukebox filled with love songs.

I wanted to stretch my arms out to all of them. I could have hugged the entire world, starting with these gnarled tree-root-men, in whom my youth and beauty seemed suddenly to have unleashed the gift of the gab, as if they'd been given a new lease on life. And why not? Wasn't it possible that now that I was a grown woman, I had something to give to humanity? Why not, for crying out loud? 'Do you want to see my birthday present?' I asked them magnanimously. I took the photos of my strawberry field out of my purse, shook Dukie's arm off me, and tottered over to the other side in my high heels.

Behind me, I heard Ludo say, 'Now you can see for yourself how happy she is with it.'

'Jesus,' said Duco, 'of course she's happy with it. We knew she would be, didn't we? That's why we did it!'

From up close, the tree-root-men reeked of seaweed and old cardboard. I didn't care; I didn't give a damn, actually, because everybody smelled of *something*, and yet they were still worth your time, even so—really, truly, everyone was. My tongue kept kind of folding over on itself as I gave them chapter and verse about the strawberry field.

'Well, well,' said the ruddiest one, baffled.

'Ye're no' kiddin',' said the tallest one, awed.

'And ye don't even have to look after it yesself?' asked the third one, almost in shock.

'No,' I said. I smiled at Lude and Duke over my shoulder.

'I say, guvs,' cried the third one, 'that's really no' bad!'

The Luducos modestly peered into their glasses. But I could tell that their eyes were shiny with gratification.

'Hey, guvs! Did ye have to make it up to her then, for sumthing? Did ye hae sumthing on year consc...' But that's as far as he got.

When, a minute or so later, we found ourselves outside again, sobered and shaken, it was still light out—gleaming with the unreal, yellowish summer night's haze of the Hebrides that you never got used to if you weren't born there. It wasn't really light; rather, there was an absence of darkness.

In silence, we walked to the bus stop in the deserted harbour. I sat down on the wall of the quay. I was shaking. Behind me the sea sloshed in and out, unhurried. It was a calming sound.

Ludo hung his head. He rubbed his bruised fist. He said, 'Sorry, Lucy.'

'It was the alcohol,' said Duco. 'Ludo can't drink.'

I looked away. But the picture that flashed through my mind wouldn't be banished so easily: Duco and Ludo holding their bloody hands under the kitchen tap, while outside the storm rattled at the windows.

'I just flew into a blind rage,' Ludo said unhappily. 'I don't know how it happened.'

'It can't be the first time they've seen fisticuffs in that bar over nothing,' Duco said quickly. 'By tomorrow, everyone's forgotten it. Don't make it into a bigger deal.' He brushed Ludo's cheek with the back of his hand.

I just wished the bus would come.

# U is for Uig

The next day, I got up early and left the house as quietly as I could. It was a brisk, fresh morning, with harsh sunlight. My hangover was gone the moment I set foot on the path. I hopped resolutely on my bike. With the wind in my back, I rode over to Callanish. I didn't come here very often these days, not since they'd put up a fence round the stones, paid for with European tourist money, and a hideous restaurant-and-information centre had arisen at the bottom of the hill. It was so early, luckily, that the large car park was still completely empty.

Leaning my bicycle against the fence, I gazed up at the giants of my childhood, my sneakers and trouser legs soaking up the dew. Saying goodbye to them had seemed the right thing to do, but now that we were eyeball to eyeball, I got that hollowed-out feeling that usually came over me whenever I thought about the child I once was. There was no point in looking back; my mother had definitely been right about that. All in all, there was only one childhood memory I was unreservedly proud of. And with that idle thought, I climbed back on my bike and, with the giants staring impassively at my receding back, headed straight for Uig.

When we had first came to live on the island, I'd been too young to appreciate the mesmerizing beauty of the Uig Sands: the grains of sand on the wide beach as white and fine as freshly milled flour, the indifferent sea a deep emerald green, the twisted rock formations sharply silhouetted against the sky. It had to be one of the most beautiful and widest beaches in all of Europe. Because it was so immense, one had the impression that there was more sky over Uig than anywhere else.

I cycled across the blooming machair; its honeyed fragrance cancelled out the seashore's salty aridity. I dismounted where the carpet of vegetation ended and the beach began. I took off my socks and shoes and rolled up my damp pant legs.

The sea was at low tide, so that the floor of the bay was nearly completely dry. The deserted stretch of sand was radiant; it seemed to be giving off light. It would have been a magnificent morning for crossing the seabed on foot, from one side of the bay to the other. The walk took a couple of hours and was never boring. Except that it was best not to attempt it unless you'd consulted the tide chart first.

I walked to the spot where our fort used to be. It had been swallowed by the elements some time ago. I sat down on the sand and reflected back on that summer, six years ago, when it had suddenly looked as if I was going to be designated the scapegoat by everyone under the age of sixteen—all over again.

After Gavin had suffered such a humiliating loss of face, all because of me, I had kept away for days. Sitting on the edge of my bed, I stared at the toes of my shoes. Filling those shoes were the feet of someone who was about to get the chop. Under my T-shirt, my heart was still beating—a bit erratically and worried stiff, but for how much longer?

They were all out to get me, and they weren't wusses. They smelled blood.

My mother and the Luducos were starting to give me funny looks, because my sudden interest in staying home roused their suspicion. All three of them tried to interrogate me whenever I returned from the loo or made myself a sandwich in the kitchen. 'Lucy, why are you hanging round the house, is something wrong?'

Sunday morning, cornered, I fled. It was a safe time to be out; my former mates were all in church with their parents. On Lewis, Sunday was truly holy. The island's numerous churches and their hard pews were always packed. So as not to give offence, even the tourists kept themselves out of the way—with a good book, or perhaps a day trip to a livelier spot in the archipelago, where at least the pubs were open at the usual hour. On the Sabbath, the entire island of Lewis was a wasteland.

The weather that morning was so nasty and grey that even the unbelievers (or unenlightened), few as they were, preferred to stay indoors. I didn't meet a soul on the way to Uig, and the beach, too, was completely empty. The tide was out.

I couldn't think of anything to do all by myself. I'd always been pretty good at finding ways to amuse myself, but over the past several weeks I had begun to rely on the companionship of other children again. In the end, I decided to go sit inside the fort. It was just as chilly in there as it was outside. I wrapped myself in a piece of fishing net to ward off the cold and finally, shivering, took the extreme measure of crawling inside the oil barrel in the corner. I began biting my nails. I couldn't stay in Lewis, I couldn't! Maybe I should simply disappear off the face of the earth. I was desperate. Why wasn't there anyone I could turn to for advice? Why wasn't there anyone to come to my aid?

And, as if for once God finally decided to hear my prayer, I suddenly heard voices outside.

'Do you think there's anyone in there today?'

'Not by the looks of it. Come on, let's go inside.'

'But they're always in there. Those wankers who think the whole beach belongs to them.'

'Here, here's the entrance.'

'Maybe they're all inside.'

'Don't worry, I'll go in first.'

'Or maybe the place is crawling with creepy insects. I bet it's pitch-dark in there.'

Dutch voices. I immediately knew who it was. My throat was parched with fear. I ducked down in my oil barrel, pulling the fishing net over my head.

There was the sound of knees scraping through sand. Then: 'Come on. It really isn't that creepy.'

'Can you see anything, then?' Vanessa called from outside. In Mr Turk's class, she'd been bragging for weeks about the great adventure they were going on in the summer hols, on some rugged Scottish island. But when it came right down to it, she wasn't very adventurous.

'Yes, I can. Come on, have a look, Vaness. It's all furnished in here.'

Her curiosity apparently got the better of her, and she crawled inside. 'Can't we stand up in here at all? What kind of shithole *is* this?'

Huddled inside my barrel, I died a thousand deaths. One of my legs started tingling, as if it would cramp up at any moment.

Vanessa screamed. 'What's that over there?'

'Where?'

'There, in the corner. There's something staring at us.'

'That? That's a jerrycan,' said Thomas. He crawled over to it and unscrewed the cap. 'Petrol. For arson, I'll bet.'

There was a brief silence. Then Vanessa said, 'Do you have a lighter on you?'

'Sure, here. But if you're gonna smoke, you'd better stay away from that petrol.'

The raspy click of a lighter. She chuckled softly. 'It works. Hey, let's set fire to the joint, shall we?'

'Come on, that's a shitty thing to do, Vaness.'

'So? Then they shouldn't have been so shitty to us. My mum says they should be grateful for every tourist that comes here. Why should we let a bunch of lowlifes chase us off the beach?'

I could just picture what had happened. Verity and Struan, the new leaders, had run the foreigners off the beach. I broke out in a sweat.

'They'll just build another one,' said Vanessa. 'Those shitheads deserve to be taught a lesson, that's all. Tell me I'm wrong.'

Thomas was silent. He'd always been good at keeping quiet, in this kind of situation.

'We're going home tomorrow,' she said. 'It's now or never.'

'Let's have a look round first and see if they've left anything of value lying around.'

'You want to steal their stuff?'

'No, I just want to take it outside, to save it,' he explained.

'Jesus, you wimp. Come on, give me the petrol. I'll have to do it myself, as usual.'

I heard her shaking Gavin's jerrycan around. The petrol sloshed against the tin walls. From the dull sound it made, you could tell it was full. Then I heard the glug-glug of liquid pouring out. There was a strong smell of fuel.

'Out of my way,' she said brusquely, 'let me get to that barrel in the back, there.' The next thing I knew, my hair was dripping with petrol. I had no time to think. I shot up out of the barrel, instinctively trying to spread my arms, but the fishing net hampered my movements. I think I screamed. But I'm not sure I did. Memories aren't always a hundred per cent reliable. In a life-or-death situation there isn't usually time for thoughtful, in-depth analysis.

For a moment, it felt as if I were hurtling back in time, and Thomas and I were thrashing about in a ditch by a new housing estate, like two leaping trout ... Did he ever think about that time, I wondered? Did he remember the rat? Or the ark?

Vanessa started screeching. She dropped the jerrycan.

I didn't know what set her off—the terrifying sight I must have presented at that moment: a squirming creature from the deep, tangled in a fishing net—or the fact that she recognized me. Did she think I was one of the ghosts that were widely believed to haunt these islands, or had she seen at once that it was her former BFF and Thomas's ex-fiancée who'd suddenly leaped up out of nowhere? Ah well, in either case it must have been a terrifying apparition.

They were already long gone by the time I had the chance to recover from my own fright. I clambered out of the barrel, coughing and choking. I tore the net off my head and shook my sopping-wet hair. It was exactly what Mrs Iedema—and everyone else, in fact, who'd ever come into contact with me—wished: that they'd see me burn, burn, burn in hell.

The air inside the fort was unbreathable, but it took me a while to work up the nerve to crawl outside. I convinced myself, in the end, that whatever awaited me outside couldn't possibly be any worse than the fate I had just narrowly escaped.

When I got outside, I saw the two of them racing off across the drying sand. Two tiny figures on the wide expanse of the flats, no longer frightening at all.

I flopped down in the sand. I suddenly got the giggles, from sheer nerves. I laughed because I was still alive, and every gulp of fresh air made me laugh even harder, even wilder and more frantically, because from the colour of the sand I could tell that the tide was about to come in, so that the flats would be at their most treacherous. It would soon start slowing Thomas and Vanessa down as they ran. Every step would take more and more effort.

Unbeknownst to them, the sea was already seeping into the outer channels of the bay. It always did that part in leisurely fashion, taking its time. But this wasn't some safe beach at home in Holland. The shape of the bay, as well as the preponderance of salt marshes and lochs, meant that here the water didn't sweep in gently, from one direction only. Sooner or later the sea ran out of patience and felt the need show its true face. Then it would come thundering in at such a clip that it had given rise to countless tragic ballads. High tide at Uig wasn't merely a flood, it was a deluge. Even Iain himself, deemed by all to be the expert on the subject of silt and mud, admitted that he had once stared death in the face out here.

The grey sky that had kept the tourists indoors this morning hung low over the beach, which was now rapidly filling with water. It could start to rain at any moment. In church they'd have to raise their voices as they sang their hymns in order to hear themselves over the loud din of the heavenly waters. I jumped to my feet and stretched my arms toward the sea, the sea that for the moment still looked like an innocent, insignificant line on the horizon. 'Hurry!' I whispered to the tide, breathlessly. 'Come on, come in quickly!'

Were they already starting to trip and stumble, those two out there? Were they sinking ankle-deep in the soft sand? And had it started to dawn on them yet? The realization that their time would soon be over?

Knowing that there's no way out anymore is almost more unbearable than the inevitable outcome itself. I had always found that to be true, anyway. All the teasing and tormenting had been nothing compared with the harsh, relentless certainty that there was more of it to come, day in, day out. For no matter what I'd tried to do, no matter how I'd reacted, no matter how much I'd squirmed, there had been no escaping it. I had been like an egg, defenceless against the approaching rim of the frying pan. Or like some impotent maggot, unable to wriggle out of reach of the pecking beaks. Or like a big fat turd that has no choice but to be expelled from someone's anus.

Tripping over my own two feet in my haste, I raced back to the fort to get the binoculars. It still stank to high heaven in there. The open jerrycan lay on its side next to the oil barrel, leaking its last drops into the sand. And suddenly I was floored by the sickening thought that I— yes, naturally, I—would be blamed for this. After all, I was the only other kid on the island who wasn't in church. And even if I had been in church, in the first row, in plain sight, they would *still* find a way to blame me. It made no difference, once they'd decided you were the one that was gonna get it! 'Och now, look here,' they would piously exclaim this afternoon. 'Someone was here! Our Luce, wantin' to let us know we'd best no' try anything with her! Shame she didna have matches on her. Aye, well, there's weans for you; her ma won't let her play with fire.'

I nearly choked on the thought that here was yet another problem for which I had Thomas and Vanessa to thank. I couldn't breathe right, and I felt tears spurting from my eyes, actually spurting. Sobbing, I dragged myself back outside.

They were now just two little dots out there on a flat, shimmering mirror.

The tide that I hadn't been able to turn, back home, had now turned for me. Only it was a real tide, this time.

Starting to feel frantic, I stood in the lee of the fort, shading my eyes with one shaking arm and holding the field glasses up to my eyes with the other.

As in a hazy TV picture, Vanessa's blond hair and Thomas's big round head came wavering into view. Pff, what a loyal friend *she* had proved to be, and he, what a faithful fiancé! I focused the binoculars. Now I could see their faces. They were looking round, panicked, scouring the beach for a dry stretch of sand. Their eyes were bulging. They galloped from here to there, desperate, pleading. That's what I must have looked like to them so many times, for six long years. Like a cornered rat caught in a trap.

You'd better believe I felt for them. I knew exactly what they were going through. What it was like to be sold down the river. To be impotent, helpless, and lost from the word go, and yet still hoping against hope that you'd be rescued.

Thomas took off his jacket with jerky movements and began waving it over his head. Through the binoculars I saw his mouth open and close, shouting for help. The sound was drowned out by the roar of the wind and the constant screeching of the gulls. How deserted the beach must look to him.

The channel that always filled up first was already full of water. It was so wide across that it was practically a lake. On fine days we used to go swimming in it.

What else could they do now except what I'd always been forced to do too: accept the inevitable? At least they didn't have a whole lot of eyes leering at them; at least *they* were spared the torment of ridicule. There was nobody egging anybody on, no jeering and yelling to give it to them good, harder, longer, nastier. There was no circle of viciously hooting and cheering onlookers, betting on their chances of survival. No one had ambushed them and forced them into this tight spot. They couldn't blame it on anything or anyone except themselves.

And suddenly the field glasses almost fell out of my hands. Because—could I, for that matter? Could I have blamed anybody else? Could I, really? True, I could never have run home and told anyone about the bullying. Ludo and Duco would immediately have wanted to go to bat for me. If they'd ever had the chance … I shuddered. But surely I could have made up a story, or found some way to draw attention to my plight? I could simply have attracted notice by screaming bloody murder as soon as the others started ganging up on me, instead of always gritting my teeth and bearing it. I could have burst into tears, or gone into hysterics. I could have shown the school nurse my bruises. I could have ratted on my classmates to the teacher, or come up with some clever ruse that would have exposed what they were doing.

I could have done all kinds of things. And I had done nothing. Nothing at all. Because all that time I had known, deep inside, that I deserved every beating, every bit of it and more, because I was bad—so bad that sometimes it made my heart sink right down into my shoes; how could the score ever be settled any other way than by continual punishment and humiliation?

Bewildered, I stared at the two dots out on the mudflats that were my ex-fiancé and my former best friend. I had *allowed* them to terrorize me—them and all the others. I had brought it all on myself. Because if I hadn't, I'd without a doubt have wound up burning, burning, burning, in hell.

I dropped the binoculars in the sand. The burden of being a thoroughly bad person was suddenly so intolerable that I was close to tears again.

The sea, meanwhile, was in so close that I could hear it roar.

Blindly, I started running. If only I could perform one good deed, just once, if only I knew how to do it! Something selfless, something kind and forgiving, something noble, something honest and true! It could never make up for the other thing, but at least it might make me feel less like a rotten apple. But I didn't have the time to sit and think it over right now. It was time for action.

I splashed into the channel, sprinting toward the mudflats. The current was already so strong that my legs were almost immediately yanked out from under me. I fell forward in the water, and instinctively started thrashing my arms and legs. My clothes and shoes were slowing me down. It seemed to take ages to reach the first sandbank. Or was it was taking so long because the sandbank was already underwater?

Whimpering, I flipped myself over on my back and swam to dry land, doing the backstroke. Nothing, nothing I did was ever right! Idiot—I should have run for help straight away. I should have raced to the telephone booth down the road, next to Uig's postboxes, all tethered down with rope against the wind. Maybe I'd even have met the postman on the way.

But it was Sunday! The postman was in church! Everyone was in church.

Everyone, except Iain.

When, soaked to the skin and bawling my head off, I'd crossed the machair and finally reached the dirt road, he was just riding up on his bicycle. He didn't see me at first—he was too busy thinking about my mother, of course. Worse, he'd probably sneaked out of church for a secret assignation. Rowan was still seated in her pew on the right side of the aisle, praising God with all her heart, but on the left, where the men sat, her husband's seat was empty.

'Iain! There are two kids out on the flats!' I screamed. 'Iain! Iain! There are kids on the flats and the tide's coming in! Help, Iain, help!'

# V is for Voyage

Ludo and Duco did their best to hide it, but when I finally returned to the house, I could tell they were disappointed I hadn't spent my last morning with them, hugging my knees by the Aga, leafing through old photo albums. 'I wanted to say goodbye to some of my favourite haunts,' I explained. It was the truth, but it did come out sounding as if the island were more important to me than the two of them, and I was ashamed of how tactless that sounded.

'Oh, there are things one would rather do by oneself, naturally,' said Ludo, immediately mollified. He had a fond look on his face, as if he longed to pinch my cheek as though I were still a little girl.

We didn't even have time to sit down together for a sandwich because the taxi was already at the door. My suitcase and rucksack were waiting in the hall.

'Don't you need to pee?' asked Duco.

'Wait,' said Ludo. 'Do you have everything? Your toiletries, too?'

'You do have your passport on you, don't you? And the tickets? For the ferry? The bus? Airplane? Remember, keep them with you at all times, in your carry-on.'

'And don't forget to check if you're getting on the right bus. It happened to me once, I ...'

'Remember to choose a front-facing seat. It makes a huge difference.'

'Oh, true. You see so much better that way.'

'That, too, but if she's facing front, she won't get carsick either. By the way, Lucy, do you have enough cash on you? For emergencies?'

'Emergencies! What could possibly go wrong?'

I said, 'Pumpkins, I'm going to miss the boat if we don't leave now.'

'Pumpkins!' said Ludo. He loved pet names.

With a face all flushed with agitation, Duco picked up my suitcase. 'But have you had a pee yet?'

'Where's that bag I prepared?' asked Ludo, looking around. 'With your sandwiches, for the trip? And an apple.'

'You didn't give her one of those hard green ones, did you?' Duco asked. Outside, the taxi honked.

'Naturally,' said Ludo, 'a green one, hard as a rock.'

'So, shall we get going, then?' I suggested.

Duco put the bag down again. 'We're not going to let ourselves be rushed. We don't want to have to come back because we've forgotten something, do we.'

'We've had three dress rehearsals!' I said. The peaty smell of the house, acrid and musty at once, assaulted my nose for the final time. I took one last look at the Swiss-cheese skirting boards and the shabby curtains we never bothered to replace.

'But that was different,' said Ludo. 'Really, pumpkin.'

'Yes, he's right,' said Duco. 'This time it's for real, love. That's the difference.'

On our way to Stornoway Harbour, I did my best to think appropriate, nostalgic thoughts. But my excitement got the upper hand every time. I was going on a voyage. I was going on a voyage all by myself; I was on my way to my own destiny. I was going to begin studying for my Early Childhood Care diploma, and once I had it in the bag, I'd be qualified for any child-care job you might think of. I could work in a day-care centre, or a nursery, or even a school for children with special needs. There weren't all that many subjects I was good at—I always seemed to bungle and fumble my way through—but this was the one area where I excelled. With little kids, it was your hands and your heart that counted; your head didn't come into it that much. I thought about the babies being born in Amsterdam this very day. They didn't even know I existed yet, but I was going to be the one taking care of them. I might even be looking after those very babies a few weeks from now, if they happened to be in the nursery where I was to do my internship. I would spoon-feed them fruit yoghurt and wipe their little noses and teach them how to make squishy monsters with playdough. And if I had to read to them— well then I'd just practise it beforehand. Or I'd read them *Clara 13*; I knew that one by heart.

'We did pack *Clara 13*, didn't we?' I cried.

To my left, Duco, who'd been staring morosely out the window, whipped his head round. 'See, there you go! I *told* you ...'

'We packed it in her suitcase ourselves, Duke,' said Ludo, on my right. 'Man, that book! Your mother definitely hit it on the nose with that one.'

'You can say *that* again,' said Duco.

They both had this casual way of bringing my mother into the conversation every so often. Not too often, but enough to make it clear they didn't harbour any ill will toward her.

I had been the one to find the note. I didn't have to open

it to know what it said. A note you found at seven a.m. on the mantel of a silent, dark room—it was only too obvious what it would say. I'd slipped out of the house, and hadn't returned until I was sure Ludo and Duco had had a chance to read it.

Later that day, we had taken the car to Stornoway. Feeling rather numb, we'd had an ice cream and then hung out on the boardwalk, watching the CalMac boat steaming into the harbour, empty. That evening, we took the trusty can opener out of the drawer again. We were all very quiet. In my room, before going to bed, I took down the drawing my mother had made for me almost a year before, when we had just arrived in Lewis, of a girl with a kite on a beach covered in pink and blue shells. I wasn't really sure *what* I was feeling, besides an immense sense of relief—at least I'd never have to hear her say she had sacrificed herself for me again.

The Luducos didn't seem to be mourning her departure too deeply, either. My mother had had this constant need to talk. Maybe it was because she'd had to keep her mouth zipped for so long in the klink, but still, she should have been the first to realize that in every family there were things that were better left unsaid. She'd been starting to make more and more open insinuations. She'd grown meaner and meaner when she'd seen there was no response forthcoming. When it had been she, herself, who'd once given her word that we would never, ever, mention it again! That promise no longer counted, apparently. 'The silence is suffocating me,' she'd snapped one evening. I'd found the note a few days later.

'Nearly there,' said Duco, next to me in the back seat. 'Right on time.'

'Unless all the lights are red,' said Lude. 'We can still get stuck in traffic.'

I kicked him. 'That almost sounds as if you're hoping for it to happen.'

'Of course not, Lucy. You just be on your way.'

The taxi rounded the last corner. We drove up to the waterfront.

It was the height of the tourist season; the ferry wharf was swarming with people. Campers, trailers, bicycles everywhere. A long line of cars was inching its way onto the red CalMac ferry. And Gavin, Iola, and the rest of the gang were standing by the ramp, waving a huge red-white-and-blue flag.

'They're all here!' I yelled, chuffed. I jumped out even before the taxi had come to a complete stop.

Iola was the first to see me. She yanked herself free of Gavin's hand and raced up to me. I crouched down with outstretched arms, caught her, and whirled her into the air, which smelled of tar and salt. When Iola thought about me, later, she'd have only good memories of me. Not too many people in the world could say the same. I lowered her reverentially onto the quay's cobblestones and then walked over to the others, beaming from ear to ear.

'You're late,' said Gavin. 'We've been standing here like eejits for a good half-hour.'

'I was gettin' worried that ye might not be goin' after all and be crampin' my style here foraye,' said Verity.

Fiona, whose blue Mohawk had turned her into the most dangerous-looking girl on Lewis and Harris combined, gave her a perfunctory kick in the shins. Then, minding her manners, she politely greeted the Luducos with, 'Hiya, guvs.'

'Well, now,' said Ludo, crestfallen, 'How very nice of you lot, to come and say goodbye *again*.'

'Boat's leaving shortly,' said Struan, generously waving a half-empty whisky bottle under his nose.

Ludo shook his head. 'I still have a hangover from the rotgut you brought us a few days ago.'

'When Lucy and me danced!' Iola crowed.

'Och well, still and always with the Noddy gang, are you no'?' Verity said to me. She pushed a rolled-up magazine into my hands. 'Here's the latest *Playboy*, loser, to read on your voyage. Maybe you'll learn something.'

'Verity,' Fiona explained to the Luducos, 'is a fuckin' cunt. And she kin stick that up her ugly bony bum.'

The ship's foghorn gave a loud, plaintive toot. The smoke-stack started spewing black smoke too. Men in hard hats appeared on deck. They were getting ready to cast off.

'Your ticket!' said Duco. He was almost in tears. 'You do have your ticket, don't you?'

I zipped open my rucksack's side pocket. 'Here.'

'No, that's not it, that isn't your ferry ticket. Ludo, which is it?'

Ludo fumbled for his glasses.

'Give it,' said Gavin. 'Well, guvs, that's indeed a one-way CalMac ticket.' He thrust the ticket into my hand and pulled me close. 'Bye, lassie,' he said in my ear.

Gavin. Thanks to him I was still a virgin. He had instilled in me a sense of decency that could have taught my own mother a thing or two. 'Hey, you soppy old thing,' I said, 'we'll see each other again next summer, you know.' Next summer he would be married—to Verity. The wedding was to be held just as soon as the peat was in.

He hitched Iola up on his arm. 'Come on, silly crybabby, give Lucy a big kiss!'

'We'll text each other, won't we, Iola!' I said. Gavin had promised that, once a week, he'd hide one of the pile of silly notes I'd written to her in the stone at Callanish.

'Maybe Fiona needs a hug too,' Struan jeered. 'The only way *she'll* ever get lucky, the ugly bag!' He pushed her into my arms.

'Bye, Fi,' I said. 'I'm coming back every summer, and I'll bring you the latest hair colour, all right?'

'Sure, then,' she said gruffly.

The ship's horn gave another blast.

'Okay, kiddos, so long!' I cried. I grabbed my bags and dragged them up the gangway. A man in a fluorescent jacket walked up to me and asked for my ticket. 'Just in the nick o' time,' he said. 'We're about to cast off.' He wasn't from the island; he came from the mainland, I could tell from his accent. And suddenly I realized I was leaving home, and for an instant everything went eerily quiet inside my head. Right as I was about to disappear into the belly of the ship, I turned round.

There they stood, squabbling over who would hold the flag. Lachlan was just giving Stru a shove. It was always a good crack, if you managed to push someone over the side.

Had I said goodbye to everyone? I had the feeling I'd forgotten someone. But perhaps that was because Iain, the hero who'd saved two drowning children, was missing from the group that had come to wave me off so enthusiastically. He was probably at work, the endless work of the croft: shearing a sheep, repairing a fence, hoeing his rows of cabbages, feeding the chickens, building a brick wall. He had never made a secret of the fact that I'd been the one who'd raised the alarm that Sunday morning in Uig. If it hadn't been for me, he had told every islander willing to listen, there would no' have been a happy ending, there'd have been two drownings on the flats that day. He never seemed to get enough of describing in his sing-song voice how I'd suddenly popped up out of nowhere in front of his bike on the machair, sopping wet and all, 'because she'd tried diving into the waves after 'em herself, the puur wee lass.'

My standing had shot up into the stratosphere, because

on Lewis, nothing was more valued than a gallant trial of strength against the elements. The fact that I was only twelve had enhanced the heroic nature of the exploit. Only twelve, and already as plucky as they come! Everyone ought to follow her example! I even received a card from the Tourist Information Office in Stornoway, with a real postage stamp, and the date stamped on it as well. Duco, bursting with pride, had bought a frame for it, to display it on my night stand.

Verity and Struan had tried to get me in trouble by accusing me of trying to burn down the fort. But Gavin had snatched the empty tin out of their hands. He'd sped with it over to Timsgarry, and returned with a full jerrycan. 'Here,' he'd said, handing it over to me as the others stood by. I didn't know what I was supposed to do with it. Shyly I just carried it over to its usual place in our fort and left it there. Apparently that was the right thing to do, because they all started cheering. As a sign of affection, little Fi murdered at least six jellyfish for me that afternoon.

Verity and Stru didn't have a leg to stand on anymore. As quickly and casually as it had been done to me, the others turned their backs on them.

Being shunned didn't seem to bother them that much. And why should it? A few weeks later the loyalties had shifted again, and it was Lachlan who had to run for his life—I don't even remember why, anymore. Lach didn't fret over it long, either; every morning we'd find a fresh skull and crossbones carved into the wet sand with his father's knife in front of our fort, signed with his name. Everyone agreed that was pretty wicked.

If you fell from grace, it wasn't the end of the world. Even if you were the underdog for a while, sooner or later you'd find yourself on top of the heap again. Alliances were forged and shattered, more often for practical than for personal reasons; usually it was the luck of the draw. They'd have it in for you from time to time, sure, but it was never because you had 'evil' stamped on your forehead.

It was a discovery that turned my world around and made the sun come out. A sun that kept shining, no matter what. Over the next six years there must have been plenty of drama in my life besides my mother's departure, of course, but those other events didn't really stand out, on the whole, in the warm, comforting light in which I now basked. At my new school, I must have done poorly on any number of tests, and then lain awake at night, hoping and praying I'd pull through by the skin of my teeth. I must have given my all to win, and more frequently lose, innumerable games. I must have got all hot under the collar about this or that. I must have ridden on the back of Gavin's moped, and later hitched rides with boys in my class. I must have had occasion to stand in despair in front of the mirror, before a party. I must have had good reason to be either seriously fed up or ecstatically happy. I must have taken great care over picking out one tie after another for the Luducos. I must have done all that, and much, much more ... but in reality, my life was as calm and unruffled as Loch Roag on an unusually windless night. I finally felt I was standing on firm ground. Even the taboos and penances that had held me so long in their iron grip seemed to have lost the incentive to stretch their tentacles out at me. Ever since that Sunday morning on the beach at Uig, they'd simply vanished, never to reappear; time was no longer broken up into phases during which I wasn't permitted to do such or such, on pain of death. I didn't quite get it. Was I really free, then, from here on? I fervently wanted to believe it—and I did just that. It was as if I'd closed my eyes to breathe a deep sigh of relief, and when I opened them again, six years had flown by.

It almost felt as though the few seconds I'd been standing on the ferry ramp had lasted longer than my entire stay here on the island. I gazed for the last time at the familiar outline of the harbour, and at my friends waving on the dock. I was leaving everything and everyone behind, with *Clara 13* in my suitcase and a photo of a strawberry field in the pocket of my windbreaker.

'I'll be back in just a sec,' I breathed at the CalMac man who was securing my luggage in the rack. I darted down the ramp. The steel plates clanged under my feet, and under them the sea lapped its grimy spume against the dock.

'Lucy! Lucy!' Iola screamed.

But it wasn't her I was looking for. I pushed aside a couple of tourists and raced as fast as I could over to the Luducos. They were standing by one of the giant bollards the ship was anchored to, looking a bit dazed. Ludo had the bag with the sandwiches clutched to his chest. Duco prodded him with his elbow and pointed at me. Relief spread over both their faces. They started toward me on their stiff legs.

'Lucy, Lucy,' said Ludo, 'you nearly left without your lunch.'

'What *would* you do without us,' said Duco, shaking his head. 'You're going to miss us, do you know that?'

'No, she won't, she won't have the time.' Ludo held out the bag to me.

'He's put one of those delicious apples in there for you, too,' said Duco.

Now I had to give them each a couple of punches to the shoulder by way of farewell, skipping round them, laughing. We'd practised it, at home, for three whole evenings.

'Are you comin' or are you no', miss?' cried the CalMac man from the top of the gangway.

When Lude and Duke returned to the empty house, they

would open up a can of soup and set two dishes on the table. While sipping their soup, they'd listen to the radio. There wouldn't be anyone around impatiently waiting for them to turn water into wine, or in some other way demonstrate their supernatural abilities. They might talk about me a bit, but they'd keep it rather light and tentative, so that the other one could change the subject if he wanted. And maybe they'd think about how it had all begun.

How had something that absurd, really, ever happened in the first place? At the time, they had already been together for so long that they'd thought they could read each other like an open book. Yet neither of them had had the guts to confess to the other that he might be falling in love with the dark-haired woman seated at her easel below the dike every morning, staring at the cows. There had been something so cheerful and engaging about the way she greeted every passer-by. About the way she always seemed to have time for a little chat. About the way she sounded so *interested* when she asked you a question. 'Really? Are you serious? Do tell!'

Both of them, bewildered, had said nothing about how strange and astounding it all was, turning their whole world inside out and upside down, so to speak. It was a phase that would pass by itself, surely. You didn't have to share every little thought with your partner. Especially not if it was likely to cause the other needless worry. Until, on the night that went down in history as the Night of the Spaghetti Sauce, they had caught each other out—arriving on her doorstep at the same time. My mother had been in the kitchen, cooking; she'd decided they should have supper early because she wanted to take advantage of the evening light, later.

Whenever they recounted this story the Luducos' mild faces would light up. Now that it was all behind them, they could look back fondly on that chapter in their lives, which was all that my mother was to them now. And, thanks to that chapter, they had me, they'd sometimes shyly say, turning red.

On the gangway, the CalMac man cried again, 'Miss! On board, now!'

Lude, Duke, and I stared at each other. It was as if a magic circle had been drawn around us. None of us was able to move.

But suddenly Duco was clutching me by the wrist. In a rush, he said, 'You haven't always seen us in the best light. We can only hope that ...'

Ludo said, 'As long as you know we always ...' He sent Duco a helpless glance.

'Oh, of course I do!' I exclaimed. There was no one in the whole wide world that I loved as much as I loved the two of them. I flung my arms so passionately about both their necks that their noses bumped. I pressed my wet face against theirs. 'Bye, Dad,' I said. 'Bye, Daddy. Thanks for everything.'

# W is for World

It was late afternoon by the time I arrived at Ullapool, on the mainland. The boat was late, and I had to rush. Fortunately, the bus depot was close to the harbour. There was just one bus waiting there, clearly identified by a large number on the front. Still, as I got on, I asked the driver if this bus was going to Inverness, then installed myself contentedly in a front-facing seat.

It was a long trip through a stark moonscape. The grey, barren hills rolled monotonously past. There weren't even any sheep grazing on the rocky slopes. Every bend in the road revealed yet another exact duplicate of the same boring view. Yet another endless glen. Yet another narrow pass choked with grit and dust whipped up into spirals by the wind. My elation gradually trickled away. Was this the world, then? Was this what, on Lewis, we used to talk about longingly—especially in winter, when the island seemed even smaller than usual, and the sea bashed against every shore, giving you the sense you were riding on the back of a small whale that might at any moment decide to dive under?

On the other hand, perhaps it was the sea I was missing.

For six long years, with every intake of breath, I had smelled the sea, I had tasted it, I had heard it, and I had seen it. Now, with those familiar sensations missing, it was as if all my senses had been corked. I felt just like the Tarot deck's poor, blindfolded Two of Swords, sitting with her back to the sea. Even when I was small, I'd pitied her; so close to the sea, and yet unable to look at it. 'Well, she's free to turn round, you know,' my mother would say impatiently, 'and she's free to take off her blindfold as well. Take a good look: her hands aren't tied, see? If she chooses to keep sitting that way, well, that's completely up to her. If you're dealt this card, it means you've turned your back on the unconscious, and can't be bothered to do anything about it. But you'll live to regret it.'

My mother and her explanations.

Inverness Airport was busy and noisy. In the departure hall, I found myself staring blankly at the other travellers, all of them families on holiday. Very ordinary families, each consisting of two adults and a couple of kids. It must be nice to grow up as part of such a conventional unit. What a lovely family, people would think when they saw you; or, better yet, they probably wouldn't think anything of it at all. Strangers would never give you funny looks.

It was still light out when the airplane lifted off. I saw Inverness disappear below me. That narrow glittering band over there must be Loch Ness. The airplane heeled over to the south-east. Not a chance of catching a last glimpse of Lewis, somewhere out there in the deep blue of the Atlantic Ocean, the only spot in this entire country that I actually knew outside of my geography books. I had to hang onto the armrest for dear life; that's how immense the world seemed, all of a sudden. People living everywhere. Billions of people, all with their own needs, hopes, and aspirations. All of them hoping to make it from cradle to grave without too many mishaps, while along the way dreaming their dreams, overcoming their fears, readjusting their goals, and getting in one another's way.

A flight attendant came by with a meal. An omelette and a warm roll on the side. It looked quite tasty. But after the first bite, I realized I wasn't the least bit hungry.

The Netherlands was a sea of flashing lights in the black of night. Or rather, it looked like a piece of dog-eared cardboard someone had pricked full of holes, hoping against hope for a fairylike effect when propped up against a lamp. Even from way up high, the staggering flatness of the land was impossible to miss.

Fifteen minutes later, I was trailing down Schiphol's endless corridors, feeling rather dazed. I heard Dutch spoken all around me, and the signs had writing with strange letter-combinations—*eu*, *ij*, and *au*. I'd forgotten what those diphthongs looked like in black on white. I caught myself mouthing the words, trying to pronounce them. The letters of the alphabet, which had never been my friends, were already ganging up on me, as a warning that this wasn't going to be a picnic.

At customs, I took my passport out of my knapsack and held my breath. With a few short, dry clicks of the keys, my name was entered into the computer. I tried with all my might to make my mind go blank so I wouldn't give off any vibes that might be construed as suspicious, but even before I'd done so, my passport was shoved back at me across the counter.

How fast it all suddenly seemed to go! My suitcase was already chugging around the baggage carousel. To buy myself some time, I went to the loo. I washed my hands meticulously and ran a pre-moistened towelette over my face. I stared into the mirror. Had I changed? Would someone who hadn't seen me in years still be able to recognize me? You'll be totally anonymous in the big city, the Luducos had assured me. But that didn't mean I might not bump into someone from my former life; the academic year was about to start, and surely I wasn't the only eighteen-year-old who was moving to Amsterdam this week.

I collected my belongings and went outside.

Warm air hit me in the face as I went through the revolving door. It was almost midnight, but the area in front of the airport was still teeming with life. Taxis, buses, and cars drove up and down. Travellers were being picked up and dropped off, most of them half-naked, in shorts and loose tank tops. I was suffocating in my heavy windbreaker, but I couldn't take it off because I had my hands full.

Just take a taxi, Ludo and Duco had advised me. They'd given me some euros in an envelope, with the address of my lodgings written on the front. Huffing and puffing, I lugged my suitcase and knapsack to the taxi rank. I thought I'd better take the first one in line; that was probably what you were supposed to do. But suddenly, as I bent down to speak into the driver's window, my heart started racing and an indescribable panic took hold of me. For a fleeting moment, I didn't know who I was. There was just one thing I was sure of: I definitely didn't belong here, amid all these people dressed for summer and the busy traffic and the dazzling neon hoardings. Then I got hold of myself again. I was dressed far too warmly, and was suffering a bit of culture shock—that's all it was.

The landlord was all flesh, a colossal mountain of a man. He was practically popping out of his shirt. Gold glinted in his chest hair, and in his ears, too. He'd waited up specially for me, he said. He picked up my luggage as if it didn't weigh a thing and had me follow him up the scruffy stairs. As we climbed, I started having serious misgivings about the actual existence of the polished wooden floors, the sunny corner window and the lofty ceiling with authentic old beams that we had seen on the website. The Luducos had been over the moon about their find. This was a room, they declared, that immediately made you think of birds chirping in the gutters, of a cosy bakery around the corner, of the happy sound of children playing in the street.

Upstairs, the landlord inserted a key in the lock and opened the door. 'It sticks a little,' he said apologetically, 'and the stairwell has seen better days, but once inside, you'll see, you'll soon forget all about that.' He switched on the light.

I tried to take it all in at once. The pale-blue window frames, the flowery sofa with just the right kind of flowers, the pendant lamp over the pine table, the odd-looking bookcase that had probably come from the Waterlooplein flea market. There was an alcove with a kitchenette, and the balcony boasted a potted honeysuckle in bloom.

'That over there was delivered for you today,' said the man, nodding at a parcel lying on the table, next to the snazzy cordless phone. Golly—where I was from, we had to place calls through the switchboard until just recently. I already saw myself sitting on the balcony with the phone to my ear and a drink in my hand.

In a haze, I heard him explaining how the cooker, the water heater, the microwave, the TV, and the central heating worked. I barely heard him, I was so happy; I just kept nodding. I accepted the keys from him, one for the front door and one for my own door. The doorbell: if it rang three times, it was for me. The letterbox: mine was the top one. And if there was anything else over the next few days, I shouldn't hesitate to come and ask this friendly ton of flesh.

Then he wished me a good night.

All I had to do was hang up my clothes in the cupboard, and I could start living here. Soon people who liked me would ring the doorbell three times, or call me on the phone. The postman would stuff thick envelopes through the slot for me. I looked at the package on the table. I weighed it in my hands. It was heavy. Hastily, I tore the paper off. A wooden box, and inside it, a bottle of champagne and one crystal glass, carefully wrapped in tissue paper. I could just see Duco and Ludo, side by side on the pavement in Stornoway, peering in the shop windows— Lude with the tartan shopping bag he always carried on his arm, Duke with the belt of his trench coat dragging in the puddles. Oh, but they'd probably just phoned an off-license in Amsterdam; the card wasn't in their handwriting. 'To your new life! xxx, L & D.'

When I had only just begun my struggle with the Word, Ludo had said to me one night, 'I'll teach you a little trick, ducks. Miss Joyce will be so impressed with you. Look, this is how you write "kiss."' And he'd drawn a big x on a sheet of paper.

I'd been jubilant. 'Miss, miss! I know how to write "kiss"!'

'That should come in handy', she'd said. 'And how about "miss," do you know how to write that as well? Or "boss"?'

Thomas had been the only one who'd been suitably impressed. He'd said …

Abruptly, I turned round. I walked into the kitchen and gazed at the dishes in the cupboards, at the drying rack hanging over the sink. I'd managed to avoid thinking of Thomas for years, and I certainly wasn't about to start now, on my first day back in Holland. I returned to the living room and picked up the bottle of champagne. I would put it in the fridge; I'd save it for when my new girlfriends from Early Childhood Care III and I had something to celebrate, someday soon. At college I was going to come clean about my dyslexia right from the start. I'd show myself to be both strong and vulnerable at the same time. And if I should ever bump into Thomas in town, I'd calmly inform him that he owed me; he owed me big. I had, for all intents and purposes, saved his life, as well as Vanessa's, that Sunday morning in Uig. Though it had been quite right for Iain to have the accolades, as well as the big fat check from Vanessa's mother that he'd received in the post. I couldn't blame Thomas for having no inkling of the role I had played in his deliverance. But still—as long as you weren't in full possession of the facts, you weren't entitled to judge, either.

The telephone rang.

The telephone! Dumbfounded, I picked it up and pushed a green button at random.

'Is it nice?' asked Duco. 'Is the room all right? Wait a sec, Lucy. Ludo! I've got her on the line, Lude!'

I heard Ludo saying in the background, 'Good, so the man did manage to get the phone installed, then.'

'What did I tell you?' said Duke. 'That fellow is one hundred per cent ...'

'Hey, are you talking to me or to Ludo?' I cried. 'And he isn't your type at all. He's dripping with gold chains.'

'Hey, no need to be cheeky, young lady. How was the trip, all right?'

Ludo said, 'Come on, first remind her she has to buy her textbooks tomorrow. Here, I have it in writing. And her schedule, she's got to ...'

'Lucy? Say something!'

'Jesus, man, I can't get a word in edgeways.'

'Just shut up for a minute, will you?' I heard Duco say in a muffled voice.

Fuming, Ludo answered, 'Right, then hand her over to me, will you?'

Feeling drained all of a sudden, I stared at the glass on the table, in a mess of shredded tissue.

'Lucy-puss,' said Ludo in my ear. 'How're you doing, sweetheart?'

One glass. They'd given me just one glass. They weren't expecting me to make any friends in Amsterdam with whom I'd share their bottle.

'Fine,' I said. 'Really, I'm fine. You don't have to worry about a thing.' Then I hung up.

I walked to the balcony. The sultry scent of the honeysuckle greeted me. Down in the garden, the landlord was smoking a cigar; I assumed it was him, anyway. From the neighbouring gardens came the sound of people making idle conversation when it's too hot to go to sleep. Somebody must have said something funny, because there was a burst of raucous laughter.

The telephone rang again. I walked inside and pulled the plug from the wall.

Maybe they'd done it on purpose; maybe they'd prefer me to drink all by myself in my new life. After all, drinking tends to make you loose-lipped.


The next morning, I set out with my reading list. It was still early, but the street already reeked of hot asphalt. I had studied a plan of the city carefully beforehand; I didn't want to walk around waving one of those unwieldy street maps like a tourist. I had to walk the entire length of Haarlemmer Dike and Haarlemmer Street, and then turn right when I got to the Singel Canal.

It had been ages since I'd been in such a crowded place. The people just barely avoided bumping into one another. At every bridge crossing, a horde of loudly cursing bicyclists would come bearing down on you, even if the pedestrian light was green. I was dripping sweat in no time, but I wasn't going to be thrown off my stride. They weren't out to get me; of course not, I knew that. But they all had such snide scowls on their faces. I had never seen so much disdain. Maybe it *was* me they were looking at; maybe they were laughing at the way I kept stopping to peer up at the street signs, worrying I might have missed the Singel Canal. At practically every crossing I got into somebody's way, and if I took a few steps back just to check and make sure where I was, I was even more of a nuisance. If only I were invisible! I had the feeling I was walking around naked, like in a scary dream, or dressed in Struan's dad's flashy kilt.

Was I dressed wrong? Was that it? Seeing me coming from afar, did people jump to the conclusion that I wasn't from here, that I was one of those country bumpkins without a clue about what was in right now? The thought cheered me up somewhat; after all, clothes were something you could buy, and it was wall-to-wall clothing boutiques down here. Even if it cost me an arm and a leg, it was worth it to me.

As soon as I started looking in the shop windows, I started feeling surer of myself. I was simply shopping, that's what I was doing. And if I had no luck on this side of the street, there was always the other side. By the time the Singel Canal came into view, I was hooked. Even though the mannequins in the corner shop's window were headless, one of them seemed to be winking at me: 'Don't you see? The outfit I'm wearing, it's *you*.' A faded pair of blue jeans and a wide belt, a shiny top the colour of whipped cream, and a short, square-cut, black velvet jacket. It was the jacket, especially, that did it. With that jacket I'd make a grand first impression at school. 'Yeah, Lucy may be dyslexic, but does she ever have taste, man, she's really cool.'

Buoyed, I went inside, where I was greeted with pounding music and two girls talking into their mobiles behind the counter. Luckily, they pretended not to notice me. The jeans were arranged in cubicles on one wall; the rest of the merchandise was hung on racks according to size. I blanched: 36, 38, 40? All I knew was that, in Scotland, I was a size 10. There was just one sample of the black jacket, size 44. Pretending to examine it, I furtively held one of the sleeves along my arm. Far too big. If the jacket in the window was a smaller size, that one might fit me. But there was no way they were going to bother undressing the mannequin if I couldn't tell them what size I was looking for. As soon as I'd gone, they'd ring their boyfriends and tell them, 'You should have seen what came in here just now! Some country bumpkin who didn't even know her own size. And she wanted to try on the agnès b. jacket, imagine!'

It was best not to give in to impulse-buying. You always regretted it later. The whole city was full of jackets; it was stupid to fall for the first one that came along—dumb, dumb, dumb.

Don't make a big deal of it, I told myself. With as much dignity as I could muster, I walked out of the store. I kept my back dangerously straight as I passed more clothing boutiques. It wasn't until some minutes later that I realized I was walking in the wrong direction; I'd already come this way once. But so what, it turned out to be all for the best, because there, on the other side of the street, was a small supermarket, and back home in my bedsit, the empty kitchen cabinets were crying out for supplies. With the deliberate stride of someone who has everything under control, I crossed the street.

Inside, I grabbed a basket. I trailed along the shelves,

gaping at the wealth of merchandise. Chocolate sprinkles. Butterscotch pudding. Fresh vegetables. And strawberries, of course. Heaps of strawberries in blue cardboard punnets. And as I bent down and inhaled the sweet smell, I was suddenly flooded with a memory from very long ago: I was lying on my back, on the green, on a tartan blanket, surrounded by the other babies from the village, and as, to our astonished eyes, a cloud in the shape of an elephant drifted through the sky overhead, little chunks of strawberry were being stuffed into our gurgling mouths. My mother's voice was saying, 'Look out for wasps!'

Absent-mindedly, I put a punnet of strawberries in my basket.

Maybe my mother, somewhere out there in the world, was doing the same thing this very minute. Was she, too, navigating the supermarket aisles, was she buying strawberries, and was she thinking of me? But why would she— my mother, who had long since ceased to be my mother? She'd informed me of that just before she'd run off. With her usual foresight, a few days before we were to find her note on the mantelpiece, she had casually mentioned that she'd been stripped of her parental rights when she went to prison. She'd agreed to it, she'd assured me, because that way Ludo and Duco could become my legal guardians, and child-protection services couldn't take me away. 'You and I,' she'd said, shrugging her shoulders, 'in the eyes of the law, we've had nothing to do with each other for years.'

It may have been that she'd been afraid I would want to leave too, otherwise. Or that it was her duty to take me with her.

There was a sale on Gouda cheese. I chose a big hunk. A package of macaroni. Olives, for the salad. A tin of tomato soup would make a delicious pasta sauce. A couple of tins of beans, for emergencies. Pepper, salt. Bread. Butter, eggs.

I should have taken a shopping cart.

It was very busy at the checkout; there were two long lines. I was crafty enough to choose the longest line, because I knew the shorter one was bound to get held up the moment I joined it. I thought about the meal I would prepare that night in my own kitchenette, and how I'd eat it sitting in front of the open balcony doors. I was already feeling a bit peckish, because I hadn't had any breakfast. The remaining rolls in Ludo's bag had been so soggy this morning that I'd had to throw them out.

My line was moving at a good clip. We were doing well, at till number two. And as I moved up a couple of steps, I suddenly saw him standing in the other queue. Larger than life, he seemed, from the back: the big head on the slight body, the thick blond hair. A linen book bag hung from his shoulder. There might as well have been a label around his neck proclaiming: First-year Biology Student.

I stood nailed to the spot.

He'd turn his head around and see me at any moment.

I put my basket down. I didn't hesitate for a second. I raced out of that shop as fast my legs would carry me.

Once I got home, I bolted the door behind me with shaking hands. I shut the balcony doors as well. Because if he was doing his grocery shopping here in this neighbourhood, he must in all likelihood live nearby, too, perhaps even in one of the very houses whose backyards I overlooked, and from whose gardens you could likewise see my room. If it had been him, that is. But even if it hadn't been, if I'd seen a ghost, if I'd been mistaken, even then, the real Thomas might very well live here! It stood to reason. And even if he didn't live right around the corner, chances were that I might still accidentally run into him, along any canal and in any square, in every café, in every park; there was no question Thomas the bookworm was here, or would end up here at some point, to attend university.

But his university didn't have to be in Amsterdam! Surely that was something I could check. Universities had admissions offices and such. I could ring them, and make up some kind of story. Except that then I'd have to say his name, the name that was his father's name and … I suddenly felt like just banging my head against the wall, like that woman in my mother's cartoon drawing, the strip in twenty frames, with the polar bear pacing up and down on the other side. If you made it into a little booklet and flipped the pages quickly, you had yourself a little animated film.

The walls lunged at me like living things. I had to get out of here. But where could I go? The only place I was safe was here, in the room the Luducos had found for me and had furnished for me, the way they'd always fixed everything for me. Everything.


That evening, Ludo rang to ask if my book expedition had gone smoothly. Yes, I said. And tomorrow you'll pick up your schedule, won't you, because classes start on Monday. Yes, I said. Are you tired? Yes, I said. Then don't make it a late night, sweetie pie.

I hung up the phone. I tore up my reading list. I sat down on the floral sofa. I couldn't go to college at all; I couldn't set foot outside the door.

It doesn't matter, I told myself; it really doesn't matter. So I wouldn't be a nursery-school teacher, so what. I probably wasn't smart enough anyway. In a few days' time, when the others were dutifully listening to their first lecture, I could slip out of town unnoticed. I'd take a train to the Westlands, to my strawberry field. Working with your hands, that was the best solution for people like me. I'd think of some fib to tell Lude and Dukie.

To calm myself down, I picked up the television remote and started zapping through the channels. My empty stomach growled. A couple of days without food—would I make it? I got up again and looked in the kitchen cabinets. They were so spotlessly clean that there wasn't a crumb or a grain of sugar left on the shelves.

Standing at the sink, I gulped down three glasses of water. Lucky for me, there was water aplenty in the tap. And what was I thinking—shit, there was bread, too! I went to the dustbin and took off the lid. I leaned down to extract the sandwich bag, which had worked its way all the way down to the bottom. The food scraps of generations of tenants before me wafted up my nose. The stale stench of poverty and rot. I stood up abruptly. I smacked the lid back in place, stomped on it with my foot, and then kicked the entire can over. I refused to be someone who ate out of dustbins—no, never again! Couldn't you just see me waiting for the landlord to put out his rubbish on the stoop, then sneaking outside to sift through the wet coffee filters for the dregs left in some tin? Panting, I righted the pail again. I drank another large glass of water.

Shit. Shit. Shit!

It was suffocating in here with the balcony doors shut. I'd have to open them a crack, or else I'd pass out. And then, of course, no lights on all evening. In view of the mosquitoes it was better to leave the lights off anyway; anyone would do the same, on a hot night it was perfectly normal to sit in the dark.

I walked past the television to open the doors. But look! The screen showed a building with two white towers. I felt as if I'd just been punched in the stomach. Bijlmer Jail—it had to be. Where my mother had slept for two thousand nights, behind the locked door with the peephole and the sliding hatch.

I stood stock-still in the middle of my room.

There was the barrier where she'd been waiting for us, in that horrendous coat, with that weekend bag. The barrier was raised. Apparently, we were to be allowed inside.

A voice-over provided a running commentary. To the left, a control room with computers. On our right, a long, wide corridor. And there, suddenly, was the commissary where my mother had sometimes bought some teabags or a bar of chocolate. I recognized the spartan shelves at once. The camera focused on a guard wearing sunglasses. 'You're very much on top of each other all day, in this place,' he said. 'But at night *I* get to go home, and *they* have to stay in here, there's the difference.' And over there! The picture showed someone who just had to be the West Indian hairdresser. To think she still worked there, after all these years! You had to be crazy to want to stay in the slammer that long. Slowly, in order not to miss a thing, I perched on the edge of the sofa and turned up the sound.

Now a corridor lined with prison cells came into view. From time to time, the camera would swerve through a door to peek inside. Then you'd see someone writing a letter, reading a magazine, or listening to music on a Walkman. The place was pretty laid-back, from the looks of it. Except that all the faces were camouflaged by these jumpy little squares. That was how the viewer could tell they were criminals. Some of them told the TV crew about their lives. They went on as if they didn't realize that half the population of the Netherlands could now see what they really were: drug dealers, rapists, bicycle thieves, crooks. Criminals, murderers.

But if you listened more closely, you soon realized that every inmate of Bijlmer Jail was, in actual fact, innocent. They weren't responsible; they were victims, most of them. Victims of the most unbelievable bad luck, and, even more frequently, victims of their own poor upbringing. Their mother had been an alcoholic, which, of course, made you more prone to hitting the bottle yourself later in life. Their father had been violent; so was it a surprise if they developed criminal tendencies as well?

The prison was full of people who had only done what their parents had done before them, apparently, who in turn had probably inherited it from *their* parents, and they from the parents before them. Why hadn't anyone thought of breaking that chain; why didn't anyone just cut one of the links? Didn't they *know* how whiny it made them sound?

In the meantime, the camera had arrived at the workshop. Here, table legs and chair frames were sprayed with a powder coating, but I already knew that. The huge machines were noisier than you could ever imagine. Suddenly I opened my eyes even wider. The remote control fell from my hand.

She was standing next to some kind of machine made up of tubes and rods. She didn't look a day older. She was wearing a denim shirt and blue trousers. She was just tucking her hair behind her ears. What, in Jesus' name, was she *doing* there?

As if her gesture had captured its attention, the camera began zooming in on her, slowly but surely.

'Stop!' I screamed. It was simply unbearable, to have her exposed like this for all the world to see. Where were the jumpy little squares that were supposed to camouflage her identity? The camera had now zeroed in on her so closely that you were struck by how blue her eyes were, and how the dimple in her cheek revealed itself as she launched into an animated description of her job as foreman.

I tried to listen to what she was saying, but all I could do was stare at her. Had she changed? She still gave off that sense of energy, but at the same time, her demeanour had acquired something quite imperturbable. She talked about her work as if she considered it the most normal thing in the world to get up every morning with the intention of going to prison.

'Oh, the slammer,' she said calmly, 'well, you know, it's all in your head, really.'

# X is for Kiss

That night I couldn't get to sleep. I could still hear the sound of my mother's voice, and the cornflower blue of her eyes was burned onto my retinas. The way she had of raising one eyebrow, the forgotten but oh-so-familiar way she tucked her hair behind her ears ... It was as if she were standing at the foot of my bed, large as life, in her denim shirt.

I didn't really know what I felt, except confusion. The thought that the documentary had been on national TV, and had therefore also been shown in the Westlands, made my throat grow tight. On Monday, the people at the strawberry farm would no doubt still be talking about it. I'd have no choice but to overhear snatches of what they were saying. 'That forewoman, didn't you see her? What's a pretty lady like her doing in *prison*?' I wouldn't be surprised if they even decided to ask *me* what I'd thought of it!

Even though no one knew she was my mother, now that she had been shown on television in the flesh, for some reason I could no longer ignore her existence. She had been right here in my room, as it were! With that sardonic look that seemed meant just for me. 'What? You really mean you don't understand how it is that I walk freely in and out of prison every day, while you've locked yourself away in your bedsit?'

By three o'clock, I couldn't stand it anymore. I got up, pulled on my knickers and a T-shirt, and opened the balcony door a little wider. What was so bad, really, about admitting you *worked* in the klink? She wasn't actually locked up, she was paid a salary and she went home every night, just like everyone else. 'Oh, so where does she live, then?' People might ask me all kinds of questions about her, and it would soon become clear that I didn't know a thing about my own mother. And one thing would lead to another, and before you knew it, I'd be trapped, with nowhere to turn.

No, I was definitely not going to the Westlands.

The decision lifted a big weight off my shoulders.

I navigated my way in the dark to the kitchen, opened the fridge, and took out the champagne. I managed to pull the cork and fill my beautiful new goblet without making too much of a mess. I carried it over to the pine table. The note from Lude and Duke was still propped against the phone. 'To your new life! xxx, L & D.'

I drank to my new life, which no longer had a purpose, and I drank all by myself, just as they'd predicted. I drained my glass in one gulp and then filled it up again. If you just kept chugging it down, you'd soon start feeling a whole lot better. In the dark, I could just make out the way the bubbles in the champagne slowly drifted up to the surface, where they burst with a little pop. Just as the magic bubble that had been my life with the Luducos on Lewis had popped without warning, sometime between my departure from Stornoway and my arrival at Schiphol.

I felt like a cockle without its shell, a snail without its little house, exposed and defenceless. I started rocking back and forth, my arms wrapped around my torso. What was to become of me now, all on my own? What was I going to do, now that my studies, my strawberry field, and even the freedom to leave my room were hopelessly out of reach? I couldn't stay here forever, could I, shut up in the dark, sitting and waiting ... waiting for what? How would I ever regain my footing, so that I could get on with my life again? The future was banging on my door, and I didn't dare let it in.

But wait: I remembered something Mr Klop used to tell us in History. If you wanted to know what the future would bring, all you had to do was look at the past. You had to carefully revisit everything that had happened before. After all, everything was cause and effect; the future arose straight out of the past.

Revisit what went before—oh, right! So memories were supposed to be the ground beneath your feet! Well, I knew better. I was raised with the understanding that it was best to be very wary of memories, just as you wouldn't trust a watch that didn't keep the time; you couldn't depend on them. Besides, if you were able to remember everything that had happened, you'd have a constant headache. There was no point in looking back! Ludo and Duco had wound up having to throw my mother's own dictum back in her face more and more often, in the end. It wasn't until she had left that we'd been able to get on with our lives in peace. *Our* clock never ran slow, we had made sure of that; we kept it under a heavy glass dome, so that nobody could come and gum up the works. The two of them always assured me that forgetting was the best way to go.

I refilled my glass. The bottle felt considerably heavier than it had before, even though it was now two glasses emptier. Was this one of their magic tricks—a bottomless bottle that never seemed to empty? I stared at the little card that had come with it. Dazed, I thought to myself, x stands for a kiss, x is another kiss, and x is the third kiss. And suddenly, I had the feeling that all the oxygen had been sucked out of the room. Half-petrified with fear, I stared at the floral sofa, the blue window frames, the goblet on the table. Their choices. Their things. With which they had chosen to surround me, now that I was out on my own—like sentries, or totem poles, or amulets, things that were supposed prevent the magic spell from being broken and the past from being exhumed.

I sat there, frozen, my fists pressed into my burning eye sockets. Were they just trying to protect me, as usual? Or was something else going on? The hair on my arms stood up. I *thought* I knew everything about them, everything, but who said? Could it be that they'd papered over the past because there was something they were keeping hidden from me? Did they know something I didn't? Or was there something I wasn't supposed to remember? And if so, why not? What kind of lie had they been trying to ram down my throat all this time?

I was overcome with despair. I gulped down what was left in my glass.

Outside, in a garden, a bird's shrill cry suddenly ripped through the silence of the night. Gavin held that once you heard the first bird, the dawn wasn't far behind. You could always count on one plucky little bird, yearning for the new day, to drive off the dark.

I sat up. I wasn't a little kid anymore, damn it, watching open-mouthed as the lemonade changed colour or twenty cents mysteriously turned into a euro. I wasn't going to let them pull the wool over my eyes like a six-year-old anymore! Granted, my mind might be a bit like the airtight bulkhead in a ship's hull, but that didn't mean the memories weren't lurking in there somewhere, like stowaways. I knew that as soon as I finally hauled one out on deck, the rest were bound to follow. And if they mutinied, I always had the option of throwing them overboard. But if I didn't make at least an attempt to face them now, I'd spend the rest of my life cowering behind the barbed-wire barricade Ludo and Duco had erected before me, biting my nails in despair.

My head was throbbing, now that I found myself teetering on the forbidden threshold of the past. But I had no choice. It did seem to me that I really didn't have all that much to lose anymore. All right. Just *do* it! I took a deep breath. I poured myself another glass, just in case. Okay, the storm. Yes, I remembered it clearly. How the wind had been howling that night! And suddenly I remembered, so vividly that it startled me, how even the streetlamps had been swaying in the wind that night. In spite of the terrible weather, I'd climbed out of the window and onto the roof, undaunted. It must have been incredibly scary.

In order to concentrate better, I clenched my eyes shut. Look! There I was, shuffling along the gutter, my arms carefully spread wide to keep my balance. The wind at my back felt like a big hand that was intent on pushing me over the edge. Remembering it gave me such a physical jolt that I had to grab hold of the table. The blood pounded in my ears. Okay, calm down, calm down.

Now I was clinging to the rainspout, but a wet strand of ivy whipped me in the face, and I let go and fell. I didn't dare scream, fearing they'd hear me inside. But there was little chance of that happening, for I had barely scrambled to my feet in the garden before I heard the unfamiliar sound of angry voices coming from the rectory, a door slamming. My mother and the Luducos were fighting as I'd never heard them fight before. I stood there listening a moment, my heart in my throat. But something told me

I would overhear things I really didn't want to know. I turned and ran.

In the street, the wind gusts sent me lurching and reeling along. It took some effort to stay on my feet. Once out in the open field, it was even heavier going, but it was the shortest way to where I had to go.

It definitely wasn't the kind of weather in which you'd want to go out for stroll before bed, so I was startled to see a figure standing under the orange floodlights of the new viaduct's building site. But I recognized him immediately. Of course, a little wind wouldn't faze someone like him; he was used to working outdoors, rain or shine. He'd go outside whenever the mood struck him, storm or no storm.

He was just crushing his glowing cigarette under his boot when he noticed me. 'Hey, there!' he cried. 'Yes, I mean you over there, little scamp! What in hell are you doing out so late, all by yourself?'

I shrank back. If I pretended I hadn't heard him, would he come after me? My whole plan would be ruined! The wind, taking advantage of my hesitation, suddenly walloped me in the back, sending me staggering helplessly into the arc of the floodlights. In the lee of the support columns there was a lull, and I came stumbling to a halt.

'Well now,' he said slowly, something hard in his voice all of a sudden, 'if it isn't Thomas's little girlfriend.'

I felt put on the spot. He had caught me in the shed with Thomas more than once, poring over our reading book. I'd always quickly scooted out of there. Thomas's dad always stared at me with a queer look, probing, yet also furtive. He must have asked Thomas about the stupid kid who couldn't even learn to read; but I knew Thomas's father had trouble with reading too, so that was no reason for him to dislike me. We had a lot in common, actually.

'Well?' he said, bending down with obvious reluctance.

'What are *you* doing here?' The orange light gave his face a creepy cast. Behind him, the new cement was already defaced with graffiti.

'My kitty's run away,' I blurted out. I hoped my words hadn't given the game away! What if he thought I'd said, '*Lucy's* run away?'

Again he looked me over from head to toe with his peculiar stare. Then he said in a bitter voice, 'Cats always find their way home eventually. Sometimes they'll turn up on your doorstep years later. Just when you thought you were rid of them.'

A blast of wind that swept unexpectedly round the pier made me totter. I heard a chain rattling that had come untethered from some crane or backhoe somewhere close by, the sinister clang of metal on metal.

'You'll get blown off your feet if you're not careful,' he said, a little more kindly. 'All right, then, run along home, kid. You'll see, your kitty's probably already been found. Off you go!'

And suddenly, I had a great idea. Home—home, indeed. Home—but of course! After all, Mum and the Luducos knew the guy from before I was born; they'd talked about it at my engagement party. So what were we doing standing out here in the cold? For someone who'd only lived somewhere for a short time and didn't know too many locals, a spontaneous invitation to visit old friends would probably be greatly appreciated. And while the adults talked about old times over a glass of wine, I'd slip out of the house unnoticed a second time, and run away to hide at Thomas's house in Shepherd's Close.

He bent down closer. 'Why are you still here? Go home!'

When Duke invited someone over, he'd say, 'So, want to come over and have a few drinks tonight?' But in this case, faced with inviting someone who was already so critical of me, I thought it best to phrase it as politely as possible. 'My mother's still up, and I'm sure she would love it if you ...'

He took a step back in the sand. 'Don't tell me your mother has sent you after me.'

'It's very close by,' I said. 'Right around the corner.' I waited a moment, then threw down my trump card. 'She baked a batch of peanut biscuits today, specially.' Our Ludo was addicted to those biscuits. He was known to whine for them like a dog begging for a bone. They were crispy on the outside, soft and chewy on the inside.

He grabbed me so violently by the wrist that I nearly lost my footing.

'She isn't going to start again, is she?' he snapped at me.

Alarmed, I tried to wriggle out of his grip.

He shook me. 'Listen, young lady, I've got a message for your mother. If she's going to start getting things in her head again, I'll tell the whole world what she's like, and I'm not kidding. Just tell her that, the horny bitch. I won't let it happen again.'

'What?' I asked, shocked.

'I won't stand for her hysterics again!' His voice rose, bouncing off the viaduct's colonnade. *Again-gain-gain-gain.* It kept reverberating, like the incessant ringing of a telephone that nobody wants to answer, and that just goes on and on ringing in the middle of the night, ever louder, ever more desperate.

'I wouldn't *think* of letting myself fall into her clutches all over again! No matter what she tries this time, it's leave-me-the-hell-alone, return-to-sender, and that's final!'

I couldn't help picturing a mountain of letters, torrents of letters cascading through the letterbox at once. Letters written in blood, but which would never receive a reply. Letters like the sound of hollow footsteps following you down a dark alley. Wherever you might go, you'd never get rid of those letters, you'd never shake those footsteps coming after you. And suddenly, it hit me like a bomb—I knew who he was. So he really did exist! He wasn't just a character in a story that some mothers whisper into their babies' ears. I yanked myself free and stared at him open-mouthed.

He stamped his foot impatiently. 'There's no need for you to understand it, little miss smarty-pants. As long as *she* gets it. If she starts up again with that nonsense—you hear me?—she'll have to face the consequences, because I'll go straight to Ludo and Duco and tell them everything. Can you remember that?'

'I can,' I said, as convincingly as I could. Was he going to tell on Mum? But so what, anyway? It was ancient history. The past was the past, in any case, and this was *way* in the past, even before I was born. Except—why had Mum always kept it a secret? She probably knew something only grown-ups understood. She knew it would be simply dreadful if this secret ever came out, even a hundred years from now. So dreadful that the Luducos would leave us if they ever found out.

My throat was parched with horror. Mum couldn't get by without Lude and Duke! If they weren't there, she'd never be surprised with a kiss in the neck, ever again, as she sat bent over her work. Without them, her cold feet would always stay frigid at night. Without them, she'd have nobody to dance the tango with up and down the long corridor. Without them, she'd have no reason to wear her red scarf, or give her hair an egg rinse to make it shine. Without them, her pencils would be drained of colour, her drawings would be bad; the pages of her sketchbook would remain blank, without them.

'We're moving,' I cried. 'Mum is making me go to another school; we're leaving.' My head was spinning with relief. It was so simple. He wouldn't have to tell on her because we were leaving anyway, the four of us, because we always did everything together, we belonged together, that's just the way it was. I wanted more than anything to run home right away and start packing. I gazed up at his orange face hopefully.

He clucked sceptically. 'Ha, right in the middle of the school year, I suppose?'

'Right, because I'm just not learning to read, here.'

Something about his eyes suddenly changed. It was the look people get when they gaze at little puppies. That's the way he looked at me: as if I were a whole litter of newborn puppies. He squatted down, stretched out a hand, and patted me awkwardly on the cheek. 'That's right, Thomas told me. It must be hard on you.'

And, for one confusing second, I sensed we shared a secret that was so big that there were no words to describe it. There was no language for what he and I had in common. I took a few steps back, into the vicious wind.

He, too, seemed alarmed by what had just passed between us. He stood up straight and put up his collar, so that his face nearly disappeared. 'So, do you remember what you're supposed to tell your mother?' he called out to me.

The cheek he had just fondled stung as if I'd been slapped. Was this really no concern of mine, just some feud for grown-ups, or had I, in some mysterious way, just been pulled into it, too?

'Didn't you hear me?' He started coming toward me impatiently.

All of a sudden, I was so petrified that I stuck my hand in my pocket. You never knew—you might meet an enemy anyplace, anytime.

'You did understand what I just said, didn't you? If I notice her stalking me again, if I so much as catch a glimpse of her, that's it, she'll regret it.' A length of construction plastic had wrapped itself around his legs, and he leaned down to pull it off. 'So you'd better make sure I never set eyes on her again, ever.'

I closed my fingers on the pencil.

My arm went up.

I nearly started to scream.

The silence in my room was so unreal that I had to shake my head, dazed. The first grey daylight was worming its way in through the window, but there was no sign of life anywhere, indoors or out. The landlord and all the neighbours were sleeping the sleep of the innocent. It felt as if the entire block of flats were gently rocking up and down to the rhythm of their tranquil breathing.

The Luducos' bottomless bottle still had some champagne left in it. Laboriously, I topped up my glass. What if the dreaded taboos returned, now that I'd started raking up the dangerous past? I felt hounded, persecuted; I was in a complete state. And the other thing was, I thought I caught a whiff of patchouli. If I turned my head, I might well find my mother standing at the foot of my bed, hands on her hips, head cocked to the side, as if she were expecting something of me.

Had I really had only her welfare in mind? Was my intention purely to make sure he wouldn't harm her? So that, late at night, I'd still be able to hear her hollering a cheerful 'olé!' and be reassured, up there in my attic room, that she was, at that moment, stepping on Duco's toes while Ludo patiently waited for his turn to tango?

She always said we were lucky to be loved by two good men. But I did sometimes find it a problem—you couldn't sit on two laps at once, could you, and someone always came up short; you were always worried that one of them would take it into his head that you liked the other one better. You were constantly trying to share yourself as fairly as possible. It was a quandary I'd often brooded about. If only I didn't have to go to school every day! Then I'd be able to run after Dukie and Ludikins with out-stretched arms from early in the morning to late at night, to convince them that I adored them both equally. Because what other means did I have to make them love me? For as long as I could remember, I'd lived with the nagging doubt—did I actually have any right to their love? I was never completely certain I did—and yet my life had been filled with their love.

So perhaps the truth was this: I had grabbed that pencil in order to safeguard my own little life. And perhaps my mother, too, had known it all along.

I glanced around furtively. The room was empty.

I staggered unsteadily to my feet. The alcohol had done a number on me, even more so since it was on an empty stomach. Clumsily, I fiddled with the balcony door latch. Blinking at the light, I stepped outside, where I fully expected to find her standing now, a sprig of honeysuckle tucked behind her ear, making her look like someone in a movie. So, Lucy, have you finally emerged? Tell me, how do you like it, out in the open?

The morning breeze gently caressed my legs. It was still a bit cool out, but all the signs pointed to another gorgeous day. Slowly it dawned on me that I was standing on the bal-cony in my knickers—alone. Befuddled, I thought to my-self, How *does* she always manage it?

When I went back inside, I left the doors wide open.

In my room, I nearly tripped over my half-unpacked suitcase, parked sideways next to the table. Underneath a pair of rolled-up socks I could just make out *Clara 13*'s cheerful cover. What did she think, anyway? That I needed her? That I wasn't able to manage on my own? I bent down and grabbed the book Ludo and Duco had so carefully packed for me. I picked it up by one corner and with all my might hurled it against the wall.

For a moment, I thought I'd cracked the spine; pages seemed to be flying everywhere, like lies finally unmasked, like stories escaping the mute iron grip of the book's binding. There was paper floating in the air. Something landed at my feet. But it turned out to be only an envelope that had been pressed between the pages. I was about to pick it up when I recognized what it was. I took a step back and let it lie there, just as I had once left it sitting unopened on the mantelpiece. Turn and run! That was definitely the easiest way out.

I sat back down at the table. I drank another glass. I tried not to look at the white rectangle on the floor. Maybe it was just the envelope. Thrifty Ludo saved the weirdest stuff for recycling, you couldn't open a cupboard without finding … But was it the same envelope? It had seemed much larger, at the time.

I snatched it up from the floor. It wasn't sealed shut; the flap had simply been tucked in. I gave myself a paper cut pulling it open. Sucking on my hurt finger, I managed to extricate the light-blue sheet of stationery, which immediately divulged its secret. Even before unfolding it, I could tell from the deep grooves, signalling determined pen strokes, that it was from my mother. From my mother, with whom, in the eyes of the law, I'd had nothing to do for years.

It was quite a short note. She must have said to herself, I'd better not use too many words, or Lucy won't read it. I felt a sharp pang of triumph, because, for once, her carefully thought-out scheme had misfired. Every carefully weighed word had been a complete waste of time; I hadn't even opened the letter. Now I began to read intently.

'Dear Lucy,' it said at the top. Underneath, in smaller script, 'Dear Ludo, dear Duco.'

Unexpectedly, my eyes began to prickle. She hadn't exactly been very lovey-dovey with us since she'd been out of the slammer. You might think they had set free the mother you'd always known, but instead you got someone who blithely said 'My arse!' if something wasn't to her liking.

Even in this letter, despite the touching three 'dears' at the beginning, she didn't mince words. She wrote that she was fed up with living with us. She wrote that what she couldn't stand anymore was that, no matter how much she provoked or badgered us, we never seemed to give a shit. She wrote that she assumed we were also getting pretty fed up with her and her constant attempts at communication, which suited her just fine, because that way we could part and nobody would shed any tears. There, now it was out in the open. And just one more thing, because, incorrigible as she was, she needed to get something else off her chest, as well. At the time, she wrote, it had seemed the right thing to do, to take the blame for what happened. 'After all, the entire tragedy was ultimately my fault. I could never have lived with myself if I had refused to take responsibility for it. But, looking back now, maybe I should have been wiser.'

I put the letter down. I was suddenly overcome with a strange, sick feeling. As if it didn't add up, somehow. Had I missed something? Painfully, I perused the letter again. But I couldn't put a finger on what was wrong. Maybe the alcohol was playing tricks on me. They were only words. It was only a letter. She hadn't signed it, as usual. She'd drawn a smiley face instead. And, underneath that, a postscript for me: 'P.S. Lucy, take a lesson from me: don't ever sacrifice yourself for another. It'll only turn you into a huge pain in the arse.'

# Y is for Yesterday

The sun had already sunk low in the sky when I awoke with a start. My head was throbbing. My neck was sore, too; I'd fallen asleep at the table with my head on my arms. The bottle of champagne was still there. It should have been empty, but it was still nearly half-full.

In the kitchenette, I splashed my face with cold water. Then I put on a pair of jeans. And as I was pulling up the zipper, I suddenly *had* it. It was that one little sentence in her letter. 'The entire tragedy was ultimately my fault.'

It couldn't have been more straightforward. It could mean only one thing: that Ludo and Duco had known all along how things stood, that they'd always known there was a chance—a one-in-three chance, to be precise—that I wasn't their daughter. It was a shattering thought, for a thousand different reasons. If a deed that had caused such havoc turned out, in the end, to have been for nothing ... Fear jabbed an icicle right through my heart. I *had* to know. I had to know for sure, before it drove me completely nuts.

Trembling, I started leafing through the telephone book. But when I found the number, I suddenly lost my nerve.

She had left, closing the door behind her. And, for all those years, she had never given even a sign of life. I could hardly expect her to be pining for me, hoping I'd show up some day. She was happy enough to be rid of me.

There was nothing else for it, though; I'd have to go there in person. At least that way she wouldn't have a chance to run away.

I practically tore the map in two in my eagerness to unfold it. There: the prison. It was on a bus route.

On the way there, I kept my eyes fixed on the floor the entire time. As long as I wasn't looking at anyone, no one would be able to see me. That's what six-year-olds did. Six-year-olds considered themselves capable of making themselves completely invisible when it suited them. What, in fact, *didn't* you think yourself capable of at that age? In a world where reality and make-believe blended seamlessly, you had absolute power.

Now I felt grown-up, and quite powerless. The imitation-leather seat made my shirt stick to my back. I was so nervous that I itched all over.

The bus was packed. It was late afternoon; people were returning from work, or, laden with bags, going home after a day's shopping. There were probably college students, too, that lived in Bijlmer. Every time the bus halted at a stop, I fixed my eyes even more rigidly on the floor strewn with paper and cigarette butts. A real prison bus.

A woman behind me with a West-Indian accent was talking into her mobile. Every sentence was punctuated with a peal of laughter. It was beyond me how anyone could laugh so heartily, as if no evil existed in the world.

When the driver announced the Bijlmer Jail bus stop, I was the only one who got out, red as a lobster.

And once the bus disappeared in a cloud of diesel

exhaust, before I'd even had a chance to gaze up at the white prison buildings, I spotted, not five yards from me, my mother waiting for the bus on the other side of the street. She was leaning against the bus shelter, standing nonchalantly on one leg. She must just have come from work. She had traded the blue shirt for a bright-red tank top with spaghetti straps over white trousers and red high-heeled sandals. She carried a straw shoulder bag. She looked young, sassy, and dynamic.

Her eyes swept absently past me. Then she turned her head to stare in the direction from which her bus would be coming. A car passed by, and then a man on a bicycle with a little kid riding on the back.

She hadn't recognized me. I'd been a child when she left, an unfamiliar child she hadn't even watched grow up.

Suddenly she started, as if she'd had an electric shock. The colour drained from her face and her head whipped back to where I was standing. Her eyes grew big. 'Lucy?' she mouthed, incredulous. Honing in on me, she detached herself from the shelter. She stepped off the sidewalk. She started coming toward me. 'Lucy! It really *is* you!'

That gravelly voice. The shiny hair cascading down the back of her head like a waterfall. That self-confident stride.

Now she was standing right in front of me. She had gone as white as a sheet.

'I saw you on TV,' I said sheepishly.

She didn't make a move to hug me. I'd seen her yesterday, but of course she hadn't seen me. She probably thought she was dreaming. Maybe this was a nightmare for her. Her lips were trembling. I hoped she wouldn't start blubbering.

How strangely exposed it felt to be standing there, facing each other in the street. Stiffly, I suggested, 'Do you have time for a drink?'

'I simply can't believe it. Since when have you been back in Holland?'

I shifted from one foot to another. 'I only just got here. And then, yesterday, I saw that programme on TV ...' I had to raise my voice because a motorcycle was roaring by. The rider ogled my mother. He didn't even glance at me, standing there in the T-shirt I'd slept in.

'And the boys?'

'They're home, on Lewis.'

'So they let you go! How about that!' She grinned, a bit unkindly. 'Well, there's a café around the corner. Will that do?'

The terrace was packed with people sipping pints in the evening sun. My mother greeted several people warmly in passing. They were probably colleagues of hers. Or men lusting after her. She had a whole life I didn't know a thing about.

We went inside, where it was cool and dark. There were no other customers. We sat down in the back, by the billiard table. We ordered two fresh pressed orange juices from the half-naked waitress. 'And a portion of *bitterballen*,' I said, suddenly famished.

'Funny,' said my mother. 'I couldn't get enough of those either, when I first got back. I must have devoured truckloads.'

I blurted out, 'Why are you working in *that* place? Aren't you writing picture books anymore?'

She picked up a coaster and started playing with it. 'You know, once you've gone through what I've gone through, it no longer seems right to make up stories about talking animals.'

I should have known—she always got straight to the point, she didn't waste a second. It was the reason there always seemed to be this dark cloud between us; she couldn't help herself, she just *had* to bring up the subject. Always. I looked away.

'You're eighteen now, right? Did you come back here to study?'

I nodded.

There came our drinks.

To break the silence, I started babbling, 'I had the best birthday ever. We went into Harris for scallops, it was totally awesome.'

'So the boys spoiled you rotten for a change.'

'The boys! When are you going stop calling them that?'

She shrugged coyly. It was nauseating. 'I can't help it, that's the way I think of them.' Her tone changed. 'What have you come for, Lucy? To rub my nose in the fact that I left you? You must have cursed me to hell.'

'Oh, not really.'

She spread her hands on the table and inspected her fingernails. 'You know, it was driving me nuts, completely nuts. That conspiracy of yours—a conspiracy of silence. Oh yes, I know, I know, I once promised we'd never mention it again, but what else was I supposed to say to a terrified child? But surely it isn't normal, that ever since, we never even ...'

I cut her short. 'You did write that you were sorry you'd sacrificed yourself.' I could have kicked myself; there I went, putting the blame on her. I had cost her six years of her life.

'Yes, there was that, as well,' she said calmly. 'Jesus, was that ever a hard thing to do. What I did—it was no little thing. So I thought it was finally *my* turn, that I deserved a little consideration. I decided I'd earned the right to a little adulation. I'd earned the right to be put on a pedestal, for crying out loud! I'd gone to jail for your sake, for all three of you. Didn't I deserve something in return?'

Her confession threw me for a loop. I didn't know what to say.

'The funny thing was,' she said with a wry smile, 'that I kept remembering how, when I was little, I used to hate it when my mother would say, "But I *always* do *everything* for you! Couldn't you, just once in a while ..." I remember how oppressive it felt when she'd gone out of her way to cook something special, buy something special, think of something special, or organize something special for me. And I was supposed to be so grateful! I'd never asked for it in the first place, but still I had to grovel. Always selfless and self-sacrificing on the surface, she was, yet at the same time busy erecting her own monument. Look, they've brought you your *bitterballen*.' She leaned forward and pushed the plate of meatballs toward me. 'I hate that, that self-righteousness of martyrs like my mother. Their moral superiority. It's insufferable. So okay, I seemed to be heading in that same direction myself. I could tell that the boys and you were beginning to loathe me the way I used to loathe my mother. And, of course, then I started loathing myself, too. Let that be a lesson to you, Lucy, and don't you ever follow my example! Never sacrifice yourself for anyone. Not even if there seems to be every reason to do so. Okay, now it's your turn. What would *you* like to get off your chest?'

I busied myself trying to cut a meatball in half with a toothpick. My head was spinning. 'Maybe he was my dad,' I said. I was so shocked by my own words that I jumped, only my legs refused to move. My startled lurch made my mother's glass wobble. Orange juice sloshed over the rim onto the table.

With her head bowed, she started blotting up the spill with a felt coaster. She didn't have to ask me how I'd guessed. Twelve years ago, she had already concluded that

I was aware of her secret. After a long pause, she said hoarsely, 'That's the reason I took the blame on myself, Lucy.'

I stared at my plate. But I'd lost my appetite.

'I'll have to carry the consequences of that mistake with me for the rest of my life. Plus, of course, the fact that because of me, the two most kind-hearted souls in the world ...'

The Luducos loomed up between us, large as life, mild and amiable. One moment they weren't there, and the next, suddenly, there they were. Just the way they had suddenly come up behind me, back then.

I hadn't seen them approach in the dark, nor did I hear them; the wind muffled their footsteps. But my two guardian angels had sensed that I needed them, as they always did. All I had to do was think of them, and next thing I knew, they were at my side. As if their entire world revolved around me, twenty-four hours a day. If there was a task that was giving me trouble, they'd patiently take over and finish it for me. They were always on stand-by to see to it that whatever it was that I'd already bungled would nevertheless turn out well in the end. Like a couple of beatific saints, ever willing to answer any prayer.

And, once again, they'd arrived just in time.

Because, just as in the orange light of the construction site, I was seeing my hand going up—my hand gripping the pencil—to rub out the man who threatened to destroy my mother's happiness, a sudden gust of wind nearly bowled me over. I staggered. The pencil flew from my fingers and I crashed into Thomas's father. Since he was crouching down, he, too, nearly toppled over. Cursing, he pushed me away. I landed hard in the sand.

And it was then that they had materialized out of nowhere, side by side. As they ran up to me, I felt such shame that it clobbered me like a block of cement. They must have seen me getting ready to strike him. They must have seen what I was about to do: stab my pencil in his eye and kill him dead. It was something that, from now on, they would always know about me; they'd know it in the morning, when they plaited my hair, and they'd know it in the evening, when they read me a story under the string of Christmas lights. They'd know it when they dug a splinter out of my foot, when they made pancakes, when they bought me a new winter coat. They'd know it every time we picked out a present for Mummy together, every time they helped me take off my skates, every time they fixed a bicycle tyre for me, and even at Christmas, when they decorated the tree, with the angel with the gauze wings on top. From this day forward, they would always know that I was capable of a heinous act.

They had no choice. He'd have gone straight to the police and reported me. There was only one thing to do.

They pulled me to my feet. 'Go home, Lucy! Run along home at once!'

I turned and ran. But I did glance back over my shoulder once. He was stretched out on the ground. Lude and Duke were leaning over him. Everything seemed to be moving, and in the orange light their thinning hair, blown in the wind, looked just like flames. They simply *had* to finish the job for me.

My mother lit a cigarette. I smelled the familiar menthol smell. Remembered sitting in Mummy's studio, on the little stool next to the draughting table, in a peppermint haze. If you wiggled your fingers in the air, you'd get to see all these transparent squiggles trailing along behind them.

She had given up smoking in prison. She had made a

funny drawing about it: herself as this little doll, surrounded by giant, lewd-looking cigarettes leering at her provocatively. I didn't have the nerve to ask her when or why she had started again.

'It's odd,' she said finally. 'I've been dying to talk about it. And here we are, and now I don't really know what to say.'

'You weren't there,' I said evasively.

'But I wasn't exactly uninvolved.' She sighed. 'Funny, isn't it? You'd think that if you'd been through that sort of thing together ... you'd think it would forge a bond, at least, wouldn't you?'

And yet that was the whole point: she hadn't really been part of it. This was it, this was the darkness, the intangible thing that divided us; only the Luducos and I knew what it was to be capable of such a deed. We didn't have to *talk* about it to know how it felt. That was the essence of our silent pact. It was a thing that was ours alone, and ours together. Amongst ourselves, we didn't have to feel shame; we were all three in the same boat. And we certainly didn't need other people, whose hands were clean, sticking their noses in all the time.

Wanting to say something nice, I remarked, 'But while you were in jail, they missed you. They missed you terribly.'

She ran a hand over her eyes. 'Oh, you were just a child. What did *you* know. They only started missing me later on. It took several years, at least. At first, there was only one reason, and one reason alone, that they didn't pack their bags and make for the hills, and that was because there was still a chance that you might be theirs—that one of them might be your father.'

I sucked in my breath.

'That's the reason they never left. They stayed on because of you. Not because of me. They were only too happy, at the time, to have me behind bars and out of their lives—you bet they were! And for my part, I did hope, of course, that they'd find it in their hearts to forgive me. What other way could I have found to accomplish that? By saying I was sorry?'

I had goosebumps all up and down my arms. I managed to stutter, 'So, uh, when did you tell them, finally?'

Puzzled, she looked at me.

'About me, I mean. About ...'

Surprised, she said, 'That night, of course.'

And finally, a light bulb went on in my head. The quarrel! That terrible argument that had made the walls quake. I had heard them go at each other as if the world were coming to an end.

'Or do you mean *how* did I tell them?' She calmly considered for a minute. 'Back then, it was still possible to make up all sorts of stories to explain to you why I wouldn't go outside anymore, and why we were going to have to move away—you were only six; but how do you think it would strike an adult? The boys smelled a rat; they weren't exactly born yesterday. That night they cornered me, and demanded that I tell them. And so I told them why we had to leave town.'

'Could I settle up with you please? It's the end of my shift.' The waitress put the bill on the table. She picked up the plate with the untouched *bitterballen* and put it on her tray without a flicker of expression.

I started fishing my wallet out of my jeans pocket.

'No, let me, Lucy,' said my mother. She fumbled in her straw handbag, looking at me out of the corner of her eye. 'It's the least I can do, I should think.'

I smiled faintly.

When she had paid, she said, 'It was the worst fight I've ever had in my whole life. Every word I uttered only made it worse. Cheating on them was one thing, but the fact that I had let them think all that time that you, the apple of their eye ... It's always the placid ones, I find, that you have to be careful never to rile. They already have to put up with so much grief from everyone, that when the shit finally hits the fan, they just can't take any more. And a betrayal of that magnitude ... You should have seen them storm out of the house, once I'd told them the whole story. And ... well, you know what happened next.'

I clenched my icy hands together, dazed. Ludo and Duco, my guardian angels? So then they had had their own motives! Their own, grown-up motives. They hadn't come rushing to my aid after all. No, they'd stormed out of the house, beside themselves with rage, their minds seething with revenge. They had taken the shortcut over to Shepherd's Close, and had happened to bump into him on our field, where they'd found him messing with me, to cap it all! I had been the last straw, that's all.

'To think it got so out of hand,' I finally said, feebly.

'Yes. I think of it this way: life can sometimes take such a sudden and unexpected turn that we lose control and spin right off the road. There really isn't any other way of putting it that makes any sense.'

It suddenly felt as if we had said all there was to say. 'Can I bum a fag?' I asked.

She gave me a cigarette and a light. In quite a different tone of voice, she said, 'What a grown-up daughter I have. I just can't believe we're sitting here face to face, you know?'

She didn't seem to have noticed how my world had been turned upside down. It had only just dawned on me how negligible my own part in the drama had been. By insisting on staying deaf and blind to all her hints, her incessant allusions to the past, I had never until this moment worked out that everything was not as I'd thought ... It turned out that even *I* was not who I'd thought I was.

'Do you want to order something else? I'll go ask for a menu.' She stood up.

I gazed at her receding back, ramrod straight, as she strode to the bar. She had turned my life into one big fat lie right from day one; that was a fact. But Ludo and Duco had kept the lie going. They had known my mother's secret, with its far-reaching consequences, as far back as the time when I was just learning to read in Miss Joyce's class!

I could see myself again, sitting in the little wooden school desk with *The Safe Way Reader* open in front of me. All the letters always seemed to turn their backs on me; all the words were in cahoots to stump me. Whenever it was my turn to read aloud, the other kids in the class would start groaning and cursing under their breath. Later, at recess, they'd make me pay, as usual, for making such a cockeyed mess of it that it had made everyone lose the thread of the story. Or they'd find some other reason to mash me to a pulp. Any reason was good enough for them, even if there was none.

In the sixth grade, Mr Turk had told us the fable of the Truth and the Lie, who took a bath together once. The Lie got out first, and sneakily put on the Truth's clothes instead of its own. Since the Truth, upon noticing the deception, would not put on clothes belonging to the Lie, she was forced to walk about naked. And so that's where the saying *the naked truth* came from. 'Just remember that, Lucy. Do you hear me?'

They'd all considered me a liar, someone who made up stories. And they hadn't been that far from the truth; it was a fact—even then, I was a living, breathing lie. Children have a nose for that sort of thing. They wouldn't leave a hair on your head intact if they felt something about you didn't quite add up. They were, in their own ruthless way, much too honest themselves to put up with it. Honesty was, after all, the most effective weapon you had, as a group, to combat the dark, dishonest world of the grown-ups.

'Look!' said my mother. She held out the menu. 'They have strawberries with whipped cream. Wasn't that always your favourite?'

I stubbed out my cigarette in the ashtray. 'Sure,' I said dully. 'Go ahead and order one, if you like.'

My entire childhood, I'd always thought that I was safe only with them—with Duco, who always carried that dumb picture of me at age three in his wallet, or with Ludo, who made sure I received my first postcard ever at Callanish. But how could you feel safe with people who'd simply omitted to tell you the truth? With the best of intentions, but even so. Oh, all the trouble they could have spared me! Not only the goading and pestering, but also the guilt, the nightmares, those awful prohibitions and taboos. The Luducos and their empty-tin pyramid, their bottomless bottle of champagne ... 'Bye, Dad,' I'd said to them. 'Bye, Daddy. Thanks for everything.'

The road to my daily torment was paved by those to whom I had given my trust. And as I was about to begin my adult life, they'd even fobbed me off with a strawberry field, instead of just opening their mouths and telling it to me straight! Just to save their own skins.

My mother returned from the bar. Her face fell when she saw me. 'What's the matter? You look so ...'

Suddenly I was mad as hell. 'None of your business!' I snapped. *Three* adults who'd only ever thought about themselves! Who'd lumbered *me* with the consequences of their thoughtless behaviour! I'd been at their mercy, helpless, as children tend to be. You didn't have a choice but to trust your elders; every child before me had had to do the same, and the ones before them, and on and on, all the way back to the very beginning of human history—an endless chain of children forced to accept blindly whatever was decided over their heads, or plotted and botched behind their backs. And, after us, there would be other children, thousands, millions, trillions—until the end of time children would be brought into this world, out of true love or sheer carelessness, and each, in turn, would find him- or herself dependent on grown-ups who had forgotten what it was like to have to depend on grown-ups.

'Come, tell me,' said my mother. 'What's got into you all of a sudden?'

'Nothing that concerns you! Just leave me alone and mind your own fucking business.'

Frowning, she lit a fresh cigarette. 'You're like this completely impregnable fortress, did you know that?'

'I bet that in *that* respect I don't take after some complete stranger.'

'Well now! Just as cheeky as ever, I see. Which is another thing you've inherited from me, by the way. Yes, Lucy, let's face it: the only one we can in all certainty blame for your less admirable character traits, is me.'

'So it's your fault I'm such a basket case.'

'Is that your way of telling me I've ruined your life?' She stared at me through narrowed eyes. 'Just come out and say it then, girl. I might just agree with you, too. So maybe you could stop going for my throat at every opportunity.'

I was so flummoxed that I couldn't get the words out.

'If you refuse to talk about it, you'll never get over it. There are words for everything, you know. Everything is ...'

Just then, a boy in a grubby apron appeared at our table with the strawberries my mother had ordered. He put the dish on the table and told us to enjoy.

'And two white wines, please,' she told him. She looked at me defiantly. 'We have something to celebrate, don't we?'

To cover up my confusion, I stuck a strawberry in my mouth. So she thought there were words for everything. That explained why she loved talking so much. But the Luducos had been right in one respect: there simply were no words for what had happened that night. Unless, perhaps, you hammered out the words yourself, if you knew how to go about pouring the hot lead into the mould of your choice. Well okay, maybe it *was* possible. If you wanted the story of your life to be the truth, for instance. If there was something *that* important at stake, you couldn't really turn you back on the thing was hard to express, or that might be painful or disconcerting to hear.

And that made me think of Ludo and Duco standing on the quay in Stornoway, getting smaller and smaller in the distance as the CalMac ferry steamed out of port, with me up on deck, standing at the railing, on my way to meet my freedom. The freedom, at last, to start on the *true* story of my life, word for word. All I needed was guts, nothing else. After all, I had someone right here with me who could show me how it was done.

Maybe I'd forgive the Luducos some day. Maybe I'd even think back fondly on the enthusiasm and energy they had devoted to being my fathers, and on how nothing was too much trouble for them where I was concerned, their little cuckoo in the nest. Except when it came to laying all their cards on the table.

Resolutely I planted my elbows on either side of my plate. I said, 'We've still got lots to talk about.'

My mother nodded. 'There's time for that,' she said laconically. 'But first let's enjoy these strawberries.'

We ate a few minutes in silence. The strawberries were sweet and juicy. They were perfect, actually. 'This is what I always dreamed of, on Lewis,' I said. 'I must have tried it a hundred times, but they just wouldn't grow in our garden.'

'I could have spared you the trouble.' At the thought of her vegetable garden, her face lit up. Or perhaps it wasn't the garden she was thinking of.

'Tell me, that Iain guy. Was there something going on between the two of you, yes or no?'

'Iain?' said my mother. She raised an eyebrow. 'Iain who ... Oh, *that* Iain!' And she began to laugh.

# Z is for Zeal

That afternoon, my mother had gone out on an errand. Lude and Duke were tranquilly at work in their rooms. In the rectory's front hall, Thomas and I took off our shoes and tiptoed upstairs, quiet as mice.

Just one pencil, she'd never miss it, he said. We had to take the biggest, fattest one, because only the biggest one was good enough for me. Gravely, he pointed at the drafting table. 'That one over there, the red one,' he whispered.

It wasn't without its fair share of danger, what he was doing. My mother might come home at any time. She'd *kill* him if she caught him in here. Even so, he took the time to sharpen the pencil he had chosen for me, using her special pocketknife, until it was as pointy as a dagger. His head was bent over the waste-paper basket, and a ray of sunlight fell across his blond head.

Never had I seen anyone perform a task with such zeal. I heard the soft crunch-crunch of the blade. I could smell wood shavings and the lead. I felt excited, honoured, and special. I was the princess for whom the brave miller's son was forging a blade that would protect her from dragons and evil goblins.

After a few moments, he held the pencil up to the light to inspect the point. Then he handed it to me, his eyes blazing with joy. 'Nothing bad can happen to you now,' he said.

I gazed at him, awestruck. One thing I knew for certain: if I stuck this pencil into the ground outside, it would immediately bring forth pink and white blossoms, simply from all the love that had been invested in it.

Sometimes, life goes in one direction, and we spin off in another direction. When you come right down to it, there's really no other way to put it that makes better sense.

## On the Design

As book design is an integral part of the reading experience, we would like to acknowledge the work of those who shaped the form in which the story is housed.

Tessa van der Waals (Netherlands) is responsible for the cover design, cover typography and art direction of all World Editions books. She works in the internationally renowned tradition of Dutch Design. Her bright and powerful visual aesthetic maintains a harmony between image and typography and captures the unique atmosphere of each book. She works closely with internationally celebrated photographers, artists, and letter designers. Her work has frequently been awarded prizes for Best Dutch Book Design.

Hellen van Meene is a renowned Dutch photographer whose work is in the collections of many museums, including Guggenheim NYC and MoMA. She took this photograph in 1999 and remembers that she loved 'the perfect combination' of the red hair, orange shawl, green grass, and yellow bucket in the composition. The photograph was taken on a warm day when the water was not too cold.

The cover has been edited by lithographer Bert van der Horst of BFC Graphics (Netherlands).

Suzan Beijer (Netherlands) is responsible for the typography and careful interior book design of all World Editions titles.

The text on the inside covers and the press quotes are set in Circular, designed by Laurenz Brunner (Switzerland) and published by Swiss type foundry Lineto.

All World Editions books are set in the typeface Dolly, specifically designed for book typography. Dolly creates a warm page image perfect for an enjoyable reading experience. This typeface is designed by Underware, a European collective formed by Bas Jacobs (Netherlands), Akiem Helmling (Germany), and Sami Kortemäki (Finland). Underware are also the creators of the World Editions logo, which meets the design requirement that 'a strong shape can always be drawn with a toe in the sand.'

**RENATE DORRESTEIN** (1954–2018) is an internationally bestselling author who occupies a unique position within Dutch literature. An extraordinary storyteller, known for her unsentimental depiction of children and their flawed families, Dorrestein's wicked humor offsets the darkness of her subjects. Her books have been nominated for the International IMPAC Dublin Literary Award, the AKO Literature Prize, and the Libris Literature Prize. Her breakthrough novel *A Heart of Stone* was a Barnes & Noble 'Discover Great New Writers' selection. Her novels have been made into films and translated into fifteen languages.

**HESTER VELMANS** was born in Amsterdam, and lived in five different countries while growing up, before finally settling in the US. She is the author of the popular children's books *Isabel of the Whales* and *Jessaloup's Song*. The recipient of an NEA Translation Fellowship in 2014, she was previously awarded the Vondel Prize for her translation of Renate Dorrestein's *A Heart of Stone*. Her most recent novel *Slipper* was published in April 2018.